Joseph

Joseph

BY

JOYCE LANDORF

grason
Minneapolis, MN

Library of Congress Cataloging in Publication Data

Landorf, Joyce.
Joseph: a novel.
1. Joseph, the patriarch—Fiction. I. Title.
PZ4.L255Jo 1980   [PS3562.A477] 813'.54 80-12686

ISBN 0-89066-034-4 (formerly ISBN 0-8007-1095-9)

My deepest thanks go to
Brenda Arnold
Patti Tyra
Sheila Rapp
Richard Baltzell
and
My Joseph—Dick Landorf

Contents

He sent a man before them,
    Even Joseph, who was sold for a slave,
Whose feet they hurt with fetters;
    He was laid in iron,
Until the time that God's work came:
    The word of the Lord tested him.
The king sent for him and loosed him,
    Even the ruler of the people,
        and let him go free.
He made him lord of his house,
    And ruler of all his substance;
To imprison his princes at his pleasure,
    And to teach his elders in the ways of wisdom.
        See Psalms 105:17–22   KJV

BOOK
I
RACHEL
AND
LEAH

1

The first *qudim ruach*, the Hebrews' most descriptive words for "hot winds," swept down midafternoon from the east and across the sandy deserts. It forced everyone who was out in it to shield themselves immediately, and it also announced the arrival of spring. But the flourishing, bustling city of Haran snuggled up to the banks of the Belikh River and took no notice of its scorching-hot breath.

The city's main corridor, the heavily traveled caravan route, connected Haran with the cities of Nineveh, Asshur, and Babylon in the land of Mesopotamia. Its Belikh River branched off from the mighty Euphrates and formed one of the great fords of that river and the Tigris River; so the city of Haran's route stretched its fingers west and south and brought trade from Damascus, Tyre, and even a few Egyptian cities.

Today this normally busy route was swollen with the great influx of people from the closest city to the farthest, and most roads had simply burst their borders. It seemed to spill masses of men, merchants, heavily veiled women, human porters with incredible burdens on their backs, mischievous children, animals, carts, and every imaginable type of merchandise into each street, alleyway, and courtyard available.

The festival which had gone on for three days was scheduled to continue for another four. For those who did not find the vast array of people amusing, there was entertainment of all kinds. One could see and hear flute players, whole groups of musicians, dancers, and magicians, some with tiny but cleverly trained animals. Scores of acting troupes presented themselves for show at every street corner and on the broad steps of every temple. The only thing greater than the crowds of humanity was the intensity of their desires to celebrate and seek pleasures at any cost. The people were caught in the contagious frenzy.

By the seventh day, the climax day when hundreds of animals would be offered up for sacrifice in the main moon-god temples, the hysterical crowds, intoxicated by it all, would finally become exhausted, and the rampage would be over for another year.

But for now, the city was ripening rather like a huge gourd and was about to break asunder. The hot winds only added to the fevered activities.

Laban, a short, fat widower, wheezing, perspiring profusely, and obviously in distress, rubbed absentmindedly at his chest. He kept wondering how he had been persuaded to bring his two daughters and three of his hired men to this mad, howling city.

His enormous weight bowed the donkey's back, but it was such an effort to dismount that he stayed on, mumbling about whose hindquarters hurt the most—his or the donkey's.

Everywhere priests and temple fanatics were shouting wild incantations to the moon-god. Some of the celebrants just ahead of Laban tried dancing in the milieu of tightly packed humanity, but what with drunken men stumbling around them and tired beasts of burden sprawled across streets and doorways, no dance step was ever completed.

"I must be completely mad!" Laban shouted to his daughters. They were riding behind him as was the custom. Both girls waved to acknowledge him, but what he said was drowned out by the volume of noise around them. *Fortunately*, he thought, *I've left my two young sons at home. Trying to keep track of them would only have added to this insanity.*

Laban wiped the perspiration from his face with the end of his headpiece and attempted to regain his composure.

"I don't even remember which festival this is or what god is supposed to be honored! So how did I get tricked into bringing you all into the city and leaving the peace of my tents and the tranquility of my land?" he called above the heads of the crowd to the oldest of his three hired men who had accompanied him.

The shepherd, a tall, dark, heavily bearded man, sat higher and straighter on his donkey. He looked at Laban, smiled, and nodded his respectful agreement with his master. In the same moment their donkeys were separated by a crude wooden wheel which had broken away from its cart.

The servant inched his animal away from Laban, leaned over, and caught the ear of one of the younger men. He said above the noise, "I really do not care *which* festival has brought us here, only that we *are* here."

The younger lad smiled mischievously. "You mean you do not miss the 'peace of your tents or the tranquility of your land'?" he asked, matching Laban's words.

Both men laughed, and as their animals bumped their plump grey sides together, they nearly lost their balance, but they managed to exchange good-natured punches.

Laban caught a glimpse of their play, and in spite of his discomfort, he smiled. *They need this adventure,* he reasoned to himself, *and so do my daughters. This city is only half a day's ride from our tents. They are hardworking, all of them, and I owe them this break from their duties.*

"Leah! Rachel!" he beckoned them to come closer.

The girls maneuvered their small grey donkeys over to Laban. He was panting and having a hard time speaking, but with gestures and half sentences, he directed them down a small street, past the shops, and finally on to a narrow, walled street lined with private dwellings.

Laban stopped, and with a great puffing effort, he dismounted his beast. He would have sank to his knees had not one of the hired men caught him.

"I must rest here for a while at least," he panted. "This one—" he said, pointing to a delicately scrolled iron gate.

The owner of the house peered over the wall and shouted, "Ah, it is Laban!" Aaron smiled broadly and opened the gate for Laban and his entourage.

Quickly Aaron's eyes darted past Laban to check exactly who accompanied him, and his whole face brightened with what he saw. Clearly he was not disappointed.

"And," Aaron rhapsodized, "you have blessed my household by bringing your lovely daughters." He raised his hands in praise and silently thanked some unnamed god for his good fortune.

Laban took quiet notice that while Aaron's tongue had said, "lovely daughters," his eyes had simply declared *lovely daughter.*

He stepped between the staring Aaron and his younger daughter, Rachel.

"Aaron, my friend, I need the hospitality of your house tonight. We shall leave in the morning, but I need to rest a bit."

Laban shook his head and wiped his forehead. "Growing old does not agree with me, I fear."

Still trying to glimpse Rachel over Laban's shoulder, Aaron said absently, "You are always welcome here at my house, and you are not old." Then he broke out of his trance and turned to look directly into Laban's wet, puffy face.

Both men had lost their wives about the same time and neither had ever taken another wife. Over the years of their friendship, they had experienced similar losses and felt some of the same keen loneliness of life The river of affection ran deep between them.

"How stupid of me not to notice! Laban, you are ill, and I've made you and yours stand out here like a bunch of sheep waiting to be watered. Forgive me! Let me look at you."

Aaron put his arm around Laban's shoulders and turned him so the afternoon sun glistened on his face. Clearly, it was the face of a sick man.

Laban protested meekly, but Aaron was more than mildly concerned and went on: "You shall stay here for as long as it takes to make you well. I will take good care of you, your daughters, and even your men. Now, come." Aaron put his arm around Laban and asked, "How are your sons, Abihu and Jubal?" Laban laughed and answered, "Much too noisy and too young to come on such a journey!"

Aaron directed the men and donkeys to a small enclosure in the open courtyard, and he walked the party of people inside. The gate was on the left side of his property with a two-story house running along the back and right side. The beauty of the house, as Laban and his daughters knew, was not in its size—actually, it was a very modest dwelling—nor for any evidence of great wealth, but rather for its furnishings.

Aaron was a master craftsman of carving and engraving, and his house was crammed with treasures of all kinds. Whether he used an anvil, hammer, chisel, or engraving tool, whatever he wrought with his hands turned out to be an artistic wonder.

Rachel and Leah had lived their whole lives under Laban's large black tents, so a house with walls was always a new experience. They peered excitedly into the main lower room for there were so many new things to see. Once it had been an exquisitely carved table. Its four sides were edged with different-hued woods, and Aaron had designed a border of tiny flowers. There were alabaster stone vases of muted colors, shiny pounded-brass lamp stands, and mirrors of polished brass which were all wonders to behold.

Another time, when they were visiting, the girls were delighted with Aaron's gifts of delicately etched golden bracelets. On Rachel's was the miniature figure of a lamb, cuddled into the arm of a shepherd. Leah's had a shaft of wheat which seemed to be floating on the wind.

Everything in the house was a product of Aaron's spare-time activities. His true talent and—yes, as everyone said of him—his real lifework, lay in his ability to sculpture.

For years now he was the highly respected, undisputed master carver of a small group of men who fashioned and formed out of stone, metals, and clay the images of gods.

The large moon-god, Sin, now standing in the main temple in Haran, was the loving product of Aaron's hands alone.

He was not superstitious or religious, nor did he believe that the gods he fashioned held any real power over men, but Aaron was totally enmeshed in the love of creating. "The only god I worship are these," he once said in confidence to Laban, as he held up his large bony hands, "and if they fail, I have lost everything."

Seeing a piece of stone, clay, metal, or wood grow into a work of art was Aaron's greatest joy, as he often reminded his fellow workers.

Years back, when he showed great promise but was not yet a master of his trade, he made several teraphim and presented them to Laban.

The gray-stone household gods were no larger than the span of a man's hand, but Laban counted them among his most prized possessions, and the little figures stood in a place of honor in his tent.

After Aaron's fingers had developed more sensitivity to stone, and when he was far more skilled, with time and experience on his side, he confessed to Laban that the teraphim he had made were crude and an embarrassment to him. He begged Laban to return them and accept new ones.

Laban shook his head no and good-naturedly shrugged off the request. "Oh, no, you old rascal!" he said jovially. "Those special gods have been in my possession and in my household for too many years for me to give them up. Why, they have sat on their shelf and with their great stone eyes have seen my joy and witnessed all my sorrows. I will have no parting from them."

Aaron sighed and eventually stopped pestering Laban about them. He turned to giving the family other gifts instead, but each time he entered Laban's tent, the teraphim struck his eyes like sharp pieces of driven straw.

Now Aaron had no thoughts about the graven images; he was too preoccupied with Laban's obvious pain. He settled Laban down on a furry bearskin and propped his back against the wall.

"I must take care of your daughters and your men," he said, as he hurriedly left the room.

Aaron saw to it that his servant Sari began preparations of a meal for the men, and then he instructed them, saying, "There is no telling when your master will be fit to travel, but you are welcome to stay and enjoy the festival. I shall make arrangements with my neighbor," Aaron pointed to his left, "for he has a large rooftop you can all sleep on."

Later, the men, pleased to be staying, finished their food and warmly thanked Aaron for his hospitality.

Finally, the two old friends dipped their crusty bread into the hot lamb-and-barley stew and thoughtfully ate. Not too much conversation passed between Laban and Aaron for, at the moment, it seemed as if words were not very important. They ate with the invisible robes of familiarity warming their shoulders.

By contrast, the cooking area was alive with Rachel's, Leah's, and Sari's bubbling laughter and gossip.

Sari was Aaron's housekeeper and cook. She was old now, but she came the closest thing to a mother figure the young women had ever known. She was about as wide as she was tall. Aaron had been considerate of her when she lost all her family in a fire, and she had ever since then made his home hers. Nothing was too good for Aaron or his guests.

They chatted endlessly about earthy and common things, but for Rachel and Leah—used to the remoteness of their father's tents and the absence of other women—the night passed far too quickly for each of them.

They were so caught up in a story Sari was telling, they didn't hear Aaron's discrete cough. Eventually, he cleared his throat rather loudly, frightening them all into, first, a startled jump, and then a fit of laughter.

He interrupted them, and his low voice was edged with concern: "It is time to retire. Sari, see to Rachel and Leah's comfort and needs. I will take Laban up and stay with him."

"Is father more ill than we thought?" Leah asked. She was instantly sober, and both Rachel and Sari matched her serious mood with their abrupt stillness.

"I think he will be all right. You know how one moment he is on his deathbed and the next he is in the finest of health. So, please do not fret; we have seen this before, and I am confident it shall pass. If I need you, I will call, but for now you should both rest. I bid you good night."

The short flight of stairs proved to be almost the undoing of Laban who wearily slumped onto the pallet in the small guest room.

Aaron pushed a soft pillow under Laban's head, brought the coverings up over his large, mounded stomach, and tucked them around his shoulders.

"There, now," Aaron said, as he dipped a linen cloth into a basin of water. "I'll wash your face. You'll have a good night's sleep. And tomorrow . . . well, tomorrow you will be as young and fresh as one of your lambs."

"And twice as weak," Laban wheezed.

"No, no. See, I've a cup of Sari's tea. She is an ancient wonder at this, and her tea is good for anything that ails you."

When Aaron finished wiping Laban's face, he propped him up so he could gulp some of the steaming, foul-smelling brew.

Laban made a face. "It's worse than I remembered," he said, and gratefully laid back his head.

His voice full of genuine affection, Aaron said, "Now, I tell you the truth, old friend. Tomorrow you are going to be just fine. In fact, you can purchase some supplies, maybe even spend a little time observing the pilgrims who overflow our city, and still be home to your hillside before dark."

Laban believed Aaron, but he did not say so. He was touched by the man's encouraging, warm words, and his acute attack of loneliness was abated and relieved by Aaron's empathy.

"You are a good man, my friend." Laban reached out from the covers and patted Aaron's arm.

Aaron pulled his low stool closer to the pallet.

"Laban?" Aaron began.

"Oh, no," Laban chuckled. "Not again! Whenever you say 'Laban' in that manner, I know we are going to have the same conversation we have had for years now."

"It's not about the teraphim," Aaron said quickly.

"I know it's not—and I know exactly what it is!" Laban said, almost defensively. "It concerns my Rachel, does it not?" He lay back on the pillow and massaged his chest.

"Laban, I do not want to cause you any discomfort, nor do I want to add to your distress, but by the gods of all ages I am a tormented man!

"Once more I am smitten . . . no, devastated with wanting. My bones burn within me, and it is as if I am a young he-goat, impetuous for my first mating. Each time I see the ravishingly beautiful Rachel, I am consumed with desire," Aaron anguished. "Words fail me or, worse, if I do speak to her, the words come slowly, and they are about as warm as the predawn frost.

"Just now," he gestured downward, "in the cooking room, I wanted to tell her what joy she has brought to my house today. Instead, I spoke and acted like she bored me, and I was merely being a dutiful host, when in truth I could barely stand before her for she is so lovely, and I have ached to have her for so long." Aaron held his head in his hands.

Laban sighed. His breathing was easier now. Quietly he said, "Aaron, Aaron. My dear friend. Why must you torment your soul in such a manner? You are putting a severe strain on our friendship, and you are grieving my heart for you know my commitment." Laban patted his chest.

"How many times have I presented my case to you? I will not flaunt your desires in the face of my ancestors' customs. You know I cannot give my younger daughter in marriage until I have suitably arranged a marriage for my firstborn daughter. Yet you continue to plague me with your dilemma," Laban cried.

Aaron shook his head affirmatively, but ever so slightly.

Laban continued and waggled a fat forefinger under Aaron's nose. "You are not the only one who is desperate with desire for my Rachel. I am beseeched and pestered with marriage offers like a camel attracts fleas and lice.

"*I* am the desperate man here—not you! It is *I* who is really suffering."

Laban's tone mellowed and, wishing not to be too offensive, he said, "I love not only my sons but *both* my daughters as well, and you, my old friend, I would give you Rachel in a twinkling of an eye and fast as the *ruach* if only I could be assured of a marriage proposal *and* consummation for Leah."

Aaron smiled a bit ruefully and said, "I suspect much of what you say is true, but forgive me if I do not believe you when you say you'd give up Rachel in a twinkling of an eye. I may be blinded with love, but I can still see through that one.

"You are my old friend, but you are also an old fox. Your daughters are the backbones of your spine. Leah has become your chief cook, besides taking care of all the cleaning and serving needs of your tents. Rachel's skin has become burnished by the sun from tending sheep on your grassy hills and fertile valleys. No, you'll never let them go, for your daughters are like the poles which hold up your great black tents. Without them, your life would come crashing down."

It is true, Laban thought to himself as he sipped Sari's odious brew, *I have never offered Leah, though I could have, nor provided a dowry to any man, for I simply cannot afford to let her go.*

"She may be plain of face, with reddened, watery eyes, and very plump of figure, but no woman is as organized or skilled at cooking as Leah. And Rachel," he sat the empty bowl down beside him and wiped his mouth, "now she is valuable to me for she does her share of the shepherding chores. I am not a wealthy man."

Aaron gestured with his hands, and then said quietly, but
with a voice of iron, "You could give me Rachel, for you know I
would treat her as a royal queen, but you will never do that. It is
utterly useless to reason with you."

Laban knew the veritable truth in Aaron's words, so he
turned his face to the wall and feigned exhaustion.

Aaron had meant to keep a vigil by Laban, but his heart was
so burdened that he paced the floor for a while and then, when
the hurt overwhelmed him, left the small oil lamp burning on the
wall and sought the soothing solitude of the rooftop.

Two days later, Laban agreed with his hired men to let them
stay on one more day, but he, Leah, and Rachel set out for home
after bidding Aaron and Sari their rather stilted farewells. Each
seemed a little relieved that the visit, brief as it was, had concluded.

Aaron's face, set in an impassive manner, gave no hint of the
keen disappointments biting and gnawing away within him.
Once again, he had asked for the hand of Rachel, and once again
he had been refused. Momentarily, as he watched them go, he
pursued the thought of marrying both Leah and Rachel, but dis-
continued that thinking when he reasoned the unfairness it would
invoke toward Leah. He could never pretend he loved Leah when
his adoration of Rachel had been obvious for years. "I will not
hurt Leah in that manner."

"Aaron, your soft heart will lose your chance for happiness in
the long run," a knowing friend had once commented.

Aaron stood, arms locked behind him, and watched until their
little caravan turned out of his view at the end of the street.

2

The trio continued heading into the warm winds, and when they
finally reached the outer road, they prodded their small beasts of
burden north. Before them lay the fertile valleys and green foothills where the black goat's hair tents of Laban; his father, Bethuel; and his grandfather, Nahor, had stood for all these years.

Now it would be only a matter of half a day's journey before they would be home, but it was enough time for Laban to gather his rambling thoughts together. He conversed back and forth with himself because he wanted to express his apologies to both his daughters. He knew the time spent in Haran had not been nearly as festive as he had hoped for, but he closed his mouth and reasoned inwardly, *One does not have discussions of any consequence with women*, and, with that settled, he pulled his headpiece over his mouth and glanced idly over the landscape. In truth, his pride was strong, and apologizing, particularly to women, seemed an unnecessary aggravation.

However, as they proceeded along, each wrapped in his or her own thoughts, and as the sun, wind, and silence grew more intense, Laban's genuine love for the girls overruled the customs of the day and slowly but surely melted his rigid pride.

He loved both girls, but years before, in the first moments of holding his second-born baby, he was overwhelmed by the tiny, magnificently formed infant. Her face was a thing of beauty, and even then, love like a tenacious vine began to entwine itself possessively between the father and his newborn. Laban, the shepherd, had cuddled and pampered more than one sweet lamb, and this baby's face, innocent and umblemished like the unspotted countenance of a lamb, touched him deeply. Immediately, he said this infant would be named Rachel which meant *ewe*. To name one's child after an animal was not a commonplace thing to do, so even from the beginning, Laban set his second born apart. He found it difficult to deny her anything, and on more than one occasion he had been accused of spoiling her. Later, when his sons had been born, he found he could never conceal his favoritism towards Rachel. He also decided he'd never let her marry, if he could prevent it.

He slowed his donkey's pace and dropped back between his daughters.

"I wish—" he fumbled and almost changed his mind about speaking, but continued, "I mean, I hoped things would have worked out differently in Haran. . . ."

To his immediate relief, he did not have to define his apology any further, for Rachel, brightening considerably, leaned over and patted his arm.

"Oh, father, it was enough just to leave our land and take this small journey. Please do not fret. Besides, we were worried that your sickness would consume you. Instead," she pointed to him, "look at you. Sari's tea has truly revived you."

At the mention of the tea, Laban made such an awful facial grimace that both girls laughed.

Rachel dug into the depths of her waistband and pulled out a short length of ribbon.

"Remember this? You bought it from that loud and funny merchant just before you got so sick."

She dangled the scarlet piece of ribbon up by her face and said, "You know this will brighten my hair and my sheep-tending days for many a sunrise." She flashed Laban her warmest smile.

He caught his breath, then marveled to himself, *Her whole face glows like a burning lamp brimming with oil when she smiles.*

They were still riding beside each other when they came upon a place in the road which opened out to a small, flat plain.

The wind swept off the floor of the valley, and, as it picked up speed, it quickly laid back Rachel's and Leah's head veils. Rachel was to Laban's right, and he noticed her first. He didn't mean to stare; nevertheless he did. Other than the browning by sun and wind, Rachel's face was flawless. Her dark eyes, fringed with even darker lashes, sparkled like the stars which filled great, black, night skies.

Now with her veil off, her hair streaming behind her, Rachel's loveliness was clearly visible. Her face was also clearly the face of his beloved sister, Rebekah. Laban winced with the sharp pain of remembering.

My dear, dear sister Rebekah, he thought. A melancholy nostalgia filled him. How he longed to see her. It had been many years since she had left the tents of Nahor and their father, Bethuel, to marry Abraham's son, Isaac. Since then she had lived in the far distant land of the Canaanites. All he knew of Rebekah was that she was happy in the household of Abraham, for she had accepted their God, and her good marriage to Isaac had been made even better by the birth of twin sons. He had heard their names were Jacob and Esau, and a pang of loneliness hit into his memory, for he had never seen the boys or any of them.

To think, he recalled to himself as his donkey plodded along, *my father and I gave my sister our blessings and sent her off to Canaan with our nurse, Deborah, and several handmaidens. Could we have dreamed we'd never see her again?*

Laban rode along and felt no small pangs of guilt. He questioned whether it really had been the right thing to do—to send her off like that. His argument back to himself was that both he and his father had sincerely believed that the marriage proposal from Isaac had been sent directly from Abraham's God.

Laban recalled that Eliezer, Abraham's oldest and most trusted servant, had made the incredibly long journey from Canaan to find Isaac a wife. When he had reached the lush green valleys of the land of Padan-aram and found the tents of Nahor and Bethuel, the old servant's pleas for Rebekah were so eloquent he could not be refused. Laban recalled that after some hasty, but definitive, consultations with Bethuel, they decided Rebekah should go and marry Isaac. Both men were impressed with Eliezer, but they were stunned with the instructions which seemed to come directly from Abraham's God. Laban wasn't about to challenge or defy such a God.

Uncomfortably, Laban shifted his weight on his overburdened donkey. Other than those long-ago memories and a day like this, seeing Rebekah's beauty reflected so vividly in his daughter Rachel's face was all he had to hold close to his heart in memory of his sister.

He put an end to his remembering by calling for a brief resting time. He was pleased to see a creek a short distance from the road, and he directed the girls toward it. He was relieved with the change of pace because he dared not spend too much time reflecting on old memories.

Laban's thoughts of Rebekah and Isaac always moved from their marriage to controversial thoughts about their God. It was always Abraham and Isaac's God versus his gods, and comparisons like that always gave him a pounding pain at the base of his neck.

Laban was very aware that the little stone teraphim he worshiped seemed remote and rarely, if ever, did praying to them produce seeable results. Abraham's God, on the other hand, could run through a whole bag of tricks, and that "living God," as

Abraham called him, could dazzle one with an assortment of spectacular changes and dramatic encounters. Yet Laban had never permitted himself to worship this living God because it always made him feel vastly uncomfortable. Moreover, Abraham's God, in return for seeable results, demanded obedience, sacrifices, and, "Yea, even a man's whole soul!" as Laban had said with no small amount of horror.

He was never sure such a high payment to a god was quite worth it, so he continued to nod occasionally to the teraphim which Aaron made, and, in the long run, it had been indeed much easier.

For the hundredth time, he admonished himself, *I must not think on these things any longer.*

The three of them dismounted by the dwindling wadi. Soon all the cool creek water would be dried and blown away by the summer wind, but for now, still early enough in the spring, the tingling, refreshing mouthfuls of water quickened their palates and lifted their spirits.

When they had finished eating the small loaves of bread and dried figs Sari had prepared, Rachel left Laban and Leah by the wadi's edge and walked up to the crest of a small knoll.

Laban shaded his eyes from the afternoon sun and watched her. Again he couldn't escape the comparison between his daughter and his sister, Rebekah. It had been said of his sister that her face was that of an exquisite goddess, but Laban thought, *My Rachel's face far surpasses even my sister's.*

He watched Rachel as she climbed the hill and finally, when she was at the top, Laban could not fail to see that the wind was pressing itself into her dark dress. The strong currents of air swept around her, and her dress clung tenaciously, revealing her amply rounded breasts, set above a leather girdle which encircled a tiny waist, followed by a flat stomach and two perfectly shaped legs.

"She is pure beauty all over," Laban exclaimed. At the same time he became aware that he had spoken the words aloud, he realized Leah had heard. She was shaking the sand and dust from the donkey blankets of wool and goatskins they used as saddles, and she avoided his gaze.

Laban, embarrassed because he could never describe Leah's plain face and lumpy body as "pure beauty all over," tried to divert Leah's thoughts by pointing up the hill and saying roughly, "Now what is that girl up to?"

"She is a dreamer, father. She dreams up there." Leah's soft voice penetrated Laban's soul.

They are so different, he said to himself, as he looked from the slim beauty on the hill to the plump young woman beside him. He wished Leah might have looked more like his long-since-dead wife, but, in truth, her stature always confirmed her kinship with him.

When the winds stretched the fabric on Leah's dress around her rotund body, Laban only shrugged his shoulders and turned away.

However, Leah's explanation of her sister's actions began to stir Laban's curiosity, and he shaded his eyes, hoping it would give him a better look at Leah.

"How do you know she's a dreamer, my daughter?" he asked.

"She has been a dreamer since the day she was old enough to tend the sheep. Each day's time of aloneness prompted her dreaming."

Leah's astute insight astounded him, so he pursued it further by asking, "And pray tell me, do you know what Rachel dreams of?"

Leah's quiet yes confirmed what he had only assumed moments before. He was seeing a side of Leah he had never seen before. Laban had concerned himself only with Leah's cooking abilities. She had become, as Aaron said, an excellent cook even if she did sample all too much. But from their brief exchange that afternoon, it was evident she had developed and hidden some commendable traits.

This girl sees much, but says little. Laban was fascinated, for the talent to see much and say little was not one he associated with very many women.

"Rachel has talked with you of her dreams?"

Leah nodded.

"What then?" Laban persisted.

"She dreams of marriage."

He frowned. It was a disappointing answer.

"Oh, does not every growing woman on every hill and valley dream of marriage?" Laban scoffed.

"Yes, we dream of marriage, father. But that one up there—" Leah inclined her head up towards Rachel, "she dreams of marrying a prince."

"A prince?" Laban sputtered. His soul reverberated with the jolt it received. "Now, where in all the land am I to find her a prince?"

Leah waited for his agitation to cool a moment, and then softly she said, "Oh, the problem is much worse than just finding a prince, my most respected father."

Laban peered at her and offered cautiously, "It is?" He asked it almost as if he didn't want to know.

Leah smoothed the goatskin and blanket on the back of the last donkey and explained as she worked, "The problem is that according to the customs of our forefathers, you have to find a man, an ordinary man, willing to marry me, your firstborn, before you can find a prince for Rachel."

Leah patted the saddle she had fashioned absently with one hand and said very quietly, "Finding a husband for me is not an easy task for you, father, and I know I have disappointed you because I am not fair of face; but my greatest fear is that I will never be wed so I will be unable to give you grandsons."

"Grandsons," he rolled the word over his tongue. "What a cherished word." Laban looked over at Leah, and the wide expanse just under her girdle sash prompted him to think, *Those broad, wide loins of hers could give birth to many fine grandsons.* His mood sobered and he thought sadly, *But she can produce no offspring unless I am willing to let her marry!*

Since Rachel was making her way down the small incline and picking a few of the tiny white flowers as she came, Laban knew he had only a moment or two more with Leah.

He pushed himself up off the ground and walked over to her. Leah wiped her eyes and squinted to see his face.

Laban put his right hand on her shoulder and, directly facing her, vowed, "You must not give up. You must be a dreamer, too, my child."

Leah looked away from him, and Laban felt her deep hurt and understood her fear for the first time. He shook her shoulder gently for emphasis and then said, "Now listen carefully to me." He bent his head closer to hers. "I pledge myself to arranging a marriage. I do not care if it is difficult or if your sister is fairer. I *shall* find you a suitable prince, my daughter." He was lying, for he had no such intentions, but he gave her his word to ease some of her hurt.

"It is a useless search," she said flatly.

"No, it is not!" He was closer to shouting than he ever had been before, and part of it was his own anger with himself, for he knew he had never taken any steps toward arranging a marriage for either of his daughters.

"I have given you my word, my honorable word, mind you," Laban answered. "And I will keep my covenant. But you must not believe the situation is hopeless!"

"What is hopeless?" Rachel asked as she heard the last of her father's words.

Laban was breathing heavily, so the soft answer, "Marriage," came from Leah.

"Oh, that." Rachel's mouth tightened into a set line. Then she wound her scarf around her head and said, "We always seem to be talking about the hopelessness of getting married."

"It's only talk," Leah countered, almost inaudibly.

Rachel flung her hands skyward, breathed a deep breath of the fresh, flower-scented air, and to change the conversation said, "Leah, I'm not going to let any of your dark moods spoil our day. Soon, too soon, we will be home, and our life in our father's tents will take up where it has left off. So let's enjoy this precious time."

Neither Leah nor Laban responded, so Rachel finished off with, "Don't you think this season with the wind is the most beautiful of all seasons?"

Leah's voice was edged with a trace of sarcasm. "All this wind makes me completely blind instead of only partially—"

She would have continued, but Rachel cut her off with, "Do not try my spirit, *dear* sister!" Then the hardness softened in Rachel's voice, and she put an arm around Leah and said sensibly,

"Now, let's try and put up a truce between us. I promise I won't make a lot of pleasantries about this season if you do not talk darkly about the wind or marriage."

"I would like peace between you two." Laban injected his opinion.

Leah's nod was stiff, but affirmative; however, she had to clarify one small matter. So in her direct-to-the-heart-of-things manner, she said quietly, "Actually, it is not your pleasant talk of winds and seasons that turns my thoughts into sourness, but the matter of finding a husband."

Rachel rolled her eyes heavenward and then toward Laban. "Father, help! Every day we talk about husbands and marriage. It would be nice if, for once, we could just enjoy the day."

Laban ignored the plea. He indicated that it was time to mount the donkeys and start homeward. He knew the girls continually squabbled, but he generally stayed clear. This was the first time he understood exactly what the bickering had been all about, and he felt a tightening about his chest. As their father, he had to find husbands. It was a duty he had totally ignored. Behind every hill, inside nearly every tent, and certainly around every corner in Haran, there was a man hungering for a marriage with Rachel. And well he knew that with Leah's being a healthy female of childbearing age, it would be no trouble to find a suitable husband. . . . He simply did not want to lose them. His head ached with his thoughts.

He mounted his donkey. The tightening in his chest escalated from merely uncomfortable to heightened pain and moved into and down his arm.

As he maneuvered his donkey around some rocks and thistle plants, he said for both girls to hear, "I am weary and eager to finish our journey. I want no more talk. Prod those beasts that we may soon come to the comforts of our tents."

Except for the light rustling sound of the wind, the soft plodding of the donkeys' hoofs, and a bird's early evening song, they rode with no words between.

The silence hung like a thick, oppressive blanket between them.

3

This season, above all, stirred and intensified her love for the land.

Each of her twenty years, Rachel had witnessed the return of summer, and it was as if she'd never seen it before. The arid heat and incessant wind sent her spirits soaring and fired up her imagination. When summer was fully upon them and she was spending long hours on the hillsides, she gave herself to unfettered dreaming.

This morning, even in the spacious sleeping tent she shared with Leah, Rachel had felt cramped and closed in. She was eager to move outside. She was glad when she had awakened before the purple and pink beams of the sun had begun their spectacular rise. A shiver of excitement played around her neck and roused her from her fitful sleep with a promise of expectation.

Ah, summer is about to begin. She relished the thought.

Rachel could never quite put it into words for Leah or her kinfolk, but the change of seasons—the immediate effect on plants, animals, people, and the land—took the sameness and boredom out of living on the plains. Being outside, in the midst of the elements, gave her the freedom she wanted, and she was able to dream privately and far away from prying eyes. The life of a shepherdess, putting her in direct contact with nature's realm and giving her time to daydream wistfully, was ideal for Rachel. She counted herself most fortunate.

Rachel lifted her head up slightly and surveyed their tent. The main overhead portion of the tent was one long awning of coarse and prickly goat's hair and held up by poles. It was not a single piece of cloth but many strips sewn together. The ends of the cloth were drawn to the ground by ropelike cords, and pegs were driven into the earth to hold it against the winds. In Laban's larger tent, there were two compartments which were separated by a hanging cloth. Rachel thought his tent *most* grand. The only light was a small lamp which burned olive oil and hung with skin bags of water from the tent poles.

Rachel traced the carpet's design with her finger as she lay on her mat and bedding. She knew soon it would be time to lift the tent sides and let the warm breezes blow. It was the season she liked best.

She looked over and saw Leah's bedding neatly rolled up and under a small table for the day. *Ah, Leah has risen earlier than usual and is probably preparing the morning lentil pottage and honey cakes.* Rachel's thoughts continued as she plumped her pillow up under her head.

Summer is best, she mused again and sighed. Rachel lay there and listened for a moment to a couple of early birds as they called to each other in shrill, high-pitched voices.

Without the threat of Leah's hearing her, she said aloud, "Summer will march from the hot, searing deserts, over the great mountains which surround us and will arrive on the plains of Padan-aram like an army of men in full battle dress!" She loved rolling the words over her tongue, and she talked dramatically on for a short while.

Talking aloud was the best of ways she had devised for coping with the lonely and barren days of sheep tending. There was deep satisfaction in dreaming aloud.

Her father Laban was not a wealthy man by some men's standards, but the enormous amount of fertile land he claimed was impressive. His diminutive sheep flocks and his small goat herd and fledgling camel herds were increasing with every year.

Rachel had been about fifteen summers old when Laban gave her the responsibility of caring for a small but specially bred flock of ewes, rams, and their tiny offspring.

The chief shepherds—Rachel could hear their voices outside now as they gathered to eat the morning's feast—were hired men who watched over Laban's great flocks. Because summer was upon them, yesterday had been their last with their flocks and herds in the surrounding plains. Now they would take their animals and journey to the lush meadows in the nearby mountain valleys where they would find easier grazing and watering. They would be gone to the high green pastures for the whole season of summer.

Rachel's flocks were treated differently. Since they were highly prized and very pampered, Rachel led them each day to small, choice pastures, as nearby as possible; watered them at a common well, just off the main road; and led them each sunset into a well-protected sheepcote near the family's tents for the night.

Now, she heard the voice of her father. He added his humor to the men's shouting and spirited conversations. Quickly Rachel dressed, splashed her face with water from the skin bag hanging just above her on the tent pole, and pulled a wide comb through her thick, reddish-brown hair. When she had tied her soft, wavy hair with the length of scarlet ribbon, she patted her head and approved her looks in the brass reflection plate.

Unobtrusively, Rachel joined her father and the men by Leah's cooking fires. Her father, brothers, and the hired men were eating outside of Laban's tent this morning instead of inside it. They sat on leather-skin mats, and Leah hurried between them and her in-ground oven and porridge pots.

Rachel held her head high without blushing as the men good-naturedly told Laban how they would never run off with his flocks because they always had to return to his tents to see such a beauty. There was a ripple of laughter. Their conversations centered on talk of the flocks; but all through it, if she listened closely, Rachel could hear a nervous, unsettled feeling. She reasoned that they didn't like the long season away—yet, it was their job. There was never any open complaining, especially in front of their master, Laban, but their uneasiness showed when the men put so much emphasis on their return home.

"We'll have a festival here when you return," Laban said, mostly to ease their leaving. The men nodded their agreement. Laban hoped it would suffice.

Rachel helped Leah but gave her most dazzling smile to the men, as if they needed anything of hers to remember her by. Of course Leah's gift was of a more practical nature. She had cooked and dried fruits and mutton for days, and now it was packed and ready for their journey.

The men made no effort to hide the fact that while Leah's gifts of food would surely fill their bellies, it was Rachel's smiles which they would eagerly carry with them to the hills to warm their minds on their lonely night watches.

Wearily Laban took notice, and Leah pretended to busily occupy herself in her clearing and cleaning of utensils.

When the well-stocked food baskets had been loaded on to the donkeys, and the goatskins, fairly bursting with wine, were all set, the men, including Abihu and Jubal, said their farewells and set out for the high country. It was the first year for his sons to join the men and flocks, and Laban suddenly felt old and bone weary.

When all the men had finished their eating, Leah dished out some pottage in pottery bowls for Rachel and herself, and, while they ate, Laban sat and talked with two remaining and obviously sad old men. Both their age and stiffened limbs kept them home to tend Leah's small garden and to do Laban's light chores, so Laban comforted them as best he could.

The girls ate in silence and respectfully regarded their father all the more because he seemed to be restoring Nadab and Azor's lost dignity. Leah and Rachel exchanged pleased and knowing glances. It was one of the few times they fully agreed with each other.

By the time the sun peeked over the edge of the mountains and sent bright pink shards of sunlight across the plains, they had finished their morning chores and had set about going their separate ways.

Leah busied herself with the gathering and cleaning of bowls and pots. Soon she would begin preparation of the evening meal of stewed mutton.

Laban went off to see about redigging a well Azor had found. The well had been filled in by some long-forgotten enemy during a past war, and, by chance, old Azor had discovered it. Laban was already calculating what another well would mean for his prosperity.

Rachel, anxious to have nothing to do with household chores, left Leah quickly, gathered her small shepherd's scrip which held some cheese and bread for her lunch, and said her hasty but courteous good-byes.

On her way to the sheep pen, Rachel gave one long, sharp whistle, and a small bundle of black-and-white fur bounded over the low gate of the sheepcote and raced towards her.

She bent down and gave the dog a hug and rubbed his ears.

"Good morning, Little Fox!" The dog jumped up on her, waggled his tail vigorously, and did everything but answer back. The bond of affection was very strong between them. For four years now, Little Fox had diligently earned the reputation of best sheep dog of the territory. He was alert, cocky, and obviously pleased with himself.

"Are you ready for today?" Rachel asked, and the dog's sparkling brown eyes never left her face.

"We will go up that way," she said as she pointed up toward a western slope and opened the main gate for the few sheep who were eager to get out to the green pastures.

The dog dashed in behind her and went to the farthest corner of the pen. Smoothly and systematically he began to run the twenty-two sheep out of the narrow gate and up the correct hillside. Rachel collected her wooden staff and flute from the small shed inside the pen, closed the gate after the last of the sheep had gone, and gave a small approving chuckle when she looked up and saw how far Little Fox had already barked, nipped, and persuaded the sheep to go.

"It's going to be a beautiful day!" Rachel's words burst from her like a song. "The gods are smiling today," she said to the dog as he circled around a few straggling sheep.

As she climbed the foothill, over grassy areas and various-sized rocks, she wondered if this would be the day—*the special day, the moment of all moments.* But just then a small cloud on the horizon caught her eye and she pondered, *Ah, perhaps not today,* and she dismissed her hopes.

Rachel reached the spot she had in mind, and the morning hours came and went uneventfully and, fortunately, without any sight of wolves, bears, or the small brown adders which menaced the sheep by popping out of their holes in the pastures. The lunch of cheese and bread was eaten, and it was routinely followed by Rachel's lyrical music from the flute. The melodies were all her own. No one had ever taught her how to play the instrument, but from the first moment Aaron had placed his delicately made flute into her hands, she had loved the slim reed pipe and determined she'd master it. Her music filled the small canyon, and its echo accompanied her. The sheep always steadied and calmed themselves when she played.

"Even if I do not play like old Azor, my sheep know my play-ing, and they seem to like it," Rachel commented, and Little Fox cocked both ears as if he didn't want to miss a command from her, in case she wanted him to get on with his herding duties.

The day was passing as a thousand other days, and finally she said, "All right, Little Fox, it's time to go down the hill and get these mothers and babies some water." The dog jumped into an immediate flurry of action.

Rachel picked up one of the smallest of the lambs to carry down the hillside. For a moment she stood still and watched the activity of her valued dog. She laughed a little and said to him, "You are eager to do your work, are you not? Diligent workers like you are hard to find. Did you know that?" she called after the dog. She thought Little Fox responded with a smile.

The girl, the dog, and the modest flock of sheep made their way down the hillside and out to the roadway.

Rachel looked beyond the flock towards the city of Haran. She could see the main well clearly in a small clump of trees ahead of her.

She recognized three shepherds—Amashai, Ezer, and Bedei-ah—who had arrived earlier than she with their flocks that day; but it was not the sight of them which stopped Rachel in the road and captured her immediate interest.

Talking with the shepherds was an older, distinguished-look-ing man. His dusty cloak and his equally dirty and tired camel had obviously traveled from afar. Rachel was sure she had never seen anyone, even from the city, who looked as impressive as he did.

The stranger had stopped his conversation with the shepherds and, standing straight and tall, he looked directly at her. Whether it was his directness—it was impolite to stare—or his handsome head set on massive shoulders, or his regal bearing and manner, Rachel didn't know, but, impolite or not, she stared back. Then, for one of the first times in her memory, she felt the hot blood rush to her face, and she knew she was blushing.

Rachel turned her face away from the man and issued an ut-terly useless command to Little Fox, but even as she spoke, she knew the stranger was examining her, from her hair to her san-dals, and Rachel blushed a deep crimson for the second time.

Long ago Rachel had accustomed herself to the looks and glances of men and boys. Always she was able to give them the same treatment; she simply paid no heed to them, whatsoever. Today it was different. Today she had been deeply affected and, without warning, it had showed.

Since she could not hide her face forever, and since it was not possible to ignore or disregard the traveler, she chose to face him head-on. She walked towards the well and met his gaze with her head lifted high.

The shepherd boys were sitting under some feathery, grey-green tamarisk trees, their eyes round with curiosity. The man stood and fixed his attention on Rachel.

With each step closer, Rachel's awareness of the magnetic presence of the stranger increased. The satchel for food was slung over her shoulder, she carried her staff in one hand, and sleeping placidly in the bend of her other arm was the tiny greyish-white lamb.

When she was only a few feet from him—the well between them—the stranger turned and, to everyone's amazement, rolled the large stone covering off the top of the well. In a voice deep as the well itself, he said, "Your flocks will be watered first today, Rachel."

She was totally taken aback to hear her name, but she was utterly stunned to find herself responding by bowing her head in a formal greeting and then saying, "I do not know who you are, sir, but I perceive that you are a prince from a distant country."

Her heart was pounding, and until the lamb in her arm bleated out a sharp cry, she didn't realize how tightly she was gripping him. She released the lamb and stood up to hear the stranger's laughter.

"I am not a prince." He was smiling at her, and Rachel found herself warmed and quickened by his spirit.

"My name is Jacob. I am your cousin on your father's side. Your Aunt Rebekah is my beloved mother."

He would have said more, but Rachel, looking at him with her deep brown eyes, said slowly and carefully, "You are wrong, Jacob. You are a prince, *my* prince, and I have waited every day of my life to meet you."

She had never been more beautiful, and when she raised her

face to his, her beauty smote his heart with a great tenderness. Tears of joy streamed down his face, mingling and glistening in his beard.

Then, as the shepherds watched, Jacob placed his hands on her shoulders and kissed her fair and lovely face. Mutually they sealed their commitment of love.

Rachel and Jacob's kisses were interrupted by the applauding and cheering of the shepherds. Bedeiah called out, "Could I be next, fair Rachel?"

She turned and shushed them over her shoulder with, "It is perfectly acceptable that he kiss me. We are kinfolk. He is Jacob, my cousin!"

"Oh that we might *all* be Rachel's kinfolk," Amashai lamented, sending the other two men into spasms of laughter.

Jacob kept his arms around her, and for several moments they stood there amid Little Fox's exuberant barking and the shepherds' good-natured laughter. Later, Rachel said of those moments, "It was the beginning of the summer of my life."

4

"But he is *my* prince. It was I who first saw him. He belongs to me!" Rachel stamped her feet, and diminutive poofs of dust and sand sprayed up through the small carpets which covered the floor of the tent.

Rachel paced. Leah sat dabbing at her swollen eyes and said nothing. Laban, his hands behind his back and perspiration trickling down the sides of his face, stood immovable in the center of the tent.

Imploringly, Rachel cried, "Jacob has loved me from the first moment at the well. The dowry he gave for me was seven years of labor. That's more than adequate compensation. Now it is paid and we have waited not one or two years, but seven. Seven! Do you hear me, father?"

Rachel, taller than her father, bent close and peered down at him. The words she spoke were venomous. "I must believe you are not a devious man by nature, my father, yet you refuse to honor the covenant you made with Jacob. It is dishonorable not to accept his dowry, and it is unthinkable that you would treat him in this manner." She leaned even closer to his stony countenance.

"Have you not seen the efforts of his labors? Do you not know of his skills in sheep breeding? Has Jacob not increased your flocks?"

Then, answering her own questions, Rachel said, "You know he has toiled far harder and far longer each day of the seven years than any six hired men put together, yet even now you will not live up to your agreement and consent to Jacob's marrying me!" Rachel's face was flushed with anger.

The air was hot and stifling. Leah longed to be outside tending to her bubbling pot of broth, but ever since the morning's meal, she had known this day would be filled with stinging accusations and bitter arguing.

Earlier that morning they had not finished their wheat-and-honey cakes when Jacob had said to Laban, "I must respectfully remind you, Laban, that because I had no money, I worked out the dowry in service, and I have fulfilled my contract. Now I ask you to give me Rachel to be my wife so I may sleep with her."

Leah and Rachel had listened as their father coldly answered, "I shall give you my decision tonight."

Jacob looked at Laban, and in disbelief he cried, "But according to your promise, there is no decision to be made. Tell me *now* that I may have my wife."

Laban shook his head and said stubbornly, "At the evening meal." And with that he strode off to his tent.

Now for two hours Laban and Rachel had refused to compromise, refused to hear the other's point of view, and most of all they had refused to give in.

Rachel's fury was fueled by the quietness of Leah.

"How can you sit there and by your silence agree to this unjust thing our father does?" Rachel railed at Leah.

Leah replied, almost inaudibly, "Speaking to him, as you can see, accomplishes nothing."

"I wish for once," Rachel pursued on, "that you would speak up. You should give a definite yes or no to problems, and when you know a man is breaking a covenant, you should say so. You are overly *tolerant* of everybody, and it sickens me " Rachel's voice thickened with disgust.

"The intolerant people of our land have never suffered." Leah's quiet comment shot like an arrow to the very heart of her sister, and it did not miss.

Rachel stood quite still. From where she was sitting, Leah continued; her voice was low, but there was no mistaking the intensity of her words.

"For your whole life, my beauteous sister, you have lived a comfortable existence," Leah said. "There has even been a certain sweetness of privacy out on the grazing meadows with the sheep. You have never suffered the loneliness of a plain woman. You do not know what agony it is to be constantly compared to a sister whose beauty only accents your plainness. You have dreamed of marriage to a prince. I have never dared even dream of marriage. And I have always asked myself the question, 'After he has seen Rachel, what man would want me?'" Leah squinted up at her sister.

All of Rachel's fury had dissipated as the truth of Leah's words sank in. She sat down crosslegged in front of Leah and said gently, "So it is the unhealed wounds within you that give you tolerance for our father?" Without waiting for a reply, she asked with a new sensitivity, "Do you despise me so much? Are the hurts so great, are the scars so deep, that you cannot or will not help me to make father keep his pledge so Jacob and I may marry?

"Leah?" Rachel touched her sister's shoulder.

There was no answer, and Rachel knew, with a sharp, painful sadness, Leah would not respond.

Nor did she. Ever.

When they gathered for the evening meal, Laban finally broke his silence. He dipped a folded piece of bread into the lamb broth, and handing it to Jacob as a sign that he would honor his word, said, "Seven days from today you may take my daughter in marriage. I will not break my promise to you."

The announcement threw the wedding arrangements, food, and festive preparations into full swing.

Jacob's joy was limitless, and he made elaborate plans to return to the land of Canaan with his bride. He reasoned that Racnel's sudden coolness towards him was simply one involving the apprehension of leaving her homeland.

"I know it will be a long and difficult journey, my dearest, but we must give birth to our sons in the land of my fathers, Isaac and Abraham," Jacob explained.

Rachel patted his arm and said solemnly, "And so we shall."

Jacob's heart swelled with even more tenderness for her, and the poet within him spoke: "These years, all these seven years, I have taken on hardships, loneliness, much work, and suffered with the winter and summer winds; but I tell you, my Rachel, the years are but as one day. The oldest and hardest trial of love is waiting, but I have endured the wait because of you."

She did not raise her eyes to meet his, and he marveled at Rachel's sweet and gentle spirit. "You will be the most beautiful bride in the land," he whispered. Still she did not meet his gaze, and love hung a curtain between the bridegroom and reality.

On the day of the wedding, Jacob was right. Rachel was dressed in a purest-white dress, with gold ornaments and a garland of flowers in her hair. Her skin and hair fairly shone with an ethereal beauty.

The day wore on as an eternity to Jacob. It was filled with a magnificent feast of the greatest array of foods and wines anybody had ever seen. Laban hired musicians who played melodies on their harps and others who beat out the rhythms on their taborets. Two old shepherds added to the merriment by occasionally accompanying the musicians of Haran with their flutes.

Both Abihu and Jubal used the wedding feast and festivities as an excuse to see which one of them could hold more wine. Their father's preoccupation with guests and arrangements provided the best cover for their youthful hilarity.

Leah had been given the help of more than a dozen women from Haran, and the supply of dishes and varieties of wine seemed unending. Laban, it was plain to see, had spared no expense.

"The bride's father is a gracious host," the guests observed. And to prove it, Laban served the bridegroom many cups of wine. Once when Jacob objected to *mezeg*, a spiced wine, Laban refilled his cup with *shekar;* but Jacob was by then so filled with feasting and mixed wines that he hardly noticed the strong, bitter-tasting wine. It exacted its toll on the groom, for it took Laban and three men guests to get Jacob to his tent.

"Bring me Rachel," Jacob said, trying to say it clearly.

"She will come to you soon," Laban replied. He took the lamps with him and left Jacob lying on the pillows and blankets of the raised platform, waiting for his bride.

"He will never consummate his love this night," laughed one of the men as they were leaving. "For he is so filled with wine, he cannot keep his eyes open." They left, and in the darkness, Jacob dreamed hazily of Rachel.

5

He didn't know if he had drunkenly slept away his wedding night or if he had lain there only a moment or two, but suddenly he was awake. He could see nothing, but a strong perfume filled his nostrils.

Jacob fought to get up. "My love? Rachel?" He called out in the blackness of the tent, and at once she was beside him.

His desire for her was aroused and stronger than all the wine and strong drink he had consumed. He fumbled clumsily with her clothing.

"I have waited so long for you." His tongue struggled to find the right words.

"I want to tell you of my love. . . . You called me a poet once, remember? My love is deep and as abounding as a. . . ." But Jacob couldn't remember what. He felt the coolness of her hand on his face.

Now they were in each others arms, and as he held her tightly, he poured out his love until fulfillment was complete. Then he nestled beside her in a heavy and dreamless sleep.

The night was far from quiet. Some wedding guests were still eating and talking, and someone was singing; but in the tent only Jacob's soft snoring sounds were heard.

She moved the pillows to support him better and rested his head on her shoulder. Only then did she speak.

Softly, she called his name. She expected no answer and got none, but it soothed her to say his name aloud and in love. She stroked his head and gently ran her fingertips over his face and beard.

"Jacob, Jacob," she sighed. "Jacob, my husband, my lord, I must talk to you." He stirred, but by the depth of his breathing, she knew he would not waken or hear her. It did not matter, for she could no longer hold the words back, and they spilled out of her like a gushing mountain waterfall.

"My husband, I must tell you something. Even though your ears are deaf to me, I would be the first to tell you." She hesitated, and then, gathering her courage from the darkness of the tent, she said softly, "It is true, Jacob, today I became your wife, and now we consummated our marriage, but before the morning's light dawns . . . I must tell you, I am not Rachel . . . I am Leah." She took a deep breath, glad it was out.

"When you wake on the morrow, your anger will be boundless. Rage will burn as a fire within you, and you will demand revenge against my father, Laban." She pictured the confrontation between husband and father and shuddered as she pulled Jacob closer to her. "I beg you, by the name of your living God, hear my father out before you bring any harm to him."

The chill of the night reached them, and Leah pulled the blanket over Jacob's shoulders and drew comfort from the warmth of his body next to hers.

"Rachel is not the only one who loves you. I do, too, my husband. I also have loved you, from the first day you came to us." She uttered a low, quick laugh. "Of course, you never saw me. Nobody ever does." She patted his shoulder slightly. "It's all right, my love. I'm used to being invisible. I am as unseen as the stilled wind.

"Oh, my Jacob," Leah sighed wearily as she tightened her arms around him. "There is an unfathomable well of loneliness way down inside me, and tonight, even though you have been cruelly deceived, tonight made the loneliness a little easier to bear. I have been loved by you, my cherished one, and you shall have sons from this union. I will make you proud. . . . You will see, my love."

Leah talked on for several hours, pledging her love and the

fruits of her womb to Jacob. She would not be still until it was all said and spoken.

Finally, when the stormy tempest within her was all out, she allowed the first tears to flow. She wept with both the special joy and the devious shame of the night; but when she had no more words or tears, the storm was replaced by a steady, peaceful calm.

We sleep together, she thought. *Our bodies have mingled, but on the morrow, and in the days and years to come, my Jacob, will we ever share the communion of love, you and I?*

Leah asked the question of the night, already knowing the answer.

To the gods she said, "It is a bittersweet cup you have asked me to drink, but I accept it gladly, for it is all of love I shall ever have."

6

When no amount of wine had been able to cut through the sour, bitter coating on her tongue, and when she could smile and pretend no longer, Rachel fled the wedding guests, leaving them to drink and gorge themselves on the wines and pretentious feast. More than anything she wanted to run, to hide . . . better yet, to disappear completely.

Pinched and smarting from the feelings which writhed within her, Rachel left the fine silk wedding clothes strewn about her tent, and, with a resentful shove, she returned the golden earrings and bracelets to their covered box. Finally, grabbing the flaxen tunic she wore when tending sheep and pulling it roughly over her head, she decided exactly where she would go to escape the guilt of being a party to the deception of this night.

Rachel's anger outweighed her guilt. *He is my prince, not Leah's,* she repeated over and over to herself, and soon she wore her anger like a cloak. By the time she slowly made her way in the darkness from her tent to the sheepcote, her anger had become a heavy, hot-molten weight which burdened her with an uncon-

trollable rage. She threw the pen's gate back with such force that
half the flock of sheep were startled into loud bleating, and her
unexpected presence plus the animals' nervous crying sent the
dog into a spasm of raucous barking. All of the noise only added
to Rachel's frustrations, but since she did not want to be discovered, she concentrated on pulling herself together; and in a few
moments, she was able to talk softly to the sheep. Slowly they all
began to settle.

Rachel tapped the dog lightly on his head. "Hush now, Little
Fox. It is only me. Everything is safe." The dog—bright-eyed,
alert, and sensing danger—blinked, became quieted at her command, and sat on his haunches. He waited in the darkness and
cocked his head to one side to study her.

Rachel dropped her cloak down on the sandy floor of the shed
and sat, crosslegged, planning. She had to decide what she would
do next. In the stillness, she determined that she'd stay the night
in the pen, but that she would be far out on the hillside by the
time dawn's light gave Jacob a chance to see how he had been
tricked. At least she would not have to see him, Leah, or her father until dusk of the next day.

"Jacob," Rachel said aloud. "Jacob, I was not a willing party
to this deception. Please believe me. My father told us he arranged for you to marry Leah, instead of me, only this past week,
and by our gods, he swore both Leah and me to secrecy. I would
have told you a thousand times these past days, but it was forbidden, and I could not disobey both father and my vow to the
gods. . . . Oh, Jacob, I think I am dying inside."

Rachel put her hand to her mouth to stifle her sobbing. The
dog, completely at a loss to understand her actions, had no training which covered his mistress's weeping, so he pressed his muzzle against her face and waited for some direction. Rachel rubbed
his ears absentmindedly, and then, as her sister had done that
very night, she softly called Jacob's name over and over again in
the darkness. While he was puzzled by her actions, Little Fox was
nevertheless pleased with her affectionate attention. He waited
with her, and even after Rachel fell into an exhausted sleep, he
kept his assiduous vigil.

The morning's light did not come in its usual way—majesti-
cally quiet and accompanied by deep pink and grey-blue skies.

Instead, it exploded across the horizon and split the air over the meadows and hills with the force of a booming clap of thunder from a thousand clouds. The sound was Jacob's voice, and it shattered the predawn calm.

He screamed and stretched the syllables of one man's name into the morning, "L-a-a-a-b-a-a-n-n!"

Rachel was at once awakened and on her feet. She realized she had overslept and instead of being out on the hills as she had planned, she was still within hearing range. Frantically, she tried to shush the panicked animals.

"Get the sheep up that way!" she commanded the dog. He obeyed instantly and scurried past her. She grabbed her things, fled the sheepcote, and began running, stumbling, and climbing up the steepest canyon.

She scrambled faster than she'd ever gone before and tried to outdistance the bleating sheep, the barking dog, and the heart-wrenching sound of her beloved's cry.

But Jacob's voice, made more powerful by the greatest rage he had ever known, filled the valleys and echoed out against the rocky hills. There was no running from it, no escaping it. His voice resounded through the crisp morning air.

"You have deceived me cruelly and beyond my belief!" Jacob bellowed into the morning like a wounded camel.

"I am bone of your bone, flesh of your flesh, yet you have dishonored our kinship. Does a covenant mean *nothing* to you?" Now he screamed, "Come out of your tent, you wretched man, you breaker of promises, you slave driver. Come out and show yourself before me and answer my charges!"

Those were the last words Rachel heard clearly, for now she had reached the crest of the hill and could go no farther.

Jacob's continual stream of words were still audible, but they were muffled and indistinguishable up in the thin, mountain air.

The very thing she had wanted to miss, Jacob's realization that Laban had tricked him, she had heard as clearly as if she had stood just outside his tent. It was bad enough that she had been forced to be a part of the deception, but to be robbed of her wedding night stirred her jealous hatred for Leah to white-hot intensity, and now to bear Jacob's agony did nothing to soothe her. However, by the time she reached the top of the canyon, Rachel was physically and emotionally spent and winded. She collapsed on a large grey rock and rested her chin on her knees for a long time before moving or showing any signs of life.

"Father will show himself to you and answer your charges, all right," she said aloud, as she breathed a little slower.

"He will tell you that here on the eastern plains, it is not an acceptable custom to marry off the younger sister before the first-born. He will plead for you to be merciful and reasonable. He will ask you to understand that because of the long-standing traditions of this land, he had no other choice. And in the end, dearest Jacob. . . ." Rachel felt the tears rushing forward and spilling down her cheeks. "In the end, father will give me to you, but only after he has driven another hard bargain with you." She wondered exactly what further payment her father would now extract from Jacob. She sat still for some time and was aware that her eyes, swollen with the day's tears and the night's weeping, throbbed with pain as the brightness of the sun intensified.

"What will hurt the most, my love," Rachel continued her discourse into the folds of her skirt, "is that should you seek some kind of recourse under the law or try to steal me and flee back to your own country, my father will have quite an argument ready. He will undoubtedly remind you that long ago you deceived your father, Isaac, and stole your brother Esau's birthright."

She lifted her head and looked down over the valley spread before her. "I can hear my father asking, 'Jacob, is my deception any greater than yours? Is it not true that what a man plants in his fields, he also harvests?'" Rachel shook her head wearily, and a heavy sadness filled her being.

The grandeur and beauty of the summer day was lost on her. Rachel missed the faded remnants of the clumps of spring flowers. She never saw the tiny brown hare which bounded and scampered across the ground near her; and only until Little Fox's impatient barking persisted, did she remember to lead the sheep to the well. Finally, she headed the flock into the western sunset and led them homeward.

When she had settled the sheep in their pen and fed the hungry dog, Rachel slipped unnoticed from the sheepcote through the trees, skirted the edges of the main tents, and silently entered her own place.

Her eyes, not yet accustomed to the semidarkness, did not see Leah, but instantly Rachel sensed her sister was there, waiting for her return.

Rachel gave no greeting, but plunged in abruptly with, "While the festivities continue for another seven days, what am I to do? Am I to play the part of the smiling bride, or do I tell the truth for all to hear?" She didn't look at Leah, but busied herself with a meticulous bathing of her own dirty and scratched feet.

Leah sat on a low wooden stool near the center pole in the tent and, in the silence which followed, she sighed and finally found enough voice to say dully, "The morning winds have carried the news of my marriage and Jacob's words with our father to everyone. I doubt there is anyone living on the plains of Padan-aram who has not heard the whole story by now."

"How does it feel to have climbed into Jacob's bed before me?" Rachel cried with saddening tears blurring her vision.

Quietly, but with some sarcasm, Leah answered, "Do I look like the triumphant victor who has just won a war?"

"Just don't tell me any details about the night," Rachel retorted angrily.

Without any inflection, Leah's voice lay flatly in the air between the two women, "I hadn't planned to tell you anything."

It seemed to Rachel that they had reached a stalemate in this confrontation, one they both had expected.

After Leah cleared her throat several times, she finally continued, in the same low tones. "It has been decided that when the seven days of my ... ah ... our wedding festivities have concluded, Jacob may have you as his second wife." Leah's voice peaked a bit on the word *second,* as if it were her only hold or her only edge on Rachel. There had never been a time in Leah's memory that she had ever had some advantage over Rachel. Having slept with Jacob first, before Rachel, felt extremely good, and Leah had enjoyed the brief triumph though she would never admit it. Also, as she sat there, she purposed in her heart to always refer to Rachel as the "second wife." She knew she was allowing her personal bitterness to show, but she dismissed the thought because she wanted to savor one victory over Rachel. *At least one,* Leah thought.

When the term *second wife* was verbally placed between

them, Rachel felt the full stabbing pain of it. She caught her breath and felt faint at the same instant.

The tent's open entrance flap allowed the soft twilight's glow to illuminate Leah's face. Rachel slowly turned and faced her sister, asking coldly, "And what will Jacob's taking a second wife . . ."; she nearly gagged on the phrase. "What will it cost him?"

"Another seven years of labor to our father," Leah replied. Her answer caused Rachel to stare at her sister in utter disbelief.

"Seven years *more?*" Rachel shouted. Now her knees gave way, and she sank down on the carpet before Leah.

"Is our father so filled with a need to be cunning and devious that he would demand *another* seven years?" She looked closely at her sister, but Leah turned away.

"Look at me!" Rachel commanded. "Answer me! And tell me! Did you agree with father to the additional and unreasonable burden?"

"You needn't be so shocked, my sister," Leah replied evenly. "Evidently Jacob thought the extra price was fair, for he has already agreed to it, and everything is settled between him and father."

Rachel got up from her knees and moved, as if she were in a trance, across the tent. She unrolled her bedding, spread it, and whispered into the pillows as she sank wearily into them, "Another seven years?" Then she lay thinking. *It is unjust for anyone to make a seven-year-labor contract for marriage; trick Jacob into lying with the wrong bride; and then extract another seven years just to have the woman he was promised in the first place.*

None of it made sense, not even the tradition's and custom's explanation; and as Rachel lay on her bedding, she was torn between her lifelong love of her father, Laban, and her newly found, all-consuming love for her prince, Jacob.

After she knew Leah had gone back to Jacob's tent, Rachel finally drifted off into an uneasy sleep. The night passed uncomfortably and was troubling to her because of a very uncomfortable dream she had been having. That night she dreamed it again, and it was fresh and vivid.

Through a misty veil, Rachel could see the tall and straight form of Jacob. He was standing by the well, much as she had seen him that first day years ago. *My prince*, she thought again and smiled. Jacob was not alone, however; for, by his side, stood a small lad of five or six summers.

In Jacob's arms was a tiny bundle, and Rachel realized it must be an infant.

Jacob called her name and beckoned her to come. The boy smiled, and Rachel thought him to be the most beautiful child she had ever seen. He cupped his hand to his mouth and called, "Mother, come to us."

Rachel's heart nearly spun out of control. She ran toward them on feet winged with joy. She knew instantly that Jacob and the two sons belonged to her, but the faster she ran, the more frustrated she became. They were unreachable.

Rachel could never cover the distance between them, and no matter how hard she forced her legs to run, Jacob, the boy, and the infant seemed always just beyond her outstretched arms.

She grew tired of running and not coming any closer, so more than once she called out to them to help her. But her words only became garbled and stuck to the roof of her mouth.

Then Jacob called her, urging her on, and she renewed and intensified her efforts to push toward them, but they remained some distance away.

Finally, the cock's crowing and the first sounds of morning put an end to her exhausted efforts, and silently, the frustrating dream drifted like a cloud off the horizon of her mind. Rachel was left anxious and puzzled, unable to fully understand the meaning of her dream.

7

During the next few weeks and months, Rachel's puzzlement over her dream was replaced with a frightening reality. All too well she was able to interpret correctly her nightly vision. Each time she failed to reach Jacob at the well, it only served to underscore the truth: she was barren. And with the same dream repeating itself, night after night, the loss she felt as a woman and the innate maternal desire to bear children was stamped indelibly on her mind.

Rachel would awaken soaked in her own perspiration, bone weary from trying to run to her beloved. Even Jacob's patient and tender kisses, when she was awake, did nothing to reassure her or to ease the suffering the dream always produced.

Wide-awake, she was able to handle her emotions a little more effectively and with a calmer perspective. She would say, "Jacob, your God *will* grant me sons." Then unsteadily she'd add, "Though I know not when; but always I see two sons in my dream, so I'll try to be patient."

However, just before Jacob and Rachel's first year of marriage drew to a close, it was Leah—not Rachel—who conceived and bore the first child.

Before Jacob could see him, Leah named their son Reuben. Then as they washed him, rubbed down his little body with salt to harden his skin, and prepared to bind him hand and foot in the linen cloth binding strips, she said to her midwife and servant girls, "I have called him Reuben, for Jacob's God has seen my affliction and has favored me with a man-child. His name means *See, a son!*, and Jacob's God has seen me and my needs."

The following year produced Leah's second son. Again, she broke with the traditional way of the father having the privilege to name a son, and before Jacob had a chance to choose a name, Leah did it for him. Loudly, as they held up the wet and reddened infant for her inspection, Leah said, "Ah, what a loud cry he makes. I shall call him Simeon, for it means *hearing*, and I know the God of Jacob has heard that I am unloved by my husband and has again favored me!"

It took no time at all for Leah's pronouncement to reach Rachel, and, when it did, it stung Rachel's heart as surely as if she had been bodily thrust into a beehive alive with a thousand stinging bees.

"Is it possible," Rachel ranted to Jacob, "that we could live our whole lifetime with Leah producing one son each and every year?" Then with sarcasm dripping from each word, she announced, "She seems to dump children into the world as easily as the biggest ewes of my flocks drop their lambs."

She gave Jacob no chance to comment and stormed at him, "And what am I to do about her righteous talk of your God favoring her each time she delivers a child?"

To Jacob, this whole thing was incomprehensible. He was at a complete loss when it came to knowing what to do with her. Once he tried wiping the tears from Rachel's cheeks and, mustering all the enthusiasm he could, he comforted her by whispering, "It will be all right. You'll see, my beloved. Maybe tonight . . . even now you will conceive, and God will bless our union."

But not that night—or any other night—did their union bring forth Jacob's issue, and reasoning with her brought no peace at all.

During the ten years which followed their marriage, Leah conceived and delivered, apparently without too much effort, and Levi and Judah were born.

Laban's health and disposition improved during those same years. He experienced no loss of breath or palpitating heartbeats, nor did he suffer from acute loneliness. The addition of Jacob to his household had been a most fortunate and timely decision.

The flocks of Laban were beginning to expand, and Jacob had organized Laban's heretofore lazy sons, Abihu and Jubal, into a small, but effective, work force.

Leah's ability to bear children had produced grandsons, and, to Laban, the pleasure of it tasted like honey cakes after a rich and satisfying meal.

"You are a man of great wealth; a man to be envied," Aaron had once commented to Laban. "You have married both your daughters and managed to keep them here with you. The women and your son-in-law have increased your family and your flocks."

"I am not all *that* wealthy," Laban countered, "but most of what you say has truth. However, there is one thing which troubles me, and that is Rachel's barrenness. Never have I seen a woman so determined to have children."

The two old friends lingered over their evening meal. "Rachel's disgrace becomes more evident each time a son is born to Leah," Laban confided.

"I confess," Aaron said, and his face wore a puzzled expression, "I do not fully understand a woman's overwhelming concern over childbearing. But I do know, from Sari, that if a woman is married and childless, other women point her out as a woman cursed by the gods."

Laban nodded his head in agreement. "Yes. Rachel feels not only cursed, but abandoned as well. I have spoken to her and tried to lift her spirits, but to no avail. The whole matter, now that Leah has four sons, is a dark and troubling cloud on my otherwise clear horizon."

Rachel remained inconsolable, and her anguish uncontainable. It spilled out of her, contaminating all her being. Trying to conceive and yet living with a barren womb became the central obsession of her life. The shame and disgrace of it ruled her tongue and shaded her moods darkly each waking hour of every day. When she slept, her dreams carried on the torment through each black or starlit night.

"Rachel, my love," Jacob pleaded desperately one night, as they lay in each others arms, and the fragrance on her skin filled him with desire. "It is so bad that you have not given me sons? We have our love."

He tried reasoning, and he touched her face in the darkness. "I worked all those years for you, and even now I am working out the second agreement of seven years labor with Laban, but the time has been only as a day or two—my love for you is so great. Tell me, why should you be filled with such envy toward Leah? You are so beautiful . . . you have more than met the expectations of my soul."

He kissed her mouth, her eyes, and then moved downward to kiss her neck, but she lay still and quiet beside him.

The stone within her would not soften or melt by anything he had to say.

"Why can't you understand?" Rachel asked sullenly.

Jacob could feel his patience growing thinner by the moment.

He used the last bit of gentle persuasion left in him and said, "Listen. The God of my fathers has promised me fertility in my family and fertility in my flocks as well. He shall do both—but in His own way, and when He pleases. He is not a deceiver; nor is He a God who breaks promises. You'll see. He is faithful to His children."

"How long am I to wait, Jacob? It has been more than ten

summers since we married, and I am still barren. I need sons, and I want them now." Rachel's frustration, always close to the surface, now mounted swiftly within her.

Jacob heard the pointed words as they pierced the darkness, and he traded his impatience for a heart racing with anger.

"Did you hear me?" she asked. Rachel leaned her elbows on his chest and held his chin firmly in her hands. She spoke with clipped precision. "Each time I see her four sons, they stab me with remorse and grief. They mock me in my barrenness. I do not know why I have this intense longing within my breast, but Jacob," she dug her fingers into his beard, "Jacob, you give me children, or else I die!"

The fierceness in her tone penetrated the depths of Jacob's soul. His anger flared, and pushing her roughly off his chest, he roared, "Am I God? Do you want me to take His place? *God* is the One responsible for your empty womb ... not me! Do not talk to me of this, again. I am weary of your constant complaining and of your continual jealousy of Leah, and I despise the bickering which goes on between you."

Rachel was glad he could not see her face in the darkness, for she was shocked and embarrassed that he had heard her complaints or ever listened in on her frequent arguments with Leah. She had never heard him speak so sharply, and since she had never been treated in any way except in loving gentleness, she held her breath for a moment. Then he continued in this new, strange tone of voice.

"Daily you have a woeful countenance," Jacob said. "Now you demand children from me, even accuse me of not giving them to you, when you know very well that *I am capable* but that God has kept you barren. Do not ever again accuse or blame me. I am not at fault!"

But even after she heard his pronouncement, she was miserable enough to risk his wrath even further, for she knew she would not drop the issue before then. Rachel took a deep breath. She felt as if she were stranded somewhere in the desert in the midst of a swirling sandstorm. To be heard over the rising wind and be spared the stinging wind-driven sand was almost an impossible dream, but Rachel knew she had to try once more, even if it meant disobeying Jacob, for she could see her life depended on it.

Loudly she cried, "Then, my husband, sleep with my servant girl, Bilhah. Give her a son, and I will, according to our custom, adopt him as my own."

The sandstorm around her subsided, the howling wind died, and she finally heard him say, "Woman, do you never give up?" He rolled away from her and placed his broad back between them as a wall.

Rachel touched his shoulder and rubbing his back, she softly pleaded, "Jacob, please sleep with Bilhah, or surely I shall die."

With a sigh as heavy as the stone cover over the well he once lifted for her, Jacob said stoically, "You do not need to entreat me any longer. It is settled. I will sleep with your servant girl, and we will see if she gives you a son. Whether she does or does not, I will not listen to your complaints any more."

A surge of hope—the first since the early days of her marriage—raced through Rachel's veins, and, in great relief, she gratefully caressed his back. He did not stir or turn toward her.

Rachel knew he had lost his keen want of her, and that, at least for tonight, there would be no union between them.

It was as she sensed. For the first time since Jacob had seen Rachel, he lay beside her now unmoved, wide-awake, staring with unblinking eyes into the tent's darkness and pondering deeply the mysterious ways of women. He shoved the even more mysterious ways of God out of his mind's door and tried vainly to sleep.

8

While it was true that Rachel said no more to Jacob about the fears and frustrations of her barrenness, she was not about to confine her worries to herself. She talked with any and every woman who would listen. "Perhaps someone will have a remedy, so I shall leave no road untraveled," she declared.

Women from other tents were questioned by her, and once

she even traveled to Haran to see if Aaron's housekeeper, Sari, had some knowledge that would help her. Rachel looked hopefully over Sari's vast array of tea and potions, but time only proved that nothing, not even Sari's magic, would fill her womb.

To Bilhah, the maid Laban had given her upon her wedding to Jacob, Rachel said, "I have spoken to my husband, and it has been arranged that you will cohabit with him and bear a son for me on my knees." She emphasized the phrase, "on my knees," for it was symbolic of adoption, and she wanted no one, especially Bilhah, to have any illusions as to whose son he would be when he was born.

"You will go to Jacob when I tell you," Rachel added, underscoring that as Jacob's favorite wife she had the dubious honor of deciding which of Jacob's wives or servant girls would share his tent on any given night. With precise authority, Rachel set down the guidelines to Bilhah, for she wanted no misunderstandings between them nor anything to go amiss.

"God was faithful to my obedient maid, Bilhah," Rachel explained when the first son was born to the servant girl. Rachel named the infant Dan, for the name meant *he argued the case*, and she felt Jacob's God had seen her predicament and, in effect, had heard, and, with great justice, argued for her petition. When the second son dropped down into Rachel's waiting hands, she called him Naphtali, meaning *my wrestling*, and no one doubted she referred to the years of argumentative wrestling battles she'd had with her sister, not only over conception but over Jacob's love as well.

Leah grew very fearful with the birth of Bilhah's second son that her own time of sharing Jacob's tent and childbearing were coming to a rapid close. Rachel allowed her fewer nights with Jacob, and even talking with him was hard to arrange. With each night, she was denied his tent. The fear grew stronger in her; and since the women did not eat with the men, the only time Leah even saw Jacob was when she served the food to the men, or as he went off to work in the fields with the flocks and herds. Eventually, out of a mounting desperation, she devised a plan and bravely set out to present it to her husband.

Leah sent her servant girls to as many tasks as she could arrange. To some, she gave the never-ending job of grinding the grain; to others, the weaving of goat's hair cloth for the tents; and in the hands of her personal maid, Zilpah, she left the entire preparations for the evening meal. She whispered to the girl, "Do not fail me today, Zilpah, and I will reward you."

Zilpah looked puzzled, but she obediently nodded and watched as Leah wrapped her veil around her head and left the tent. Leah quickly walked a circuitous route so no one would see or follow her out of the encampment, and when she was sure she was safe, she headed straight for Jacob. She found him tending some of her father's flocks in a nearby meadow. All the way, Leah rehearsed what she would say to Jacob, and she prayed to her gods that the smells of the field grass would not make her sneeze and that the sandy winds would not cause her eyes to cloud up with fluid. Most of all, she hoped she would be heard.

He saw her before she reached him, because the dog announced her presence. Shyly she approached him. "My husband " she said and bowed before him, "I have brought you some water." Leah offered him the small goatskin. "May I speak with you awhile?" she asked.

Jacob's eyes twinkled and quietly reflected his amusement. He found himself chuckling and pondering the mysteries of a woman. He plugged up the ram's horn of olive oil. He had been rubbing the oil into some scratches on a lamb's head, and now he put both the horn and the lamb on the ground before him and drank deeply from the skin.

"The water is cool, and I am grateful to you," he acknowledged with a compliment and smiled. Pointing down beside him, he bade Leah sit on the cloak which was spread beneath and said, "So you want to speak with me? Am I like a great ruler or king that you must steal away and ask permission . . . looking fearful as you do it?" he teased.

Leah relaxed a bit and sank down beside him. Her round, plain face softened with a slight smile, and she said quickly, "Oh, no, my husband. I know I can speak with you freely anytime. . . . It is just that there has been so little *anytime* lately."

Jacob breathed out a short "Ha," and added, "well, now you have your time. Just please don't talk about barrenness or of having sons. My ears are filled past their ability to hold all the talk on that subject!" He took another drink of the satisfying liquid.

"But, my lord, that is exactly what I have come all this way to talk about," Leah cried.

Jacob's jaw dropped, and his face mirrored his surprise. He wiped the remaining droplets of water off his beard with the back of his hand and stared at her.

"Do we have four sons or do we not?" he finally said, when he found his voice.

"Yes, we do, my husband, and fine men they will be, too, for your God has blessed the fruit of my womb, but—"

Jacob reached over and took Leah's plump hand in his and asked, "But what, then?"

She put her head down. It flustered her to have him touch her, and the love she felt for him rose swiftly within her. It was distracting and made her even slower of speech. She withdrew her hand and pretended her veil needed adjusting.

"It's just that with Rachel, myself, and now Bilhah as your concubine, I fear my time of bearing children may be over. . ." she ventured.

"Ah, so it is the addition of Bilhah to my tent that disturbs you?" Jacob mused to himself. "The jealousies of women are almost as complex as their tears."

"No, my lord," Leah answered evenly. "It is not Bilhah . . . she is a loyal servant girl to Rachel. . . . It is just that I would have as much of God's blessing as possible, and I would like to have more sons for you. However, I do not see too much of you, and I am not allowed to come to you very often; so I was wondering if you would consider taking my maid, Zilpah, as you took Bilhah, so that I might bear you more sons, also?"

Jacob had never kept a record, but it took very little remembering to tell him that Rachel had allowed Leah to sleep with him on a very limited basis. He knew Leah had been deeply aware that he had been unable to love her as he did Rachel, and so he was pleased that Leah had not openly accused Rachel of biased decisions. He marveled at her acceptance of the whole situation involving their marriage.

With a greater degree of respect for the woman who sat beside him, Jacob placed his hand on her shoulder and said with affection, "Leah, go back to our encampment now and tell Rachel that I have said I would sleep with your servant girl, Zilpah."

Leah's eyes, already teary, filled with more tears, for she was greatly relieved. Her errand and purpose accomplished, she kissed Jacob's hand, murmured she would be always grateful and left him by the vast flock of sheep.

So it was that when the next spring season to be born was come upon the land and the tents of Jacob, Zilpah gave birth to a son. Leah rejoiced and called him Gad. Leah's joy was evident when she said to the women helping in the delivery of the infant, "I have called his name Gad because it means *fortunate*, and I am most fortunate to have another son!"

Then, after that boy came, another was born to Zilpah, and he was named Asher which meant *happy*. Leah gushed and confided to Zilpah, "How happy am I! Now women will call me happy!"

The two sons of Leah, given her by her servant, made her very happy and extended her childbearing days. But for Rachel, they only served to increase her restlessness, and the moods which came upon her became darker than ever before.

Rachel had tolerated Zilpah's two sons, but she was genuinely pleased with her servant girl Bilhah's two children. She took pleasure in them, and they consumed a good portion of her day. Gradually, however, she understood that only one thing—bearing a child herself—would ever give her the peace she sought so desperately. So, she retired to her tent and spent less and less time with Bilhah's children.

Rachel allowed Leah and the two concubines only a few nights with Jacob, for fear they would use up his seed and there would be none left for her. Daily she continued her search for fertility, and nothing slowed or stopped her fervor. To both Jacob's God and the teraphim in Laban's tents, she prayed regularly and continuously.

One day, after praying to the stone gods, Rachel left Laban's tent, and she spotted Reuben, Leah's firstborn, playing in the field. She watched him idly at first and then with quickened interest. He seemed to have found something in the ground; something so unusual and exciting that he jumped up suddenly, grasping what looked like a plant in his hands, and he ran to his mother's tent.

Rachel shivered with a small thrill, for the boy carried what appeared to be mandrake roots. *If only I could have them*, Rachel thought. The mandrake plant, with its dark green leaves and tiny white blossoms, was hard to find, but it was believed that, if eaten, the roots—fleshy white and shaped like the lower portion of a human's body—would induce conception. It was a very favorable and acceptable superstition, and Rachel, fevered with desperation, ran to Leah's tent. She pleaded with her sister to give her the plants. But Leah felt no charity toward Rachel who held Jacob's heart. With much hostility in her voice, Leah said, "It is not enough that you have taken my husband, now you would take my son's mandrake plants as well?"

Long after the bitter exchange of words that afternoon, and months after the heated confrontation had cooled, Rachel realized with despair that she had lost in two ways. Bitterly she wept and went over the losses. After successfully negotiating an agreement with Leah, she had eaten the prized roots only to face the reality that she had been taken in by the superstitious lie, for nothing had happened. But the thing which ground down her spirit the most was the fact that the very night she used as barter with Leah for the mandrake plant was the night Leah conceived.

Some nine months later, Issachar, a fifth son, was born to Leah, and once more Rachel plummeted into a pit of despair.

Eventually, Rachel stopped praying to Jacob's God and Laban's gods, for she knew they neither listened or cared. She became unshakable in her belief that no god existed; especially when the following year, Leah gave birth to another son who was named Zebulun, meaning *honored*. The final blow came when, after that, Dinah, Leah's first girl, was born.

Rachel counted up the heavy score. Of one thing she was sure: dream or no dream, god or no god, she would never give birth to any child. "I have lost the war, and the enemy of my womb has won every battle," she said dramatically, but realistically. "Jacob now has six sons and one daughter by Leah, and four sons by his two concubines, and none of those eleven children are *really* mine." Her mouth tasted of ashes as she spoke to the wind one cloudy morning.

Rachel had left their encampment, wrapped herself in her thick brown-and-white-striped wool mantle, and went off into the cold morning's air to seek the seclusion of the mountains.

She stood now, a drizzling rain dampening her veil and cloak, on the highest vantage point of the hills. She surveyed the familiar valley and fields below her with a detached numbness. The thin column of smoke rising from Leah's cooking fires could be seen through the grey light, and the tents of Laban and Jacob dotted the landscape with their blackness against the feathery-green tamarisk trees.

Why should I ever go back there? she asked herself. *Even for the love of Jacob, do I want to go down there to live in such poverty of spirit? Do I want to be daily reminded by Jacob's sons of my empty womb? Would the gods have me live my life in mourning forever?*

No answers came out of the mist. The only sound was the screeching cry of a field hawk which huddled on a small tree branch across the hill, on the other side of a deep canyon from her.

Directly beneath her feet, the rugged precipice she was standing on dropped sharply off and extended down deeply into the valley. Rachel looked over the edge and rationalized, *It would only take one step forward, and then I would no longer hold this grievous burden in my heart. Giving birth to a son would no longer matter.*

Before Rachel had a chance to act on her thoughts, something moved and caught the corner of her eye. She turned in time to see the red-tailed hawk swoop out of his tree, fly up the canyon, and dive down behind her. The large-winged bird missed his target, a small brown hare, and he flew up and disappeared over the next crest. The hare had seen the hawk coming and had popped down into his burrow. Then, sensing the danger had passed, he jumped up out of his tiny home and sat like a stone statue before her.

Rachel moved slowly away from the cliff's edge, as to not startle the hare, and said softly to him, "Even you multiply your numbers and have many children. But I cannot."

Just then the rain stopped and the wind rose slightly, and it seemed to whisper in a strange way. "Did someone speak?" Rachel asked, now fully alert. "Is someone there?" she called out.

"I have lovingly remembered you, Rachel. Now you shall have your heart's desires."

She heard the words distinctly and was instantly alarmed. "Who are you? Where do you hide?" she cried. Only profound silence greeted her. The brown hare was back in his burrow; the hawk was gone; the wind had died; and no voice spoke again. Rachel stood there, and, as she did, the clouds moved and sent the barest amount of sunlight to the hilltop. It caressed her face, and she slipped her cloak off her shoulders to stand in its warming glow.

The voice had come out of nowhere, but she knew instinctively this voice was of Jacob's God. *It certainly is not one of my teraphim!* she smiled. *They never speak nor promise anything. It has to have been Jacob's God, for I did hear it.*

After she had stood there awhile pondering His words, "remembered you," she picked up her mantle, left the cliff top, and thoughtfully made her way down the mountainside. Hope sprang like some fresh, new bubbling spring over her parched and aching soul. *Do I dare believe it?* she wondered, as she picked her way between the rocks and boulders.

Rachel half ran, half walked, back to her own tent and stayed there in seclusion all day. She would speak to no one, nor did she eat. To Bilhah she said, "Please leave me today. I am well. . . . I just do not want to see anyone." And after she made the statement, Rachel sent the girl off to tell the others.

Rachel wanted to see no one—no one, that is, but Jacob; and so at dusk, after she had bathed and anointed herself with perfume, she ran out to search for Jacob in a large meadow east of their tents. Since her marriage to him, Jacob had taken over her sheep, and Rachel had learned to cook and tend the domestic duties with Leah. It had never suited her. She was fully alive out here on the plains. Finally, after she spotted some of his flock, she called his name, and suddenly they were in each other's arms.

They kissed, and then abruptly Jacob stopped, stepped back, and looked down into her glowing face.

He cried out, "My love, you are radiant with joy. What news do you bring me? What has happened?"

"Everything is changed. Everything!" Rachel replied. But try as he would, Jacob could get nothing more from her. They walked home together, her small hand held snugly in his; the sheep bleating and following after.

Jacob left the evening meal with the other men early and returned to his tent where he knew she would be waiting.

Their lovemaking filled the cool evening's air with the sound of their satisfied joy. They could not get enough of each other, and Jacob worded it accurately for both of them when he whispered, "This time for us is as it was when we were first married. My youth has returned this night. You, my beloved Rachel, are truly the most beautiful woman in the land, and you know how to pleasure your husband beyond any expectations."

She had told him nothing of her day. She had simply entered into loving him with a renewed passion, and she knew she was desirable. That knowledge and the words she'd heard on the hill only increased Rachel's capacity to love.

The night passed in an incredible celebration of love, and out of the gratefulness of a joyous heart Jacob said, "Rachel, I would buy you a gift. What would you like? Would a gold ring for your finger or a bracelet please you? Or perhaps there is some cloth in Haran that you have seen and want? Oh, my love, let me shower you with gifts. You have made this old man young and virile again." His torrent of words finally ended, and he waited for her to speak.

"There is one thing," she said, in the quietness of the moment, and for an instant Jacob thought she would plague him about a child. Instead, the question which came softly from her lips stunned him.

"Tell me, Jacob, about your God . . . the living One . . . the One of Isaac and Abraham. Is it true that He lives, and nowhere is His likeness to be found?" Rachel took Jacob's face in her hands, and by the light of the small oil lamp she asked, from her heart, "And is it true that He speaks to men, and you can hear the sound of His voice?"

"Why, after all these years," Jacob asked, "do you want to know of my God?"

"Because I think I heard Him today," she said hesitantly, "and I must be sure it was He and not my mind or the wind playing games with me."

He pulled a large pillow towards him and settled Rachel's head gently on it. Then he held her in his arms, at his side, and began to speak as she had never heard him speak before.

"Once, before I met you, my love, in fact on the way to Haran from my home in Canaan, I pillowed my head on some very hard

rocks and dreamed the dream of my life. I have always wanted to
tell you of it. Perhaps now is the best time. I saw a remarkable
stone staircase rising out of the ground, and the top of it was en-
cased in clouds way above me."

"It sounds as if you saw all of our Mesopotamian temple
towers," Rachel put in.

"Yes, it did resemble a ziggurat," he said, using the technical
name, "but where the heathen temple towers represent confusion
and the voices of many gods, my staircase was an open, clear
pathway to the one true living God. In fact, the very angels of
God came down, collected my needs and my prayers of worship,
and went back up to give them to my God. When the clouds
cleared, I saw God Himself standing at the top and, my dear, He
spoke, indeed. He spoke to me!"

"You never doubted?" Rachel asked. "You knew instantly?"

"No, not instantly," he replied. "At first I was frightened
when I awoke; but after a while, as I remembered the things
which He said, I realized it *was* God. Then there was no doubt."

"I took the rock which had been my pillow, and I set it up as a
monument, and after I poured oil over it to consecrate it, and
since God promised me the land, I changed the name of the
nearby town of Luz to Bethel, for it means that the staircase or
tower I saw was 'the house of God.' "

Jacob fell silent and Rachel asked, "What did your God say?
And what else did He promise?"

Jacob smiled down at her lovely, upturned face and said, "Oh,
my sweet lamb, my God promised me so much."

"Like what?" she prodded.

"Well, as I said, my God promised first that I would inherit
the land beneath my feet; and secondly, that I would have many,
many descendants. His words, my wife, about our children were
that they would number as many as there are specks of sand or
dust. Imagine that, my love."

Rachel's heart began beating so hard she thought Jacob would
notice the movement at his side, but he was caught up in remembering, and so he continued.

"My God said He would always be with me and that He
would protect me wherever I went . . . and, most of all, He said
He would bring me into this land and not leave me until He had

accomplished all He had promised. Rachel, do you understand? My God is not merely a tribal god, like one who is restricted by borders and local territories, as your teraphim are supposed to be ... but He is an all-compassing God. He is here in the tents of Laban, in all of Mesopotamia, and far over in my land of Canaan and Egypt. In fact, He is everywhere!"

Jacob sat up beside her. He was filled with a new vigor, and recalling his dream to Rachel reminded him of his own promises he made the night of the tower and the stone pillow. He took her face, lovelier than ever by the light of the small lamp, in his hands, and said, "My beloved, that night was the night of turning for me. God was not the only one who made promises that night. ... I did, too. I vowed that if He kept His covenant with me, protected me while traveling, and gave me the necessities of life so I'd be able to return home ... then ... *He* would be my God ... my only God. I promised to worship Him, and I vowed I'd give Him a tenth of all my possessions. Those are vows I gladly keep."

Jacob lay back down on his pillows next to her and explained softly, "Now, as to whether or not my God is a living God and talks with us ... do you understand my heart? Do you see that once having seen Him and heard Him, I know He lives?"

"Yes, Jacob, I do," Rachel said peaceably.

"I intend to give the God of my fathers my life for all my days, dear wife." He spoke the words into her ear.

"Then the God of your father will be my God, too." Rachel's voice seemed laced with a new strength. "I am sure now it was He who spoke out of the wind today."

Jacob leaned up on one elbow to see her better. "So that is what happened to you. What did He say to you?" he asked excitedly.

"Oh, Jacob!" Rachel gave a long, deep sigh and then said wistfully, "Your God ... I mean, our God, simply said He remembered me and that I would bear a son. I have never been so happy, for I really believe this God is a living God, and He will bring forth the issue of our loins!"

"And so He shall!" Jacob's tears ran freely down his cheeks. "My beloved, I have always known that when the God of my forefathers promised that my seed would number as the dust of the earth and that I, Jacob, would be spread abroad to the west, east, north and south . . . He would not break His covenant.

"But over the years of our marriage, I have wondered if the issue of sons would be denied you," Jacob continued. "It was wrong of me to doubt God, but the years have gone on, and I was old when we met. Now you say God has talked with you this morning; then I know surely it was He, and the promise of fertility is open to you, too." Jacob rejoiced aloud and would have clapped his hands and danced had Rachel not reminded him that the camp was quiet, and the night was far spent.

Jacob held her close and, just before he finally went to sleep, he whispered for only her to hear, "My cherished one, we shall name our first son Joseph."

She agreed, saying, "It is perfect, for it means *may he add*, and our God will add to our joy and give us more sons."

They said no more. Soon Rachel heard the sounds of Jacob's deep and even breathing. She felt at peace with herself, her family, even Leah, and now with the living God.

She fell into a tranquil sleep, but briefly she dreamed her dream again. It was as if a small, dark shadow drifted over her soul to cloud her joy, so she moved out of its way. Gradually the dream faded, and before Rachel slept, she *knew* for certain two things: Jacob's God was her God; and she had, on this glorious night of nights, conceived!

9

Later, as if she needed anything to confirm her heartfelt secret, Rachel's flow disappeared, and nothing she ate stayed safely lodged down in her stomach. Rachel began to understand that, for some, bearing children was a difficult and treacherous road to travel, but it was a journey she was willing to take—no matter what the cost.

Each day she watched and waited for all the signs of life to blossom within her, and when Rachel's small, wispy waist disappeared, and she began to look bottom heavy, she checked with a local midwife to see if a prediction could be made as to whether the child was male or female.

"It is much too early for me to even guess," the midwife said, with a slight chuckle at Rachel's impatient naiveness. "But I *can* tell you one thing for sure."

"Yes?" Rachel asked eagerly.

"You are definitely with child," the woman teased.

Rachel knew she was acting like a young girl, by the inexperienced kinds of questions she was asking, but watching Leah breeze through childbearing without so much as a hiccup and having sons by your servant girl was nothing compared to bearing your own. So with *this* baby, she had to know everything!

Rachel hadn't counted on the strange, queasy sickness in her stomach which came one morning and never went away. She did not know that Leah's cooking, which always smelled and tasted so fragrantly delicious, would now cause her to throw up anything she'd barely been able to get down.

She also didn't know that as she grew heavier with child her early sickness would increase its intensity. Even the day she felt the first stirring movements of the baby within her, the joy of the experience was eclipsed by the illness which commanded her full attention. It was a maddening frustration to be with child and yet to be so sick she could not enjoy it.

"I am sorry, my husband." Rachel's tone was truly apologetic. Jacob had broken with tradition and had asked her to join him for the evening meal. "I just . . . cannot be around food," she stammered.

Jacob's silence prompted her to broaden her explanation, so she said, "You are being very understanding and patient with me, but I know my sickness, day in and day out, does irritate you . . . still there is nothing I can do about it."

Jacob studied her momentarily, and then with no accusations or judgments in his voice he said retrospectively, "For years you have been desperately ill because you could not bear children, and now you are ill because you are with child. It is a mystery." He shook his head, and a slight smile played across his face.

Rachel listened as he continued, "I do not pretend to understand it all, but you are right about one thing—I am a patient man, and we will weather out this storm together."

Jacob's solicitous words gave her some comfort, and gently she advised, "Thank you, dear Jacob.... Now go on. At least one of us should enjoy the evening meal."

"I will," Jacob said with conviction; then he teased, "On the way over I think I smelled Leah's delicious roast lamb, her lentil soup, some fresh onions...." He ducked his head to the left, and the small wooden bowl she threw at him sailed right on by.

They parted, and their laughter soaked into the tent walls. It was the last of happy times, for after she was seven moons into her time, Rachel—weakened by her inability to eat—turned very pale and took to her bed. Desperately she wondered how it would all end, and when she discovered that a small issue of blood trickled from her daily, she grew fearfully despondent.

She said nothing to anyone of her pain or blood, or of the despair that came with it. "I'm fine, really," she said to Leah. "It's just that I am not as fortunate as you in childbearing, but I'll be all right."

With Jacob, Rachel pretended she was still the confident about-to-be mother she had been earlier, but each time he knelt down by her bed, the truth of her illness—plainly visible—smote his heart with sadness. Tenderly he held her trembling hands in his and rubbed her cold, grey fingers. He tried to ignore the deep purple shadows under her eyes and the overall pallor of her skin. He hoped his voice sounded confident and that his words would bring comfort when he said, "Our God will bring you through this, and we shall have a son, my lamb."

"Yes," she answered weakly, without even a show of enthusiasm; but he noticed she parted her lips and tried to smile. Inwardly Jacob was shattered by what he saw, and the thought of losing Rachel crouched in the corners of his mind like some hideous beast of prey.

When Bilhah could stand the obvious decline in her mistress's health no longer, she touched the arm of Jacob as he left Rachel's tent one night and whispered frantically, "She has no strength. Were the baby to come tonight, she would die in the struggle. My lord, day after day she lies on her bed. She grows weaker with each dawn. I fear for her life," Bilhah sobbed into the fold of Jacob's tunic, and he held her head against his shoulder.

"I know . . . I know," he said softly, and then he made a decision.

"Bilhah," Jacob said, as he straightened up to his full height. "You will send a runner to Haran to fetch a physician. I'm sure Aaron knows one who is the best. Instruct the runner he is not to come back without the physician." Then he added, "Rachel must live. I am going to that mountain there," he pointed northward, "to beseech my God in Rachel's behalf. Come and find me if there is any change between now and tomorrow's dawn."

Bilhah did as she was told, but there was no change in Rachel's condition. A day later, when the physician shrugged his shoulders and returned to Haran, the tents of Jacob and Laban stood silhouetted against the cloudless blue skies; there was nothing left to do but the waiting.

Abruptly, several mornings later, near the time of her delivery, Rachel awakened and reached over to rouse the sleeping Bilhah. The girl became instantly awake and responded, "What is it, my mistress?"

"Ask Leah for some barley broth. I'm hungry," Rachel whispered. Bilhah's eyes instantly filled with tears. "How good it is to hear you will eat something!" she cried.

"And Bilhah," Rachel continued, "there is a new pain down low in my back. Send for the midwife. I think my time has arrived." She lay back on her pillow, her limited strength spent; but she thought, *It will be today!*

Then Rachel watched her very excited servant girl as she collided abruptly with a sturdy tent pole. Bilhah picked herself up and, turning to look at Rachel, asked sheepishly, "Has that pole always been there?" It was the first time Rachel had laughed since she had thrown the bowl at Jacob, and it had been too long for either of them to remember.

The pains gradually grew stronger and in between them Rachel, wan but alert, watched the comings and goings of the women and noted each and every detail of preparation with the keenest of interest. Jacob and Laban came to see her, but the flurry of activity around her kept their visit brief.

"I will be back, my beloved," Jacob whispered to her, and she gripped his hand tightly, knowing precisely what he meant.

Zilpah and another servant, Achsa, brought in the birthing stools that Rachel would half sit, half recline upon for the delivery. Everyone called them stools when, in fact, they were a pair of smooth, slightly mounded stones. Leah spread a large, clean cloth over the carpets and then arranged the stones, leaving a small space between them, and covered it all with another clean linen cloth.

Merab, the midwife who had attended all the births of the children of Jacob, knelt beside the softly moaning Rachel; and when the pain doubled its intensity, causing Rachel to scream out, Merab gave the order saying, "It is time to lift her up."

Leah and two other women moved Rachel the short distance. They sat her up, braced her back and placed her left hip on one stone and the right hip on the other for the moment of birth.

Rachel, sitting on the strange stone arrangement and feeling the intermittent and mounting pains, said weakly to Leah, as she leaned against her, "I cannot bear the pain in quiet dignity. I will have to scream again if it gets worse."

Leah removed a fallen strand of hair from Rachel's perspiring forehead. "It is acceptable to scream. None of us will mind," she said crisply.

"But you never cried out once . . . never once," Rachel remembered aloud.

The older sister's sad eyes grew pensive, and then, almost like a flower opening its petals to the sun, Leah's manner grew warm. She said softly, "I know how long you have prayed for a child. I would not deny you anything at this moment. It is not a time for remembering me, for I have never been visited by as much sickness as you . . . so scream, cry, and do whatever you have to do, to push this baby out into the world. We are all eager to see him!"

Leah had barely spoken the words when, with one long scream piercing the predawn's solitude, Rachel pushed with all the strength she could summon and heard Merab cry, "I hold his head . . . now once more . . . one more push. . . ."

Rachel's breath came in short, panting bursts, and she called upon her God, the living God of Jacob, with one word, three times: "Now . . . now . . . now!"

The tiny infant boy dropped into Jacob's ready and waiting hands.

Although Rachel had not seen Jacob rush back into the tent, she knew he'd be kneeling there to catch his son at the moment of birth. He had told her months before that some Hebrew fathers, when they were sure the child would be a boy, would come in at the moment of birth to have the privilege of catching the infant during the first seconds of life. Jacob had not disappointed her. He had arrived at the right time.

She looked at him holding the baby, and after Merab cut the cord with a sharpened stone knife, Jacob stood and said, "Yes, my sweet lamb, God has remembered you indeed, for He has given you Joseph . . . as I told you . . . *Joseph!*"

Jacob held the wet infant near her face so she could see and touch him firsthand, and even in her exhaustion, Rachel could see the baby was perfect in every detail. "My God has remembered me," she said to Leah, as she was gently lowered down on her bed.

"Yes, He has remembered you. Now rest, Rachel, and regain your strength. For now we will take care of you and your Joseph."

Mercifully, Rachel sank into her pillows and was only hazily aware of what was happening around her. But nothing mattered. God had lifted the curse of barrenness from her. She had given birth to one exquisite man-child, and God had spared her life in the process.

Suddenly, amongst the milieu of activity around her, she recalled her dream. She realized that the beautiful boy who had always stood by Jacob at the well was *her* son. *Oh, the boy is Joseph!* she said to herself and smiled. *No wonder he is a beautiful baby. Wait until everyone sees him as he grows into manhood.* She delighted in the remembering, and then a bright new thought crossed her mind and exploded into joy. *The baby Jacob holds in his arms must be a second blessing from God!* She laughed and said aloud, "Joseph, you are my first. God has remembered the dark slur against my name, and He will give me another son."

"You have reason to be so happy." Rachel opened her eyes and saw Leah's face above her. "He is perfect," Leah said. "We have washed him and given him his salt rub, and now the binding strips are being wound around his arms and limbs so they will grow straight and tall."

Rachel nodded her approval, and then, with the first pangs of a guilty conscience, she listened as Leah said softly, "My sister, he is so perfect . . . absolutely perfect. I am genuinely happy for you and the fruit of your womb."

Rachel was stricken with guilt at the tenderness of Leah's words, and the memory of the hateful years loomed into her memory with an incredible jolt.

Leah's words and the spirit in which they were spoken had broken through the barriers and brought the first measure of healing between the two women.

Rachel reached up and pulled Leah's face close to hers, whispering, "Forgive me, Leah, for the vengeful things I've said to you and about you. I have treated you unfairly and have acted as a spoiled child. . . . I was torn with jealousy because you bore children so easily—"

Leah cut Rachel's words off midsentence and said with gentle sternness, "We shall let no more hatred come between us. The living God blessed us both, so from today on, we shall live peaceably in the tents of Jacob. Now, lie quietly and gain your strength back so you can be well enough to nurse this little man."

Rachel kissed her sister's face and noted that, like her own, it was wet with tears. Old wounds covered with the oil of forgiveness began to soak in the healing.

Jacob quietly observed all this from one shadowy side of Rachel's tent, and when he was overcome by his emotions and no longer in control of his tears, he stole silently out into the brightness of the cloudless day.

Without a word to anyone, he slipped away to his favorite place of worship, high on the crest of the hill, and there—with no one to hear—Jacob sobbed out his praise to his living God and spent the day worshiping in great joy.

10

The year Joseph was born was one of challenges, setbacks, joys, and—as Jacob remarked one day, his voice showing a marked sharpness—"definitely the year of mixed blessings."

Rachel's happiness was clouded by the fragile status of her health. Instead of gaining her vitality back after the birth of Joseph, she seemed to lose a portion of her strength daily. Valiantly, she nursed Joseph for two months, but when Bilhah told her of one of their shepherd's wives who had an unusually large flow of milk, Rachel was reluctantly persuaded to give up nursing. Gradually, and with no small amount of misgivings, she gave Joseph to the woman at his feeding times.

Everyone could see Rachel's health disappearing, but almost as visible was the fact that her mind was just as strongly set as always. A semi-invalid, Rachel spent much of her day lying on her bedding; but she made it very clear that she, and she alone, would take over the duties of training and teaching Joseph as he grew.

She purposed in her heart to leave no area of his education unexplored, and until Joseph was five or six summers old, Rachel intended to do her best in instructing her son in the ways of his father.

She understood that part of her teaching would involve religious training. The night of her conception, Rachel had hurled a barrage of questions to Jacob concerning his God. From then on, right up to the present time, Rachel set about to deliberately learn all; not only about the living God, but the history of the people who worshiped Him. Carefully, she questioned Jacob and studiously prepared herself so that when the boy could comprehend and understand, she would be ready with the answers.

Even during the first year of his life, as she held the tiny infant to her breasts, Rachel whispered about Jacob. "He is strong and clever, your father. You will grow up to be a prince like him," she crooned over the sleeping baby. "And wait until I tell you about your grandfather, Isaac, and his father, Abraham! Oh, Joseph, the faithfulness of their living God . . . now, there is something! I will teach you your father's fear, love, and respect of this living God, and you will hear, over and over again, of God's magnificent blessings toward the men, women, and children of Abraham's tents." Rachel hugged the baby and kissed his diminutive rosy cheeks.

The first year of Joseph's life was also the culmination of his father's services. In that year of "mixed blessings," Jacob completed his fourteen years of wage-free labor given to Laban for the hand of Rachel.

One night after the evening meal, when Joseph was about six moons old, Jacob sat on the carpets beside Rachel, who was playing with the smiling, gurgling, contented baby. Joseph was delighting his parents because he showed all the signs of recognizing them. And even though Jacob had fathered eleven children before, he threw his head back and roared with laughter the first time Joseph's face had lit up with a smile for him. It was as if no other child had ever existed for Jacob.

"He will grow into a fine man of God!" Jacob's immodesty knew no bounds or limits. He boasted to everyone and anyone whom he could catch about his newest son.

When Joseph, nestled down into his mother's arms, had drifted off into a baby's guileless sleep, Jacob's mood shifted from high exuberance to deep thoughtfulness.

Rachel caught the change instantly and was troubled by it. She asked, "Are you ill, my lord?" She studied Jacob closely for a few moments; then, taking a guess, she said, "It is your parents, is it not?"

Jacob expelled a long sigh. "Yes," he answered, and he took her hand in his.

"I have heard no word from them, nor do they have any news of me . . . I mean, us."

He looked down at the sleeping infant and explained, "I fear I am homesick for my kinsfolk and my country."

"Have you spoken to my father about leaving and taking us all back to the land of Canaan?" Rachel asked cautiously.

"Yes . . . today."

The "today" jarred Rachel's sense of balance because she feared much had transpired between her husband and father, and she instantly understood that unless she got it all from Jacob now, she might never hear the whole story.

Hastily, Rachel laid the baby in the small, hay-filled wooden trough by her bed, and after she tucked the small blanket around Joseph to ward off the night's chill, she gave her full attention to Jacob.

Intensely she demanded, "Tell me everything."

Jacob's face, before her, bronzed and weathered by the searing heat of the sun and wind, had become even more handsome of character with his aging. Rachel felt the deep stirrings of love rise within her and knew if she ever had to make a choice between going with her husband or staying with her father, her love and loyalty would go with Jacob. He held her heart as no man had ever done.

"Tell me," she repeated.

Jacob was under no obligation to tell his wife, or wives, anything—but he could deny Rachel nothing. He took her hands in his and began to relate what had been spoken that day.

"Early this morning I found your father at the sheepcote. There is a sickness upon the flocks . . . perhaps you heard?" Rachel nodded. "Well," Jacob continued, "this morning we began counting the afflicted sheep to see how widespread this is, and what we can expect in terms of losses—"

"I was a shepherdess," Rachel reminded him impatiently.

"So you were," he acquiesced. Jacob winked an eye at her and teased, "But I thought you wanted to know *everything.*"

"Stop that," Rachel said with mock irritation.

Jacob sobered and said, "When we had finished with that flock, we talked as we walked to the pasture where Amashai is tending the camels. It was there, on our way, that we discussed the matter of our leaving here."

"What did you say, exactly, and how did father seem?" Rachel asked, anxious to get to the heart of the matter.

"I told Laban that the fourteen years of labor were over and fulfilled and that it was time for us to leave. I explained further that I wanted to see my parents once more before they died. I told him that I would never leave here without you, Leah, my concubines, and children; and that it is my intention to leave here as soon as it can be arranged, for I must go back to Canaan. And, finally, I reminded him that I had worked out my contract for all of you in my labors and that you and Leah had been fully paid for by the efforts of my toiling."

Rachel's expression and voice seemed to harden noticeably, and she asked, knowing in her heart what the answer would be, "And father said we cannot go?"

Her husband's explosive and sarcastic laugh split the air between them. "You know your father well!" Jacob said. He scratched his beard for a moment and pondered Rachel's keen mind before he continued.

"It seems that Laban has consulted a fortune-teller in Haran and has been advised that the blessings and unexpected wealth he is enjoying are all due to my being here.

"Your father is wise in a crafty way, and it took only those few words to convince Laban that he must not lose me. I am a good-luck charm that has done more for him than the teraphim in his tent."

"And well he knows it," Rachel scoffed.

Jacob stared up absentmindedly at the tent top and continued his recitation. "Then, after he said he would not let us leave, or rather, he politely said he wanted us to stay, he offered to pay me wages! He even went so far as to promise he'd pay whatever wage I asked."

"My father!" Rachel's temper was rising. "My father knows very well, without the assistance of any fortune-teller, of your value!"

She carried on, indignantly. "He also knows you are a skilled shepherd and herdsman. He owes his blossoming wealth to your superb talents and management. Well he knows, too, we had precious little before you came into our lives." Rachel's voice was raised so loudly Jacob put a finger to his lips and then pointed to the sleeping baby, but she would not be hushed.

"Furthermore," Rachel concluded, "your steadfast laboring cost my father nothing but two daughters, and he would have had to find us husbands anyway. In my opinion, he has paid very little in the way of wages for fourteen years."

Rachel's face, flushed with anger, gave her skin a healthy tint, and Jacob thought her more beautiful than ever. He leaned over and gently settled her back down on her bed. Then, bending close, he said, "My beauty, my lamb, fortunate is the man whose wife is filled with such a reserve of unconditional loyalty as yours." He smiled down at the treasured face and would have consummated his love for her except she took his hands away from her and held them.

"Please," she said quietly, "I want to know what was decided. Did you accept father's offer, or what?"

"Actually," he gave her a bright smile, "I said almost exactly what you have just said. Your father knows very well how faithfully I have served him. He has seen his flocks and herds grow, and he knows he has become a rich man in these fourteen years. It is an undeniable fact.

"I was moved by his genuine sincerity when he pleaded with me to stay—"

"My husband," Rachel interjected bluntly, "my father is a cunning man. Do not be overcome with his sincerity. Given another chance, I'm afraid he will once again try to cheat you."

"Oh, I have not forgotten his deceptive ways. Nor have I forgotten my own deceit with my father, Isaac, over my brother's birthright." Jacob's tone of voice was mingled with regrets and old guilts.

"Then you must be *more* cunning if we are to ever outsmart my father. And if you are not crafty enough, we will never have our own possessions. Leaving here will forever be impossible. You'll just have to be more clever," Rachel said softly.

"I fully intend to."

Jacob's answer did not completely satisfy Rachel, for she knew the devious ways of her father. She looked closely at Jacob in the lamp's glow and without words asked, "What will you do?"

"I have decided to remain a while longer, but I did not ask for wages as Laban wished."

Now the look on Rachel's face formed the unspoken question, "Why?"

"Because I have a different plan," Jacob said with considerable confidence. "I am going to build my own flocks from Laban's; and if I can accomplish what I have in mind, then we shall leave, take our possessions, and journey back to the land of my fathers."

Rachel was now totally speechless, but her eyes asked, "How?"

Jacob moved closer to her, smoothed the hair from around her face, and gently said, "The 'how' of my accomplishing this will have to be my secret for now; but trust me, my beloved. I will not be denied what is mine, nor will I go home empty-handed. I believe God will crown my efforts with success."

Rachel met his gaze with teary eyes, and as he kissed her cheeks, she heard him whisper, "My God has a covenant with me. Remember, my beloved? So He will not fail us. He cannot."

11

It was weeks later that Rachel began to hear bits and pieces of gossip, from the whispering of her servant girls, as to the strange actions of both Laban and Jacob.

Finally, it was Leah, excited and bursting with stories, who told her the straight of things.

"It seems," Leah said breathlessly, "that when Jacob told father he wanted to leave, our father begged him to stay on and even offered him wages as a reward for working."

"Yes, yes, I know that!" Rachel cried impatiently. "Go on."

"Then do you know what he asked for instead of wages as payment?" Leah questioned with an air of triumph.

"No. What?" Rachel asked, as she moved up on one elbow to face her sister.

"Jacob asked father for some livestock to start his own flocks. But, Rachel," Leah leaned close, "he asked for only the speckled, off-color, spotted, or black animals of father's flocks and herds! It seems that he wants only the poorest of specimens. He asked for only the blemished animals. Jacob explained to father that when it was time to settle what father owed him in wages, there would be no doubt in anyone's mind as to whose flocks and herds belong to whom, for none of Jacob's flocks would be white. Father agreed readily because he saw those animals as no great loss."

"If father agreed," Rachel shook her head, "then he probably even found some way to cheat Jacob out of those animals, right?"

She grimaced and waited for the inevitable answer.

Leah replied, "Yes. I found myself unwilling to believe it of him. After all, look what our husband has done for him; but what you have just said is true.

"Father's shepherds, Amashai and Ezer, told me that before Jacob could get to the flocks and herds, a scheme was set into motion against Jacob. Father rushed to pastures and removed many of the marked, blemished animals, leaving only a few for Jacob.

"Then, without my knowledge, father used my sons Reuben and Simeon to cover up his deceitfulness. He sent the boys and animals off into hiding in a pasture three days' journey from here, hoping Jacob would not notice the loss."

"Father!" Rachel's voice exploded in disgust. She knew it was useless to be angry with her father as so little could be done. "I only hope," she said, "that our Jacob has in some way outsmarted him, but it is all so puzzling. Jacob's flocks and herds must be pitifully small, and surely he realized immediately what father had done. . ." her voice trailed off.

"Oh," laughed Leah, "there's more! Ezer said he and Amashai spied on Jacob not long after he had gathered the remnant of marked animals that were left. They watched Jacob the better part of one whole morning. They reported that Jacob spent a good deal of time gathering white and spotted poplar tree branches. Then they said that Jacob put some twigs and branches beside the watering troughs and others he put into the trough itself. What do you think he—"

Excitedly, the shepherdess in Rachel cut Leah off with, "Ah, ha! There is an old superstition that declares when animals see speckled or mottled wood near their watering troughs where they usually mate, they will give birth to mottled and colored young. How clever of Jacob! Of course, if it works, he will have many spotted and black sheep, but my, how it would increase his flocks." Rachel savored the moment of deep pride and then suddenly wondered aloud, "Will this work because of an old superstition or because of the power of the living God?"

"Our husband is a great man. I think both God and superstition will work in his favor." Rachel had never heard Leah sound so confident.

Whether it was one or the other, or a combination of both reasons, it didn't really matter too much, because as Leah announced one morning, months later, "It worked!"

Actually, it worked beyond anyone's expectations, for by the time the first spring birthing season was upon the plains of Padan-aram, Jacob's scrawny flocks had decidedly been hit with an epidemic of fertility.

When Rachel congratulated him on his cleverness, he shrugged his shoulders and said that besides the wood-in-the-trough trick—perpetrated when he discovered Laban's craftiness—he had divided the ewes in Laban's flocks, for he was still tending some flocks for Laban and set them apart. Then Jacob had let Laban's ewes mate *only* with his fat and healthy black rams. He never told Rachel how or when he used Laban's flocks like this, only that he had. Moreover, he confessed that he never placed the mottled branches before the sickly or old and feeble sheep—only before the strongest animals. That way, Jacob explained, he was assuring himself of breeding good stock right under Laban's nose, as it were, which would produce strong and healthy flocks and herds.

Rachel was readily impressed.

When the rumor circulated around the encampment that Laban's flocks were looking a little peaked and puny and that they seemed to be shrinking somewhat, everyone—with a few exceptions, like Jacob and Rachel—was puzzled.

The first spring which brought the initial increase to Jacob's flocks was followed by a second. By the time a third spring had expanded his cattle, goats, and sheep beyond anyone's belief, Jacob's ebullience was as great as Laban's dismay.

One night, as they lay together, Jacob whispered into Rachel's ear, "We are on our way."

Their eyes met, and she asked, "When?"

"Oh, it will be soon, my lamb. Soon. I have a good number of servants now; camels, goats, donkeys, and, of course, vast flocks of sheep. When I have enough . . . then we will leave. My God has remembered me, too, as He did for you when He gave you Joseph." In spirited warmth, he hugged her, but she pressed him again, asking, "When?"

"Perhaps one or two more spring seasons. Then I will probably have accumulated the necessary amount of wealth for a triumphful return to my home. I must have large flocks and great herds to show for my years of laboring."

Jacob turned his head and glanced over at the sleeping boy on the other side of Rachel's tent. He loved the tender tradition of the children sleeping in their mother's tent until they were ten or so summers, for it reminded him of a mother hen who, each evening, safely tucked her little brood under her wing. Jacob saw Rachel as the loveliest mother hen of all, and he visualized the boy as the most precious of all the chicks.

"He is a treasure, you know . . . he is part of my wealth, and I want my kinsfolk to see him. He is perfect, is he not?" he mused aloud.

"Yes, he's a perfect treasure," Rachel agreed. "He is now three summers old. He weaned well, my lord, so I know he will be a great and strong man . . . as you, dear Jacob."

Jacob said nothing, but smiled and continued to study the mound of bedding. He wondered exactly what kind of a man Joseph would be. Rachel interrupted his thoughts with, "You know, when he was born, I could hardly wait for him to talk with me so I could teach him in your ways. I was so eager to get to know this son of ours. . . . Now he talks, and he never stops. His words are not like an endless stream of chatter, like the women gossiping at the well, but rather, he asks well-thought-out, even logical, questions." Rachel laughed, "My, how many questions! I've never seen so young a child with such an inquisitive desire to learn and know about everything. It's almost as if he thinks his time of living will be short, so he packs each day with as many questions and answers as he can."

As soon as she said the words, a dreadful thought pounded through her head, *His time is not short . . . mine is! Will I not be around to see him into manhood?* she asked wordlessly and blindly shoved the notion out of her mind.

She heard Jacob say, "You will be a good teacher, and you will give him the best of answers." His words covered over the starkness of her face. "And when it is time for me to take over,"

Jacob was saying, "I will know Joseph's mother has prepared the way!"

His compliment, and the tone of voice he used, was all the praise Rachel felt she'd ever need, and she was greatly warmed by it.

By the time the handsome and spirited lad was almost five summers old, Rachel had poured her whole heart and small re- serve of strength into Joseph's training. She knew it was custom- arily a mother's duty to teach her son until the age of six or so; and from then on, the task would go to the father.

Rachel, still ailing and daily sensing that it was she, not the boy, who had little time, tackled teaching like no other mother had ever done.

Her love of Joseph was fierce and amazing. No mountain was as high, no wall as deep, and no valley so wide as her uncondi- tional love for her firstborn.

"Mother!" Joseph stood just inside the tent's entrance and called to her, waking her from an afternoon's nap. Rachel raised herself up and for a moment took her little boy in with loving eyes.

His light brown hair, curly and tousled, framed his manly face. He held a small leather sling in his hand, and his short tunic, dusty from the fields, revealed that both of his knees were scratched and skinned.

"Did you fall?" Rachel gestured to his legs.

He smiled, shook his head and explained, "Lots of times! I am learning how to aim my sling and how to make the stones go where I want them to go. I was watching the stone, not where I went."

Rachel lovingly studied him as he talked. He used his hands to show her his progress, but while she watched him, her mind wan- dered. She was silently delighted by his unusual looks and gentle spirit, but she questioned in her mind why she could never fully understand that Joseph was so different from his brothers; only that he was vastly different. His looks were an obvious departure, for his face, fair skinned and topped with light brown hair, con- trasted deeply with his half-brothers' swarthy complexions and dark, raven-colored hair.

On special and rare occasions, when she had been well enough

to leave her tent and she had seen Joseph and his brothers together, the lad always stood or sat with them; yet somehow he always seemed to be set apart.

Maybe it's his eyes, Rachel thought. At his birth, his eyes had
been the typical blue-grey color of many babies; but instead of
turning darker and becoming brown as he grew a few days older,
Joseph's eyes lightened. The blue that stayed could only be described as pure sky blue. Many times when Rachel looked
directly at her son, she was transported back in time to her girlhood days as a shepherdess. She could recall that the blue of the
sky was now the exact same shade of blue of Joseph's eyes as he
looked across the tent at her. The thick fringe of dark eyelashes
had been her contribution to his facial beauty, and perhaps the
fair skin, too—but the blue eyes? "They must be from Jacob's
kinsfolk," she decided.

Rachel called for Bilhah, and moments later the young woman
obediently appeared.

"I want you to bathe Joseph's knees and pull out any thistle,
stone, or splintered wood for me," Rachel instructed.

Joseph protested meekly, but whatever Rachel wanted done,
even if it was only small wounds tended, it was done.

When Bilhah had finished and had left the tent to fill the
water skin, Rachel asked, "Is Dan or one of your other brothers
teaching you to use the sling?"

"No," Joseph answered, with some hesitancy; and then, with
just a small touch of pride surrounding his words, he said, "*I* am
teaching Joseph."

Rachel saw his ears redden slightly, and she suddenly com-
prehended what before she had only surmised.

"Do your brothers ever let you play in any of their hunts or
games?" she asked, forcing her voice to be controlled.

He hesitated a second time, and softly he said, "Sometimes."

So! she thought. *"Sometimes" means not very often—maybe
not ever.* Instantly Rachel steamed with a fiery resentment. She
would have brought down her quick-tempered wrath on Leah's
head and Joseph's half brothers had not Joseph's calm voice totally changed the entire subject. For in that moment, Joseph, with
innocent simplicity, said, "Mother, when I sleep at night, I close
my eyes, and I see things, people, animals, and I go outside the

tent. What is that? And why does that happen only when night is upon me?"

An eerie chill raced down Rachel's back, and she thought, *It is an unnerving experience to have such an adult child.* She sensed he had asked her the question to keep her from consuming strength in an outburst of anger. Yet, how did one so young know these things? Rachel rationalized that the question Joseph asked was the original one he had come in with earlier.

She regained her composure and called, "Come here, my love. Sit by me."

Sitting crosslegged beside Rachel, Joseph gave her his fullest attention, and the beauty and love of him broke over her afresh.

"It's called *dreaming*," Rachel said, and the boy silently repeated the word without taking his eyes off her.

"Dreaming happens to most of us at one time or another. Dreams are stories which happen while we sleep. Sometimes the stories are true and believable; sometimes they are false and filled with mystery; sometimes dreams are good or bad, but usually, parts of them at least are very real. You should know, too," Rachel said, "that instead of being told the story, like I tell you the stories of Abraham and Isaac, when we dream we *are* the story. We live it, and the story happens all around us.

"I am so pleased you are having dreams, my son, especially since we are a family who worships the living God."

"Why is that?" Joseph asked.

"Ah, why?" Rachel repeated. "Well, because. . ." she hesitated, and then with some intrinsically good wisdom which came just in time from her God, she responded, "Our God has no priests to chant out His wishes or commands, like the ones in the moon-god temple in Haran. He has sent no prophets to tell us how and when to worship, and He has given us no fortune-tellers to predict the future. So our God often uses dreams."

The boy nodded gravely. "I see," he said soberly.

"Your father has had dreams, and they are wondrous. Sometime I'll tell you about one which God gave him as he slept on a stone pillow."

"Mother, has father had a lot of dreams?" And before she could answer, he said, "I have many. Almost each night."

"I shouldn't wonder," Rachel thought out loud.

Nothing the boy said should have surprised or shaken her, for he was so extraordinary, but she took a deep breath and in silent desperation she prayed, *Living God, I need a river of wisdom to flow through me with this one. I am a needy mother. My illness has robbed me of strength, and many times my answers come slowly, so visit my soul with the proper words that I might not fail to wisely instruct my son in Your ways.*

He was still looking at her intently, and she took his hands in hers.

"Joseph, it is important that you hear my words, for you are very blessed of God. I know He has chosen you for something very special. As I just said, there are many kinds of dreams. There are even plain dreams or stories or ordinary, everyday things with no significance, nor are they of any importance. But there are *other* dreams. While they may have ordinary experiences in them, they are—because of God—very high and holy dreams."

"What are high and holy dreams?" the boy asked, looking perplexed.

"Those are dreams that may predict something which will happen many days from now, in the future. They are also dreams which are given as a goal to set before us. Sometimes the dreams will give you hope and courage when you feel you are failing. Oh, there is so much to teach you."

Rachel laid back on her pillows and said, "My son, Joseph, just know that when God gives a high and holy dream it will mean He is going to do something very special in your life."

She looked over at him and asked, "Can you remember anything of your dreams?"

He wrinkled his brow and then said, "Only when I first wake up, and then I forget." He paused, frowned again, and replied, "This morning I remembered that in my dream I was playing in a field—"

"Were your brothers there? Were you playing with them?" Rachel interjected.

"No. I was by myself, except there was a whole flock of sheep around me. I think I was the main shepherd boy in charge, but I don't know."

"Is that all you can remember?"

"Yes."

"Then," Rachel straightened the pillows behind her, "you probably had an ordinary dream, but I want you to promise me something."

Joseph nodded.

"When you have a dream you can remember, no matter how strange it is or what mysterious thing takes place, I want you to tell your father and me about it. You see, we never know when, exactly, God will give us a high and holy dream; and perhaps, some night soon, He will visit your soul."

While Joseph didn't understand everything she had said, Rachel could see by the nod of his head that the gist of what she had explained was sinking in and being absorbed. They shared the silence of the tent for a few moments, and then Joseph kissed her and left for the evening meal with his father and brothers.

Rachel lay for some time, wondering how many boys would experience dreams at such a young age. *How many dreams would he have, and of what significance would they be? Is he so special just because he is my child, and I can only see him through my eyes of love? Or, is he special because God sees him in love as His child?* The questions blew in and around her mind like unpredictable bursts of gusty desert winds; and answers, like leaves, were blown hither and yon, never to settle.

Later, when she recounted the episode of the boy's dreams to Jacob, he refused to treat it as seriously, for Joseph was so young. He teased Rachel by saying, "So, we have given birth to a child dreamer, a child of high and holy dreams, have we?"

Rachel took his humor good-naturedly and then softly said, to no one in particular, "Joseph's *father* is a dreamer of dreams. In fact, once he laid his head upon a stone pillow and found the stone was placed in the center of the crossroads of his life. The dream he dreamed *that* night changed the course of his life forever.

"Who is to say Jacob was too old or too young to dream his high and holy dream?"

Rachel's gentle accusation sobered Jacob instantly. For hours he pondered about the holy destiny God might have in store for his little son, Joseph; and, in the end, he decided that one's age was not a factor to God. *Only to be a chosen one matters when it comes to holy dreams*, Jacob said to himself. *And just think! Joseph, my little son, may be one of those men . . . chosen!"*

Jacob shook his head in wonderment, and sleep would not come.

12

Jacob continued to pursue and enlarge his fortune in livestock. His efforts were ceaseless in building up the flocks and herds. He worked like a madman, so much so his menservants and undershepherds were convinced the master never sat to eat or lay down to sleep.

When Jacob had amassed several hundred ewes, rams, goats, and almost matched that number with camels, cows, bulls, and donkeys, Rachel timidly suggested they had enough wealth. "Is it not time to leave?" she queried. But Jacob shook his head stubbornly and said, "We wait a little longer."

Abruptly, however, he changed his mind when, through the encampment grapevine of gossip, Jacob learned that Laban's sons, Abihu and Jubal, were bitterly and publicly critical of him. It was rumored that they had complained to Laban, saying, "Jacob owes everything he has to you, father. All his wealth is at your expense. Are you going to let him do this to you?"

Jacob knew he could not count on Laban's willingness to divulge his devious ways to his own sons, so he knew Laban would let their vitriolic words stand unchallenged. Laban's silence took the form of lying; the kind where one simply says nothing, and so an untrue statement rides along, picking up credibility as long as it is not challenged. The news left Jacob fuming and longing for vindication.

Coupling what Abihu and Jubal said with Laban's chilly, withdrawn attitude, Jacob could easily see life and coexistence on the plains of Padan-aram was strained beyond any amount of mending. "My father-in-law has become less than friendly," he remarked sarcastically to his son Reuben.

In the next few days, so sharp was the air around Jacob and

Laban, and so brittle the brief exchanges of conversation between them that Jacob went off to his place in the mountains to seek God's direction.

"Maybe it *is* time to leave," Jacob muttered to himself as he picked his way through the boulders and climbed up the first of several sharp inclines. But hours later, when he descended, he was sure.

The next day, he sent a servant boy with a message for Rachel, only if she were well enough, and Leah to come to him in the pasture where he was tending one of his flocks.

The servant delivered Jacob's words and both women, suspecting what they were about to hear, eagerly agreed to leave as soon as possible.

Leah politely forced Rachel to drink down some lamb broth, in hopes it would add to her strength; and when the servant brought a donkey, Leah helped Rachel up. Then, walking along beside her, Leah steadied Rachel as they began their short journey to the field.

None of the activities of his mother or his aunt escaped Joseph's curiosity. He knew his father had not mentioned that he come along, but when he stepped in front of the small, grey donkey and most seriously said, "You must give me permission to accompany you, for you need protection," both women laughed outright, and Rachel said, "So be it!"

In the midst of the flock, Jacob straightened up to look for them, as he had done five times already; and when he finally saw two women and the boy, he startled the sheep with his whoop of delighted satisfaction. He disentangled himself from two large ewes and directed the women and boy to the edge of a small wadi.

"I am glad to see you all." He directed his greeting to Joseph, and the lad—a little anxious about his father's approval, yet pleased with himself—explained, "They needed me to come so no harm would befall them." Joseph didn't see his father's quick smile.

Jacob nodded gravely, and turning from Joseph, caught Rachel's twinkling eyes as parents do when their children please them. When the saddle blankets were spread on the ground, Rachel sat down and leaned against the trunk of an acacia tree. Joseph sat beside her, eager to hear the adult conversation because he sensed it would be important.

Leah gave Jacob the goatskin of water and after he took a long drink, he idly toyed with the goatskin. He then grew thoughtful, as if he did not know quite where to begin.

Finally, it was Leah who broke the silence with, "We are eager for any news you have for us, my lord."

At first Jacob averted his eyes from them and said softly, "I am both saddened and reluctant to tell you this, for I wish to speak evil of no man, but your father has turned against me. I have no options or alternatives but to leave."

Looking at Rachel, he continued, "You were right. You said a while back that it was time to go, but I wanted to add to my flocks and finish a few more things. Now, I find, it is time to go.

"Yesterday I climbed that mountain," he gestured and inclined his head toward the hill.

Joseph studied the rocky foothills and rugged peaks to see if he could find the place his father might have built an altar. Then he heard Jacob say, "I talked and worshiped with the living God. I sought out His face and asked for guidance, and He met me there."

Joseph's eyes were wide with attention, and he missed nothing of his father's words, facial expressions, or the look of respectful fear on Jacob's face as he talked of the living God.

"The righteous God of my forefathers told me unmistakably to leave here and return to the land of my birth, the land of Canaan." The magnificent, rich tones of Jacob's voice rolled on. "Moreover, He promised to go with me so my family and I will have His journeying mercies.

"My son," he tossed Joseph the half-empty goatskin, "when our God promises something, it *will* come to pass, for He never breaks or even bends a covenant. He is a faithful God, and He can be trusted."

Then to Leah and Rachel, Jacob said, "If we are to leave, and we are, it must be done quickly and with as much secrecy as possible. I wanted to talk this over with you, for there will be a lot of work, and the effort will take all of our ingenuity and strength. I fear, Rachel, the preparations alone and the long, exhausting journey to come may be more than you can bear."

Rachel straightened up and said with unshakable confidence,

"You must not concern yourself with my well-being. Give your attention and efforts to our leaving.

"It is good that we leave. You have heard our brothers' complaints, and our father will continue to let them slander you. I can see no future here for us as father will simply renew his efforts to make your life miserable here."

Joseph sat watching his aunt, mother, and father and intently stored each and every word in the back rooms of his mind. He looked and listened as Jacob, striking one fist into his other open palm, said heatedly, "Your brothers spoke out of their ignorance, and Laban never corrected them or informed them of the truth. You know that while it is true that I outsmarted your father in the breeding of animals, I never broke out of the limits of my bargain with him."

The women shook their heads vigorously.

Jacob continued, "Your father knows how hard and how long I have worked for him, but time and again he has deceived me and unscrupulously broken his wage agreements with me!

"The one reliable factor in my favor is that God has not allowed Laban to harm me. In fact, I have prospered in spite of all Laban's tricky maneuvering."

Jacob gave out a short laugh and said, "God has seen to my success, for when Laban said I could have only the speckled animals, the flocks produced speckled. Then, when Laban changed his mind and said I could only have the streaked ones, all the lambs born that season were streaked! It is almost humorous, the way God has made me wealthy at your father's expense." Jacob's smile widened across his face and then, directly at his son, he said, "Even in my dreams, Joseph, my God directed me. Did you know I dream dreams, my son?"

"Oh, yes, I know." Joseph's eyes danced with a special interest.

So to his captive audience Jacob said, "During the animal's mating season, I had a dream and saw that the only he-goats mating with the flock were streaked, speckled, and mottled. And in the dream, an angel of God called to me, and I answered, 'Here am I.' Then the angel told me that I should mate the white nanny goats of Laban's flocks with the streaked, speckled, and mottled he-goats; thereby enlarging my goat herds immensely with colored goats.

"The angel also told me that God had seen all the unjust things Laban has done to me. Then, just before my dream ended, the angel said, 'I am the God you met at Bethel, the place where you anointed the pillar and made a vow to serve me. Now leave this country and return to the land of your birth.' "

Jacob finished his story, and Joseph said excitedly, "I know about Bethel. Mother has told me of the dream, the stairway to God, and how you vowed you'd serve this and only this God."

Jacob affectionately rumpled the boy's hair and whispered, "Your mother is a good teacher."

Then Jacob, turning and looking at the two women, asked, "Are you willing to leave your place of dwelling, the familiar tents of Laban, and journey to my country? Do you have any idea how difficult and how long such a trip will be? What are your thoughts on this?"

Leah and Rachel exchanged glances and knew simultaneously they were in complete agreement, so almost together and as if with one voice they cried, "This is fine with us, and we are eager to get started. Let us leave." Leah, not usually so outspoken, surprised everyone when she exclaimed, "There is nothing here for us. None of our father's wealth will come to us, anyway. He has reduced our rights to those of some distant, foreign women. He has sold us and what he received for us has disappeared."

Rachel picked it up and continued, "The riches God has given you from our father were legally ours and our children's to begin with—so go ahead and do whatever God has told you. We go willingly, gladly, and all our household shall move with you."

It took Jacob only a matter of a few days, but secretly and with great stealth, he instructed his wives, children, and servants to put his household goods, tents, and vast holdings of livestock into a state of readiness.

Rachel's illness forced her to go at a slower pace than Leah, so in order to conserve strength for the trip, she kept as quiet as possible; but she refused to be hampered completely. With decisive actions, she directed several of her servant girls in preparation for the move. The carpets were rolled, tied, and made ready for the ox carts; and the low stools, lamps, and most of their clothing were stacked in readiness at one end of her tent.

One afternoon when she thought no one would notice, Rachel stole cautiously and quietly out of her tent. The going was not easy, and she stopped several times on the way, but slowly and deliberately she headed for Laban's dwelling. Once, when she sank to her knees to rest by some caper-berry bushes, she was startled to look up suddenly into the face of Joseph.

"What are you doing here, mother?" he asked, his eyes full of concern.

"I was about to ask you why you have followed me." Rachel said, evading the question. "Come, we will go together." She rose up and, taking his hand, they continued on.

When they reached Laban's tent, neither mother nor son spoke, and Rachel would have gone in alone, but Joseph firmly clutched her hand. Only when she took the stone teraphim gods down from their shelf and put them snugly under her waistband did Joseph let go of her hand, and she heard him whisper, "Mother, why are you taking grandfather's gods?"

Without answering the boy, Rachel simply put one finger to her lips and gave him her sternest look. Then slowly they made their way back to her tent. Once they reached the safety of her dwelling place, and she was sure their journey was undetected, she said into his ear, "Just because you went with me does not mean you may tell anyone what you saw. Do you understand your mother's words?"

Joseph nodded, and she repeated, "No one, do you hear? *No one.*"

"I will not speak of it nor break this promise," he solemnly pledged. Puzzled, Joseph wondered why they could not speak of this when they had no secrets between them. But still he kept his vow.

Two more days of secret preparations were concluded, and then finally, early one morning, Jacob made his move. He knew Laban would be on the most distant pasture fields, busy with shearing the sheep of their wool, so Jacob selected his best camels and oxen and brought them to his encampment.

It took four men only a few moments of time to take down each tent. It required two more men and lots more time to fold the heavy goat's hair canvas which was stiffened and matted with age and dirt. Once folded, the tents, poles, and pegs were loaded on to large wooden carts which would be drawn by Jacob's robust teams of oxen.

The scene was one of frenzied activity. The men, women, and children worked with as little conversation as possible; but swiftly the large encampment of Jacob—with its many tents, pens and cooking fires—vanished, leaving only the sand disturbed and furrowed with black fire holes dotting the ground in an odd assortment of patterns. Their dwelling places had been removed and dismantled in a few hours.

When everything was packed and loaded onto carts or onto the backs of animals, Jacob helped Rachel, Leah, and his sons mount up on the camels.

Joseph would not be separated from his mother. "I will keep her safe," he assured his father. So, the boy was hoisted up in front of his mother, and bravely he held the reins. At that moment, Jacob had more concern than time, but quickly he asked Rachel, "Do you fare all right?"

She reassured him, "You must not fret over me. I shall be fine." Then hugging Joseph closer to her, she said, "My son is looking after me."

"I wish I could say we will stop and make camp to give you many times of resting, but for now we must press hard to put land between your father and us. Try and bear it, my wife. I must leave now. May the glorious God of my fathers go with you both."

After kissing Rachel and Joseph, Jacob jerked the camel's reins sharply, and the beast groaned in protest but obediently got off his knees without delay, straightened out his spindly legs, and lifted up his load. As if that was the signal for all the others, men and camels rose. Then, with the sound of many tinkling camel bells ringing in their ears, they began their long journey.

Maidservants and menservants rode donkeys, and Jacob, with his family and all his possessions, moved like a mighty army of people and animals. They left twenty years of living behind them and fled the plains of Padan-aram without a single farewell to anyone.

Jacob, his son Reuben, and several menservants rode out

ahead and drove their goats, camels, and flocks with intense and relentless efforts. Jacob's merciless pace and the demon of determination which stabbed at his soul were so effective that his company crossed the great Euphrates River in record time, and he headed his mammoth entourage for the territory of Gilead, northeast of the Sea of Galilee.

Only when he was several days out into the desert area did Jacob finally slow the pace, and to everyone's great relief, when he spotted a small group of green palm trees by an oasis, he signaled his sons and men to stop.

He called for the small sleeping tents to be set up for their first night of real rest. By the time the tents formed the outer perimeter line making a circle around the tall palms, and the animals were watered and bedded down, the central cooking fires were lit, and the fragrance of hot food filled the air, Jacob finally allowed himself to take what seemed to be his first breath of air since their frantic departure. His first question was about Rachel. "Find how it is with my wife Rachel." He issued the order, and the young servant sped off across the encampment circle and soon returned with Joseph.

"My mother sends her greetings," the lad said, after he kissed and hugged his father. "She said to tell you she is fine, and I am to remind you that she does not want you to worry."

"The truth, son; that is what I want," Jacob said sternly, but kindly.

The boy grew quiet and jabbed at the dirt with the toe of his sandal. "She is pale and tired, but she rides well."

Joseph reported only what he knew, and the father patted his head and replied, "Tell her, after I have seen to the needs of men and cattle, I shall come and say good night to her, but she is not to wait up for me. It will be well if she sleeps long tonight, for we will stay only one more day, and we leave early the next morrow." He watched the boy scamper off and coveted the child's boundless source of youthful strength.

Back in the fertile fields, just beyond the city of Haran, it took the news of Jacob's departure three days to reach Laban.

Then, in frantic haste, he left his shearing pens and returned to Jacob's community of tents. To his great disbelief, Laban looked over the empty plain which once held all Jacob's family, their dwellings, livestock, and sheepcotes; and Laban cursed the day Jacob was conceived, the day he was born, and all the days that followed as well.

He ranted on into the late afternoon to his sons and his men. "Never, never have I been so taken and so outwitted!" He rent his tunic and wailed loudly, again cursing the source of his humiliation, Jacob, until it was pointed out to him by his son Jubal that he was wasting precious time.

"We must catch up with him, father!" Abihu shouted, "and bring back all that Jacob has stolen from you!"

Laban removed his headpiece and, as if still in a state of shock, absentmindedly he used it to wipe the heavy trickles of perspiration which were beginning to cascade down his face and into the massive folds of his neck. Silently he began to seethe with anger, as agitatedly he pondered his sons' words. Finally, without any verbal exchange among themselves, Laban agreed, nodded his head in the direction of the great river, and stalked off to his tent. When Laban discovered that his teraphim were gone, he determined not only to catch up with Jacob, but to kill him as well for stealing such a valued possession.

Their trip to ensnare this thief and to return all their possessions was put into reality and motion as soon as they were able to gather camels and provisions. Laban plotted their course and, in order to make up some lost time, the men set out in hot pursuit west toward the great river, in the last hours of daylight.

It took one whole night and five hard-riding days across the desert sands, with only a brief stop at a small green oasis, for Laban, his sons, and their men to ride into the beautiful hill country of Bashan.

It took two more days before they reached the base of the largest hill called Mount Gilead.

But it was, as Laban—panting from their thunderous desert ride—shouted to his men, "Well worth the chase!"

They could see the cattle, sheep, and livestock peacefully grazing on the lower plains beneath Mount Gilead while the flocks and herds spilled out onto the smaller slopes in pleasant disarray. Then, by looking up the largest slope, they could see the edges of an encampment at the top of the first ridge which could only be the tents of Jacob.

With their prize in plain view, Laban and his band of weary fighting men made camp in a small meadow and ate their first warm meal of wild goat, which one of their men had killed, dressed, and roasted. When they had eaten the meat and drunk their wine, they went to sleep with Laban's plan and battle cry very much on their minds: *Attack in the morning.*

While sleep came easily to his sons and men, it completely evaded Laban. His stomach seemed to be on fire; his hindside, saddle sore and aching, made his efforts to get comfortable impossible; and try as he may to sleep, the vengeful thoughts of Jacob kept both his eyes wide open.

It was in the deepest part of darkness, just before dawn, that Laban finally drifted into a disturbed, uncomfortable sleep. Even then, he wasn't too sure whether he was awake or dreaming; and what made it worse, he thought he heard the voice of Abraham, Isaac, *and* Jacob's God speaking to him out of the fire pit beside the sleeping men.

No one moved or awakened, so Laban concluded that he must 'definitely be dreaming.

The voice said loudly, "You must make sure that you watch out whatever you say to Jacob. Do not give or take, bless, or curse this man."

Laban woke and sat up stiffly. He was shivering, so he pulled the camel blanket around his shoulders and pondered the awesome and puzzling words he had just heard. He sat like that until the auroral purples and greys lit the dark skies. Then, eating nothing, for his stomach was still burning, Laban tapped his sons on their heads, waking them, and said, "Come. Get up now. Break bread quickly, for we go to Jacob. Do not say anything to him. God has warned me in a dream about any revenge we would take, so let me do the talking."

Up on the mountain, the guard—a young manservant of Jacob's—sat on a high vantage site and saw the small band of men as they passed the flocks. He left his station and brought the report to his master.

Jacob went to meet them. He stood his usual way: straight, tall, hands behind his back, and feet firmly planted apart. The wind off the rim of the crest blew his headpiece and tunic against and behind him. Standing into the wind as he did, he looked as if he were a ruler or king in complete control.

Jacob watched the men climb the last few feet with a great deal of apprehension strangling his throat. He was relieved that his fear and nervousness did not seem to be apparent to the young lad by his side. He counted on a brave front for the benefit of Laban as well as Joseph.

"What will grandfather do to us?" Joseph asked before the grimly determined Laban and his men reached them.

"I am only sure of one thing, my son, and that is this: The angel of the Lord commanded me to leave and go back to my homeland. I will do just that; though, at this moment, I am not sure by the looks on their faces what price I will have to pay."

"Jacob! My kinsman," Laban called, and without a smile, yet surprisingly without a show of hostility, he lifted his hand in a peaceable greeting.

Jacob formally welcomed Laban and his sons and his men. Then, without another wasted moment, Laban, still puffing from the climb, demanded, "What do you mean, sneaking off like this behind my back and taking my daughters and my possessions with you?" He gave Jacob no opportunity to answer, but continued, "Tell me, are you holding my daughters prisoner, as if you captured them in battle and then forced them away with you as the spoils of war?"

Both men faced each other, and Joseph saw that his father never took his eyes off Laban nor even blinked an eye, but remained calm and steady as he listened to Laban's protest. About that same moment, Laban realized Joseph was there, and his face warmed with a smile. He bent over and kissed the boy's cheeks and then implored, "Jacob, why didn't you give me the honor of giving you and the boy here a farewell feast with singing and dancing to the tambourines and harps?" Then, gesturing to Joseph and the tents farther up on the slope, he said, "You didn't even let me kiss my grandchildren, like Joseph, nor did you let me tell them good-bye. Are you so calloused to the ways and customs of families that you forgot I would want to say my appropriate farewells before your long journey?" Laban scratched his head and then his beard. "You have behaved in a foolish and strange way."

Then stepping closer, Laban waggled his finger under Jacob's nose and cried, "We are armed, and it is within my power to snuff you out as simply as one puts out the light in a small lamp."

Joseph gripped his father's hand tightly and listened as Laban continued. "But you have been spared my wrath, for the God of your father, Isaac, spoke to me last night, down there," he pointed to the smoke rising from their fires. "And your God said not to be hard on you."

Jacob squeezed Joseph's hand in two quick movements, and the boy thought it was as though Jacob had said, "See, our God *is* taking care of us!" But the victory was short-lived, for Laban's tone turned caustic as he shouted, "I am a reasonable man, and when the God of your father speaks, I listen; and I am willing to obey. But see here—" Laban's bloodshot eyes bulged in their sockets, his face reddened, and his breath came in short, angry bursts. "Though you feel you must go home . . . that perhaps you are committed to going to your country, and you long intensely for the sight of your parents . . . but does that give you the right to go to my tent and *steal* my teraphim?"

Joseph saw the shocked expression on his father's face and heard his sharp intake of air. When his father did speak, Joseph heard Jacob defend his position.

"I fled because I feared you would never let me take your daughters and that if you knew of my plans, then you would *forcibly* take them away from me!" Jacob cried.

"But," Jacob straightened to his full height and with great dignity said, "as to the household gods that are missing . . . a curse on him who took them. I say let him die for his theft. Furthermore, my kinsmen will assist you in a search of all our tents and possessions, and if you find anything—teraphim, livestock, or material possession that is yours—you take it! I swear before your sons and mine, I'll give anything back, anything that is yours, without hesitation or question."

Laban grunted, "So be it," and took his sons to find and search Jacob's tent first.

Jacob's sons Reuben and Judah joined their grandfather and uncles. Together they systematically went through Jacob's, Leah's, Bilhah's, and Zilpah's tents and to Laban's incredible dismay, they found nothing.

Protective of his beloved wife, Rachel, Jacob and Joseph accompanied Laban while he finished the search at the concubines' tents. Together then, they made their way to the last tent: Rachel's.

Laban found her near the back of the tent, reclining against her camel's saddle.

Joseph stiffened with fear, for he knew somewhere in that tent or on her person, the teraphim rested in hiding. Rachel caught the boy's eyes and in a glance reminded him of his vow and silenced anything he might have volunteered. Though she had taught him to be truthful, she did not want any evidence of her training to show up and divulge her secret.

"My father, greetings," Rachel said graciously. "But if you think your coming here will change our minds, I must tell you plainly. We will not be deterred from our journey. Leah and I have chosen to live in Jacob's land—"

Her father cut her off, saying, "It is not my purpose to change your plans or stop you. I only want what's rightfully mine, and Jacob has stolen the teraphim of my house."

Laban pulled up carpets, looked in what few boxes held clothing or blankets, and left nothing untouched. But when he got to where Rachel lay, she held up one hand in a weak gesture of protest.

"Forgive me, father . . . I hope you do not object to my being unable to get up, but the cursed custom of all women is with me today."

When Laban left her tent, Rachel knew the teraphim she had stuffed under her camel's saddle were safe. Joseph looked at her and saw the slight smile of satisfaction spread across her mouth. He wondered why someone who worshiped the living God needed the stone gods, and he resolved in his heart to make that the next question he would ask his mother as they traveled.

When Jacob saw that the search was ended and none of the teraphim had been found, he stalked from Rachel's tent and angrily waited for Laban.

Joseph had never seen his father so angry, and he watched the confrontation between the two men with a dreadful sick feeling in his stomach. He wanted to deny it, but the plain truth was his mother had deceived both his father and grandfather. He couldn't begin to understand why.

Jacob took Laban's hands in his, turned the open palms up, and spit into them. "Laban, you false accuser! What did you find in your elaborate search? Nothing! See, you have come up empty-handed!

"Set what you have found and discovered in my tents, whatever it is that I am *supposed* to have stolen, here in front of your men and mine, and let them decide whose it is!"

Laban looked steadfastly at the tufts of grass on the ground beneath his sandals and shifted his bulk uneasily.

Joseph started to say, "But, father, there is nothing to bring out to set down for my mother sits upon it." But he remembered his mother's menacing glance and kept still.

Jacob's anger flowered and came into full bloom as he howled vociferously, "Twenty years! Do you hear? Twenty years I have been with you, and all that time I have cared for your ewes and nanny goats so that they have produced healthy offsprings, and I never touched one ram of yours for food.

"If any were attacked or torn apart by wild animals, I bore the loss of it. I never asked you to reduce the count of your flock. Yet you made me pay for each and every animal stolen from the flocks whether I could help it or not."

Laban sat down on a large flat rock so he would be out of direct line of Jacob's vindictive words of scorn.

"I worked for you," Jacob flung the words angrily into the air, "through the scorching heat of the day; and I endured, for you, the cold frost of sleepless nights.

"Yes, you hear me, clean out your ears my father-in-law! Twenty years . . . fourteen of them earning Leah and Rachel, and six to breed a flock of my own. And," he bent down, hissing like a snake into Laban's face, "you have reduced my wages ten times!

"In fact, were it not for the promise of God, the God of my grandfather, Abraham, even the glorious God of Isaac, my father . . . you, you miserable excuse of a man . . . you would have sent me off without a single possession to my name!"

Jacob's anger spent itself and cooled somewhat, so in a voice a little more controlled he said, "You would have left me with nothing, but my God has seen your deceptive cruelty and the hard labor of my hands. That is why He spoke to you in a dream last night. He keeps perfect records, and the deeds of all men are recorded in His mind. His words to you on that plain down there were His rebuking chastisement of your actions."

The circle of men and boys which stood around Jacob and Laban waited in silence to hear what Laban would say. Each man and boy took sides, in their minds, and predicted the outcome. But none foresaw it in the way the matter was settled.

Laban rubbed his eyes and then stood up to face Jacob. In a helpless gesture, with both arms outstretched beside him, he answered, "These women are my daughters, and these children my grandchildren; and these flocks and all that you have are from my flocks and possessions . . . so, how could I harm my own flesh and blood?"

"You evade the issue, Laban," Jacob said soberly.

"No, I am not evading the issue. I simply have come to·understand, as you have talked," Laban replied, "that I do not want to harm or take away anything from my daughters and my grandchildren. Besides, I recognize that my daughters must be allowed to accompany you, their husband, back to Canaan if they want to.

"So, come, Jacob." Laban took the taller man's arm. "Come and let us make a covenant together . . . a peace pact, and you and I will abide and live by its terms."

Joseph saw Jacob momentarily lift his face to the effulgent sun overhead, and then he watched as his father moved a good-sized boulder to a small clearing. Calling the men, Jacob told them to gather stones and make a heap around the big stone. Then Jacob and Laban named the monument, "The Witness Pile." Both men agreed not to deceive each other or to trespass into one another's territory.

"This heap of stones will stand as a witness against us if either of us trespasses across this line," Jacob stated.

They agreed also to call it "The Watchtower." Neither Laban nor Jacob was sure they could ever fully trust each other, so Laban put Jacob's thought into words when he said, "May the Lord watch between you and me when we are absent from one another." He said for both of them that they would decide to let the *Lord* watch for cheating or deceiving ways.

Joseph looked on, his eyes wide with wonder, as his father and grandfather solemnly took the oath to abide by the terms of the covenant.

The feast, later that starlit evening, was not remembered for its fun and festivity, but for the gentle, healing fragrance which filled the air. Laban, his sons, and his men, while not victorious, were nevertheless peaceably satisfied.

After a sacrifice was made to seal their covenant, and after their quiet time of eating roast lamb and fresh bread together had drawn to a close, they all spent the night in Jacob's mountain encampment.

The morning sun rose and, with its coming, Laban kissed Leah and Rachel and all his grandchildren. With one final speech, he gave them his honest blessing and departed for his place in the fertile valleys near Haran.

Jacob watched them go until they were mere specks on the valley below him. "We shall not see your grandfather again, my boy," he said softly to Joseph. "This is our final parting. We, the descendants of Abraham, are free of our ties. We shall not go back to the land of our forefathers, but ahead to the land of Canaan. We will be a nation of our own . . . chosen of God."

The boy wondered what it all meant.

13

The formidable tents of Jacob rimmed Mount Gilead's most prominent ridge for several weeks.

There was no need to hurry now. Jacob, wanting to restore Rachel's strength as much as possible, instructed his sons and servants to use the down time for fattening and resting the flocks and herds. "There is still a long journey ahead of us," he cautioned.

The setting was perfect for restoration of both man and beast. A fresh, copious water spring gurgled and surged out of a canyon above their tents and supplied them abundantly as it flowed down the hillside. The crystalline air, cool in the morning and evening and free of sand particles, smelled invigoratingly fresh. The weather surrounded them with a comfortable warmth totally unlike the intense white-hot heat of the lower desert floor they knew so well.

So they passed their time of waiting in what Joseph thought was their most pleasant of days.

"It is so beautiful here," he said to his mother one morning after he had brought her the goatskin filled with cool spring water. "Could we not stay here and make this mountain our home?"

Rachel and Bilhah were sitting just outside Rachel's tent. They had a small stone handmill between them and were grinding grain. Rachel was feeling stronger so she had told Leah that she would do "her share" of the work. Each morning now, she and Bilhah ground the grain into flour; and while it wasn't very much, for Rachel tired easily, she was pleased with herself and felt good about her contribution.

The comforting, almost musical sounds of the stones, as the two women alternately pushed and pulled together, hummed into the morning air. It seemed to lull them all into a protected sense of well-being.

Rachel looked over Bilhah's head and said to Joseph, "My son, it appears that we are all taken with this place. You are very happy here, are you not?"

"Oh, yes," he eagerly replied. "When I was at the mouth of the spring a few moments ago, I saw two wild goats." Joseph gave out a short giggle and said with sparkling eyes, "I watched *them* a long time before *they* saw me! Mother, I wish I could run and jump the rocks like they do."

The women exchanged smiles.

Joseph hung the goatskin of water inside the tent on the center pole and then, moving a basket of grain over towards Bilhah, he sat beside his mother and watched the grinding process. He grew quietly thoughtful as the flour fell silently between the stones and onto the sheepskin spread below. Finally, he spoke, but his voice had lost all the childish wonder over the mountain goats. He was filled with what seemed like adult concern.

"Mother," he said genuinely, "I fear that while we might love this place, it is not so with father. Something sad troubles him."

Joseph looked out past the tent flap and added, "He spends much time out there looking over the valley below, and sometimes he does not even know it is I who sits beside him."

"You mean he is quiet and does not talk with you?" Rachel asked. Joseph silently shook his head affirmatively.

His mother took her hand off the grinding stone's handle, turned the boy's face towards her, and said gently, "Your father knows you are there, dear one, but sometimes it is possible to be together without requiring words. It is an acceptable thing," Rachel assured him, "and very often there is a need for silent companionship.

"He was probably very pleased that you were there, but simply not inclined to speak . . . or to answer questions. You *do* ask a lot of questions, you know." Rachel winked at Joseph, and he brightened instantly with a smile. Then he turned serious again and countered, "But it is more than that, mother. I think he has wide-awake dreams as he sits and gazes out over the valley, and I fear they deeply trouble him."

Rachel caught her breath in surprise, and Bilhah, leaning over the stones, whispered with some degree of awe, "This one misses nothing." She would have said more, but Rachel beckoned her to continue grinding.

The women continued pushing and pulling the stones without any conversation until finally Rachel, eager to have private words with Joseph, said tactfully, "Bilhah, this is enough for today. You may take the flour to Leah. Tell her I fear it is not much, but we will make it up on the morrow."

When they were alone, Rachel laid down on her bedding and calling Joseph to her side she said, "You are keenly perceptive, my son. I think one day you will be a prophet who is able to foresee future events . . . if not by your dreams, then surely by your ever-alert eyes!"

Rachel studied him and thought, *How extraordinary! You see not only surface things, but, Joseph, you have the ability to see through people. Your powers of observation are more developed than a person three times your age. What has Jacob's God planned for you?*

"About father—" Joseph's words interrupted her thoughts.

"Yes, about father . . . well, your father cannot help but be troubled for the closer we come to his homeland, the more he has to deal with old, almost forgotten fears," Rachel said. Silently she pondered how much she should tell the boy.

"But," Joseph said with puzzlement, "my grandfather has gone back to Haran, and he and father have made peace between them. See . . . even up there is the stone which marks their promises."

"Oh," Rachel smiled, "your grandfather, Laban, is not the problem. Jacob fears someone else."

This "fear of someone else" Joseph did not understand and said so.

Rachel leaned back on her pillows and stared at a slim, golden shaft of sunlight which beamed down on the carpet from a small hole in the tent's cloth above her. She spoke without looking at the boy.

"You see that one shining beam of sunshine? It looks as if it is a tent pole made of beaten gold, but when you take a closer look, you see the pole is not solid at all. In fact, it's filled and alive with a moving sandstorm of dust.

"It is the same with life," his mother explained. "Our lives are not one solid experience, but a whole moving collection of experiences, events, and happenings. Each day in life can, and often does, add a new facet to our lives."

Rachel turned on her side and faced her young pupil. "Like this morning for you," she said. "You saw the goats and wished you could jump as they do. That was an experience. It's now an event that happened in your past, your recent past, but nonetheless your past. Chances are the meaning of that experience will never trouble you. But in life, it is possible that you will find one of those swirling swarms of dust in your sunbeam, and it will cause you no end of heartache."

"Is that what ails father, an experience from his past?"

Joseph's astute question penetrated Rachel's soul, and she decided to treat him as an adult. She said with candor, "Yes. His experiences in the past, before he knew us, now lurk about his soul, and he is haunted by his awful memories.

"My poor Jacob has reason to fear. When he was young and lived at home," Rachel continued, "Jacob desired the birthright and blessing of the firstborn so badly, he cruelly deceived his father, Isaac, and with great cunning cheated his brother, Esau, out of his rightful inheritance.

"I imagine the closer we come to your father's homeland, the stronger his guilt becomes.

"Time has changed your father, Joseph. He is a different man now. We must remember that his dealings with his own father and brother happened *before* his life–changing dream at Bethel."

Rachel stopped and pondered what kind of a man her husband might have become had he not climbed the great stone stairway to God. She shuddered with a quick chill and then resumed her talk, directing her full attention to the boy.

"Your father faces a difficult dilemma. He fears meeting Esau because the last time they were together there was much hatred and strife between them. Yet . . . the living God transformed your father's heart and mind. And now, before he can live out his life in peace, old accounts must be settled, old wounds closed to heal, and old swords buried forever.

"God and the years of growing have changed Jacob, and I fervently pray that one or both have softened and melted the hard, revengeful heart of Esau."

"To which god?" Joseph asked

"What?" Rachel leaned up on an elbow to see him better.

"When you pray about Esau, which god do you pray to—the living God or grandfather's teraphim?" A slight, teasing smile played around his mouth.

"You rascal!" Rachel broke into laughter. She shook her finger at him and confessed, "I *knew* I was going to have to explain those teraphim to you one day!" Then almost to herself she muttered, "As Bilhah says, 'You never miss a thing.' "

Rachel sat up and poured her heart into the explanation. "Well, my young discoverer of secrets," she began, "there is not terribly much to explain, but I will try.

"You see, when I pray, it is to the living God—the God of Jacob's fathers. But when I embark on my first long arduous journey, leaving my childhood home to live in a far distant land, I take the teraphim. I could not bear to go so far away without something familiar from my home as a keepsake.

"The teraphim are a part of my 'golden tent pole' of experiences and are as much a part of me as my old dog, Little Fox."

Rachel caught the slight reproach in Joseph's eyes and hastily explained, "I know that stealing the teraphim from my father and then lying about them to both my father and husband were completely wrong, but maybe when you are older you will understand."

Joseph made no comment.

Rachel looked pleadingly at Joseph's face. "A woman . . . a woman needs familiar things—seeable, touchable things—sometimes, and the teraphim comfort me. They restore good childhood memories within me and are rather like good luck charms from my past."

She silently thanked the luck of the stone gods when Joseph did not ask if she had showed the teraphim to Jacob. The less Jacob knew about the stone gods, the better. Rachel was relieved when Joseph's next question changed the subject.

"When will we continue our journey?"

"Tomorrow." Jacob's voice startled both of them. Rachel's eyes took in the large, tall, and straight form which was silhouetted in the tent opening. Jacob's head was held high, and every inch of him looked like the stalwart leader he had become. *My prince*, she thought.

He greeted his son and then sat down by Rachel. He kissed her hands and said, "I have given my men their orders, and tomorrow we shall break camp early. We shall travel southwest. Are you rested enough?" He was still holding her hand, and she returned his loving gaze warmly.

"Yes, I am fine and ready to move on," Rachel answered. "Now, your son, on the other hand—he would like to stay here. Shall we leave him in this beautiful place and go on?" Rachel asked in mock seriousness.

"Why not? He can take care of himself," Jacob answered without looking at the lad.

"I certainly can. You two go on without me," Joseph said, and the three of them burst into laughter like families do when everyone is winning at the same game.

Their orderly and regimented departure the next morning was vastly different from their first hurried and perilous flight from Haran. Yet when Rachel met Jacob's foreboding look, as he helped her onto the camel's back, she knew they were still vulnerable and open to the ominous and inevitable meeting between Jacob and his brother, Esau.

She spoke soothingly to him as he arranged the blankets and layers of kidskin against the saddle; but knew, even as she talked, that Jacob was unable to hear her comforting words.

A few days later, Rachel was dazzled by the change in her husband. He even rode back toward her with the look of a man who had worked everything out to perfection.

"Look!" he cried, as he brought his camel alongside of her. "See those men? They have just joined us. We must praise the Lord in a mighty way, my wife. God has kept his promise about our safety." Jacob's face was glowing, and the confidence made him ride tall on his camel.

"But who are they?" Rachel shouted into the rising wind.

Joseph, who shared his mother's saddle, turned his head slightly and, leaning back into her, said with credibility, "They are angels, Mother. Angels . . . sent by God to protect father and all of us on our journey."

Rachel looked in astonishment from the boy in front of her to the man beside her and then back again.

Jacob cried in approval, "The boy tells the truth! They *are* angels sent from God!" Then he exclaimed loudly, "*This is God's camp.* I will call it Mahanain for it means *two camps* or *two armies*—God's camp and my camp. Praise the living God for His unceasing kindness and His unbreakable covenants!"

Jacob was buoyantly filled with courage, and he took the presence of the band of angels as God's signal to arrange a meeting with his brother. Then, with a large degree of blind faith, he sent messengers down to Edom, which was south of the Dead Sea in the land of Seir, to find Esau.

"Go!" Jacob said. The tone of his voice was filled with authority, but his words conveyed pure diplomacy for he said, "Find my master, Esau, and tell him I send my greetings. Explain that I have been living as a stranger with Uncle Laban all these years until recently. Tell him that now I own oxen, donkeys, sheep, camels, and many servants, both male and female. Impress on him that I have sent you in the fervent hope that he will be friendly to us, and that I will find grace and favor in his sight."

The messengers hurried off on the fastest beasts, and Jacob

gave orders to set up their tents along the north bank of the shallow Jabbok River.

Days later, as Jacob sat along the riverbank, he spotted the returning messengers. He called for Joseph, and the two of them waded across the small, narrow neck of the river to meet the men.

The news at first was reassuringly good. "We found your brother, Esau, and he is coming here to meet you." But there was more, and Jacob paled visibly as the messenger said, "But he comes with an army of four hundred men."

Jacob's impassive face revealed none of his inner turmoil, but Joseph quickly sensed that his father was frantic with fear. He was sure of it when Jacob grabbed his hand, and together they hurriedly splashed back across the river. The lad ran beside his father in order to keep up with Jacob's long strides.

Quickly, Jacob's sons and menservants were called, and Jacob divided their entire encampment of people and animals into two sections. "If Esau attacks one group, then at least the other group will be able to escape," he hurriedly explained to them.

Then, before them all, Jacob lifted up his head and implored into the heavens above, "O God of Abraham, my grandfather, and of my father, Isaac, O Jehovah, who told me, 'Return to your land and to your family, and I will treat you kindly.' I do not deserve the least of your kindness and faithfulness that You have rendered Your servant. Indeed, for when I left home I owned nothing more than a walking stick . . . and now I am two armies strong.

"O Lord, deliver me from the destructive hand of my brother, Esau, for I am frightened and terribly afraid that he is on his way here now to kill me, these mothers, and my children.

"Yet You promised to deal kindly with me and to multiply my descendants until they became as the sand along the seashore . . . too many to count. Help me, my God, I pray You." Jacob begged fervently.

They spent the night by the river, and with the first early light, Jacob devised another plan. He prepared a lavish present for Esau in hopes that it would appease his brother's anger. Eagerly, out of his vast possessions, Jacob set aside two hundred nanny goats, twenty billy goats, twenty rams, forty milking camels with their colts, forty cows, ten bulls, twenty female donkeys, and ten foals. To his sons, shepherds, and servants, Jacob instructed: "I want this livestock divided into two droves. Keep them separate and drive one a considerable distance ahead of the other."

Joseph watched and listened as his father said to the chief manservant in charge of the first drove, "Now, when you meet Esau and he asks, 'Where are you going? Whose servants are you? Whose animals are these?'—you will reply, 'These belong to your *servant*, Jacob. They are a present for his *master*, Esau. He is coming right behind us.' "

Jacob repeated the same message to the other servant in charge of the second drove, and when he was satisfied that the men understood, he sent them off.

"Are we going to follow them now?" Joseph looked up eagerly at Jacob.

"Not yet," he answered. "I hope the presents will cool your uncle's wrath. It is my peace offering, but I think there should be some time between the presents and our arrival."

Jacob wanted no more discussion, and so they walked slowly toward their encampment to join the remaining company. The evening meal was prepared and eaten by Jacob and his sons in thoughtful silence; and shortly after, with very few words, the entire encampment settled down in an uneasy sleep.

Jacob's restlessness, however, finally propelled him out of his tent in the middle of the night. He went first to Rachel and Joseph, and waking her, said, "I hope my gifts will appease Esau's anger, but I cannot be sure. I think, for your safety, you, Leah, my concubines, and all the children should seek shelter away from this encampment."

Hurriedly, each person was awakened, and they waded south across the river Jordan at the Jabbock ford. When Jacob saw they were safely settled, he recrossed the river and decided to spend the remaining part of the night on the north bank even though he was wet and shivering with the cold night's chill.

Joseph was awake before his mother and the others, and his curiosity was near the breaking point over the whereabouts of his father. He rubbed the sleep from his eyes and slipped down to the riverbank in time to see Jacob coming towards him.

Joseph saw that his father seemed to be in great pain, and as

Jacob limped towards him, the boy ran and offered himself as a walking stick.

"You are hurt. What has wounded you, my father? What wild animal attacked you? Did Esau come in the night?" The questions poured out of Joseph.

"No, my son. Esau did not come, but I had another visitor," Jacob replied. "I have wrestled with God, and I've left my fears on the other side of the river."

Joseph looked up at his father and said, "Sir, I do not understand. Please tell me more."

So, Jacob sat down on a large rock a few feet up from the river and explained. "Last night, because I could not sleep, I went across the river and waited. I lit no fire but sat in the darkness. I wondered how Esau would respond, and I wished for a confirming sign from God to tell me that all was well.

"Suddenly, from behind, I heard the snap of a twig as if it had been stepped upon, and I knew someone was there."

"Were you frightened?" Joseph quizzed.

"No," Jacob continued, "I felt no fear or bewilderment for even as I saw the man come out of the shadows toward me, I knew it must be the sign I had hoped for." Joseph nodded and urged his father to go on.

"The man took ahold of my arm and an immediate battle ensued," Jacob said. "It was a wordless and strange wrestling match. We fought and continued to fight throughout the night, with no apparent winner. Finally, in an attempt to break the tie between us, and thus to end our combat, the man gathered his strength and struck me. I think he wrenched my hip loose from its socket, but still I was determined that I would not give up my viselike grip on the man.

"He was tired and soaking with perspiration when he finally uttered his first words: 'Let me go for the day is breaking.'

"I perceived this was no ordinary man, Joseph, for I was convinced he was a messenger or angel from God. My fear of Esau was still so real, and I felt I needed all the assurance from God I could get. I summoned all my strength and said, 'I will not let you go until you bless me.'

"The man asked me sternly, 'What is your name?' When I told him he said, 'Your name will be Jacob no longer. You shall be called *Israel* because you have been strong with God and men, and you have won.'

"The stranger finished his blessing as the first rays of dawn lit the eastern sky and now, as before at Bethel, I knew I had spoken and wrestled with God."

The boy's face was filled with wonder. "There is more, my son, for I would not let the man go. I wanted proof that I had wrestled with God.

"So, I pleaded, 'Tell me your name, I pray you.'

"The wrestler answered, 'You need not know my name, so do not ask. I have given you your blessing, and that shall be sufficient.'

"Then I watched the man disappear into the trees, and I would not have stopped him even if I found the strength."

Jacob pointed across the river, and Joseph could see that the sun's slanted rays revealed the matted grassy bank where the two had wrestled, and Jacob said, "I shall name the place Peniel, meaning *The Face of God* because I have seen God face-to-face and yet my life was preserved."

Then looking directly at Joseph, he said, "My son, you are known now as the son of Jacob, but I am Israel now, and someday you and all my descendants will be known as the children of Israel."

Joseph would have asked more, but Jacob stopped, put his hand up to shade his eyes from the early brilliance of the morning sun, and pointing to the large cloud of dust on the southern horizon he exclaimed, "Your Uncle Esau and his men!"

Joseph marveled at his father's calmness for he remembered his panic the night before. Yet now, even though in pain, Jacob seemed at peace. By the time the thundering herd of four hundred men and beasts came within hearing range of their encampment, Jacob had everything arranged.

He at once organized his wives, concubines, and children into a long column. Joseph was sent off with his mother. The line of people began with the handmaidens, concubines, and their children in front; stretched to Leah and her children in the middle; and had Rachel and Joseph—Jacob's most precious possessions—as the last.

Then, without a trace of any fear, Jacob led the procession of loved ones toward the advancing men. Jacob bowed to the ground seven times on the way to show his repentant heart and his respectful humility.

"He suffers more than you know, mother," Joseph whispered to his mother while they watched. "When he bows and walks there is great pain in his hip."

"What happened?" Rachel asked.

"He had a visitor last night—an angel from God—and I fear they fought. Yet father won a great victory. When he came across the river this morning, he was in pain, but his soul was healed; he is not troubled anymore."

"I still do not understand what happened," Rachel said, a bit desperately.

"I am sure father will tell you, for it is wonderful," Joseph replied; and so they stood, far back in the line, and watched the limping form of Jacob as he bowed his way to Esau.

Esau—his dark face almost hidden behind a thick, massive beard—recognized his brother, dismounted, and ran to Jacob. The two men melted the hateful events of the past by embracing and mingling their tears together.

When they could tell there was to be no war between the brothers, Jacob's family and the company of four hundred sons and men of Esau crowded around, eager to hear how life had been for the other.

Esau saw the women and children and, with his arm still around Jacob's shoulder, he asked, "And who are all these people with you?"

Jacob laughed and said, "They are *my* people. Here, come. Meet my womenservants and their children, my concubines, their sons, and my wives, and our children." They each came and stood directly in front of Esau, bowed low and paid their respectful homage.

Esau was delighted with the steady stream of kinsfolk, but his interest quickened when he looked past Leah's last son and saw a small boy standing beside a woman.

"Pray tell me, Jacob, just who are they? The woman is too beautiful and delicate to have anything to do with you," he jested and moved forward to meet her.

Jacob shielded his mouth with his hand and said in confidentiality, "She is my very *favorite* wife, Rachel, and the boy is our son, Joseph."

The pair bowed low before Esau, and then the big, broad shouldered, dark and hairy brother of Jacob picked Joseph up in one swoop and lifted him high above his head. As he swung the boy around, he shouted to Jacob, "I can see this one is special. It's a good thing he looks like his mother and not you." Esau's laugh was hearty; and while in some ways he frightened Joseph, the lad was captivated by the rough goodness of his uncle.

When Joseph was put down, he said quietly and a little breathlessly to his mother, "Things change quickly. Is this the same man my father feared? Perhaps your prayers have been heard, my mother."

Rachel shushed and silenced him by putting her finger to her lips, and at the same time she raised her veil around her head. She gestured for him to listen to the conversation of his father and uncle.

Esau was asking about all the droves of flocks and herds he passed on his way. Jacob's face showed a crimson flush of embarrassment. He feared Esau knew full well about the droves for he had instructed his servants in what to say. He also guessed that Esau knew a bribe when he was offered one. So, he answered straightforward, "They are my gifts, my peace offering to you. I had hoped to gain your favor."

"Oh, my brother!" Esau's easy laugh boomed out above the heads of the children who stood around him. Then, with a measure of humility, Esau said kindly, "Jacob, I have plenty—more than I need. Keep what you have."

"No, Esau," Jacob implored. "Please do me the honor of accepting them. Actually, it was a relief to see your friendly smile for I feared facing you as I fear facing God. Take all my gifts for God has been most gracious to me, and I have enough."

Jacob insisted and continued to insist until Esau finally shouted, "All right, Jacob. You win! I'll take them."

Then without warning Esau said, "Let's break camp and travel to Seir together. My sons and men will be a protective army covering your flanks."

Rachel looked on with renewed interest for she knew it was not Jacob's plan to spend his days in Seir, but more south in the heartland of Canaan. She wondered how Jacob would graciously get out of this without being offensive to Esau and without starting a new conflict between them.

Jacob, not to be deterred from the route he had chosen, pointed to Joseph and some of his servants' youngsters and said carefully, "As you can see, some of the children are small, and the flocks and herds have their young. If they are driven too hard, they will die.

"So why don't you go on ahead of us," Jacob suggested, "and we will follow slowly, at a more leisurely pace. We will see and visit you eventually in Seir."

Esau was not easily convinced, and he proposed as a compromise that he leave some of his men to assist Jacob so they could serve as guides; but Jacob refused. Finally, after much discussion, it was settled; Esau, his sons, and his men would take the gifts of livestock and return to Seir. They left in high spirits, before the afternoon sun slipped behind the hills, and the peace of God rang like a song in the distance between the brothers.

In the days following, Jacob and his entourage moved south, deeper into Canaan, to a place on the west bank of the Jordan river called Succoth. There Jacob called a temporary halt to their journey and set up his camp. To give the young animals a chance to mature, he built huts and pens for the flocks and herds and utilized a copious spring and the fertile plains to the best advantage.

Two uneventful moons later, the order was given by Jacob to break camp and move on.

The whole assembly traveled due south once more toward the prosperous city of Shechem.

When they reached the lovely plains and meadows of Moreh, Jacob found the small terebinth trees which looked like the oak trees his grandfather, Abraham, had once described, and he said, "Here, under the trees my grandfather knew and in sight of the Hivite city of Shechem, we shall stay."

Before the tents were raised, Jacob took his oldest son, Reuben, into the city. He found Prince Shechem, a son of Hamor the Hivite, and paid him one hundred pieces of silver for a large portion of the tree-filled plains land.

That evening, in the tent of Rachel, Jacob sat on a stool and chuckled out loud. "What is amusing?" Rachel asked.

"Oh, I was just thinking that everyone expected me to be in Padan-aram only a few days.

"But, of course, that was because no one knew how clever your father, Laban, would be or . . . how smitten I would be with you, my love.

"The 'few days' have stretched into many years; but oh, my lamb, God has been good to us." He bent over and touched her cheek as she sat before him on the floor. Softly, he promised, "I will dig a great well here so we will never need to depend on other sources, and in this place you will grow strong again."

Rachel patted his hand and said nothing about the vague but growing fears she had about the city just down the road. God had given her no dream, so there was little proof, yet even the sound of the city's name, Shechem, sent a wave of panic through her. *He will think I am a silly woman if I tell him of my concern, so I will not spoil his homecoming,* she said to herself.

"And it will be called El-elohe-Israel," Jacob finished triumphantly.

"What will?" Rachel was jerked back into the moment and realized that she must have missed something.

"The altar, of course!" he replied. "My grandfather always built an altar to show his gratitude to God, and I shall continue the tradition. The priests of the moon-gods and sun-gods are always erecting temples and shrines, but our people always build altars; and then, because our spiritual experiences are real, we show our gratitude by worshiping and praising our God at those special places."

"Yes, I see," Rachel replied. "I must remember to teach Joseph the importance of both your projects. Now, let's see; the well will be dug for our bodies' thirst, and the altar will be built for the dryness of our souls." He nodded his approval.

Jacob studied the remarkable woman and hoped that their time in Shechem would restore the color to her cheeks and the flesh to her bones.

It was not to be. But only Rachel knew that.

14

"Shechem ... *Shechem?*" Rachel repeated it ominously. "Who would ever want to go to *Shechem?*" She spit out the ancient city's name as if it was an abhorrent disease.

It was true: Rachel had traveled the short distance to Shechem only once, but it had been enough. Her fears that the city was an evil place had been confirmed. From then on, the terebinth trees—Abraham's "oak trees"—of their encampment seemed intensely too close to the city's boundaries.

"It's an evil, smelly place." Rachel looked closely at the women seated around her in her tent and verbally questioned their state of sanity.

"But I *want* to go," the usually timid Zilpah spoke up.

"Me, too."

"And I."

"Bilhah ... and you, too," Rachel stammered.

"Aunt Rachel, we *all* want to go! It's our big city. Have you forgotten the excitement of going into Haran during the growing-up days of your girlhood?" It was Dinah, Leah's raven-haired and strikingly beautiful daughter who voiced the opinion of the rest of them.

"Haran was hardly the shockingly sinful place that Shechem is," Rachel said scornfully in reply.

"Oh, no?" Leah quietly retorted. "I remember Haran in much the same way my sons tell me Shechem seems to be. Big stone walls, houses of wood and mud bricks, temples to different gods and much, *much* corruption!"

Rachel turned sharply toward her sister and snapped, "You would allow your only daughter to go there unchaperoned? That's like sending her into the hills alone to face a pack of winter-starved wolves."

"No, not alone," Leah replied. "My sons, Reuben, Levi, and Simeon, maybe others, would accompany Dinah and the girls. Besides," she added, "it's only for a day's visit, my sister. They are not moving there on a permanent basis!" The girls laughed and tried to tease Rachel into a change of heart, but she would not be moved.

Strongly she advised, "Mark my words. No good will come out of this. I have a feeling here. . ." Rachel touched her chest, "and I know we shall all remember this talk and rue the day of Shechem."

Despite her casual warning, an outing to the city became the central theme of everyone's discussions among the tents of Jacob.

Leah's oldest sons had been there once or twice and their enthusiastic endorsements of the city only served to fire Dinah's and the servants' curiosity and desire to a white-hot fervor. They practically demanded to go.

The girls' first excursion into the city and even the second one was uneventful as far as Rachel's gloomy prediction of evil befalling them was concerned. Dinah made a point of coming to Rachel's tent after one such adventure into Shechem and twirled slowly around for her aunt, saying, "See, my aunt. I have been to that evil place, and I am *perfectly* fine! Your fears are merely in the shadows of your tent."

Dinah was tall, solid boned, and blessed with a voluptuously full figure. Her facial features, though large, were perfectly proportioned, and the visual sight of her was stunning. Rachel wondered, as she watched Dinah perform a graceful dance before her, how it would be to have the girl's sturdy, reliable and blossoming good health. With some sorrow, she compared her own fragile vitality with the robust beauty before her and decided she'd take health over beauty any day, if she had the choice.

"What do you say, Aunt Rachel?" Dinah's dark eyes sparkled with a glint of triumph.

Rachel smiled and acquiesced, saying, "All right, my dear. You seem fine! After all, what do I know?"

They were interrupted by Joseph's cheery, rather breathless greeting.

"Hello and good-bye, little brother. I must help mother with the evening meal." Dinah swooped down and kissed the top of his head on her way out. From the tent flap she called, "Joseph, ask your mother if you can go to Shechem with us next time we go."

Rachel pretended she didn't hear the remark and, partly out of curiosity but mostly out of wanting a change of conversation, she calmly said, "You look as if you have some interesting news, my son. Where have you been all day?"

Joseph sat down beside her, and using his hands in excited gestures, he said, "Early this morning, father and some of my brothers found a man just past the farthest grouping of trees. The man is old and seemed very sick. They brought him to our tents."

"Where did he come from?" Rachel asked, to be polite and to cover up her disappointment at such a trivial piece of news.

"He was left by his master. The man had been in a caravan traveling to Shechem when he became too ill to continue. He asked that in return for his years of service to his master they let him die in peace by the side of the road."

"How sick is he?" Rachel asked idly.

"That's just it. He is not sick at all. After the caravan moved on and before father could summon Aunt Leah to see to his care, the man picked himself off the ground and asked to speak to the father of the household." Joseph's face was glowing with the deliciousness of surprise, and Rachel sat up with a quickened interest.

"Go on. . ." she insisted.

"Well, father introduced himself, and then he let me go with him and the stranger to his tent. There the man said his name was Sapher."

Upon hearing the visitor's name, Rachel abruptly got up from her bed and began to make herself presentable.

"Are you going to father's tent to meet the stranger?" Joseph was puzzled by the suddenness of her actions.

"Yes, I am." She found her head veil in a small chest and then explained, "The name Sapher means 'scribe' or 'writer,' and if he *is* a scribe, I'd like him to be your teacher. Perhaps someday you could be a big help to your father. Just think . . . if you kept records and learned number writing—"

"Mother," Joseph caught her arm as she was about to pass him and leave. "Mother, it is already settled."

"What?" Rachel's mouth dropped open.

"He is here to teach not only writing and numbers, but also languages. He speaks several dialects, and because his former master traded goods with the people of the Nile, he writes with pictures, and he speaks the Egyptians' language."

Rachel sat down abruptly on the low stool in front of Joseph. "But why did he choose your father's tents?" she asked the boy.

"Because of a dream," he answered simply. "Sapher said a man appeared to him in a dream and commanded him to leave his master that very night. He was told to walk toward Shechem and on his way, the man said, he would find an encampment of tents in the terebinth trees. Sapher was then instructed to teach all of his skills to the person who showed the most willingness to learn," Joseph finished.

Rachel cleared her throat and, looking at Joseph's bright blue eyes, she said, "And you said *you* had that willingness. Is that true?"

"Yes," he answered simply. Then he added, "And starting with the morrow, I will have a teacher."

"Ah, I see . . . I have been replaced," Rachel teased the boy.

Joseph instantly grew serious and with determination said, "Oh, no! You are my *best* teacher. I have learned so many—"

"Joseph, Joseph," Rachel protested. "I am only testing your humor." She gave him a hug and then said, "I am very pleased for this scribe to be in our tents. Come, I think we should welcome him properly."

Without moving Joseph said, "Mother, will you still be my teacher in other things?"

Rachel assured him that she would, and then he surprised her once again by the adult depth of his next question.

"Then tell me why you fear for anyone to go to Shechem? You won't let me go with Dinah and my brothers, will you?" The lad stood looking up at her, his face gravely somber.

"No, I will not let you go to Shechem . . . ever!" Rachel's voice was fierce with determination. "Here is a lesson for you, my son. Now, listen closely.

"Do not go any place where you know evil exists and thrives. It will be best to avoid that place completely. On the other hand, should you be in someone's tent and then find an evil thing happening, leave immediately. And if you can't find an open tent flap, *make one!*"

Joseph laughed as he got her message and would have said no more about Shechem except that a few moons later his half brothers were engaged in a full-scale war of revenge with what seemed to be the whole population of Shechem.

"Sapher," Joseph said one morning, in the middle of his numbers' lesson, "what is 'rape'?" The old scribe dropped the wax-covered wooden tablet he had been holding. Joseph recovered it quickly, and the old man collected the board and his poise.

"I am here to put words and numbers into your head, Joseph. I would be taking away someone else's teaching privilege if I discussed your question. Who is it, your mother or your father, who answers your questions and helps you to learn about the delicate mysteries of life?" Sapher asked kindly.

"Sometimes both," Joseph replied. "But mostly it is the task of my mother."

"Then go to her. She should be the person you ask. I shall finish off this lesson quickly, and then I want you to go directly to your mother. And Joseph," the old man took the boy's chin in his hand, "ask her gently."

Joseph went to Rachel's tent, then to Leah's, past the cooking fires, out to the east pasture, and finally he found his mother at the main well.

Rachel was sitting on the edge of the stone top Jacob and his men had made for the well. She warmed her back with the slanted rays of the afternoon sun. No one was with her, and Joseph surmised—she knew the women came in the morning for water—she came now to be alone. He also sensed she was deeply troubled about something.

When he was a short stone's throw away, he called to her so his presence would not startle her. He did not fully understand Sapher's meaning about asking gently, but he thought giving his mother warning that he was coming was a good place to begin gentleness.

Rachel turned, looked into the orange sun and recognized both his voice and his silhouette. "Are you through so soon with Master Sapher?" she called to him as the boy ran toward her.

"We will continue tomorrow. He let me come to you as I have a question." He reached her, kissed her cheeks, and continued, "My teacher says this question is just for you to answer."

"I see," Rachel said, and suspected immediately that the

question would involve something about the dreadful events which had taken place in Shechem. They were a small community. Gossip, small talk, news, and information was their dinnertime mainstay. Everything was discussed, and she shuddered, even with the sun on her back, at the possibilities of what Joseph had heard. There was an openness between them, and no subject was forbidden. Still, she breathed inwardly, "O living God, I would like his young and tender ears to be spared such ugly knowledge. Must I teach him about lust, greed, and the devious ways of sin?"

She heard inside her soul, "Who better than you? Do you wish him to learn by painful experience what he could have easily learned from his mother's loving teaching?"

"No," Rachel whispered back to the living God. "You are right, my Lord, who better than I? But what if I fail him or make a mistake?"

Once more, from the depths of her soul, she heard the voice of the living God, "The wise woman is one who keeps herself open to Me daily and obediently keeps My instructions. Have you taught Joseph as I have led you?"

She answered with a silent yes.

"Then," He continued, "you will have to entrust the outcome of Joseph's training with Me."

"Yes, Lord," she breathed.

Then she rose, took Joseph's hand and said to him, "I will lean on you as a walking stick, and you can ask your question as we walk homeward."

Joseph remembered Sapher's instructions so he began, "Every night, mother, during and after our evening meal, my brothers sit around the camp fire and hurl their curses into the air. They all seem very angry at Hamor's son, Shechem, and they shout of revenge and killing." He looked up at his mother's impassive face, unsure if he should continue.

"Go on," she said softly as they walked.

"Well, I do not understand their anger. Once when I asked Reuben why they wanted to kill the prince, he struck out at me with his fist."

Rachel looked at him in alarm, but Joseph smiled, "I ducked, and he missed." Rachel shook her head, knowing she should not be so anxious for she would not always be around to shield him from physical or verbal blows. She asked, "Did any of them tell you the reason for their anger?"

"No, not exactly. But I think it has something to do with Dinah for I have not seen her since the last full moon," Joseph reasoned. "Then finally, when I asked Judah why all this talk of killing Shechem, he gave me an answer; but I did not understand the terms he used. He said Dinah had been raped by Shechem, and for that the brothers meant Shechem to pay for his crime with his life."

Rachel's small cup of ominous foreboding spilled over and made a lake of fear within her. *So,* she thought, *the brothers are not going to be satisfied with just punishment for the rapist—no, they will not put away their knives and spears until they have taken his life.*

Joseph's voice pressed into her thoughts, and she looked numbly at him as he said, "Sapher said to ask gently, but I can only ask it bluntly. What does *raped* mean?"

The two had reached the outer perimeter of the terebinth trees. The sun was close to settling into the horizon, and the air, still holding the day's heat, was fragrant with the purple and yellow blossoms of the saffron plant which brightened the meadow.

Rachel took off her head veil and, pointing to one tree whose branches were far enough off the ground, she said, "I've grown weary. Let's rest there, under that one before we go on into camp."

They sat watching the sunset, each wrapped in their own world of thoughts until Rachel knew she had overriden her fears. So, she broke the silence with, "Do you remember what I have already told you about the marriage vows?" The boy nodded.

"Then you may recall this. . . . I told you that when a man marries a woman, he then has the right to lie with her. Do you understand what 'lying with her' means?" Rachel faced him with her face and her directness.

"Yes," Joseph acknowledged. "To lie with his wife means from his loins to hers he plants the seeds to grow his children. I have watched the rams with the ewes as you instructed, so I know about that. I have . . . also seen my father when he lies with you in our tent," he finished with a smile.

"I suppose you have," Rachel said easily. Then, because she knew the boy would learn more from forming his own conclusions than by her straight lecture, she asked, "Tell me, then, why do you smile when you recall your father and I together, and not at all when you spoke of the sheep?"

Joseph's eyes brightened and without any hesitation, he answered, "Because the sheep and other animals are very serious and sometimes violent about it, but you and father seemed to enjoy lying together."

"Ah, then you've caught the difference!" Rachel clapped her hands in approval. "Our God has given the animals to each other for mating and giving birth to their young, but for us ... oh, for us He has done something special.

"Your father's and my love reaches the highest expression when we are joined in such an intimate way. It was the living God who said to the first of our forefathers, 'It is not good for man to live alone,' so He created a woman. A unique creation, in fact, a wife. And only to humans has He given the power to think, to reason, and to respond.

"One day God will lead you to the special woman who will be your wife, and you will be with her and know, for yourself, the joy which that act brings."

Joseph said almost timidly, "Then, mother, what does *raped* mean?"

"I was getting to that." The pain and fear of what was to come to the tents of Jacob crashed in around her again, and she stood up and dusted off her skirts. "I only wanted you to know how extraordinary the act of marriage is, for then and only then can you understand what a crime it is to violate that act.

"It seems as Shechem, the young prince, who bears the name of his city, saw your sister, Dinah, and he took her to his house. Then, without marriage and without her consent, he forced her to lie with him, disgracing and dishonoring her. That is called *rape*, and it has brought much shame to the tents of Jacob," Rachel explained and then continued.

"Your brothers seek revenge for that shame, and they would have killed Shechem on the day they learned of Dinah's plight; but an odd thing happened. So vile is the act of rape that usually both the man and woman despise each other from that day forward; however, in this case, it was different. Shechem has fallen in love, deeply in love, with Dinah. Now he has asked Jacob for her hand in marriage, and has offered your father and brothers as large a dowry and as many gifts in payment as they want. But there is something terribly wrong in all this. I do not know yet, but my soul flutters like a frightened bird everytime I hear the name Shechem."

The woman and the boy left the trees and walked along the back edges of the tents towards Rachel's dwelling.

"Has my father agreed to a wedding?" Joseph asked.

"Yes . . . but only after certain conditions were laid down. Because of the disgraceful shame brought to Dinah, your brothers have insisted that Shechem may not marry her until he and all the men of the city are circumcised as your father, brothers, and you are.

"Several days ago, the men of the city agreed to be circumcised. Schechem is the favorite son of Hamor, and he is well liked, even pampered; so the men submitted to our circumcision ritual as a wedding gift to him."

Rachel unconsciously slowed her step, paused, and shuddered inwardly as a thought projected itself more persistently upon her mind. *On the morrow, it will be three days since the circumcisions took place. I don't know why, but everything within me is desperately afraid.* Aloud, she said to Joseph, "I pleaded with Jacob to free Shechem of this agreement, but he refused, saying the shame of Dinah had ruined his reputation with other men, and that the circumcision of every male in the city is a fair and just payment for the evil deed."

As they reached Rachel's tent, Bilhah appeared from around the side and spotting Joseph admonished, "Your Aunt Leah told me to fetch you. The evening meal is already served. You are late. Hurry now." The playful swat she gave him was ignored, and since he left without making some kind of retort, Bilhah asked, "What is the matter with him?"

"I had to tell him about Dinah and Shechem."

"Oh." Bilhah nodded her head in understanding.

"It was painful for me, and I know he has caught my anxieties over all of this." Rachel poured some water into a basin and rinsed her face. As she dried off, she said, with weariness, "You know how accurate and sensitive he is when it comes to judging feelings and assessing situations. He learned today about the meaning of rape, and I think the innocent child of seven summers has waded into the muddy river of manhood."

"Those fears will be only confirmed for him as he eats with the men tonight," Bilhah said with conviction.

"Why? What have you heard?" Rachel cried.

"Nothing. Absolutely nothing. And that's what is frightening. Ever since the men found out about Dinah, their evening meal has been a boisterous time of threats, insults, and much shouting about taking their revenge. Yet tonight they ate in silence, complete silence. It was eerie, and the other servant girls refused to finish serving. It was as if the brothers have settled on a plan . . . like they have made a secret agreement and have come to terms about the prince and the city of Shechem."

"So," Rachel said softly, "they will not settle for circumcision or let a marriage take place . . . they have stiffened their necks and will demand their revenge. Oh, Bilhah, they will kill him. I know they will. They want to spill blood, and they will.

"Shechem. All along I've said it's an evil, cursed place. It has taken a while, but, Bilhah," Rachel said shaking her finger at the servant, "my warning about that wicked city should have been heeded. God does not live in Shechem. I wish we could flee this valley and put as many hills and mountains between us and that city as it is possible."

The following afternoon all of the other inhabitants of the tents of Jacob learned the shocking truth of Rachel's statement that God did not live in Shechem, and their horror increased when they found that since morning, no man lived there either.

Rachel joined the other women, and together their faces contorted with angry disbelief: they heard the devastating story from Simeon and Levi as they boasted and paraded before the encampment.

"We knew today, when they would be sore and barely able to move from their circumcision wounds, that it was time to take our revenge!" Levi shouted.

What little color she had drained from her face, and Rachel held her ears as though it would shut out the awful news.

"There was no opposition," preened Simeon, "so we entered

the city early this morning and took our rightful revenge." He continued with odious pride, "With our swords, we slew every man in the entire city, including the rapist, Shechem, and his father, Hamor." Rachel heard Leah's sharp cry, and instantly she moved over to her and put her arms around her sobbing sister. Simeon set his jaw forward with the smug satisfaction of a job well done. "See, we have even rescued our sister, Dinah, and have returned her to the safety of her father's tents."

The brothers cheered wildly. Some applauded; others clapped Levi's and Simeon's backs in hearty approval; and still others admired the bloodied swords and tunics. The women began a low moaning sound, and Leah repeatedly screamed, "What have you done? What have you done?" It was as though she hoped they would change their story or tell her something different.

Jacob stood stone-still, his face ashen and frozen, and for the moment, he could find no voice with which to speak.

To Rachel's horror, while Jacob mutely stood there, all of his sons—except Joseph—hastily mounted their camels. The men whipped their camels' flanks in a hard ride back to Shechem. Obviously, they intended to plunder the ravaged city and bring home the spoils of their war.

They rode home hours later, drunk with the wine of their victory. Everyone in the encampment could hear them coming. They had confiscated all the flocks, herds, and donkeys, and had taken everything inside and outside the city. They were barking like jackals over their bloody victory.

Rachel was appalled at the sight of all the sheep, oxen, and donkeys being herded into the open part of their valley, but her heart was truly panic-stricken when she spied what came next. Teams of oxen were pulling carts. Some of the creaking wooden conveyances were loaded to the bursting point with women and children; but others were jammed with what appeared to be anything of value.

"See, father! We, the sons of Jacob, have gained great wealth today," they shouted and proclaimed with reckless abandon.

When Reuben's camel was close enough to Leah, he called out to her above the noisy din, "Wait until you see what I have brought for you, mother!" He pointed back to a small ox cart which appeared to have several large baskets, a wooden chest, and a pile of blankets or clothing packed within its rough splats.

Leah had stopped crying but seeing her son, she pulled her veil across her face. She believed her sons had committed these atrocities, but she could not begin to accept it. She said vehemently to Rachel, "I want nothing from this degrading, murderous adventure. Tell him to keep his spoils. I will not be a part of this fiendish act."

"Take it back! She does not want it. . ." Rachel said as she moved forward to meet the servant who was holding the muzzle of the ox. Reuben brought his camel to its knees and dismounted. "But you haven't seen your prizes yet!" He was in high spirits, but Rachel blocked his path.

"I said your mother does not want to be a part of any of this." Rachel's tone was icy with contempt.

"Fine! Fine!" Reuben shouted and threw up his hands. "That's just fine with me. I shall keep all of this to myself, including. . ." he pulled at the bundle of clothing at the bottom of the cart, and a disheveled but somehow engaging young girl struggled to stand upright, ". . .this!

"I plan to be a part of this one just as soon as possible." Reuben lunged at the girl, but she ducked down into the cart. He caught her by the hair and roughly pulled her up and over the side into his arms.

The girl struggled and wrenched free of Reuben's grasp and headed for the safety of the women. She ran to Rachel's outstretched arms.

Leah, deciding to speak for herself, uncovered her mouth and said scornfully to Reuben, "If you are to be a part of this young woman, it will be only *after* marriage and not before. Make up your mind to it for that is the way it will be." Rachel thought Leah had never sounded so full of authority as she did in that moment.

"Child. . ." Rachel brushed the heavy entanglement of hair away from the girl's face and looked deeply into the dark, expressionless eyes. Before she could finish her question, Rachel wondered, *Whatever those eyes have seen today, the girl will never forget. Her eyes are not the windows of her soul anymore. They are merely for seeing now. It's as if all the lights have gone out at one time.* Rachel pulled the girl close. "What are you called?" she asked.

"My name is Sherah," she answered uneasily and in a low and husky whisper

"You are safe now, child. We will see to your needs. This is my sister, Leah, and I am called Rachel."

Reuben edged closer and when the girl saw his movement towards her, she said to Rachel defiantly, "I will never forgive these men for what they did today...." Then in a louder voice and pointing to Reuben, she finished, "Nor will I ever marry that wild jackass."

Suddenly, from the center of the encampment, Jacob found his tongue, and loudly he commanded everyone to gather around him. He climbed up on to a rock which was about half the height of a standing camel, and he shouted for Levi and Simeon to come forward.

The two young men lost little of their braggadocious swagger, and with much waving and bowing to their brothers, they made their way through the crowd of carts, animals, and people to stand before Jacob.

Rachel watched the spectacle with Joseph's hand squeezed tightly in her own. In the midst of all the crush of people, she bent down close to the boy's ear and whispered, with a severe urgency, her warning: "If the day ever comes, Joseph, that you meet your 'Shechem,' you remember what I have taught you. Let these unspeakable crimes burn in your heart and vow to me that you will remember the evil shame of what you have seen and heard today. Promise me that with this memory you will flee from the sinfulness of your Shechem."

Joseph could not imagine that he would ever face his own "Shechem," but because of his love for her, he pledged his vow and promised to remember.

As Rachel straightened up, she realized for the first time that day the horrendous news of the killings that her mind was rejecting as true, *was* true. And now again ... she was hearing something she simply could not believe or accept.

She had fully expected the wrath of Jacob to descend, and mightily so, upon the heads of his sons for their wickedness, their wholesale slaughter and their senseless plundering of Shechem, but it never came!

Jacob's words were only of himself. *He cares only of what others think of him.* Rachel formed the thoughts in her head. *His reputation is more valuable than the lives of those men who died today.*

Instantly she felt a wave of weakness sweep over her. She let go of Joseph's hand and moved behind him. Then, when her nausea became intense, she turned aside and spilled out a stomach full of sour juices.

Jacob's voice filled her ears as she recovered. He was still screaming about his reputation. "You have made me stink!" he roared in rage to his sons. "Stink! Do you hear? I am but an offensive smell to the Canaanites and the Perizzites of this land.

"And mark my words well," Jacob ranted on, "we are so few in number here that when word reaches them about today's bloodshed, they will band together and come after me to crush me. And because of your actions, you and I will be killed, and all the household of Jacob destroyed!"

Levi lifted his head defiantly and without the barest display of respect or honor for his father he said, with much sarcasm, "What you should have done in retaliation for the rape of your daughter, you did not do; so we settled accounts for you. Or should we, too, have let the fair-haired prince of Shechem treat our sister like a prostitute?"

Jacob sucked in his belly and stood tall, his fury now fully developed so much so, in fact, that he could produce no logical argument for Levi. His anger, his wounded ego, and his damaged reputation blinded and deafened him to what he should have said or to the punishment he should have meted out.

He flung himself off the stone and, in a voice close to a growl, he snarled to Levi and Simeon, "The least we can do at present is to provide these women and children with lodgings. See to their needs." Then as he started to leave, he turned back sharply, caught Levi by the throat, and hurled his threat.

"There will be *no more bloodshed!* Do you understand? And, furthermore, if you and your brothers do not treat these widows and orphans with the utmost care and respect, I will personally sever your head from your body!"

Hours later, when there was at least a semblance of order about the camp and places for everyone had been made, Rachel stood in the cool evening's air outside her tent. She could hear the low moaning sounds of the captive women, and some babies were shattering the quiet of the night with their unsettling cries.

The moon and star-sprinkled sky stretched out in the heavens above. Rachel looked up, and aloud she asked the unanswerable question, "How could anything so beautifully created as the sky look down on something so ugly?

What a merciless slaughter ... all those men crushed into nothingness like pieces of brittle pottery underfoot, she thought; and then, as if to add to the day's filthy crimes and her own dismay, she grew violently nauseous and vomited out her evening meal.

When her stomach had quieted and her breathing had become more normal, she wiped her mouth and thought, *The wickedness of Shechem has turned my stomach inside out. Twice today I have lost my food. I haven't done that since the days of. . . .*

Rachel stopped in mid thought, held her breath, and then quickly she tried to recall how many moons had passed since her last issue of blood. *It has been two moons. . . I am sure.* Her surprised cry cut into the night with sharpness, and she covered her mouth with one hand and clutched her stomach with the other.

Vividly she remembered her old dream. *This must be the baby which Jacob holds*, Rachel thought with elation, and then for a few moments she stood lost in praise to the living God.

It still puzzles me that I can never reach them, she pondered with sadness, *but at least I will have another child.*

Abruptly her thoughts ended for out of nowhere, as it were, Joseph appeared and tugged on her arm.

"Mother, are you all right?" he asked. "Was it you who cried out?"

Joseph spotted the glistening pool of vomit at her feet, and he surmised the worst. "You are very ill. The day of horror has been too much for you, and the cold air is not good for you. Come inside. Shall I get Aunt Leah?"

"No, dear Joseph. She deals with her own grief tonight, and Dinah desperately needs her." She patted his shoulder to calm his fears. "Besides, I am not sick . . . far from it . . . I think I am with child again."

He turned to see her better and there, by the light of the full moon, he searched her face.

"Does this bring you pleasure?"

"Yes, indeed, it does. It gives me *much* pleasure." Rachel answered, and then in hushed tones she said, "Joseph, for now—because of the terrible crimes committed today—let us keep this small joyous secret to ourselves. Other women have lost so much this morning. Your Aunt Leah is like a raging wild woman over the actions of her sons. I would not flaunt my gains in their faces. So, not a word to anyone for a while. All right?"

"All right," he pledged.

They were quiet for a moment, and then his mind formed a tantalizing question, so he asked, "Mother, what will I get when your time has come? A brother or a sister?"

Rachel smiled and said with mock seriousness, "Which do you want, son?"

He thought a moment, and then his poignant answer stung her heart with both its beauty and its sadness. For there, under the glorious skies of the night, she heard him say wistfully, "If you can, mother, I'd like a brother, please . . . a good brother . . . and one who likes me."

"I will try very hard, my love," she replied softly. She could not see him for her eyes rapidly blurred with tears.

"Oh, God," she prayed, "answer the child's prayer."

15

The small but adequate fields of summer wheat and barley grew into autumn's harvest, and Jacob, his wives, children, and servants slid tentatively and cautiously into the stream of daily living.

An unspoken, bare, and shaky truce existed between the father and his sons. The brothers went about their daily chores as though things were right between them and their father. But there was an unavoidable amount of tension cracking in the air.

Adding to the tension was the brothers' unmistakably sharp stab of guilt everytime they caught sight of Dinah. Ever since she had been returned to her father's tents on the day of the killings, Dinah's inner fire left her soul, and she spoke no words. Mutely, she followed Leah to the well and back and occasionally to the cooking fires. She didn't go anywhere without holding on to the sleeve or skirt of her mother and besides the empty smile which played on her lips, her vacant eyes revealed that no vibrant being lived there anymore. Soon the brothers understood that the high-spirited sister they knew before was now gone forever.

Fearful at first of someone retaliating, they were careful to set a day-and-night watch guarding their encampment. The viable fear of retribution which might ride over the hill at any moment and destroy them hung heavily on their minds.

However, three full moons appeared and dissolved without the brothers having had a battle or skirmish, a sword lifted, or a single drop of blood spilled into the soil.

When each day began to pass uneventfully into another and the sight of Dinah shuffling along behind their mother became more routine, the sons of Jacob lost much of their guilt and apprehension. Their conscience dulled about their sister, and the remoteness of a battle lulled them into a false confidence: their cocky pride in the taking of Shechem returned. They talked of it when no women were present.

"See, they deserved to die," Levi boasted one night as the brothers sat around the evening camp fire. He spoke partly out of a need to cover his own remaining fears and partly to condone his murderous act. "Their kinsfolk and allies will not rally for them. They know we were right to avenge our sister's rape."

"Our father, however, does not seem of our persuasion," Reuben, the oldest of the brothers and in his twenties, commented pessimistically.

"I've noticed that," Judah broke in, "but what I want to know is—where has he disappeared? Lately he is nowhere to be found. He is not with the cattle, or flocks; nor is he down in the fields. . . ."

"I know where father is and what he does." Joseph's strong, young voice of seven summers sliced the evening air, and immediately the warm, brotherly flow of conversation died a quick death.

Joseph, eager to share his knowledge and anxious to be a part of their fellowship, was oblivious to their coldness. He waited for their response.

"I don't remember anyone asking you if you knew anything." Asher, Zilpah's son, broke the icy silence. "But *naturally, you know.*"

Asher's sarcasm was lost on Joseph, and in bright, undaunted innocence, the boy continued. "If you need our father by day, you can find him up at the stone altar. There he sits and talks out loud to the living God," Joseph said, tilting his head in the direction of the altar on the hill. "By night he keeps to his tent and takes his meals alone. He sees no one these days." Joseph finished, flushed with his knowledgeable input.

"He doesn't even see your mother?" Reuben chided.

"No. In fact, father does not even speak with me these days."

Joseph did not intentionally aim his words at his brothers' jugular veins, but nonetheless, they slashed and found their victims. The verbally wounded brothers were bitterly incensed by Joseph's words and obviously favored position. The boy seemed to have gained access to Jacob's heart and mind, while they were denied. It bothered Levi so much he said to Judah, "I will not waste my time listening to the meaningless clicking of a lizard's tongue." Gradually all but one of the brothers stole away into the night.

When he realized most of the men had left, Joseph could not miss or deny their intent. The brothers' jealousy and resentment hung odiously like fresh camel dung in the pure night air.

Joseph, frustrated by their obvious resentments, queried Reuben, the remaining one: "What have I said that has sent them off to their tents? How have I offended them? Reuben, tell me what it is that I do so wrong? I would be friends; yet, it never comes to pass."

Reuben's face already tanned by the sun and heavily bearded fortified itself and became as hard as a bronze breastplate of armor. The older brother had been chewing on a wheat stalk, and now he took careful aim, spit the juice out, and hit a hot coal at the fire's edge. Reuben watched the spittle as it hit the target and hissed itself into steam. Then, in a low voice filled with bitter reality, he said into the night, "Will you never understand? You are *not* the firstborn. *I* am! No one . . . I repeat, *no one* wants to hear anything you have to say," he growled as a wounded wolf. "If anyone is to be our teacher, it will be father or me, the firstborn, *not you.*"

Joseph thought, *They hate me because I am the youngest born?* Out loud he reasoned, "Reuben, I do not understand. I am not trying to be their teacher. I am a student . . . I'm learning and Sapher is my teacher . . . I'm not teaching." Joseph's puzzlement was overwhelming.

"Sapher." Reuben spit again. "That Sapher is another thing!" he said with disgust. "Why is it *you* are being taught? Why not *me?*"

Reuben bent close to the lad. Joseph's eyes took in Reuben's dark and hairy face; his nose was assaulted by the garlic and sour wine of his brother's breath, and his body smelled as bad as an old camel. Joseph's ears were blasted by Reuben's thunderous question: *"Who do you think you are?"*

"He is nothing but a boy!"

They turned from their camp fire to see Leah with Dinah and Sherah. The girls stood a little behind Leah, as shadows. Dinah gazed unperturbed at the fire, but Sherah stared at Reuben, her dark eyes glaring contemptuously. "Leave him alone, Reuben, and go back to your tent," Leah ordered in an iron-stern voice.

Without another exchange between them, Leah and the two girls turned and walked towards Leah's tent. Reuben angrily threw a small rock in the direction of the hill where the altar stood and then glared at the disappearing figures as Joseph fled, as fast as his bare feet would take him, to Rachel's tent.

"My child, what has frightened you?" Rachel cried, in dismay, as she turned the oil lamp toward him for a better look.

"It is nothing, mother . . . nothing." Joseph hoped his words would dismiss the subject and that his mother would ask no questions.

Joseph could not put into words, even for her, whom he loved, his deep longing for his brothers' approval. He desperately desired to be a part of their evening discussions; yet, whenever he spoke up, it seemed he always said the wrong thing. *My presence or my words, I don't know which, always irritates them,* he cried inwardly.

"Did your father eat with you and all the men tonight?" Rachel asked, to change the subject. She had long ago learned with this one that prying into his soul simply closed doors. She would always have to be patient and wait for him to open up to her.

Joseph gave his head a negative shake and quietly he unrolled his bedding mat to make ready for sleep. His "Rest well, mother," were the only words from him, and she sensed he was hiding a fresh inner wound of some kind.

His brothers, maybe? Rachel wondered. *No ... it is probably just this terrible place and the horrid events of Shechem,* Rachel surmised as she drifted off to sleep.

Only three days later, when the sons and menservants had harvested most of the grain in their fields, Jacob suddenly materialized in front of Rachel's tent.

The sides of her tent had been tied up, and Jacob, ducking under a low one, came in with the soft afternoon winds. He seemed the same Jacob; yet, Rachel sensed a difference about him somehow. His face, leaner from his sparse eating habits of the past few months, broke into a broad grin when he saw Rachel and Joseph.

As a stranger would have done, only somewhat more awkwardly, Jacob pronounced his formal greetings and salutations to his wife and son.

Rachel, stunned to see him after so long an absence, put down the dress she was mending, and with elaborate concentration slowly and carefully stored her sharpened bone needles and folded up her dress.

Jacob waited uncomfortably while she placed the dress in a small wooden chest.

The boy, eager to save the delicate moment, assumed the role of host, and with respect and genial hospitality offered, "Welcome, father! Sit down ... it is good to see you." He poured water from the goatskin into pottery bowls, and all three of them sat cross-legged on the intricately patterned carpets and drank the lukewarm water.

Jacob was the first to speak. "You are looking well." He gazed at Rachel's face and her beauty stirred, as it always did, the most intimate feelings within him. "My leaving you alone for a while seems to have agreed with you. Your beauty is more enchanting than ever. . . ." Jacob paused, and then, squinting and focusing his eyes, he observed, "I see there is more flesh on your bones and the color in your cheeks is rosy as the pink skies of dawn."

Rachel blushed and bowed her head slightly, acknowledging his compliment, but she said nothing for she still found it difficult to feel her usual freedom to speak. She was very aware that ever since the evil day of Shechem a thick curtain of silence had been hung between them. Rachel wondered if Jacob would try to talk through it or under it, or was he about to take it down altogether?

The pleasantries dispensed with, Jacob came directly to the subject matter which held first priority in his heart. He stated, strongly but peaceably, "God has spoken to me."

Rachel breathed a breath of relief, as she marveled to herself, *Oh, so that is why the curtain between us is down and gone. He has made his peace with God over Shechem.* Rachel surmised, *He could not live with the unspeakable crimes his sons committed, so he has made his peace with God and now he has come to make his peace with us.*

"What did the living God say, father?" Joseph took the question out of Rachel's heart and mouth.

Jacob looked lovingly over at his youngest son and replied, "God's exact words were, 'Move on to Bethel now, and build an altar to worship the God who appeared to you when you fled your brother, Esau, so many years ago.'

"So . . . we will go, son, and very soon now."

Jacob looked hopefully to his wife for her consenting sanction. Rachel was quick to give it.

"My husband, it is well that we leave this wretched place. I have never felt at ease with the wickedness of Shechem, and ever since Dinah. . . ." Rachel blocked out the painful memory. Looking straight at Jacob, she assured him with her eyes that what had been done was done, in the past, and that it would be good to be moving on.

"Besides," she said, her mood changing and an impish smile playing around the corners of her mouth, "I don't want our child to be born here. Bethel will be an ideal birthplace for him."

Jacob did not move; it was as though his ears were momentarily deaf, and he was so hushed and solemn that Joseph felt compelled to enlighten him.

"Did you hear, father?" Joseph said. "She is making me a brother!"

Rachel could tell from Jacob's genuine expression of surprise and awe that, once the women in the encampment knew or suspected, none of them had told Jacob. She was pleased that they had loyally kept her secret.

"I heard, my son." Jacob smiled at the boy's eager, upturned face. Then brushing her hair gently off her forehead, he said, "Woman, you are truly remarkable, but why have you kept this from me?"

"For a while," she said, thoughtfully, "I did not know myself. I had almost given up that God would bless my womb again . . . but by the time I was sure He had . . . well, you were not around to tell."

He moved away from Rachel and her gentle rebuke and sat on a low stool. "How long have you been with child?" Jacob asked kindly.

"Almost five full moons now," she replied.

Jacob rested his chin in his hands as he leaned over to formulate his plans. "Let's see," he said to no one in particular. "It will take at least two moons to reach Bethel. Do you feel strong enough for the journey?" Jacob reached for her hand to see if it was as fragile as it looked.

"Oh, my husband, I am stronger now than I have been in a long time, and. . . ." She looked past Joseph out the open tent flap towards the road to Shechem, "It will be good to leave this place."

He turned her hand over, kissed her open palm, and stood to leave. "There is one more thing . . ." Jacob said, straightening his shoulders. "I want to make a clean break with this valley and with the city of Shechem. So, before we leave, I am instructing everyone from our tents, including the widows and orphans of Shechem, to destroy all the idols and stone gods they may have in their possession. We shall go to Bethel as God's people, clean and pure of false gods."

He started out of the tent, but stopped midstep when he heard

Rachel say, "Then you had better take these. I do not need them, and I should have never taken them from my father's tent in the first place."

Jacob turned around, came towards her, and stared in total disbelief at the stone teraphim she held out to him.

"So it was you who took them? Laban was right?" Jacob's mouth slackened with awe. Then his face drained itself of color as he remembered he had cursed the one who stole the gods, and that publicly he had vowed to put the thief to death.

"But where were they hidden when Laban searched our tents and belongings?" he asked, to fill in the gaps of his knowledge.

"She sat upon them, father," Joseph—ever eager to be a part of things—explained.

"I see," Jacob said, breathing a little easier and with a slight smile on his face. He found Rachel's ingeniousness a most engaging part of her character.

He took the idols from her outstretched hands and said, without condemnation, "I shall bury *everyone's* foreign idols and god-engraved earrings and jewelry this afternoon, and then ... we will speak of them no more." Jacob moved toward the side of the tent where he had entered, and finished his visit by saying, "Tomorrow, early, at the first sign of dawn, we shall break camp. I will be instructing everyone to wash themselves thoroughly and to put on fresh, clean clothes. I want my people to leave here purified in soul and body ... and ready to walk in God's direction for a change."

"Will we take Sapher with us?" Joseph asked hopefully.

"Yes, I suppose so. He is an old man, but having a scribe with us ... and teaching you is a valuable thing," Jacob conceded. "Do you learn much from him?" he asked.

"Oh, yes! He is right now teaching me the pictures and signs of Egyptian writing." Joseph's eyes sparkled as he warmed to the subject of his teacher.

"Tell him what the Egyptian man, Dua-Khety told his son," Rachel interjected.

Joseph, the diligent student, flashed a smile at Rachel and then proudly repeated the tale for his father. "Sapher told me this ancient man took his son and sailed south to a school for scribes, and on the way, the father, Dua-Khety, said, 'It is to writings that you must set your mind. I do not see an office to be compared with like that of a scribe. I shall make you love books more than your mother, and I shall place their excellence before you.' "

"I see," said Jacob.

"So, you follow Sapher and this Egyptian and you will become a scribe?" Jacob patted his son's back affectionately. "It is good that you are growing in the wisdom of writing, and it well may be that the dream which sent Sapher to us was given to him by our God. Who knows, eh, my son?"

"Who knows." Joseph answered, a wide grin stretching across his handsome face.

Jacob kissed his wife and son and left their tent and their pleasant conversations of moving, babies, and scribes. Once outside though, a slight chill ran down his spine.

"What if Laban had found those wretched teraphim in Rachel's tent?" Jacob looked down at the idols in his hands and remembered vividly the death penalty he had placed on the thief. "I could have caused Rachel's death. . . ." The chill returned; this time it shook his frame as he walked.

Judah spied Jacob just as he was about to enter his tent. "Father," he called, "how does the day go with you?"

Jacob waved a greeting and answered with the look of a man who had been given a last moment's reprieve, "I am blessed with the living God who takes my mistakes and turns them into lessons instead of irreversible grief.

"I was about to call you," Jacob continued, "Call your brothers, Judah, and have them come here. We will be moving on."

Judah said his "Yes, sir," and hurried on.

Jacob stood for a moment watching him go across the encampment, and then shaking his head clear of the thoughts about the stone idols he turned his thinking to the enormous task before him.

The trip was not accomplished in the two moons Jacob had promised. Rachel grew heavier with child, and in her inner depths she feared the journey would be her last. She was, however, so pleased to be leaving Shechem and heading for Bethel that she refused to become discouraged.

"I think," she said dryly to Bilhah, "I and this camel are one, and tonight when we stop to make camp, I fear I will have to sleep with old Jez here." She patted the beast in a show of strength and good humor, but Bilhah was not deceived. And when, a few days later, they came within sight of the city of Luz—which Jacob had renamed Bethel—Bilhah grew frantic with worry. She relived the time of Joseph's birth, and she sought out Jacob and pleaded, "She tries to say she is all right; but, my lord, it is worse this time. I feel she will surely die if we do not stop."

Jacob comforted Bilhah. The servant stopped wringing her hands, but she was not put to ease until he promised that they would stay in Bethel for a few days. "Rachel will be fine. I've never seen her look so well," he said with unshakable certainty. "It's only a little distance to Bethel; see, it lies just over that ridge, so we will move on." The matter was settled and Jacob called for them to continue.

Bilhah walked slowly back toward the place where Rachel and the other women had stopped. Merab, the midwife who traveled with them from Haran, met her and asked, "What does the master say? Will we move on or stay here?"

Bilhah replied, "He said that we will go and stay in Bethel, but. . . ."

"But what?" Merab questioned.

"It is just that Jacob does not *see* her. I mean he does not really see her. He thinks she is well, and no matter what I tell him, he is convinced Rachel is as immortal as the gods."

Nothing could be said to Jacob about Rachel. They reached Bethel by the next afternoon and immediately Jacob began to fulfill his part of the covenant. He built an altar, as God had commanded him to do, and he named it El-Bethel, *the God of Bethel*, and he spent several days praising and thanking God for the safe journey they had survived.

Joseph was with him at the great stone altar when a breathless runner arrived with the message that the kinsfolk of Deborah were bringing her body to Bethel to be buried.

Who is Deborah? Joseph wondered; and, as if his father had read his thoughts, Jacob said, "Deborah was my mother's nurse. She went with my mother, Rebekah, from Haran years and years ago when she left the land of Padan-aram to marry my father, Isaac, in Canaan. Deborah, that kind nurse, was deeply loved by my mother, and both Esau and I were alternately hugged, swatted, or taught by her." Jacob's eyes grew misty with the memory.

"Was she your friend when you were a boy?" Jacob listened with his heart.

"Yes, my lad. She was my friend . . . and many others felt she was their friend, too," Jacob said with a trace of melancholia in his tone.

Jacob had always been aware of the sharpness of the division between his sons and Joseph, and he knew that even though it was his great desire to see his sons as comrades and friends, it did not seem that it would ever come about. Joseph would never be accepted. "What troubles me the most," he once confided to Sapher in a rare moment of openness, "is that I cannot figure out the why's and wherefore's of the brothers' differences. I have tried to be a fair and just father. . . ."

Sapher, with a teacher's wisdom and the benefit of being a bystander, said, "You and I have a problem, though, when it comes to Joseph." Then kindly he added, "It is hard to deny the boy anything, so it is natural the brothers would see this and resent it."

Jacob, unwilling to see the truth, had brushed aside Sapher's remarks and would have all but forgotten them had it not been for Joseph's question about Deborah being a friend.

To Jacob, a friend was someone like the beloved Deborah; a person who cared and loved you enough to win the right to be open with you. Deborah could hug the brothers, Jacob and Esau, but she could also insist on their obedience or their diligence at finishing a task.

He had so wished that all his sons could be friends like that but as he had known, it was not to be. Sapher would have to fill that place for Joseph, and so Jacob explained, "Our Deborah, Joseph, was to Esau and me what your Sapher is to you . . . an honest friend, a dedicated teacher, and a creative spinner of tales."

"Then you will always miss her?"

Jacob made no answer for they both knew it would be so. Wordlessly they walked down the hill to meet the mourners.

Jacob supervised the burial, and the small cloth-wrapped remains of Deborah's shriveled old body and brittle bones were placed beneath an oak tree in the valley just below Bethel.

The sound of weeping was heard around the countryside, and Rachel, in her tent and too encumbered with her pregnancy to walk, said to Joseph, "Listen to the sounds of mourning. The place where they buried her will forever from this day be called *The Oak of Weeping.* Deborah was much loved."

I wonder, she said to herself, *when I die, who will weep for me? Joseph? Yes, and Jacob. But Leah, and the others? I don't know how I will be viewed and remembered.* These dark thoughts and others had troubled her a little more each day, so she began setting her affairs in order. She had made apologies where they were needed, and had given her thanks to faithful servants. In the days which followed, she gave secret instructions to Bilhah. The trusted servant girl was to hide in Leah's belongings Rachel's favorite gold bracelet, the one Aaron had made, some gold earrings with precious stones set in them, and a small kidskin bag which held her treasured gold, ivory, and silver trinkets. To Joseph, Bilhah was to give the most treasured gifts of all—a narrow gold ring that Jacob had given her after Joseph's birth and her beloved flute from her days as a shepherdess. Tearfully, Bilhah listened well and promised to carry out the sad tasks.

Rachel came out of her thoughts and realized that Joseph was watching her with intense interest, so casually she said, "We have mourned the passing of Deborah. Now, we continue to live. It will be this way when any of our beloved die. We will have a time of mourning, then we must resume the living . . . as painful as it may be."

"Who else is dying, mother?" As always, his questions robbed her of instant answers, so she stalled by saying, "Son, I am only teaching you about dealing with the sickness of grief and mourning when it comes to you."

An older man somewhere within the boy said a quiet, "I see," and the mother and son waited for the mourners to make their way back to the encampment.

It was only a few days after Deborah's burial that Jacob came to Rachel in great excitement.

"God has spoken to me again, my love, and given me His blessing once more!"

Rachel ponderously heavy with child, shifted her bulk and reached for a pillow to give her back some sturdy support. Jacob plumped and positioned the pillow behind her and continued in his joy, "God has reminded me anew of my name change. My name is not be be Jacob, *the grabber*, but Israel for it means *one who prevails with God.* Israel, that is my name! Oh, my dear Rachel, I may not have followed the Lord my God all the days of my life, but since the first time here at Bethel, I *have always prevailed!*" His enthusiasm was contagious. Rachel smiled and said with as much strength as she could muster, "Your name should simply be shortened to *Prevailer.*" They laughed together.

"What brings you so much happiness?" Joseph stood by the tent flap.

"Ah, come in, my son." Jacob warmly embraced the boy. "Our God has blessed me all over again. Remember what I told you by the Jabbok River, that my descendants will be called the children of Israel? Well, God confirmed His promise to me, again!"

"You usually build an altar when God speaks to you. Will you do that here and now?" Joseph asked.

"This son of mine," Jacob whispered to Rachel, "reads my mind like a fortune-teller!

"I'll tell you what I'm going to do, Joseph, and you listen closely, for I commission you to be my number-one helper.

"We shall build a large stone pillar on the exact spot the living God appeared to me. And we shall pour wine over it as an offering, then we will anoint the pillar with olive oil as our token of gratitude to our God for His goodness!" The man and the boy glowed with anticipation.

The day the pillar was finished, consecrated, and the sacrifice made, Joseph thought was the most exciting day of his life.

The lad, swathed in wonder, had watched and listened as his father renewed his vows to God and heard Jacob as he once again committed his life to the service of his living God. Joseph felt he himself had never been so close to God. He was jubilant about the time spent at the pillar. Even his brothers' lack of interest, when Joseph told them of his day, could not dampen his spirits. Nor was his joy squelched when his brothers left him standing alone by the side of a large flock of sheep.

Once the pillar was completed, Jacob itched to be on the move again, so the following morning, the great entourage of people

broke camp and with their large droves of animals pushed southward to the Canaanite city of Bethlehem.

Rachel, unable to ride a camel or donkey, was bedded down in
one of the ox-drawn carts. Even though she sat atop a mound of
bedding mats, made softer with wooly sheep skins, and Joseph
and Bilhah rode with her to steady her, the trip was a bone-jolting
ride.

The rough coarseness of the terrain started the severe birthing
pains on the second day of travel. Rachel's wild animal-like
screams stopped the caravan, stampeded some of the flocks and
herds, and brought a panic-stricken Jacob flying to her side.

He was shaking and palsied with fear. "Merab!" Jacob
shouted above the frightening racket, "Can't you help her?"

"Don't just stand there, quaking in your sandals, asking me
what I can do for her. Go put up a tent so she can have some shelter!" Merab screeched back.

Joseph stood inside the cart, his eyes round with fear, his
body rigid with shock, and his hands locked like eagles' talons
around the wooden slats.

When Rachel had been lifted out and moved to the shade of
the tent, Sherah disentangled herself from the crowd of women
who stood by, and she approached Joseph.

She pried his white knuckles loose and helped him move his
stiffened limbs over the back of the cart. "I will stay with you,
Joseph, if you want me to." Sherah had never spoken a word to
him before, but because she sensed he was the only son of Jacob
who had nothing to do with the death of her people, she broke her
vow of silence and offered her protection.

Had it been any other time, Joseph would have welcomed the
friendly gesture; but his mind was filled and bursting with his
mother's screams, and there was room for nothing else.

Joseph broke away from Sherah and pushed his way into the
crowded tent. He put both hands over his ears, but the sound of
Rachel's screaming would not be drowned out.

Rachel could feel herself falling. The pain was still pushing at
her from within, and she could tell she was falling faster each
moment, tumbling and plummeting downward. It was dark, and
the walls of the long and endless pit which surrounded her flew
past her faster than arrows from a thousand bowmen.

Rachel screamed for help, but nobody answered; and nothing, absolutely nothing, stopped or slowed her fall.

Then suddenly it was as if she struck a side wall or a jutting rock, for momentarily she stopped her flight, and miraculously her pain eased and began to fade. A moment later she resumed her downward plunge at the speed of thought.

As she pitched down in the darkness, someone, *Merab*, she thought, shouted to her. The words echoed and rang against the dark and dank walls, "How wonderful, Rachel! You have another boy!"

Desperately Rachel tried to respond. She reached out to grab at the walls, in an attempt to slow down, but her body only fell faster and raced on. The air grew cold, and she shivered with its dampness.

If I had another son, then he must be called the son of my sorrow, she thought; and then, mustering all the strength she could, Rachel screamed upwards to the faces she could barely see above her, "His name shall be called Ben-oni!"

As she fell, a vision of Jacob holding an infant, with Joseph standing by his side flashed into her mind. It was her old, oft-repeated dream. "So this is how it ends. The riddle of my dream has been solved. I will never reach them, for I am lost in this bottomless pit. At least God blessed my womb, and I have lived to give my husband and the earth two sons."

Rachel never heard Jacob's command, "No! He is not a child of sorrow. This tiny babe will be known as the *son of the right hand*, so his name will be called Benjamin."

She didn't feel Jacob's body as he flung himself across hers, and she never heard his shrieking sobs or knew he stayed there until long after the sun had set.

Rachel never viewed her newborn son nor pressed him closely to her breast, and she never guessed her other son stood watching everything in the shadows of her tent. She did not know that Joseph's hands were still covering his ears, nor did she see his agony in the wash of tears which steamed down his beautiful face.

She simply fell away from them all.

BOOK
II
SHERAH

16

Her fingers were nimbly weaving a wide piece of prickly goat's hair cloth, and in a moment or two she would have the material ready for Jacob's tent.

Sherah smiled as she remembered how the bulky material had scratched and bitten at her fingers when she first worked with it. But that was shortly after her arrival so long ago. Her fingers had toughened over the years, and her hands had picked up a great deal of agility, so now the strips of cloth did exactly what she wanted them to do.

Tent dwellers, she had learned, rarely if ever, except for an occasional newly married son, made a new tent. They simply cut off the old or torn pieces, wove a fresh new strip of material, and sewed it on, ever enlarging or mending their hearts' pride and joy—their great black tents.

One of Sherah's tasks was to collect goat hair clippings for a season or two, and then weave the replacement strips. As she worked she whimsically wondered how long or how wide a strip of her goat's cloth would be if all she had woven and sewed were collected and stretched out end to end before her.

It would probably cover half the desert, she said to herself good humoredly. Sherah's hands kept working and she gathered her thoughts and grew serious.

All of ten summers have passed since I was torn away from Shechem .... She paused because, as usual, a thick, unswallowable knot rose in her throat. The strangling sensation happened each time she thought about her last horrifying day in Shechem and her macabre arrival at the tents of Jacob. To push the knot away from her throat, Sherah resorted deliberately to thoughts of Rachel and Leah. It seemed to help, but only a little.

Recounting the day, she said to herself, *I will always be grateful to those two women for befriending me in the presence of my enemies.*

A few years later she had said with candor to young Joseph, "They helped me pick up the shattered parts of my soul, though I doubt if I'll ever find all the pieces."

The girl and the young boy had been gathering wool clippings at the sheep-shearing pens when Sherah recalled how she spent the first night in Rachel's tent. She had dreamed the night away with hideous dreams filled with the grisly details of her final day in Shechem. In her dream Sherah vividly saw Reuben walk over the bleeding bodies of her parents, breaking their bones as they lay dying. "I remember that I awoke crying and shaking, for in the last part of my dream I relived how Reuben seized me and pulled my arm behind me, forcing me up and over the wooden slats of the ox cart," Sherah tearfully repeated to Joseph.

"Had it not been for your mother, Joseph, and her outstretched arms ..." Sherah shuddered as the memory washed over her, "I dare not imagine what might have happened to me." Joseph patted her shoulder.

"I grew up quickly that day," she continued, "for I learned that safety and sanity would only be found in staying close to your mother and Leah."

Sherah smiled to herself as she wove the black goat's hair together, for she would never forget the genuinely loving look on Joseph's face for as young as he was, he had definitely cared for her and was full of concern.

She sat for a moment thinking how, in those early days, the only retaliation available to her had been a vow of silence against Reuben and his brothers. She had taken up that vow with a single-minded vengeance.

The knot finally subsided, but a small reminder of pain stayed lodged in her throat, and Sherah knew that even time would not remove it completely.

The dark-eyed young woman reached for a handful of goat-hair clippings and skillfully continued to infuse them into the wide strip of material before her. It was the woman's work, and the fact that she was good at the task filled her with a satisfying sense of pleasure.

By now the weaving was a familiar and mindlessly tedious job, and its only drawback was that it provided her with an unusual amount of time to remember and daydream.

Sherah recalled that it had been Leah who first noticed her skill and quickness with the needles and camel-hair thread. It had also been Leah who, after one spring had passed into summer, put Sherah in charge of most of their sewing and mending. She even gave the young seamstress several servant girls to train as helpers.

In return, and out of a grateful heart, Sherah gave Leah and Rachel meticulously mended garments and her unswerving loyalty which was as constant and dependable as the morning sunrise.

On the sad and grievious day that Rachel died in childbirth, Sherah found that her own acute suffering had added some maturity to her life and that, if she was to continue to grow, she had to be willing to change some of her attitudes. Her thoughts began to solidify. *It is a time to accept my life within the tents of Jacob. Merely making or mending garments in gratitude is not enough. I must either live here with my whole heart or not at all. My hopes of returning to Shechem have to cease for I know there is no Shechem to go back to.*

So Rachel's death marked the first time Sherah had found some independence, and she came out from behind the folds of Leah's skirts. It was also the first time she broke her vow of silence and talked to the boy Joseph, a son of Jacob. She never dreamed she'd ever dare break such a vow, but it was as though Rachel's passing had closed the door to the past and opened a new one to the future.

After Sherah watched the grieving Jacob at Rachel's burial proceedings and had wept with the mourners, she faced a final and terrible truth: *I will always live with these people. I cannot go back, even in memory, to a place and a family who do not exist. So, I will stay with Jacob's people and I will try to live peaceably among them.* Sherah rolled the factual thoughts slowly in her mind and the truth of them began to turn the direction of her life around.

Sherah's kind words and helping hand which reached out to

Joseph the day his mother died initiated the beginning.

She found the boy enchanting, guileless, and as lonely as she was for a friend. The unlikely pair began to enjoy the liaison sometimes found in an unstrained and benevolent comradery between an older sister and a younger brother.

Springing from her frankness with Joseph, Sherah found she could open the windows of her memories and let Leah, as well as Joseph, see her soul. She told Leah of the life she had lost, the deep family love that had surrounded her in childhood, and, lastly, of the mother who had been a gifted seamstress.

"Leah, my mistress, you think my skill with a needle is good—you should have seen my mother's handiwork! She was the best!" Sherah's eyes glowed, and she continued her acclamation. "The reason I can sew today is because of the lessons my mother pressed on me. Even when I was little I knew how to spin flax, weave wool, and thread a needle on the first try." Both women exchanged smiles.

"In all of Shechem," Sherah recalled with pride and a touch of wonder, "there was no finer teacher or seamstress. Hamon and all his family had garments fashioned by my mother." The pitch of her voice rose with a fierce ring of pride.

Leah agreed and added, "The skills she has passed on to you, dear Sherah, are your inheritance; and, in a way, as you sew and mend, your mother's talents will live on, even though she is gone."

Sherah had not thought of her sewing skills as a birthright, and her eyes suddenly rimmed with crimson and filmed over with tears.

To change the seriousness of the moment, Leah cocked her head to one side and teased the girl ever so slightly as she said gaily, "Well, now, I'm not sure any of us will need finely sewn clothes or hand-embroidered tunics, but your mending skills are remarkable! Actually, what I need to know is how are you at tent making?"

"I've never woven tent cloth or repaired them before; but if I can't do it, then I am not my mother's daughter. And if it's done with the hands, then these hands accept the challenge."

Both women enjoyed the cheerful exchange, and a mutual bridge of respect and friendship began building between them

Given time, Leah proved to be Sherah's loving mother figure, and a fiercely protective one at that. On one occasion, Leah's staunch stand may have saved Sherah's sanity from crumbling into a thousand pieces.

Reuben had staggered drunkenly into Leah's tent one night, wild-eyed and incoherently roaring about "his woman." He had just come from the campfire where he had bragged and proved that he could drink an entire goatskin of wine in one sitting. He also had claimed that he, and he alone, had the rights of sexual ownership for the woman named Sherah. It was after his brothers egged him on with the challenging dare to make good his right that Reuben broke into Leah's tent, demanding that Sherah sleep with him.

The trembling and once more terrified girl had barely managed to escape, partly because Reuben was too far gone to be quick enough to catch her, and partly because Leah planted herself in her son's path like the branches of a great solid tree of oak.

By the middle of the next morning everyone including Jacob, had heard that Reuben had failed as far as his conquest of Sherah was concerned. But they knew also that he had stumbled out of his mother's tent and had forcibly taken Bilhah in Sherah's place.

"I want him dead for what he tried to do to me and for what he *did* do to Bilhah!" Sherah cried in anguish into Leah's shoulder. Joseph had rushed to Leah's tent as soon as he heard, and visibly angered by what had happened, he stood in red-faced silence as he listened to Sherah and Leah.

The older woman, torn by her love for her son Reuben and her hatred of his evil ways, patted Sherah and said with sad wisdom, "I am sure that Jacob will not let the defilement of one of his concubines go unpunished. And if I know Jacob, and I do, his chastisement will be severe, perhaps worse than death."

Leah's prophetic words came true later that afternoon.

Jacob, the great old father of the tribe, shouted for all the camp to hear, "Reuben, you wicked wild ass, you spoiler of everything you touch, you will regret the fact that you have dishonored me!"

Several of Jacob's sons home early from the tending of fields or flocks, stood mute and fearful as their father brought down his verbal wrath and punishment on Reuben's head. Sherah, Leah, and Joseph stood together and watched with mounting apprehension as Reuben cowered before his father.

"You are my oldest son, my firstborn, the first fruits of my loins. You head the list of my sons in rank and honor." The old man spoke with a calmer voice, but his thistle-like words punctured and bore down into Reuben's soul.

"But you," Jacob snarled, "you are unruly as the wild waves of the sea, and you shall be first no longer! You have climbed up into your father's bed, and you defiled my couch with your climbing. You will never claim the firstborn's birthright."

Sherah, along with all the other spectators, would never forget the sound of Jacob's wrath or the acrimonious look which spread across Reuben's face as he realized that he had just lost the one thing he had ever cherished or valued: his God-ordained rights as the firstborn.

"You wish him dead, don't you?"

Sherah had been standing with Leah and Joseph, absorbed in the angry confrontation before them, and so she was unexpectedly startled by the voice behind her. Instantly she turned and was face-to-face with Judah.

Sherah turned to Leah for help as she felt the panic rising in her, but Leah whispered, "It's all right. Talk with him. My son Judah will not hurt you."

Sherah believed Leah, but she eyed Judah suspiciously.

"Girl," Judah asked mindful of her past, "do you hate us all as much as you hate Reuben?"

He had never spoken to her, at least not so directly, and though from time to time she had caught him watching her when she served the evening meal, she had never given Judah too much of her thinking time.

"Do you?" The heavily bearded young man persisted.

Sherah was still a bit unnerved by him, but she was relieved that her initial panic was subsiding.

"Do I what?" she asked, because she honestly had lost track of his questions.

"Do you hate the other brothers as you do Reuben?"

The impact of his question focused on her budding dilemma. She thought of her tender, sisterly love for Joseph and his baby brother, but somehow her feelings for the *other* brothers were vastly different. Joseph and Benjamin were not, in her eyes, in the same evil league as the wicked sons of Jacob.

"I don't know," she answered lamely and moved away from Judah, hoping she could end his questions, but he fell into step beside her.

They walked away from the center of the encampment and circled along the back sides of the tents. Sherah found that in one afternoon she went from being totally revolted by one man, to actually enjoying the experience of walking and talking with his brother.

By evening, she felt as if the walk had helped her take giant strides in conquering her hatred and her fears of at least one of Jacob's sons.

Judah's logical and persuasive ways were not lost on Sherah, for though she was pleased with Joseph's friendship, still she yearned for someone closer to her age and marriageable.

The day Judah questioned her she found her heart was primed and ready to be warmed by the conciliatory tone of his voice, and his words aroused a warm tenderness within her. It was a feeling she thought could never be awakened.

"You are very different from Reuben," she finally admitted, "but still you *are* a son of Jacob."

He shrugged his shoulders and kicked idly at the small stones around his feet.

Sherah, her back turned from him, said, "I know it was Simeon and Levi who plotted and actually slew my family, kinsfolk, and friends, but you must bear some of the guilt and shame . . ."

Judah knew she wasn't through with him and he braced himself for her major thrust. He didn't have long to wait.

"You don't deny you rode back to the city with your brothers, plundering and taking captives, do you?" she cried judicially.

"No, I do not deny it." Judah's voice broke in places as he huskily pleaded, "But I do ask you to hear my side of it. We were all caught up in revenge for Dinah. The matter of circumcisions and the mass slayings gathered like rolling stones at the top of a mountain. There was no stopping my brothers, and like a great avalanche we came crashing down into the city; it was out of control before we knew it."

They stopped and sat down on a flat, grassy mound. Judah

leaned back on his elbows and as he looked at the sky above him he said pensively, "I have learned much from the crimes of that wretched day, and I pledge to you ... nothing of that sort will ever happen again. I will see to it!" He looked over at Sherah. "You can tell by our father's rebuke and by the way he revoked Reuben's birthright over the rape of Bilhah that he has changed. We all have ...."

"Your father, Joseph, the baby Benjamin, and you, perhaps, but not *all* the sons of Jacob," Sherah retorted coldly.

Emphatically Judah said, "I *have* changed!"

In the days that followed this encounter Judah spent a number of late afternoon and evening walks with Sherah, talking about the lessons that had been learned. In the end, he eloquently and with convincing credibility proved his claim.

Within a few moons the two young people had shared much time together, and their hours of conversation had planted, as Judah had hoped, the small but definite roots of friendship. After that, as so often it happens, their friendship flowered into full-blown love.

Jacob and Leah found no objections to their union, and so with genuine parental blessing the wedding of a Shechem captive and a son of Jacob took place.

Sherah laid down her weaving and sat there for a moment or two, fingering the narrow band of gold on her left hand. "It's been a good marriage, constantly on the move, but a good one nevertheless," she mused as she stretched her arms above her head and unfolded her stiff legs out before her.

I'm spending most of my days sewing or weaving, she thought. She remembered that when she had said, "However, I'd rather spend my time sewing than riding on a camel ..." Judah had laughed aloud at her lighthearted complaint.

"Your father is certainly a traveler." Sherah had commented one night to Judah as they lay together in their tent.

"You'd best get used to picking up and moving at a moment's notice, Sherah, for you have married Jacob's son, and I like to pick up and resettle almost as much as my father."

"Oh, dear!" Sherah jested mockingly. "I wonder how long we will be here in Kirjath-arba, perhaps a sunrise or two?" She expected a teasing retort, but the only response from her husband Judah was the soft sound of snoring.

"Yes, it is a good marriage, but where have the ten summers flown to?" she asked of the small oil lamp which flickered and burned above them.

17

"Could you use some goat clippings?" Joseph called to Sherah late one afternoon as he lifted up one side of her tent. "Leah sent them," he added.

Sherah grinned at his willingness to help in women's work. Rare was a man who would stoop to touching goat-hair clippings, much less become a messenger boy for a woman. "He is a man set apart from other men," Sherah thought, and her face brightened.

"Not too many goats are giving up their warm coats during this season," she answered aloud to Joseph, so I am grateful as always to Leah and you." She meant it, even though the handful of clippings he offered was pitifully small.

Sherah broke into downright laughter when he came in and stood directly in front of her. His full head of curly hair was wet and plastered down over his head.

The unusually heavy winter rains were drenching the land with torrents of water. The herdsmen of the tents of Jacob were already eagerly rubbing their hands together in anticipation of the fat and healthy sheep the pastures, heavily greened by all the rain, would produce. Dealing with the rain day after day, however, was beginning to wear thin on everyone's disposition. Jacob, his sons and menservants, long accustomed to bountiful sunshine, grew restless and exceedingly short-tempered. Joseph was, Sherah noted, the exception.

Even dripping wet, Sherah welcomed him warmly for his optimistic enthusiasm for life was constant and contagious. "And I could use some cheerfulness around here," she mused to herself.

He didn't visit her very often, but when he did she could

count on his breaking the monotony of a dismal day with his humor, or the recounting of an interesting tidbit of news, or just sharing some good-natured conversation.

"You look like a lion cub who fell into the river and drowned!" Sherah teased. Joseph raised his hands, pretending they were paws, and growled at her to impress her with his viciousness.

"Oh, I am so frightened!" she mocked, playing his game as she motioned for him to go behind the hanging carpet petition which divided the tent. "Take off your wet things and put on a dry tunic of Judah's," she said, enjoying the role of a mildly annoyed mother.

Sherah had mothered Joseph every opportunity she was given. Since she planned to bear no children to Judah—a promise she had made to herself not too long after she married him—adopting Joseph as her secret son produced a sweetness within her breast she would not stifle.

At one end of her tent the flap had been propped open by several long sticks and, because of the wet weather, Sherah had dug a fire pit just under the flap and out of the rain. The firewood was burning brightly and to one side a pot of stew was bubbling away, filling the air with its savory fragrance.

"You must be thoroughly chilled, Joseph. So when you are into dry clothes, come talk with me and warm yourself by the fire," she called to him as she added more small tree branches to heighten the blaze.

In the licks of fire and shadows which played against one side of the tent, Sherah imagined she saw the outlines of two faces; one, her husband, Judah's; and the other, Joseph's. As suddenly as she saw them, they were gone; but it was enough time to set her mind silently comparing the two brothers.

She longed for just a little of Joseph's warm openness and gentle tenderness to somehow rub off on to Judah. It never had, and as Joseph had grown out of boyhood into his young manhood the differences between the two brothers only grew sharper; Joseph grew more fragrant with wisdom, and Judah simply turned sour as rancid cheese.

"He is a good man, my Judah is, and we have a tolerable marriage," Sherah reasoned to herself. "But my husband is without mercy to Joseph, and with me. . ." she paused, "Judah is about as soft and warm as the high, cold ridges on the bleakest of mountains."

Even though she was by the fire, she shivered at the memory of the first night of her marriage, ten summers ago.

Sherah had gone to Judah's tent as his bride, trembling with fear. Desperately she hoped the woeful stories told among women about men's unsatiable sensual appetites were highly exaggerated.

Judah's tongue had thickened with many wine toasts, and if she had expected any sweet words of love, her hopes died instantly when she saw him. Sherah's worst fears were realized when he saw her, aroused himself, and struggled up from his bed. Pulling at her robes, Judah roughly forced her down beside him, and yanking on her sleeve he said drunkenly, "Take this off. . ." Sherah had felt that had she not complied quickly he would have ripped her tunic to shreds.

Standing by the fire, she reminisced: *I wished for some kind words of endearment, but he gave me orders. I hoped for a gentle time of caressing, but he bruised my arm pulling me to him. I dreamed of wedding-night kisses but none came.* The thoughts lay in her mind like the grey ashes around the fire's edges.

The next morning Sherah had awakened to find her husband sitting up beside her with a most contrite expression. She sensed instantly that Judah realized how he had treated her, but knew of no way to ask forgiveness or to wipe out the damage already done. Suppressing a small smile, Sherah bid him, "Good morning," and, pushing the coverings back, started to get up.

"A moment, please," Judah whispered, his voice tight with apprehension and colored with guilt. Sherah said nothing but lay back down.

He took a deep breath, as though to fortify himself, and plunged in: "I fear I was harsh with you last night. . ." Sherah closed her eyes so he could not read *how* harsh he had been.

"I thought our first time together would be different," Judah stumbled on, "but I drank too much strong wine. Was it bad for you?"

She wanted an apology, but she readily settled for his explanation, and she had to admit she was touched that he would consider her feelings for generally this was not the way with men.

Sherah opened her eyes and rolled over on her side to face him and said, "Yes, it was bad, but not terrible. It was more disappointing than anything. I, too, dreamed our first time together would be more..."

"Go on," he prodded. She turned from him and stared up at the tent's ceiling above her.

"It is just that we began our friendship by talking together... remember?" He nodded. "I had hoped that we would mingle our bodies together as we had our souls, slowly and with words."

"But I have no way with words," Judah protested.

"Oh, no. You are wrong." Sherah corrected him with both her words and her face. "It was you who talked to me first, and it was you who started me talking even when I had vowed I'd never speak to any son of Jacob except Joseph and Benjamin. So it was natural that I would expect..." her voice trailed off.

They had reached a standoff, and Sherah knew Judah had said all he could or would say and that she would have to be the one to give if a healing was to begin between them. Slowly and deliberately she leaned up and bent over him. She kissed him lightly on his ear, then his bearded cheek, and finally she pressed her lips softly against his mouth. She felt his body, tightened in response, and his arms folded her to his chest. She said playfully, "Perhaps these kisses will linger with you today, and tonight you can begin afresh by returning them to me." Sherah was pleased that when Judah finally found his voice he said hoarsely, "I can see I have much to learn about the ways of loving."

Sherah had broken away from his arm, sat up beside him, and reached for her small comb. He watched her as she combed out the long strands of dark tresses; and as she plaited them into one long braid he confessed, "I have boasted much with my brothers about my magical powers with women; but, in truth, I know very little about women." Sherah stopped her braiding and looked at him closely. He continued, "As I said before, I have much to learn about loving."

With her husband's honesty came the first tears which made

Sherah's eyes sparkle. "Then we shall learn together," she promised with genuine conviction.

"And so we have," Sherah thought as she waited for Joseph. But the experience of growing together and the deepening tender courtesies she longed for in Judah had never developed to any great degree. Over the years their marriage had eventually settled into a tolerable, if not acceptable, routine.

It was also childless for Sherah secretly prepared herself with special ointments and oils to prevent conception. There was, buried deep within her, a part of her that would always remember the horrible atrocities Reuben and Levi had committed in Shechem; and so, to appease the hurt, she vowed to never give Judah, also a son of Jacob, a child.

She was startled back to the reality of the rainy day by Joseph's remark, "This is too small for me, but it is dry. I and my cold bones thank you, gracious lady." He squatted down by the fire and warmed his hands.

Joseph's presence seemed to fill her whole tent, and Sherah turned from him to busy herself with adding small onions to the stew simmering in front of her.

Sherah always found one part of herself wholeheartedly loving Joseph. At first it was a sisterly love; then, as a few years went by, it became a type of mother love. Recently she had discovered another side of loving him, and it disturbed her ease and peace of mind. Even at this moment, Sherah felt it was a bit disconcerting to be inside her tent and in such close quarters with one whose face, body, and mind had gone from a sensitive and rosy-cheeked childhood beauty to an incredibly perspective and handsome man overnight.

The growing awareness of her sensual feelings towards Joseph flashed danger signals in Sherah's mind, so she was careful to limit their times together. However, she loved their occasional moments of conversation and missed them dearly when for some reason she did not see Joseph. She had been charmed when Joseph wrote her name on a clay tablet and presented it as a gift to her. Sapher had taught his prize pupil until there was very little more to teach about writing, reading, counting, and the scribe's way of keeping accounts and records. On the day Joseph gave her

the clay tablet, Sherah was very aware that something more than
gratitude was welling up within her. She managed their brief in-
terlude together by blocking out these disturbing feelings of desire as best she could.

"Joseph," she asked, moving away from the fire and him to
discourage her own line of thinking, "exactly how old are you
now? I've lost track." It was a lie. She knew precisely how old he
was, but she used the question to bring her own thoughts under
control.

"Come next summer, it will be the seventeenth anniversary of
my birth. Why do you ask?" he questioned her, as he rubbed the
remaining droplets of water off his legs. Deftly, Joseph caught a
piece of wool cloth which Sherah threw to him, and he toweled
off his curly head of hair and his beard until it fuzzed out and resembled, to Sherah's thinking, the full mane of a young lion in his
prime.

She looked at him and pronounced to herself, *He is as
strongly built as a mighty man of battle, yet his heart is that of a
wise scribe. He is one who sees much and records all the terrible,
true, yet tender things of life. What a unique combination!
Jacob's God has outdone Himself on this one.* Sherah's mouth
curved in a smile.

Joseph left the fire and settled himself crosslegged on the carpet before her stool. "Tell me, Sherah," he looked up, his blue
eyes dancing with life. "Are you smiling and asking about my age
because you still think of me as a helpless little boy? Haven't you
determined that I've grown into a man yet?" His questions could
not be easily answered because he struck the heart of Sherah's
feelings. She realized all too well just how much the "little boy"
had grown into a man.

He played with a small bundle of flax which Sherah was thin-
ning in preparation for weaving. "Well, what do you think?" he
asked.

"What *I* think," she laughed to conceal her tension, "is not of
great significance! What is important is what all those mother
ducks think who quack at the main well each morning when we
draw water together. Once they have seen the next to the youngest son of Jacob, they begin pairing off their daughters with that
certain young man!"

Joseph's cheeks above his beard turned a pomegranate red, and hastily he denied that anything like that was happening.

"Oh, but it's true, my friend!" Sherah insisted. "You have bewitched all the women who see you, so much so that the village women and the women from other tent dwellings rattle on and on about you, as though their mouths were those little wooden clappers the musicians use to keep the song going!"

"Even you, Sherah?" Joseph's voice was suddenly serious. "Have I bewitched you, too?"

As calmly controlled as possible and without even a glance which would give her away, Sherah willed herself to blandly ignore his question. Then, with a gaiety which was much more forced than she would have liked, she continued lightly on as though she hadn't been interrupted. "The mothers are pretending to take wagers on whether you will marry while you are young or wait until you are older as they have heard was the tradition of your father's. They hope it is very soon and not later, for they fear Jacob will move on again." She had passed the awkward moment and, pleased with herself, she allowed herself to wink at him teasingly.

"So they take wagers, do they?" Joseph laughed and shook his head. "I shall be clever and fool them all. I think I shall be a scribe, never marry, and give my life to the writing and keeping of records."

"Oh, how awful," Sherah said in mock horror. "Think of all the brokenhearted mothers and daughters you will leave behind you!"

The two broke into gales of laughter, and Sherah blessed Jacob's God again for His goodness in fashioning such a joy as Joseph.

Their laughter was short-lived however, because suddenly Judah stood before them. Wordlessly, he pulled off his rain-soaked outer garment and accepted the wool drying cloth from Sherah.

Then, abruptly, as he dried himself, he changed his mind about speaking to them, turned to Joseph and said tensely, "Why are you here and what do you want?"

The hair at the base of Sherah's neck rose, and the remnant of a cold shiver of hatred ran down her spine. Her memories of a long-ago day in Shechem and the murdering, scheming sons of Jacob filled her once more with contempt.

Angrily and defensively Sherah answered before Joseph could utter a word. "The boy was only trying to be of some help to me. He brought goat-hair clippings; your mother sent him. Look for yourself." Sherah pointed to the wet clippings in the basket. "I am grateful for they are scarce, as you know."

Joseph was on his feet now. "I was just leaving," he said to Judah's back, and then glancing down at himself he gestured to Sherah in a desperate attempt to find out what he should do about Judah's tunic. She signaled him to just leave, so the young man eased himself out, backing carefully towards the entrance of the tent. Then, just before he ducked under the flap, he said, "Forgive me, Sherah, but I forgot. My father asked to see you this evening."

"What does he want with my wife?" Judah asked quickly. He was puzzled as to whether it was meant to be a private meeting or not.

"He did not say, my brother," Joseph answered solemnly, "only that I should tell Sherah that after the evening meal he would speak with her."

Sherah nodded, and when Joseph was gone and out of hearing distance, she flung the full force of her frustrations at Judah. "Why, why, must you always be so inhospitable and uncharitable to Joseph? He is your brother, whether you like it or not."

"*Half* brother," Judah corrected her as he muttered the words under his breath.

"All right!" Sherah snapped. "So he is only your half brother, but you do share the same father. Surely there is enough vile hatred around and men who are anxious for war with one another without your *adding* to it!"

Judah looked at her fiery brown eyes which were filled with amber sparks of anger, and incredulously he raged at her, "Who do you think you are to talk about hatred between men? You, who sleep in my bed but give me no sons. And why no sons for Judah? Have you put a curse on your own womb, woman? Is not your barrenness due to your own hatred of Levi and Simeon? Do not ever speak to me of my treatment of Joseph until you are ready to put down your own hatred and fully open your womb to me!"

Sherah sucked in her breath, and, with vehemence, silently reaffirmed the vow she had taken so long ago: *Never! Never will I bear you a son! I will take my own desires and loves and become a wanderer in the vast deserts of this land before I open my heart or my womb to you. I promise you, Judah, I'll vanish as the wind before I add one child to the line of Jacob.*

Judah had never been able to prove his suspicions about her barrenness. He wished he could read her mind, but since he couldn't do so, with typical surliness. he ordered sarcastically, "Prepare the meal for me so you can keep your appointment with my father." He narrowed his eyes and watched her as she bent over the bread and stew. Then. drinking deeply from the wine skin, he slowly shut her out.

18

"Greetings, Israel," Sherah called, using Jacob's formal name to show proper respect as she lifted the flap of the impressive tent.

"Come inside, wife of Judah. Has the rain stopped altogether?" Jacob's voice, deep in timbre, called out, and his tone was the same he used to greet an old friend. It made the corners of her mouth tilt upwards for she guessed he was getting ready to ask her to do something for him.

Sherah answered politely, "The rain is gone and the night sky shows the stars. Perhaps the clouds which have disappeared will stay away, and hopefully it will not rain tomorrow." She pulled off her veil and laid it around her shoulders. Her eyes, quick to observe everything, took in Jacob's spacious "main room." Several oil lamps were burning, the carpets had been brushed of any dirt, the tables and chests were free of the wind's fine sand; and Jacob lay comfortably, half sprawled against some brightly upholstered floor pillows. He motioned for her to sit across from him. He did not offer her any of the wine he sipped, but instead pushed a small pottery bowl of dates toward her.

Sherah marveled at Jacob's physical ability to weather the test of time. The durability and longevity of his health was a remarkable thing to see. His body had retained its youthful leanness. The years of hard work had ruggedly toughened the sinew and muscles of his limbs. He looked and drove himself like a man half his age.

The young wife of Judah felt just a little uncomfortable seated before him. It was as if his endless stamina and drive reached out and prodded her into some action besides taking her ease.

Jacob was a man to respect, and she was honored and more than a little curious as to why he had sent for her.

"I have a task for you, Sherah," Jacob said as she bit into the dried fruit.

She flashed a quick smile at him, and looking at the tent roof above her said, "I thought so. I was beginning to wonder how much wind and rain we might have before our Father Israel would ask me to mend or weave new goat's hair cloth for his leaking tent."

She had caught him at his game, and Jacob was delighted that she called him on it in such a skillful way. He chuckled out loud for he could not fool this daughter-in-law. Both of them knew he never sent for her unless he needed his tent repaired. In fact, most of the time Jacob treated her like he would a woman servant. The exception to that rule came when he needed her skills. Then, and only then, he offered dates and hospitable talk. She was accustomed to his traditional treatment of herself and the other women of the encampment and had long ago stopped thinking it unusual behavior. That too pleased Jacob. Only Rachel had been respected and treated as a man, an equal, or a partner by Jacob, and Sherah longingly envied their rapport.

"You are right in assuming I need your special skills, but as you can see, my tent is in fine condition." Jacob said, breaking into her thoughts. "The last strips you wove have shrunk with all the rain pouring on them, and no water is seeping through anywhere, even between the seams."

Sherah felt a glow of satisfaction flush her face, but now she was interested and curious. No tent to be mended? Then what? She gave him her undivided attention.

"I want you to make me a very special tunic," Jacob said. His words were uttered simply enough, but something about the rather piercing look in his eyes prompted her to catch her breath.

"A short workman's tunic, my lord?"

"No . . ."

Jacob seemed to be having some difficulty, so Sherah volunteered, "You mean a long tunic, made of linen or perhaps wool, reaching the ankles and with sleeves to the wrists?" She didn't want to be coy or use tricks, but she wanted to get as much information as she could without it appearing that she was curious for the sake of gossiping.

"Mmmm," Jacob stalled for a moment more, trying to decide how much of his plans he'd have to share with her to get exactly what he wanted. Finally he said, matter-of-factly, "I'd like the material to be your best flax, woven into linen. I want it of white linen," he continued as he took a sip of wine, "and I understand from my wife, Leah, that you learned your mother's skills in embroidery as well as weaving and sewing. Is that true?"

Sherah nodded but kept still, hoping he would continue, for by now she knew as much as she needed to know but was fearful of pursuing the subject. He had vaguely described a tunic embroidered with many color-dyed threads, and probably embellished with a design in gold thread overlay. With surprise, she realized Jacob wanted her to make the type of garment worn by a nobleman, a very rich man, or a man of kingly power.

Sherah had a reputation for honest directness, so heading for the heart of the matter, she took a date pit from her mouth and spoke as nonchalantly as she dared. "I can embroider with all kinds of threads. The task always comes easily for me. It is the best part of sewing or weaving, and I enjoy it greatly." She took another date and asked, even more casually, "Will I be making this tunic for you, my lord?" With a small show of humility, Sherah looked down at the carpet as she awaited his reply. Then, as he answered her, Sherah abruptly snapped her eyes open to sit wide-eyed before him.

Jacob spoke with quiet authority. "You will be making the

tunic for me, that much is true, but I will not be wearing it. I want to give it as a gift of my esteem to one of my sons."

"One of your sons?" she whispered, and leaned forward to not miss a word.

Jacob nodded.

"Which one?" She knew to ask directly was presuming on his hospitality, but she asked anyway. Her heart was racing within her because she instantly guessed that the son designated to wear the tunic would be heir to a prestigious birthright. Quickly her mind spun a series of facts before her: Reuben was the firstborn of Leah and that gave him the birthright, but because of sinning with Bilhah, he lost it. The sons of servant girls, or concubines, as these Hebrews called them, were not recognized as valid sons. Then her heart skipped a beat as she thought, "Joseph is the firstborn of Rachel. . . ."

Sherah put everything together in that moment, and calculated that Jacob determined to give this tunic to Joseph as his announcement that Joseph had inherited the birthright. She covered her mouth with her hand as her discovery became more of a truth within her. Finally she recovered enough calmness to ask cleverly and cooly, "Shall I make the tunic to fit the height and breadth of Joseph?"

It was Jacob's turn for wide-seeing eyes, and his mouth dropped open to match. He knew Sherah was a skilled worker, but the sharpness of her mind had never before revealed itself. His heart suffered with a sudden pang of grief because the girl's mental quickness reminded him of his beloved, long-departed Rachel.

He managed to nod affirmatively.

"Do you have any other instructions?"

He nodded again, this time negatively, so Sherah continued: "I have, in my possession already, a fine piece of woven linen. It is bleached to snowy whiteness, and I'll use that for the tunic unless you wish it otherwise." She peered at him, waiting for other information or instructions.

Jacob raised himself from his painful thoughts of Rachel, and said passively, "Yes, yes that will be fine. I trust your judgment, and I know you will make a garment worthy of my son."

Before he had a chance to wave her away or dismiss her with a "Good night," Sherah stood, gave her farewells and left the mighty presence of Jacob. She was grateful that apparently no one had seen her enter her father-in-law's tent, and now no one was around to ask her about the visit.

As she walked back to her own dwelling, the moon came out and helped her skirt the edges of the puddles made by the heavy rains. Her mind was full of Jacob's commission, and she wondered why it was that she felt, at once, both highly elated and yet strangely depressed.

"What part of father's giant tent needs mending now?" Judah asked her, without really caring to know the answer, as she entered their place and slipped off her wet sandles.

"His tents are fine. Your father, Jacob, called for me because he wants . . ." Sherah hesitated a moment and then finished unsteadily, "some other sewing done."

Judah caught nothing amiss, and Sherah was relieved when he replied, "Fine," and rinsing his face with water he asked if she was ready to go to bed. He asked no more questions that night.

The word was not "fine" a fortnight later however, when Judah came home from the flocks to find Sherah working on a large piece of white linen.

"It's too big for a baby son," he tossed the words sarcastically at her as he pulled up one edge of the material. Sherah reacted too quickly and gave herself away when she shrieked, "Don't touch it with your dirty hands. You'll soil it."

Judah dropped the tunic as if it had been a hot ember and straightened up before her. "So what do we have here? A nobleman's tunic for my father?" Then very loudly, and as if to some unseen audience he asked, "But if it is just for my father, why has Sherah appointed herself chief protector of the material? I didn't realize she cared and respected her father-in-law to such a great degree, or . . . is it for someone else?" Judah's eyes narrowed and, stunned with a glimmer of an idea, he bent down and looked directly at her and asked incredulously, "Is this for Joseph?"

In that brief moment of time Judah put the whole thing together—his wife's obvious devotion for Joseph, and the humiliating significance of the tunic, with its birthright. His hatred for

Rachel's sons awakened with new passion, came fully alive, and exploded within him.

With one muscle-wrenching whack, he grabbed his shepherd's staff and brought it and his right knee together! The wood cracked, splintered, and shattered with the force of impact. Leaving Sherah staring in horror at the broken pieces, Judah charged wordlessly out of the tent.

The rain disappeared as quickly as it had begun, and Sherah saw one new moon followed by another, and finally a third without any sight of Judah. She used the time to pour herself into the highly detailed and wide, colorful borders she was stitching and working around the edges of the sleeves and hem of the tunic.

She was grateful to Leah who occasionally gave her bits of information on Judah and the others in the camp. It was the only oasis in her silent desert. The brothers, when they heard of the tunic, arrogantly denounced Sherah for making the tunic, Leah reported. Reuben arranged for Judah to stay with him in his tent for as long as it took her to finish the garment.

"Is he well?" Sherah asked of Leah one morning, some weeks after Judah had gone.

"Well, he eats his fill of my cooking, if that is what you mean. But I fear Judah's heart, though he would have you think it is made of stone, is raw and tender with loneliness for you, Sherah," Leah comforted the girl. Then, unexpectedly, she answered Sherah's unspoken question when she said, "Jacob has sent Joseph out to the hills as the chief shepherd over some flocks and herds. The sons of Bilhah and Zilpah are his under shepherds and assistants. For the most part, the boys stay in the valleys with the flocks, but when they do come back occasionally I can hardly wait for them to leave.

"Dan, Naphtali, Gad, and even Asher, complain all the time that one of *them* should be chief shepherd as they are older than Joseph. There is much muttering between them, but they dare not oppose something Jacob, their father, has ordered. I fear that all the brothers, including my own sons, are very hard on Joseph. There will be real trouble when that," Leah pointed down at the tunic which covered Sherah's lap, "your labor of love, is completed. I know, from the way they talk even now, that there will be grave repercussions."

"But what am I to do?" Sherah's eyes joined with her voice, and she pleaded, "I sew this because Jacob told me to do so. I must finish it. Yet, as long as I sew on it, my husband stays away; and when I finish it and Joseph wears it, the sight of him wearing the garment may bring down his brothers' wrath on him. As you said, I too feel there will be trouble, but I seem to be caught in the middle."

"Finish it, my child." Leah patted the younger woman's shoulder. "It is the task which is set before you. We will have to leave the consequences in the hands of the living God, my husband, Jacob, and his sons." Leah straightened up and turned to leave. "We both know that Jacob is going to give the tunic to Joseph. What we don't know is what Jacob's sons will do or what the living God will allow. Finish it," she repeated, "and then, Lord willing, we will see what happens."

Long after she left, Sherah pondered on Leah's accurate assessment of her dilemma. After some time, she decided to pour herself even more into the exacting embroidery work and finish, at all costs, the tunic which lay on her lap.

When the resplendent garment ended up being even more beautiful than Sherah had hoped for, she sent word to Jacob that she had completed her task. She also advised she would bring it to him the next morning.

After the bright, white dawn softened into a rosy pink, Sherah took the tunic, asked permission to enter Jacob's tent, and, when it was instantly given, she went inside and spread the exquisite piece of her labors on the carpet before Jacob.

The father's eyes moistened with tears.

"Is it fitting, my lord?" Sherah asked, knowing the only answer he could give.

"It is more than fitting—it is perfect. It is my finest gift. I weep now only because I wish his mother were here to share the joy and delight of watching Joseph's face when he sees it." Jacob wiped his eyes with his sleeve, and then picked up the hem of the tunic and examined the colorful border closely. "It is a marvelous thing you have fashioned," he said truthfully. Then, looking directly at her, he stated, "I want to reward you for your diligence and your skills." Jacob held out a small box, but Sherah shook her head.

"Come, take it," he urged. "You have more than earned this."
Reluctantly, she took the box and opened the lid.

"Those earrings are made of ivory," he explained, leaning
over to point them out. "These of gold, and of course the bracelet
to match, is gold, too." He settled back against some cushions
and, because he knew she was speechless with pleasure, he
waited.

"But this . . ." Sherah held up a delicately wrought needle.
"This needle is made of gold too . . ."

Jacob smiled approvingly and added, "You have earned a
golden needle, bone or bronze would not do, so I had this one
fashioned. Even before I saw the finished garment, I knew you
would do your best."

Sherah had grown so silent and ever so pensive that Jacob inclined his head towards her and inquired, "Is it not enough? I can
give you something else, if you are not pleased."

"Oh, no, my lord. It is *more* than I deserve . . . it is just that
. . ." she stopped.

"What then?"

"I would like one favor granted."

"Name it, child."

Hesitantly, she explained. "I'd simply like to be here when
you present the tunic to Joseph. I know I am not as worthy as
your beautiful Rachel, but I'd like just to see his face when he
understands why you have given him this loving gift. May I
stay?"

Jacob laughed, "I was going to ask you to remain here anyway. Now, sit down. Joseph is on his way."

To Sherah it felt as though one whole day and one long night
passed before Joseph came; but when he did, her heart nearly
burst with joy at the sight of him.

Joseph greeted his father first, and then surprised at seeing
her, he smiled a welcome towards Sherah. His eyes quickly accustomed themselves to the tent's shadows, and then, with what
seemed like a quick step backward, he bent his head downward
and looked at the tunic spread out on the carpet before him.

Sherah watched Joseph's face closely and realized that not
even for a second did he think it might be a gift for him.

"What a magnificent tunic!" he cried. "Father, you will look majestic in it; and it is fitting and right that you, the head of our household, should wear it." Then, turning to Sherah, he said with a wide grin on his face, "I see now why you are here. This is your handiwork, is it not?"

"Yes, Sherah made the tunic." Jacob spoke. His voice was smooth; and evenly he added, "But she did not make it for me to wear."

Joseph turned his head toward his father and, with uncomplicated innocence, asked, "Who then?"

The old man sat upright, straight and tall, and looked into Joseph's face as he answered, "The firstborn son of Rachel shall wear this tunic, and let all who see him in it know that his father's love of him is as solid as the mountain and as constant as the sunrise."

Joseph bent down and picked up one corner of the tunic's hem. Then, fingering the raised grapes' and leaves' designs of gold threads which overlayed the many colored threads, he asked incredulously, "This is mine?" Suddenly his infectious laugh punctuated the air. "Father," Joseph teased, "the only ones who will see me in such a treasure are the sheep that the sons of Bilhah and Zilpah and I are tending, and I hardly think the sheep will notice!"

Jacob smiled at his son's humor, but said seriously enough, "Take it, my son. It is a token of my love. You deserve it, for in you I have seen the budding blossoms of faith such as your great grandfather, Abraham, possessed. Also, there is about you the gentleness of my father, Isaac. . . ." Sherah wordlessly agreed and watched as Jacob got up from his couch, his eyes moist with tears and, in a voice unable to hold firm, he finished: "But the real beauty of your character, Joseph, is your unswerving obedience to me. I can only pray that in the years before you, you will give the same kind of obedience to the God of our forefathers; for if you take your vow of obedience to Him, as you have to me, it will be your greatest inheritance and birthright."

Joseph went eagerly into Jacob's outstretched arms, and the two stood warmly enbracing each other. They kissed each other's cheeks with fervor; and Sherah, who did not believe or disbelieve

Jacob's God, wondered why she felt suddenly that the tent was no longer a tent, but perhaps a shrine, a temple . . . or, most intriguing of all, a tabernacle filled with a living God's unseen presence.

Out of the corner of his eye, Joseph saw Sherah start to slip out the tent opening, so he left his father's embrace, caught her wrist, and said, "I have appropriately thanked my father, and now I must tell you how beautiful your work is; however, I am at a loss for words." Sherah bowed her head and accepted his thanks—not by the words which would not come, but by the look she had seen on his face when he had first looked down at the tunic.

When he could find no expression of thanks adequate to describe his gratitude, he took Sherah's face in his hands. He kissed one cheek and then, as he kissed the other, he whispered, "Sherah, truly you are a loving sister to me. I shall cherish the tunic, even when it is threadbare and old, for I shall remember the hands that fashioned it."

Sherah's face burned where he had touched her, and her heart swelled with joy over his praise; but the ecstasy of the moment was instantly over. As Joseph returned to his father, and as she turned to leave, she stood face-to-face with Judah and Reuben.

Both men stood like stone sentinels, just inside the tent. Their eyes were staring down at the tunic before them, and their faces were glazed with their immediate comprehension.

Sherah heard Jacob say, "I have summoned you here, Judah and Reuben, to tell you firsthand that it is I who gives this tunic to Joseph . . ." as she ran blindly out of the tent and disappeared into the foliage of a small cluster of olive trees.

I am a seamstress, not a fortune-teller! Sherah thought. But as she sat in her private tree shelter, unable to control her trembling, it was easy to foresee that Jacob's gift to Joseph would bring a tangible disaster to every one of the tents of Jacob.

19

Tantalizing stories of Joseph's magnificent tunic and the implied birthright which came with it swirled through the encampment with the force of a powerful whirlwind. The tunic which was almost immediately dubbed by all who saw it, "Joseph's coat of many colors," was the main, and sometimes only, topic of conversation.

Everyone from tent dwellers, villagers, shepherds, and farmers, to women and children, added luster to the already preposterous story.

Sherah took to the seclusion of her own lodgings and refused to be drawn into the "tunic" discussions with everybody, including Leah. Even when Judah appeared unannounced one night after his long absence and moved back into their tent, Sherah never spoke about Joseph or the tunic. When she did speak to Judah, it was only of mundane things and in the sparsest of terms.

One afternoon, just when Sherah thought interest in Joseph and his garment was dying down and that the brothers' resentment seemed to have cooled, a whole new controversy presented itself. The half brothers' hatred of Joseph flared up as if someone had put a torch to their souls.

Sherah put away the small weaving loom and the wool she had been working on and drank from the goatskin of water. Feeling refreshed, she gave herself to the task of fixing the evening meal when, without warning, Judah angrily flung back the tent flap. In a fit of evil temper he stormed, "Woman, why is not my evening meal ready?"

What now? Sherah thought, but quickly she offered, "You are early tonight. I was just about to see to the food." Her soft answer made Judah instantly regret his outburst, but he was not sure he knew how to take back his spoken demands.

The slim young woman passed close by him, intending to go to her cooking fires outside, but he caught her arm and held her firmly. It was not the tightness of Judah's grip that surprised her but the sound of the first and only apology she had ever heard coming from his lips.

"Sherah, I ..." his voice cracked with hoarseness, "I am sorry. Truly sorry."

"What for?" she asked, cooly masking her curiosity and surprise.

There were so many things which had never righted themselves in all their time together that Sherah dared not let herself believe they were about to reconstruct and rebuild some of the damaged feelings of their lives. Yet Judah stood beside her, unable to look directly at her, and it seemed he really regretted the real or imagined hurts that he had inflicted on her. Still, she made an apology difficult for him, and he inwardly cursed her silence for it demanded an explanation. Barely able to manage his feelings he went on: "I am sorry for ... I mean, I feel badly about everything." He looked directly at her dark brown eyes now, and pleaded his case before her with no little anguish.

"It is just that the hatred I feel for Joseph and his kinship with my father, Jacob, boils inside of me continually, like your pots of broth. I am never free of it." He let go of her arm, but he did not move away.

"Then," Judah continued in a low voice, "just when I tell myself to ignore Joseph and simply be the man the God of my forefathers would have me to be, *something else* happens and I am right back with my brothers, neck deep in new hatred, and my skin crawling for revenge."

Sherah studied him a moment and then asked perceptively, "And today, what was the 'something else' that happened?"

She was so close to him that he caught the faint fragrance of her hair. In that moment, he successfully dismissed the monster of envy that lurked in the shadows of his mind, and, in a rare moment of tenderness, he pulled her to him and held her close. For once she did not stiffen in his arms or back away. He was relieved, and into her dark silken tresses he whispered, "Sherah, Sherah, I've missed you. Come to my bed." Her eyes asked, "Now?" and he answered, "Make me forget this miserable day ... please, Sherah ..."

She had never seen this Judah before, and terribly hungry for the gentle way he was caressing her hair, she said softly, "I have to tend the fire of the baking pit for a moment, but I will be right back." He understood and gestured for her to go.

Sherah arranged the stones in the fire pit with a thick stick and knew they would take a while more to heat. She watched the fire flicker over the stones and recalled that Judah had never begged her before. She found she was fascinated as well as curious. *What has Jacob or Joseph done now?* she wondered.

When she returned to him, he took her respectfully and gratefully to bed and, as Sherah noted, never had he been more gentle.

After Judah's passion was depleted he did not, in his usual manner, push away from her or fall soundly asleep. Instead, and to Sherah's pleased surprise, he lay quietly beside her. When she raised up to take a better look at this stranger she had just shared her bed with, she found Judah staring absently at the center tent pole, and she was frightened by the coldness of his expression.

Carefully, not wanting to lose the closeness of their time together, she moved with concerned curiosity asking with kindness, "My husband, what troubles you so?"

It was as if he didn't hear her, so she repeated her concerns a little more urgently. "Judah . . . please tell me."

Still he said nothing. Sherah's heart sank for she feared the sharing they had just experienced in their bed was not the beginning of some much needed healing but merely a brief glance at something which could have been. She tried once more: "Judah, we must not close ourselves to each other . . . we need to open the doors between us." Her words, so long pent up, tumbled from her. "I am sorry, too. I am sorry for my indifference to you and for the countless other things which I have done, or worse, led you to believe I've done. Can we start afresh like a new sunrise? Or is it too late for new beginnings? I wish," she said wistfully, as she lay back down beside him, "I wish I knew if there was any chance of our growing up together."

Judah leaned up on one elbow and looked over at her as though he had heard her, and yet he hadn't, for when he spoke it was not to her particularly, but in a flat, monotonous tone. He recited, "Now, besides telling father about the misdeeds of his brothers in the field—now, he tells us his dreams."

"*What?*" Sherah blurted out. She stared incredulously at her husband, not ready to believe the intensity of his jealousy and that the old hatred was back again, or rather, *still* there. It lay as a cold mask on his face.

Continuing in his flat unvaried voice, Judah said, "First he flaunts his coat of many colors before us. The way he wears that wretched garment he lets the whole community know that he is better than us. We are made to feel that we are nothing more than common laborers, born to toil our lives away. Then he reports the actions of his brothers to our father."

The quality of Judah's voice finally took on some human characteristics, and it became louder and higher pitched. He sat up, laid a heavy punch into one of the pillows behind him, and almost shouted, "Then, as if Joseph's tunic and his carrying tales were not enough—now, he has the insolence to wipe our noses in his disgusting dreams of his exaltation—"

"And your humiliation," Sherah finished for him.

"Yes, it's our humiliation he plans. He connives to remind us always that, of all of Jacob's sons, he is the crown prince!"

She had reached the end of her patience with the brothers' hatred of Joseph, and with disgust dripping from her voice Sherah said, "As usual, you make far more of this than can be imagined! Joseph is just a young lad. Why can't you forgive him for accepting the tunic?" She tilted her head in a defiant gesture and didn't wait for any answer, but went on. "Surely if Jacob had given the garment to you, you would have not folded it up and stored it in a chest or a basket. You would have taken it proudly and worn it, just as he has done!"

Judah continued to stare sullenly at the ceiling. She watched a twitching facial muscle which moved his beard and gave away the fact that, though he was quiet, he had heard her. She could see the anger was boiling and seething within him, but Sherah knew what needed to be said.

"As to his telling Jacob about the sons of Bilhah and Zilpah's behavior, I know about that." Sherah paused before going on. "Your mother told me about it. Jacob made Joseph overseer for his concubines' sons. It appears they are not diligent in their tending of the flocks and unworthy of trust, so your father wanted Joseph to report any of their wrongdoing.

"There is no reason to believe Joseph took pleasure in carrying the bad news. It is simply that Jacob will never forget all the brothers' evil and cunning ways, and he trusts Joseph to keep the family name pure."

Judah turned his face to the tent side as her words made his stomach cramp together in a rigid knot. He needed no reminding of his father's feelings.

"And as to the boy's dreams," Sherah continued, "they are nothing more than that—just a boy's dreams."

Judah sat up, faced her, stabbed a long accusing finger in her direction and thundered, "That proves then, woman, you don't know what this 'boy' dreams!"

"No," she admitted, "but can anyone's dreams be so bad, so terrible, or so threatening, that you—a grown man, sit beside me—your eyes bulging in contempt and your hands trembling in rage? Do you Hebrews worship dreams and their interpretations?" Sherah asked sarcastically.

Judah quickly folded his hands together to disguise their trembling and, with as much patience as he could possibly force, he said huskily, "Sherah, this *boy*," he spit the word out with bitterness, "this boy you admire so much has openly boasted of his dreams . . . and to answer your questions about Hebrews and dreams . . . yes, we do attach great importance to dreams. It is many times the way the living God chooses to speak to us. Joseph taunts us now for he swears his dreams are from God."

"So, what if they are?" Sherah asked unwittingly, exploding a powerful spark of fury within him.

"*What if they are?*" he repeated, like a man crazed by the burning desert sun. "Let me tell you what his dreams are about!

"In one of them, Joseph said we were all out in the field binding up sheaves of wheat when his bundle of grain stood up. Then he said our bundles all gathered around his grain and bowed low before his!" Judah smote his fists together and began to pace the confines of the tent. Sherah listened to him, appalled by his vehemence.

"Then today, in front of Jacob our father, he boasted of another dream. He said that in *this* dream the sun, moon, and eleven stars bowed low before him!"

When Sherah asked if Jacob had said anything, a small smile of satisfaction passed over his face and Judah responded almost gleefully, "Did father say anything? Oh, yes! He definitely did.

He was as incensed as we were over all that bowing down, and he took Joseph by the shoulder and rebuked him by asking, 'Joseph, what is this you say? Indeed, shall I, your dead mother, and your living brothers come and bow to the ground before you?' "

"How did Joseph answer Jacob's charge?" Sherah asked as she searched his face for answers.

Judah looked at her and shrugged his shoulders. He suddenly seemed to have lost the angry fervor of the moment. Almost off-handedly, he said, "Oh, I don't know. Joseph just said something about his dreams coming from God and that he had not made them up to provoke us."

Judah left his pacing, took a large pillow from their bed and sat leaning against it while Sherah pulled her robes on and tied her sash around her waist.

"There, you see," Sherah picked up defensively, "Joseph is not telling you of his dreams to hurt you, only to share them with you. I suspect even he does not know what exactly they mean."

"Of course he knows full well what they mean!" Judah scoffed. "And he tells us in order to wave the flag of defeat and humiliation in our faces."

"This is ridiculous. You are a fool, Judah!" Sherah's agitation and lack of patience put a fine, sharp edge on the tone of her voice. "Joseph doesn't expect, or demand, that your father and you all bow down to him. Nor does he expect his mother to bow down to him from her grave. He merely believes, as he has been taught, that dreams are from God, and he tells you about them. He has no gift for interpreting them and, as a matter of fact, neither do you!"

To change and soften the line of her verbal attack, she asked, "Did your father say anything else to Joseph?"

Judah shook his head and replied, "No, he was very quiet and just walked away. We all did . . . we just left the dreamer in the middle of the pasture by himself." Muttering more to himself than to Sherah, Judah mused, "Bow down to him? Never! Not even if I outlive my sons and my grandsons." Then he directed to Sherah, "Should I *ever* have sons or grandsons."

Ignoring his remark, Sherah said, withour rancor or smugness, "I think I know why your father left the fields quietly. It is because while he may not understand the meaning of Joseph's dreams, he has built up a lifetime of faith in God-given, holy dreams. He has probably gone to his tent to ponder as to what it all means."

Suddenly her heart softened, and she opened her soul just a crack and found that a small lump of compassion had formed within her. She bent down before Judah, took his face in her hands, and said without any malice or forethought, "Judah, the innocent, boyish dreams of Joseph can be like an adder's poisonous bite to the man who is filled with envy and hatred. I see you constantly bitten by this evil snake, and I am horrified, for one day it will claim your life. I know it will."

He jerked his head roughly from her hands. "Sherah," he said, his voice devoid of any emotion, especially love, "you know nothing of what is involved here. As a woman you cannot understand a man's thinking nor can you see how Joseph has robbed us of our father's affection, our birthright, and now our pride.

"You only know Joseph as the handsome, fair-haired heir to the throne . . . perhaps what you feel for him is more than mere sisterly affection . . . but, in any case, you do not understand any of this. Stay out of it, lest you embarrass me in the presence of my father and brothers."

Sherah scarcely breathed except to curse herself for her vulnerability. She had opened her soul to him, and he had rewarded her by wiping his feet all over it.

Jackass! she thought with a sour bitterness. *I understand much more than you do. You are a foolish child and someday, somehow, you will live to regret your stupidity.*

Out loud, she snarled caustically, "Then you tell me where all this hatred ends, if it does not eat you alive."

"It is not your concern!" Judah glared at her. "You just take care of the baking of bread, the meals, the sewing, and weaving of goat's hair cloth, and I'll take care of the rest . . . and in my own way!"

His stubborn, unyielding words embedded themselves into her soul like the brittle, sharp pieces of iron in the tips of a flagging whip.

Sherah fled the tent and wept blindly into her cooking fires. Her soul screamed out for the loving arms of her dead mother and father, and once again she felt the searing pain of fresh grief. She longed to be back in Shechem and to have things the way they were before.

"Sherah, my child." Leah's face appeared through her blurred vision. "What has devastated you?" Leah questioned softly, her own face lined with concern. She wiped the girl's face with her veil.

Deciding not to lie to the mother-in-law who had befriended her, yet not wanting to tell her of her son's words, Sherah said carefully, "I am weeping for my departed parents. I would gladly walk all the way back to the ashes of Shechem if, just for a moment, I could reach out and touch them."

"They are all gone from there, you know." Leah said somberly.

Sherah agreed by a slight nod of her head. Her tears slowed down, leaving her eyes rimmed and fiery red, her breath coming in sporadic hiccups.

Leah astutely ignored the unspoken but implied message that Sherah might want to go back home—permanently; and she was struck by an interesting thought. With guarded enthusiasm, Leah offered Sherah an alternate plan.

"Child, listen to me carefully," Leah whispered as Sherah blew her nose and sat across from her on the other side of the fire pit.

"In just a few days Jacob is going to send all my sons north, out of this vale of Hebron, to find greener summer pastures for his vast flocks. The sons of Bilhah, Zilpah, and Rachel are staying here.

"Jacob will not break camp in this valley for it is our home now, but he will be sending my sons."

Sherah was puzzled as to what this had to do with her, but she gave Leah her respectful attention.

"I don't know exactly how far north they will go," Leah offered, "or how long they will stay. Perhaps they will go as far as Shechem. But I know someone should go to cook for that many shepherds." Leah hesitated and then asked, "Why not you?"

Sherah did not reply immediately because her mind was instantly filled with bits and pieces of plans. To herself she thought, *Even if I got close to Shechem, then I could . . .*

"Perhaps they will camp in one of the neighboring villages

near Shechem," Leah was saying. "That way you could find an old acquaintance or two. It may be just what you need . . . an old friend to help assuage your grief somewhat." Leah smiled a consoling smile. "Maybe, child, it will even restore some of the lost joy to your soul."

It was a moment or two before Sherah was able to take a break from devising plans. She asked logically, "But, Leah, do you think Jacob would let me go? It is not customary for a wife to follow the shepherds to summer pastures."

"Jacob is a wise provider, and he knows that if six of his sons are away from home and not eating well, they are apt to be surly tempered and get into mischief. If that happens, his flocks will suffer. Besides, Jacob is not your problem. I'll take care of him. It is Judah you must convince."

Leah said no more but rose, gave Sherah a warm hug, and went back to her own fires, leaving the troubled young woman to her baking bread and tumbling thoughts.

Sherah watched her short and stocky mother-in-law until she disappeared behind a tent and then vowed silently to herself, *Oh, Leah, you have just saved my life! I'll convince Judah to let me go or I'll die trying.*

After all, didn't my husband just order me, like a maid servant, to tend to cooking chores? She brightened at the irony of it all, and then her head began to fill and swirl with decisions, conclusions, and, best of all, plans.

The young woman thought the flat, newly baked loaves of bread before her smelled sweet with the fragrance of hope.

"No, not hope," she said aloud, "it is the fragrance of freedom and the scent of victory!"

Someone, probably Joseph she thought, was playing the flute at the far edge of the encampment, and Sherah hummed a small melody from the almost forgotten song as she brought the food together for their evening meal. She moved swiftly and with a lightness of step because of the incredible escape route which had loomed on her horizon. She would put her ideas and itinerary into motion when the timing was just right; but, until then, it was her own precious, exuberant secret.

Sherah hugged herself in excited anticipation.

20

The pastures in the vale of Hebron, as lush and bounteous as they had been to his father, Isaac, and his grandfather, Abraham, were still not sufficient to feed and support all of Jacob's vast flocks and herds.

So in the days that followed Judah's envious and hateful denunciation of Joseph, Sherah finally saw Leah's prediction come to pass; Jacob told the brothers to seek pasture lands farther north.

Sherah presented her case for accompanying them with utmost tact. "You will need a woman to bake the bread and someone to simmer the broth without burning it to death," she ventured one night, after she was sure Judah had eaten his fill of her carefully prepared roasted lamb. "Who among the brothers can cook?" Without waiting for the obvious answer, she said, "Besides, have you not told me I should take care of the household chores and be mindful of nothing else?"

Judah looked up at her as she sat before him. She was delicately biting off a small piece of flat bread, and mildly surprised, he asked, "You would leave the safety of these tents and the security and friendships of other women here—including my mother—to face the hardships of a journey in search of pastures?" He was puzzled but so pleased that he only heard her soft yes and saw her mouth curve in a rare smile. He did not notice that her eyes were cold and masked.

Then, as an afterthought, he added, "You do know that Joseph stays here? He will not be coming with us. How will you get along without his pretty face and his flattering words?"

With quiet dignity she summoned up a plausible response. "Whether he goes or stays, it is of no concern to me." She lied. Then convincingly she said, "You, my husband, are the one who has put so much importance to my feelings for Joseph, not I." Sherah hoped she had successfully covered her affections for Joseph because, in truth, she counted on the boy staying with his father. She wanted just as much time and distance between Joseph and his brothers as possible. She could easily lie about her stirring emotions for Joseph if she felt she could help keep him safe by avoiding bloodshed between the brothers.

In the end it was surprisingly easy to persuade Judah to let her go with them. So one day, after thanking Leah privately for the friendship which had flourished between them and without a farewell of any kind to Joseph, Sherah supervised other servants who checked and rechecked the supplies; then she joined Judah and his brothers, mounted her camel and began the arduous journey north.

The task of moving so many flocks and herds was not complicated to Jacob's sons—they were well trained in shepherding—but the work was slow and tedious. Their journey consumed many hours, days, and weeks.

As Judah, Sherah, the brothers, and the flocks traveled north and eventually came to the place where the ruins of Shechem stretched out before them, Sherah saw the familiar mountains rising on each end of the valley like natural sheltering walls of protection, and she was filled with the exciting tingle of expectation. Sherah would have put her plan into immediate effect except that when they camped that night Judah instructed her to leave the carts of household goods and supplies as they were.

"But I need to unpack these things for our stay here." Her tone was submissive for she was trying to figure out what he was about to do.

"It is Reuben's feeling that we will not be here too long. So leave the cart as it is. Just continue to use our traveling supplies," Judah said with no other explanation. Then he quickly left her to join his brothers in tending the flocks.

So the brothers are afraid of a battle here, so close to Shechem, Sherah thought, and she liked the idea that the Canaanites or the Perizzites who despised these men as much as she did might be alive. *I'll stay awhile longer,* she promised herself, *and then I'll leave Judah and all his murdering brothers. I will vanish from their lives and no one will ever find me.* Her thoughts warmed her.

Sherah did unpack her cooking utensils, for it turned out they stayed in the valley of Shechem the length of time it took two

moons to come and go. It was too long for Reuben because at the
end of a sunfilled summer's day, he stood beside her cooking fires
announcing his decision to the brothers as they ate their evening
meal. "We shall rise before dawn tomorrow and move on."
Sherah's curiosity was piqued, and she was grateful when one of
the brothers asked where they would be going.

"Farther north," Reuben explained, "to the upland plains of
Dothan. They have excellent pasturage, and since they are on the
caravan route from Syria to Egypt we will not have to live like
hermits, seeing only our own faces and the faces of the flocks."

Dothan ... Sherah repeated to herself. *Ah, from there I
will disappear and take my leave from Jacob's sons. If I stayed
here they would immediately know I could be found in the Shechem area, but if I go to Dotham with them they will be too busy
with the flocks to come and find me or to send anyone to bring me
back.* Instantly she wondered if Judah would feel anything at her
leaving, and yet—just as suddenly it didn't seem to matter.
Dothan would be the place to leave them.

When their camels and flocks reached the plains of Dothan,
Sherah behaved as expected: dutifully. Then, not to arouse any
suspicions, she routinely unpacked the supplies from the household carts. As soon as the tents were firmly pegged into the
ground, she dug her own fire pits. It took her days to settle her
supply tent and to organize the cooking equipment and foodstuffs, but she had been taught by the best, Leah.

The men ignored her but tolerated her presence because of
the delicious meals she served each night.

The first few weeks kept Sherah busy with organizing and
finding two young serving girls from Dothan who would help
with the chores. *You don't know it yet,* she said to herself, as
she taught one girl the finer aspects of churning goats' milk into
white leben, *but you had better learn your lessons well because
you are going to take over for me after I've left the tents of
Jacob's sons.*

Several mornings after the camp routine was working
smoothly, Sherah went by herself to wash some of her garments
at a shallow brook just beyond their encampment. When her
soiled clothes were pounded and shaken clean she climbed up an
embankment and stretched the wet pieces over the small but

sturdy bushes to dry. Once everything was laid out, Sherah straightened up and, using her wet hands, she wiped several strands of fallen hair off her face. The coolness of her hands and the fresh country air were invigorating, and she sat down on the side of the grassy hill to look over the valley.

She was about to slip into her favorite pastime of planning her escape when idly her eyes traced the main caravan road on the eastern edge of the valley and there she saw the lone figure of a man riding a donkey.

The man was dressed in a long white tunic, and as she watched, he dismounted and shaded his eyes with his hands to look over the valley and the surrounding slopes. Sherah thought he looked for all the world like Joseph.

She stifled a cry, jumped up, and ran up the embankment to get a better view.

"It is Joseph!" she shouted. "The tunic," she cried breathlessly, "it's the one I made for him. I would know it anywhere! But what is he doing here?"

Wildly, Sherah scrambled back down to the bushes and snatched off one of her still wet under–tunics. Enthusiastically, she flagged Joseph down just as he turned to scan her direction. He recognized her and, leaving his donkey behind, hurried toward her.

Eagerly Sherah ran to meet him, and the closer they came the more her heart pounded with happiness. The sight of him, tall and bronzed by the sun and running towards her, was overpowering and she could not hold back the jubilant tears which streamed down her face.

They met in the middle of a grass-green, flower-strewn meadow, and in the exuberance of the moment they embraced. Joseph swung Sherah off her feet and around him until she was dizzy with joy!

"Hello, little sister," Joseph cried out. Then he set her feet on the ground but held her out at arm's length and examined her face. "You are crying. Why?" he asked.

"It is nothing sad, Joseph. They are tears of gladness. I didn't know I was so lonely to see you! But why are you here? Has something happened to your father?"

Joseph slipped his arm around her shoulder. "No, father is

just fine," he assured her as they retraced his steps back towards the main thoroughfare to retrieve his peacefully grazing donkey. After they had the animal in tow, the two walked back to the brook where Sherah's clothes were drying and Joseph said, "My father is well, but he was fearful and uneasy about my brothers' well-being. He had not heard from any of you for so long that he, and all of us, were concerned for your safety."

"Especially since we camped near Shechem, right?" Sherah added. Joseph silently agreed with her.

Seeing her young friend brought back a flood of memories and she asked, "How does it go with your aunt, Leah? Is she well?"

"Yes, Leah is as round as ever, and her eyes trouble her as they always have, but she is well." Then Joseph's face grew thoughtful and he said with sadness, "Sapher, my good teacher, died shortly after you left."

"It is hard to lose someone like Sapher," Sherah reflected with her own dark experiences tempering her tone. "You miss him, don't you?"

"I will always miss him. He was much more than my teacher . . . he was a friend. . . ." Joseph shifted his gaze towards the distant hills.

"Tell me, then, of your father. You said he was well?" Sherah asked brightly. He looked over at her with affection.

"Yes," he replied quietly. "He suffers no painful illness, but he grew anxious in his love for my brothers. Shechem and the memory of the events that took place there still cripple my father's spirit, yet he loves my brothers. I'm sure he did not want to send me on such a difficult journey, but he wanted to know about his sons. So, after much inner conflict and even hesitation, he called me and asked that I would find you all and bring him word of your welfare."

They came to the clear, bubbling brook and sat down on the grassy bank. "When I reached Shechem," Joseph continued as he chewed thoughtfully on a long stalk of tender green grass, "I found evidence that large flocks had been on the plains, but I had no way of knowing where you were or what had happened. Finally a man saw me looking at the remnants of your encampment, and he told me he thought he had heard my brothers say they were going to move northward to Dothan. So here I am, and now I must see the brothers with my own eyes and then go home with the good word to my father."

For a moment or two they sat together beside the little brook, with only the twittering of birds and the slight hum of an occasional bee. Then, Sherah, unable to keep her thoughts to herself, said, "You are a most unusual and remarkable young man, dear Joseph!"

He smiled at her and protested his innocence at such a charge, but Sherah would not hear of it. She continued. "Yes, you are a remarkable man, and I'll tell you why! You could have gone home to your father and given him the news that your brothers had survived their time at Shechem and had moved to Dothan. Since that's all Jacob wanted you to do, it would have sufficed. However, you came on to Dothan today, braving the treacherous caravan road, the perils of robbers, animals, and the loneliness of journey to find your brothers and to see with your own eyes how they fare." Sherah paused and then breathed, "As I said, you are one of a kind, little brother!"

"Sherah . . ." Joseph took out the blade of grass and looking down at it he said softly, "I have not done anything one would not have done for his brother . . . and besides, I love my brothers in spite of . . ." He left the last of his sentence unspoken for he knew Sherah understood.

In an attempt to change the course of their conversation and to relieve the pain which crept up within her, Sherah pointed eastward across the valley as she said, "See? Just at the base of those cliffs." He nodded. "The few sheep you see there are the stragglers from the flocks. Your brothers are grazing them today around the last outcropping of rocks."

Sherah sent him off in the direction of his brothers and called as he waved his good-bye, "I'll see you tonight, back at our tents. You'll eat well for I will make you a good hot meal!"

Joseph flashed her his marvelous smile and, after mounting his donkey, he pulled out the slim shepherd's flute his mother had used and piped a lilting melody as he rode toward the hills.

Sherah listened until the sweet sounds faded, and then hastily she gathered her still-damp clothes from the bushes and hurried across the brook towards the encampment.

The servant girls guessed something exciting had happened by the way Sherah flew like a whirlwind into their midst. She had high color in her cheeks, her eyes were dancing with fun, and within moments of her arrival she had changed the evening meal from mere food to an extravagant feast.

"Are we having a guest tonight?" timidly ventured one of the girls.

"Oh, yes. You will see for yourself—one of the youngest sons of Jacob—and I promise you it will be the most pleasant thing that's ever happened to you!"

For the rest of the morning the servant girls giggled, gossiped, and worked very hard with Sherah to get everything accomplished.

Midday she stopped them in their tasks and told them to eat their meal of bread and leben to keep up their strength.

"Are you not eating with us?" they asked.

"No, I will just concentrate on getting the feast prepared. I want the food to be ready by sundown when the men come back." Sherah began preparing the flour mix for honey cakes and explained that she wasn't hungry. In truth, her stomach had gathered in a tight, excited iron gate, and no food could have ever passed through it.

The afternoon crawled by as slowly as a lazy lizard sunning itself; and eventually, when Sherah had run out of things to do, she told the girls she would walk down the valley to see if the brothers were coming. Twice she made the trip, and twice she had seen only the meadows, the virtually empty caravan road, but no shepherds.

The sun turned from a small golden circle, high in the western sky, into a large, brilliant orange ball before it slipped behind the horizon and still there was no sign of any men.

"Why are they so late?" Sherah began to fret. "What has kept them?" Her thoughts grew desperate as twilight began to cover the land.

Finally, after the lamb had to be taken off the roasting spit because it was overdone and drying out, and the darkness had fallen, the brothers, one by one, straggled mutely into camp.

Their mysterious silence panicked Sherah. However, the sight of Reuben carrying a familiar white linen tunic now marred and spattered with blood totally terrified the young woman.

With a quick count of the men, Sherah's anguished cry wrenched as if it were from the depths of her bowels, and she screamed, "What has happened to Joseph? Where is he? What have you done?"

Reuben's eyes silently questioned Judah as to how she knew about Joseph. Judah shrugged his shoulders, so Reuben folded the tunic and laid it beside a tent and then walked over to the animals' watering trough. He was about to plunge his head and face in the water when Sherah grabbed him and demanded an answer.

"We have done nothing to him!" he answered with the unmistakable ring of guilt in his voice.

She pointed to the tunic, her eyes filled with suspicions, and with fury said, "What about *that?*"

"It was an unforeseen accident. A wild boar, incensed by our flocks invading his territory, cornered Joseph in the rocks as he was almost to us."

Sherah found her voice and marveled sarcastically, "What is a wild boar, Reuben, that you or any of the sons of Jacob could not have beaten it off with your rods and saved Joseph's life?" She was crying now and, without waiting for an answer, she turned around and flung herself on the ravaged tunic.

The moaning sounds of sobbing would not be still within her, and as she gathered the bloodied garment to her breast her moaning increased and passed into earsplitting screams. The men stood like stone statues until Judah came to life and roughly yanked the garment from her and threw it to Levi. Sherah was still screaming so he slapped her hard across the face, snapping her head backward, and he shouted, "It is as Reuben said! We could do nothing about it. Joseph is dead. It is finished." He bent down and pulled Sherah up and propelled her across the center of the encampment to their tent.

She lost count of how many days and nights she lay on her bed. She was only vaguely aware of the servant girls as they came and went monotonously and silently. Only one thing passed from Sherah's lips; it was the words, "You could have saved him . . . you could have saved him if you wanted to . . . you could have . . . "

Then one day, when the darkness in her soul gave way to a

small light and she could see things more clearly, Sherah looked up into Judah's face as he bent over her bed. She asked perceptively, "There was no wild boar, was there? You and your murdering brothers killed Joseph, didn't you? It's like Shechem all over again, isn't it? He died at your hands, did he not?" By now she was sitting upright on her bed again, her head was pounding in pain, but she demanded answers to her penetrating questions.

He turned from her so with all her strength she reached up and grabbed his beard, pulling his face to hers. "Tell me the truth, or I will go to Jacob and tell him what I know *here*." She tapped her breast above her fiercely beating heart, and she thought the guilt on Judah's face confirmed her worst fears. Still he denied it.

"We did *not* kill him," Judah insisted.

"You are lying!" she shot back at him.

"No! It is true, we did not kill him—but neither did a boar . . . " He stumbled over the words.

"But the tunic . . . " Sherah's face showed the frustration mounting within her. She wanted so badly to believe that Joseph was alive, but she knew Judah had lied before, and now it was hard to tell fact from fiction. Once more she questioned desperately, "Then, tell me, what have you done? The truth, Judah, the truth!"

He sighed deeply, and then, looking only at the carpet, he said hesitantly, "When we saw him coming up the canyon slopes, we . . . well, some of the brothers wanted to kill him right then."

"Reuben, Levi, and Simeon, right?" Sherah glared at Judah. "No. It was not that way. Reuben was the very one who warned us that Joseph's blood should not be spilled." Judah fell silent.

"Go on!" Sherah ordered. "What happened then?"

"Nothing. We just, ah . . . we waited, talked . . . and when we saw a camel caravan of Ishmaelites, it gave us an idea, and so it was decided that we would . . . send Joseph with some caravan."

"Send Joseph? How could you *send* him?" Sherah's eyes were wide with the horror of her thoughts.

"All right," Judah raised his hands in a gesture of argument, "we did not *send* him. After the camel caravan had passed, another Ishmaelite caravan bound for Egypt came by, and . . . we sold Joseph to them."

"*What?*" Sherah exploded. She lay back on her pillows, her face drained of color, and silently she repeated Judah's words. *We sold Joseph . . .* Then aloud, "You sold him? Your brother Joseph? You sold him into bondage like a slave?"

Slowly truth persisted and dawned over her mind like a brand-new day. It made her catch her breath; and then, finally, she cried vehemently, "Not 'like a slave,' but to *be* a slave!" You sold him into slavery—to be chained, manacled, and marched or dragged down to Egypt? You considered it evil to murder your brother but found it permissible to sell him into slavery? How noble!" she spit out scornfully. Suddenly she sensed she had not been told the whole of the day's ugly truth, but what she had just learned was enough to last forever.

A small spark of defiance broke in Judah's voice as he said sharply, "Yes, we sold him. Despite Reuben's warning, one or two of my brothers might have tried to kill him, so even you should see that I showed mercy for it was I who exchanged Joseph's death penalty for a life of servitude in Egypt. At least none of us has his blood on our hands."

"What of the blood on his tunic?" she asked, without looking at him.

"We butchered a kid of goat. Then we dipped Joseph's garment into the blood. We will show it to father and let him think Joseph was eaten by an animal."

It was as if she hadn't heard Judah at all, for Sherah's next words burned through Judah's tough conscience and singed his soul. He heard her as she cried, "So you killed him after all."

Judah gave her some bitter tasting water to drink, and Sherah, wan and pale, fell back onto her pillows for what could have been days or weeks, she didn't know which.

Sherah closed her eyes and slowly put what she could together. *Soon now, Judah and his brothers will go back to their father, Jacob, with their lies and what's left of Joseph . . . they are stupid men. Judah, Reuben, and the others think that just because they sold Joseph they have ridded themselves of him, but I know better. The memories of Joseph will haunt them all their lives. As to old Jacob, this loss will break his heart, and he will die of grief. Then the blood of both father and son will be on the brothers' hearts and hands.*

I will not go back with them, for I want no part in any of this. Sherah felt the time to leave was not today, but certainly it could be tomorrow or the day after. As she wondered exactly when she would leave, she realized she needed to simply wait until she was strong enough or when the time was perfectly right—whichever came first. Finally she fell into an exhausted sleep.

During the following days, Sherah meekly and with no verbal protest, submitted herself to the care of her serving girls. They bathed, fed, and restored her body to the degree that color returned to her cheeks, and Judah suggested that she was well enough to travel.

"Travel?" Sherah repeated. She went on combing her hair.

"Yes, I said *travel*," Judah answered sharply. "We will return to Hebron, and, mind you, woman ..." Judah's eyes, dark and sinister, bore into her as he threatened, "you will never speak of Joseph to my father when we get back. Nor will you discuss any of the events of his time here—not with anyone. Do you understand me?"

"What is this?" she chided, "Are you afraid if I tell Jacob the real truth about Joseph your father's anger will destroy you and your brothers?"

Judah turned from her and clamped his lips tightly together.

Sherah finished plaiting her long braid and retorted sarcastically, "Wouldn't that be terrible! All those nice boys crushed and hurt by their mean and insensitive father!"

Judah whirled around and slapped her across the face. The impact spun her whole body across the pillows as if she had been made of straw. He reached over, pulled her up by her hands, and nearly crushing her fingers he snarled viciously, "You say one thing ... just one thing about any of this and you will never use these hands to braid your hair, cook, spin, weave ... or sew another coat of many colors!"

She listened in ashen silence and understood. His words became the catalyst for all her plans.

Ten days later, and after Judah's preparations for the journey were in readiness, Sherah made her move. On a dark, moonless night, she slipped out of her tent. No one expected her—so slight and so spent of strength—to do anything but be a dutiful wife to Judah and return to the tents of Jacob.

They had all, however, underestimated her secret reserve. Sherah, fully aware of Judah's fearful temper and obvious threats, was powerfully motivated to leave, and when she counted up her enormous losses of recent years, she had discovered a reservoir of strength just waiting to be tapped and tried. She committed herself to leaving.

Taking only the clothes on her back, the golden needle, and the jewelry Jacob had given her, Sherah left the tents of her husband, Judah, forever and resolutely walked south towards the ruins of Shechem.

At one point along the route from Dothan, she thought she heard someone in the distance playing a simple tune on a shepherd's flute. Instantly, in a sweet but painful memory, Sherah's mind glimpsed Joseph—beautiful in his resplendent tunic, playing and riding off down the road—but she shut out the scene.

She never looked back.

BOOK
III
KHNUMET

21

Khnumet knew she had been sitting idle before her dressing table fiddling with the vast array of cosmetic pots, paint spatulas, and jars for an inordinate amount of the afternoon; but time was the one thing she had in abundance. She quelled the almost imperceptible needle prick of guilt over her nonproductive day by rationalizing that it was still mid afternoon and she needn't be anywhere until Pharaoh's birthday dinner feast at sunset.

I will be ready when the time comes, but for now . . . she sighed and glanced across her room to the deepening blue skies beyond her open doorway and plant-lined balcony.

The hottest part of the afternoon was descending upon the golden city of the pharaoh, and in this region, the eastern part of the Nile delta, everything from palace to peasant houses absorbed the sun's penetrating rays and was saturated by the heavy heat. The near-oppressive, Egyptian warmth produced a euphoric laziness, especially among those like Khnumet who were wealthy enough to "eat the bread of idleness," as her mother had once said.

The delicately flecked white-marble floor was cool beneath her feet, and a slight breeze scurried across the length of her spacious sleeping quarters, yet Potiphar's young and exotically beautiful wife was unmoved by her position, her access to Pharaoh's court, or by the material wealth which surrounded her. Khnumet was warm, bored, lonely, and desperately tired of being tired. Even though the bath, in tepid, scented water, that she had been given earlier by servants, had refreshed her body, it had done nothing to invigorate her soul.

Once she had heard someone at the temple say, "Boredom and failure give birth to fatigue." Out loud she said, "I have both. No wonder I am always tired. At least the dinner tonight at the palace will be a diversion."

Daily, now, she was having to deal with an ever-gnawing sensation deep within her being over her lost sense of purpose. Once, Khnumet remembered, she had eagerly looked forward to each new day, especially the days she spent serving in the temple. But since her marriage forced her to retire from the temple duties, the burgeoning monotony of life began to close in on her. Khnumet felt a real stab of guilt as she realized that there she sat, in the midst of the luxurious elegance of her bedroom, feeling sorry for herself.

What's the matter with me? she wondered. *Here I am—the highly favored, much-pampered wife of an Egyptian official— and I'm drowning in a pool of self-pity.*

The magnificent villa she shared with Potiphar was grander and larger than any house she had lived in as a child. The social life they enjoyed in Pharaoh's court was a powerful, heady experience. Khnumet looked at the intricately carved wooden couch piled high with cushions which served as her bed, the chairs with their ivory inlaid designs, and the glorious paintings which covered the walls. *I must be the most ungrateful woman in the world ... why is not all this enough?* she pondered as she studied her reflection in the polished-bronze hand mirror. Then without answering herself, she put down the mirror and rang a small gold bell.

In moments a dainty, fragile-appearing servant girl stepped into the room as if it were from nowhere.

"Zeneb, has the master returned home?"

"Not yet," the girl answered, appropriately lowering her eyes.

Khnumet hid her disappointment and issued crisply, "I'd like you to fetch my braided wig from the wig stylist. It should be finished by now; and if it is, I shall wear it to the dinner tonight."

Zeneb bowed quickly and murmured, "Yes, mistress." She moved silently out of the bedchamber.

Khnumet dabbed her slim paint spatula into one of the four kohl tubes before her. The narrow tubes were drilled and spaced into the back of a small sculptured limestone hippopotamus. Carefully she applied the black kohl around her left eye and was skillful enough to leave no smudges. She finished the tracings on both eyes and returned the spatula to the hippopotamus. The expensive cosmetic pot had been a wedding gift from Pharaoh's wife, Makara, and though Khnumet had seen it every day for three years it always offered her a tiny moment of pleasure.

The young woman traced her finger around the fat, smooth sides of the animal and down its short, stubby legs. The gift never failed to stir her memories, and she loved the fairy-tale magic of her first meeting with Makara.

She let her mind stay in the rooms of her past. She recalled that she had been ten summers old before she could convince her mother to let her join the temple dancers. Finally, her mother had reluctantly agreed. To her overwhelming joy, Khnumet had been dedicated to the service of the goddess Hathor and had taken her vows of servitude.

All the gods seemed to join forces as they smiled down on Khnumet that summer. She was convinced she had the favor of the gods when Amset, the most gifted priestess of the temple and the most undisputed mistress of the dance, decided that she and five other girls showed promise. Amset, to Khnumet's everlasting gratitude, became their teacher.

After only a few weeks, Khnumet reflected, *the great Amset stood before our group and planted the new seeds of ambition in all our hearts.* Amset had declared bluntly: "All my students show a desire to serve Hathor well, and many of you possess the potential to be the finest dancers in the temple. But there is one here," she had waved her thin boney arm gracefully but ambiguously over their heads, "who excells even now!" Khnumet remembered looking at the girl next to her, and both girls had wordlessly wondered which hopeful student Amset had spoken of.

Then, with a sage's wisdom, the teacher had stated, "I'll not tell you who the girl is so that *all* of you will work hard to be that special one."

There had been a funny kind of fluttering in Khnumet's heart that day, and it had returned a few weeks later when she accidently overheard the priestess talking to someone in a small chamber off a temple hallway.

"I have one student who is a rare find," Amset was reporting, "and she has a great future in store for her." The young girl's heart pounded like the temple's drums, and the sound increased its tempo when she heard Amset finish with, "Her name is Khnumet, and though she's young, she moves with the beauty and agility of a supple gazelle."

Two years later, when nature had added the curving softness of full breasts to Khnumet's straight figure and after Amset had fine-tuned her natural dancing ability, the girl had been called out of class. Amset had ushered her outside to a small courtyard. There, beside a long pool covered with lotus blossoms, Khnumet stood face-to-face with a serenely beautiful woman.

Instantly Khnumet realized the vulture headdress which spread its protective wings over the woman's head could only be worn by the queen. The girl gasped, and Makara, main wife to Pharaoh, smiled down at her.

She remembered the terrible pressure she felt because of the presence of this virtuous queen. Pharaoh had several wives, but it was established by the king himself that Makara was his first choice. Khnumet remembered, as if it had happened only the day before, the words of Amset.

"Khnumet," the priestess had ordered quietly, "you will dance for our lady. Dance well, for I want the pharaoh to know that this old priestess knows her calling and still does her best for him and for the goddess Hathor."

Khnumet savored the memory of her dancing that day. She flushed with pleasure as she recalled that Makara had been graciously outspoken. Her comments, brief as they were, had removed any age or social barriers between them. The woman won Khnumet's heart when she had said decisively, "I am smitten by this girl's beauty and grace . . ." then, turning directly to Khnumet, she spoke with serious purpose sparkling in her eyes. "I will be watching your progress, little one, as well as Amset's." That moment brought the beginning of their friendship.

And watch me she has, Khnumet breathed to herself. She looked about her spacious room and marveled because even her marriage to such a rich and famous official had been due to Makara's intervention.

Makara, the matchmaker, Khnumet smiled, but her face grew wistful. She recalled that when she had reached her eighteenth summer the pharaoh, prodded by the enthusiasm of his wife, had called the highest military officer of the royal court, named Potiphar, and had "suggested" a marriage between the Egyptian captain and a young temple dancer named Khnumet.

She smoothed the green malachite on her upper eyelids, and all the green flecks in her hazel-brown eyes took on a glow. When she was satisfied that her eyes and well-tweezed brows were all they should be, she dipped her finger in the ivory shell dish of ochre and touched her high cheek bones with its red tint.

Zeneb coughed discreetly, and Khnumet bade her enter. "Ah, they have done a good thing with my wig," Khnumet responded pleasantly as she examined the intricately braided hairpiece. Expertly the servant coiled her mistress's black, shiny hair into a low, flat bun at the nape of her heck, secured it with pins, and began carefully adjusting the wig on Khnumet's head.

With her hand mirror, Khnumet surveyed the final outcome and was about to send the girl for her dinner gown when a disturbance down in the street below erupted and could not be ignored.

Khnumet crossed the floor quickly and from behind some small potted palms on her balcony, she looked down on a curious scene.

"Zeneb," she called, motioning for the girl to join her, "who is old Metenu bartering with?" The servant glanced down at the little man who was the chief overseer for the house of Potiphar and squinted her eyes to get a better look at the man he was decidedly yelling at.

"Oh!" Zeneb's giggle slipped past her mouth before she could smother it. "That's the Ishmaelite camel merchant."

By focusing her attention on the man, Khnumet could understand why Zeneb had been amused. The merchant's face was small, round, and deeply etched with lines of age. His skin was bronzed by the desert sun, and Khnumet thought he looked like an old leather-faced monkey. His wispy beard, almost nonexistent, moved up and down as he agitatedly argued. Khnumet found herself enjoying the sport of eavesdropping.

"Does he have a name?" Khnumet smiled.

"Yes. But I'm not sure what it is. I remember him because of his face and his haggling with Metenu over prices."

"We buy camels from him?" Khnumet asked surprised.

"No. But he has come a long way, and always in his travels he picks up other wares for sale. Today it must be the prisoners." Zeneb pointed down behind the trader.

Khnumet moved one of the plants to the side and stepped further out on the balcony to get a better look.

Metenu and the merchant were heatedly disagreeing about the price of something. The ancient Metenu seemed to be holding his ground and shouting *"No!"* every moment or two.

The merchant kept acting out his feelings, gesturing with his hands and shrugging his shoulders in disgust.

Across the road two men sat on their donkeys, apparently waiting for the merchant. They held the reins of a third donkey. Close behind them stood four rather bedraggled men. They were lined up along the wall across the narrow roadway and squatted wearily together. Each of their wrists was manacled with a thick iron cuff, and they were held together by a long, connecting chain.

"Come!" Khnumet ordered. "I want to get closer so I can hear what is going on."

The mistress and the servant slipped down a back stairway and half ran, half walked out of the house and into the tree-lined courtyard. They stopped just inside of the outer walls, and by crouching behind some blossoming henna bushes, they were hidden enough to be unseen but close enough to watch and hear without being detected.

Metenu was shouting, "Asher, you thief! I am not going to pay sixty rings of silver for that Hebrew. I don't care how strong he looks."

"But he cost me a fortune!" Asher whined as if he were in severe pain.

Khnumet whispered to Zeneb, "Metenu is buying that big slave over there?"

"I think so," the girl nodded in reply.

Khnumet wondered why their household manager did not go to the regular slave block near the temple as everyone else did.

"Does Metenu get all our servants and slaves in this manner? Did you come to our house this way?"

The girl smiled and answered quickly, "No. Metenu usually goes to the slave market, but when this merchant has something special he comes here to show Metenu. I think they are old friends.

"As to me ... I came to this household because my brother was a soldier in Master Potiphar's regiment a number of years ago. When the enemy killed my brother in a northern battle, the master himself came to tell us of his death. There was only my mother's sister and I left of our family, and the gracious master brought us that day to work for him here. My aunt died within a few moons, but I have remained."

Khnumet wanted to hear more from the girl, and she felt ashamed that she had been with the girl daily for three years and had never encouraged the servant to talk. She sensed they might have a limited but loyal friendship, if she had allowed it. Khnumet made up her mind to do some cultivating in that line, but for now she put her finger to her lips and cautioned the girl to be quiet.

The merchant was saying, with an apologetic tone, "But Metenu, my old friend, how can I sell him to you for less than sixty when I paid fifty for him? I would make no profit at all. Am I in business or not?"

"You paid fifty silver rings for just one of them?" Metenu pulled back and gave Asher his most skeptical look.

Then Khnumet was taken back in surprise when out of the corner of her eyes, she saw the largest slave shift his weight as if to get Metenu's attention. The slave gave a slight but definite nod of his head to the left and right. When he saw a flicker of recognition, the slave purposely glared at Metenu.

The old man caught on quickly and said to Asher, "You paid more like thirty for him, didn't you?"

Khnumet watched the slave, and once more, before the merchant could answer, the slave shook his head to the left and back slowly to the right.

Metenu took the neck folds of Asher's tunic and said, "My sly old fox, you paid only twenty silver rings for him, did you not?"

Again Khnumet saw the slave nod and this time his affirmation was done by a slight lifting of his head. There was also a suggestion of a twinkle in his unusual, blue eyes.

Asher was rendered speechless for a moment and then he said, "You win, Metenu. I'll sell him for thirty pieces of silver, but I only do that because I like you . . . not to make any profit."

"No, Asher. I shall pay forty pieces of silver for that one," he pointed to the largest of the slaves, "and that way you will have doubled your profit, and we will remain friends."

The two men embraced, Metenu counted out the silver, and Asher had one of his hired men take off the chains around the wrist of the tall slave at the end of the line of men.

When the transaction was consummated and Asher and his company of men gone, Metenu stood, his hands on his hips, and looked into the face of the heavily bearded and filthy, dirty slave. Khnumet heard him demand, "Now, tell me your name and where you come from."

The young man rubbed and held his wrist where the iron cuff had cut and bruised it.

"I am the son of Jacob," he replied softly. "My name is Joseph, and my father's tents are pitched in Canaan in the valley called Hebron."

"You are lying, and I will have you flogged for it!" Metenu exploded.

"My lord . . ." the slave was startled by the accusation, but he quickly said, "I am not given to lying. I have spoken the truth."

The old man then hissed suspiciously through his teeth, "Then explain this riddle to me and watch your tongue for I am an old man, but everything in here," he tapped his forehead, "is bright and new. Now, tell me how a Hebrew from Hebron was sold to Asher in the upper regions of Canaan, a far distance from the tents of his father, and how this Hebrew understands and speaks our Egyptian language effortlessly!"

All of Khnumet's senses were pulsating with excitement. She had found a new game, a diversion, and suddenly she was not content to hide in the bushes. She wanted to be a part of it.

She straightened up, left Zeneb, and walked out over to the paved-stone entrance way. Both men instantly fell silent. Metenu bowed low and ordered the slave to follow suit.

"I'd like to hear this Hebrew's answer," she said cooly. "We may have a spy here, Metenu, or perhaps this man is the first well-planned step in a conspiracy against our king." Metenu, his eyes widened in the horror of such a thought, silently agreed.

The slave stood transfixed and as silent as a statue. His eyes fastened themselves on Khnumet, and it was as though no one else were present. He was filled with the sight of her.

Metenu said sharply, "Answer my lady!"

Still the slave stared wordlessly.

The old servant, not used to his orders being ignored, slammed the side edge of his palm down on the slave's bloodied wrist. The action commanded and received the slave's immediate attention.

Khnumet was impressed that he had not cried out. *This slave is very different,* she thought.

"Forgive me," he said to both Khnumet and Metenu. "I had not meant to stare." Then, again, in his low, soft-spoken voice, he began to explain. "My father sent me on a mission to find my brothers and their flocks. I was to see to their safety and then report their state of well-being. I finally located my brothers in Dothan . . ." He paused and, though his face was streaked with perspiration and dirt and his beard was clotted and matted with sand, both Metenu and Khnumet could see he was genuinely pained and hesitant to go on.

Metenu urged, "Then what? You found your brothers. Asher has told me about the cities on the caravan route, so I know Dothan is one of them, but how did you get sold to the trader Asher?"

"I fear I am not in good standing with my brothers . . ." Again his words left him.

"Your *brothers* sold you for twenty pieces of silver to Asher?" Khnumet asked, appalled by the enormity of the idea.

Slowly and solemnly he nodded his head and said softly, "Do not ask me why for I honestly do not know the reasons for their actions."

Both Khnumet and Metenu accepted his words because they both had enough experience at lying to know the truth when it rang loudly and clearly around them.

Metenu said with hesitation and a slight bit of awe, "But when Asher spoke to me in Egyptian, you alone of the slaves understood our conversation. You told me by nodding your head how much Asher paid for you. Now you stand before me, and I do not understand how you, a Hebrew, can speak our language without showing hardly a trace of foreign accent?"

The slave smiled, and Khnumet was suddenly shocked at how very handsome he was. Even though he was dirty, scratched, bruised, and covered only with a tattered waist cloth, she was strangely attracted to him. He was still smiling when he answered, "You, my lady, called me a spy. I am not that. I am a scribe. I have been taught and tutored by the best of scribes. He was called Sapher, and I not only speak and understand your language, I can count and write it."

Everything he said and the manner in which he said it simply took their breaths away. First, he spoke as their equal. He did not merely answer the question as a slave or servant was required; but, rather, in the hospitable manner one uses with friends and kin. And secondly, Khnumet marveled, he was more highly educated than she and Metenu's whole staff lumped together.

"Metenu," Khnumet said with directness, "you have made a good purchase here. I shall tell the master about your astute judgment of character."

The old servant beamed under the light of his mistress's praise.

"Now, before you assign him any work," she continued with authority, "clean him up and tend to his wounds." Then, looking a little closer at Joseph, she asked, "How did you manage to get all those cuts, those welts, and bruises?" Some of the wounds oozed a yellow pus; and as she saw that, Khnumet asked Metenu, "Does Asher take the whip to his slaves?"

"No. Asher treated us fairly," Joseph answered before the old man could speak.

"He would whip his camels, but not his human cargo for fear it would lower his profit," Metenu offered with a sparkle of humor in his eyes.

"Then how . . . ?" Khnumet asked again pointing to the ugliest of his wounds.

"I fell into . . . ah, it was a dry water cistern. I fell . . ."

Khnumet sensed he was not telling her the whole story, and she had the feeling he was being loyal to someone by his reticence. *Perhaps his brothers*, she thought. *Sometimes the love of one brother towards another is steadfast, no matter what test their love is put to.*

"I want to see you in a few days, Joseph. I have a few questions for you," Khnumet said, quietly thinking he would be a welcome diversion for her.

It was his dismissal, and Metenu pointed the way to the servant's quarters.

Khnumet called Zeneb, and the two women turned toward the house, but just before they reached it, Khnumet turned and issued one more directive.

"Oh, by the way, Metenu, before I see him again . . . cut his hair and shave off that ridiculous Hebrew beard. He speaks and writes Egyptian. I want him to look Egyptian as well!"

"Yes, my lady," Metenu obediently promised as Khnumet left the open courtyard and disappeared into the main entrance of the house.

22

Later that same afternoon Zeneb had just secured the gold and turquoise jeweled collar around Khnumet's neck when they both heard the rumbling sound of Potiphar's chariot and the staccato beats of Beeta's hoofs clicking on the stone street and courtyard below.

Khnumet reached her balcony in time to see the fine figure of her husband as he reined the large black horse to a stop inside the inner gates of the courtyard. He stepped wearily out of his chariot and greeted Metenu.

The white-haired man, prompt, in spite of the stiffness of his age, welcomed his master with unconcealed pleasure. Khnumet observed Metenu's silent order to another servant and watched as the boy quickly took Beeta's reins and disappeared with horse and chariot.

Vibrantly Metenu's words of greeting floated upwards. "Hail, master! I trust the gods have treated you favorably today!" Khnumet could hear the sound of the old servant's loving loyalty from where she stood. Giving the men some moments together, for whatever it was they so eagerly talked of, Khnumet lingered on the balcony; and then, dismissing Zeneb, she hurried down the staircase to the central hall.

Pharaoh and Potiphar's friendship had been established for years, and this spacious villa, protected and isolated by its tall mud-brick walls, was indeed Pharaoh's tangible statement of trust. Khnumet had never forgotten her first glimpse of what was to be her new home. It had taken her breath away for it had all seemed so wondrous. Even today it had lost none of its original grandeur. From the beginning, she had loved the pleasant cool gardens and the long narrow pool at the garden's end, fragrant with its lotus plants which floated lazily atop the water. The surrounding double row of palm and acacia trees, the blossoming plants and shrubs, the separated servant quarters, not one kitchen but two, the stables, cattle pens, grain silos, their own well, and the small but elaborately decorated chapel for private worship, had all been a marvelous eye-filling wonder to her. As Khnumet had surveyed the vast estate which was now so much a part of her life, she marveled to herself for she could never fully believe that it was she who lived here. It always seemed as if she were visiting, and that one day the time for her to leave would dawn, and she would have to go to her real house, leaving all of this.

At the foot of the stairway, Khnumet stepped down into the main reception room. The deeply carved and brightly painted columns of the central hall took on life and meaning when she glided soundlessly across the polished marble floor of the vast chamber and went willingly into Potiphar's open arms.

"You look fatigued. In fact, you look as if you fought some enemy with words instead of swords on some indoor battlefield," Khnumet observed as he held her close.

Potiphar's deep laugh penetrated the hall, and he held her out an arm's length from him as he conceded, "How apt! That is exactly how my day went."

"I'll serve that." Khnumet turned from Potipher's embrace and took the tray out of a startled serving girl's hands.

Potiphar crossed the hall and sank into the welcome comfort of a couch. From there he let his eyes rove over the unblemished beauty of his wife's face and figure as she poured some delicately spiced pomegranate juice in his silver cup. "Let this cool your throat," she said softly as she offered the goblet.

He drank almost the entire portion in one continuous swallow, and then, obviously refreshed by it, he declared thoughtfully, "I think I liked the simplicity of life much better when I was only the king's first envoy. I traveled, took care of disturbances and disputes between men in the outlying precincts, and came back with a sense of having met the problem or the enemy and having known the sweet taste of triumph. It was dangerous work at times. I was gone from home, and I was not always victorious. But at least I understood what the problems were, and I recognized the faces of the enemy. Here, issues and people are not clearly defined in black and white, but rather in shades of grey, and I find it hard to take score.

Khnumet refilled his cup and let him go on uninterrupted, as he leaned back against a couch across from her.

"Now that my duty is centered in the palace around Pharaoh, I am not as sure of things as I was once. On the plus side, I have received this incredible promotion, this house, and," winking an eye at Khnumet, he added, "a beautiful wife. On the minus side, there is the enormous burden of seeing to the pharaoh's total security—all the palace guards and the soldiers at the royal prison who serve under me. The constant responsibility is enough to make me long for the good old days when I was just an envoy or, better yet, an armor bearer in the army.

"This pressure," he rubbed his forehead and eyes with one hand and gestured with the other, "has me wondering if there is such a thing as an 'honest and decent' man left in the whole of Egypt. I am beginning to imagine that the men who appear each morning in Pharaoh's court sessions are spies, liars, assassins, or, at the very least, opportunists eager to put their hands on Pharaoh's gold. I seem to view each man with a basketful of real or imagined suspicions!" Potiphar studied his wife a moment, over the edge of his cup. "Which is going, Khnumet . . . my eyes or my mind?" he quipped, smiling broadly.

"All you need is a cool bath," Khnumet urged; and then, rising to her feet, she took Potiphar's hands in hers and gently pulled him up and off the couch. "A bath will wash away your deceptive vision, a change of clothes will brighten your outlook, and Pharaoh's birthday feast will fill your empty stomach and divert your tired mind from your serious responsibilities."

He groaned, "Oh, no! How could I have forgotten the dinner? The palace was a beehive, buzzing with preparations for tonight's feast. I worked in and around that madness all day ..." Then, looking down at her, he said almost childishly, "I don't want to go. Do we have to?"

Khnumet ignored his question, and together they left the main hall and walked up the staircase. When they reached her bedroom door, Potiphar stopped and released his arm from around her waist. He meant to leave her there and go on to his own room alone, but she shook her head no and steered him past her bedroom to his chamber next door.

Their entrance surprised Metenu in his preparations, so Khnumet explained, "Tonight I'll see to the master's bath." After a nervous glance at Potiphar, Metenu reluctantly but obediently gave Khnumet the towels and ointment jars he was holding. He was confused as to whether he should go or stay and help, but since he didn't leave, softly but distinctly, Khnumet ordered, "You may go."

Potiphar protested after the servant had closed the door behind him, "But you are all dressed ..."

"My dress is no problem," she replied as she deftly untied her waist sash and slipped the finely spun linen dress off her shoulders. It fell, and effortlessly she stepped out of the white folds lying at her feet. Just as quickly she undid the gold buckle on Potiphar's wide leather belt. He let his pleated kilt, the short skirt under it, and his belt drop to the floor, and he clutched Khnumet's hands. Carefully, and to not hurt her feelings, he said, "Please ... you know I do not want you to do this ... I cannot bear for you to see my wounds."

"I know," she whispered, "but just this once." And she kissed his cheek and led him off into the bath chamber adjacent to his bedroom.

Metenu and the other servants had filled the long but shallow mosaic-tiled pool with warm water and soothing oils. Khnumet gently pushed her mildly protesting husband toward his bath, and, as she did, she said convincingly, "There, you see. Your bath is ready, and while I know you prefer Metenu to help you, there are times when I wish you would let me."

"And this is one of those times?" he grinned.

"Absolutely."

Potiphar surrendered and sat down in the pool. He sank into

the scented water, grateful for the oil's milky white cloudiness which covered his legs and came up to his waist.

Khnumet perched on the tiled edge of the pool and poured some cleansing oils on the soft cloth.

She started with his back. As she washed the fine, almost imperceptible patterns of thin lines which ran across his broad shoulders, she wondered how many whip lashes he had endured before the lashing was called off, or before a darkness closed mercifully in on him.

"Besides the time you told me about, my lord, how many other times were you captured?" Khnumet questioned.

Potiphar roused himself from his thoughts and answered abstractly, "Oh, I don't know . . . it seems as if I have been with the military all of my life, and I've certainly been engaged in battles and conflicts with the enemy many, many times."

"But captured?" she pressed, "and this?" She ran her fingertips over the whip scars.

He reached her hand and kissed it. "I've been in the hands of the enemy several times, I guess. To me it is unimportant how many times you are captured. What counts, actually, is how many times you escape and survive." His voice was laced with a congenial thread of humor.

The two fell silent as Khnumet continued her washing, but when she finished with his back, neck, and chest and moved towards his stomach and thighs, he uttered a soft but unmistakably brittle, "No."

His wounds have closed and healed, but the scars are still festering and inflicting their pain every moment of the day, Khnumet thought to herself. She left her kneeling position, turned from him and dried her hands. Leaving him as he wished, to finish his bath in privacy, she walked into the master chamber and sat on the edge of his large, gilded couch.

Vividly Khnumet remembered how she had seen Potiphar sitting in this same place three years before on their wedding night.

She had waited what seemed like hours after their wedding feast—all bathed, perfumed, and swathed in her sheerest robe—but he never called for her. She had been sure that Zeneb had said, "When the master is ready, he will send for you," but she had paced the floor, stood quietly by the double doors listening for any sounds, and still he did not summon her.

By the time the sun's scant light was pushing over the eastern horizon, Khnumet wearily decided to take matters into her own hands. Taking a deep breath, unsure of the proper protocol, she opened the highly carved doors which connected their rooms and prepared to take the consequences for her actions. She was totally taken aback, for she could have never predicted the revelation which followed nor could she have known the sadness that would eat away her soul in the years to come.

On the edge of his couch, with his head in his hands, sat the tall and muscular commander of Pharaoh's palace guard. A quick look at the undisturbed pillows and bedding told Khnumet that he had been there on that exact spot all night.

He did not look up, even when the door hinges announced her arrival. Finally she ventured softly, "My lord?"

Potiphar slowly lifted his head and turned to her.

"You are so beautiful," he murmured, "too beautiful for me . . . too beautiful . . ."

Khnumet dropped to her knees before him. "My lord," she cried, "whatever has happened? Are you unwell? Let me call the physician . . . only pray tell me, what troubles you!"

He cupped his hands around her face and tried to talk to her, but the words seemed frozen within him. To help him, Khnumet said, "I am your wife . . . now, what is this dark demon which has come between us? Tell me, and I will fly to the priestess Amset, and we will beseech Hathor to destroy this evil thing and bless our union."

Potiphar bent over slightly and brushed her forehead with a kiss. "No god can restore what man has destroyed . . . not even your patron goddess, Hathor," he said grimly.

"Tell me," she insisted.

"I've told no one. Only Metenu and two of my soldiers know," he said wearily, and then, taking a deep breath he began haltingly.

"Ten winters ago when I was a field officer, I was outmaneuvered and outflanked by the warring tribes of the Kush people. I was separated from my unit, captured, and then taken prisoner along with two of my men.

"We expected to be killed for it is well known that the Kush rarely, if ever, take any captives. And, indeed, both the men who were with me were instantly beheaded."

"But not you?" Khnumet waited for his reply.

"I would have suffered their fate, but one of the Kush officers saw the insignia of Pharaoh's hawk on my belt and told the others that because of an old score he wanted to settle with Pharaoh, I belonged to him." Potiphar got up and slowly paced the length of his chamber. Then, continuing, he said coldly, "I don't know what he originally planned for me, but at that exact moment the officer was notified by a scout that the rest of my regiment was heading in our direction. We both knew that the oncoming unit of men severely outnumbered the pitifully few Kush, so the officer in charge made a quick but lasting decision."

Potiphar sank into a thronelike chair, stretched his long legs out before him, and said evenly, "He decided to let me live. So I was reunited with my troops and returned to my Pharaoh, but not before the swine used his dull dagger to mutilate and destroy my manhood." Bitterly Potiphar rubbed his eyes as if to wipe away the remembered horror.

Khnumet sat perfectly still on the edge of his couch. It took many moments for her to comprehend the full measure and force of his words. But before she could say anything or react in any way, Potiphar interrupted her thoughts by continuing.

"When my men reached me they knew I had been wounded, but only Peheti and Kharu knew that I had been castrated by the Kush savage. I swore the men to absolute secrecy and allowed no one but Metenu to treat me. When I was recovered enough to return to battle, I fought with the ferocity of a wild, cornered beast. I determined to personally kill as many Kush as I could find. Pharaoh and others misread my frantic murdering drive as fearless, courageous soldiering. He rewarded me with medals and advancements. How could I tell him that the great, manly warrior, Potiphar, thought to be so valiant was nothing more than a newly made eunuch with only enough passion running through his veins for revenge?" Potiphar flung out the words into the golden dawn's light which filtered through the loosely woven blind over the window.

Khnumet quickly crossed the floor between them, and standing behind him, she gently massaged his neck and shoulders. "My husband, it is all right. We will live with this . . ."

Vainly she tried to assure him, but he countered with, "No, it is not all right! It never will be. I was wrong in not telling Pharaoh. If I had, then he and Makara might not have pressed me to marry . . . you would not have been involved, and I . . ." his voice trailed off.

"But that is *not* how it all happened," Khnumet replied, controlling her voice. "Now we must go on from here." Then with sudden inspiration, which she thought must have been sent from the goddess Hathor, she announced, "If the only thing lacking in our marriage or the only thing wrong or disappointing in our lives is that we will never lie together, we are still more fortunate than many others." She came around his chair, sat on his lap, and took his chin in her hand. "My dearest, I fell in love with you the first time I saw you riding at the head of a group of your soldiers. I watched for your colors on your horse and your chariot every time Pharaoh was on parade."

Potiphar started to protest, but she covered his lips with her finger and went on. "A woman loves a man in his entirety. If he is blind, without a limb or an arm, short, tall, fat . . . it doesn't matter! If she loves him, she loves him!" Khnumet paused. "I shall love you like that . . . unconditionally."

"It will not be enough for you," he murmured.

"What did you say?" She bent closer to catch his words.

"I said I think you should take a lover," he lied. "I will put that into a written contract. You would be free to physically love someone else, that way . . ."

"No!" Khnumet shouted vehemently. "Never! I shall rot with the desire smoldering in me before I'd stoop to that. I would not humiliate you in that manner," she declared.

"Khnumet, it is a perfectly acceptable arrangement. There are certain situations in which taking a lover is allowed. Certainly my wounds make this one of those times. Besides, even Pharaoh, as much as he loves Makara, has other wives and access to many concubines. Why should you not take a lover?"

"I will never be *that* desperate, nor am I like some animal in the heat of the mating season."

He turned a deaf ear to her rationalization and said quietly, but clearly, "You are forgetting that my castration came well after I reached manhood. I have no ability now to lie with a woman, but I have a few glorious memories." He grinned, and she felt a sharp stab of jealousy. Then he continued, "All I'm trying to say is that I am realistically acquainted with the fires of desire which build and sometimes rage out of control in our loins ... even your loins," he finished gently.

"Khnumet, where are you?" His question abruptly startled her out of her memories. Potiphar stood before her, dressed and ready for Pharaoh's dinner. He held out his hand to her helping her to her feet. Then he said quietly, "You were gone, just now. What were you thinking about? You were very intent and very lost to me."

She laughed and said almost flippantly, "I was remembering how you told me to take a lover and how I vowed I'd never do such a thing. Well, my lord, you didn't believe me then, but time has proved me right!" Khnumet held up three fingers and preened, "Three years, and no lover. See!"

"So what do you want, a public statement that you were right and I was wrong?" he teased.

"That would be a start! We could work out some more materialistic compensations later," she countered.

Metenu observed the beautiful couple as they came down the stairs. They were laughing, talking, and arm in arm with each other. The old man felt himself blushing with the joy of it all.

"He looks very proud of himself," Khnumet remarked of Metenu as they walked out to the courtyard.

"Yes, he does look pleased," Potiphar agreed. "He likes to see us happy with each other, but I suspect he is equally pleased about his purchase today."

"The Hebrew slave?" Khnumet questioned.

"Yes. Several moons ago I assured Metenu of his home with us for the rest of his life, but I suggested he train or hire someone to help with his duties. I also asked him to find someone who could eventually take over. He's been searching ever since; and many times, when I have asked him how his search is going, his eyes have twinkled and he's answered, 'When I find someone as

remarkable as myself, I'll train him.' But today Metenu was genuinely excited. He says it's too early to tell, but he thinks he may
have found his replacement."

"Is that what you two talked of earlier this evening in the
courtyard?"

"Mmmm." He smiled and then said, "And it seems we have a
slave who doubles as a scribe. Have you seen him?" Potiphar
asked as he drew back the curtains of her litter and helped her in.

"Yes. I've seen him," she replied. She adjusted the folds of her
skirt, "He seems to be the answer to Metenu's prayers, and if he
is half what he claims to be, your old servant can retire from service within the year. I only hope Metenu's hopes are not too high.
You can never tell about those Hebrews."

Potiphar closed the curtains and signaled the four servants to
carry her to the palace. Then he mounted his horse and led the
way.

"All things considered, Beeta," he patted the horse's well-
brushed mane, "I am a very wealthy man."

Khnumet heard his statement, and whatever vague disen-
chantment or slight depression may have visited her earlier in the
day, passed on as easily as a lotus leaf skims the top of the River
Nile.

23

The delicious euphoria Khnumet tasted on the eve of Pharaoh's
birthday disappeared quickly. It was only a matter of days before
the sourness of boredom and frustration began to coat her tongue.
One morning a few weeks later, she ordered Metenu to fetch her
servants and litter chair. In anguished haste, she left her home
and made an unscheduled trip to the temple.

"Amset," she cried, "I am simply at my wit's end! I ache for
sleep, yet it eludes me. I am tired all the time, and I don't even
know why."

"Have you consulted your physician? Perhaps you are with
child," Amset suggested quickly.

"No!" Khnumet blurted out, "I am physically fine. There is no child." She turned her head away from Amset and changed the direction of their conversation by saying, "I heard someone once say, 'Boredom causes fatigue,' and I thought maybe if there was some work I could do here at the temple, I could change the circumstance of my life a little . . ." Her voice trailed off, and idly she played with the scarlet sash around her waist.

"It was I who said that, but I said fatigue was brought about by both boredom *and* failure," the priestess announced quietly. Then, resuming, she pierced the air with, "Besides idleness and boredom, what has failed you, my child?"

The only answer Amset heard was Khnumet's soft sounds of sobbing. The old woman put a protective arm around Khnumet's shoulders, and the two of them walked wordlessly down a shrub-lined path in the garden adjacent to the temple.

A very thoughtful Amset was the first to speak, and carefully she said, "My child, first of all I want you to know that I would like having you here in the temple again. Secondly, your dancing skills were . . . no, *are* superb. You would be an experienced teacher for the young, but just a few days ago I gave those duties to the priestess Mimut. I wish you had come to me sooner."

When they came to a narrow stone bench beside a lotus pool, they sat down, and Amset silently asked her goddess Hathor for wisdom.

Cautiously Amset finally whispered, "Perhaps I could help you if you opened your heart up to me. I am quite good at guessing and have years of experience at it, but I'd like it if you would explain why the wife of a noble and respected official like Potiphar appears to be desperately anxious to leave his house. How has this marriage failed you, and how have you failed it?" she pried.

Khnumet wiped her cheeks with her fingertips and said, without looking at Amset, "You are wise above all sages, dear teacher. Am I that obvious about my marriage, or is it just that you always could see through my masks?"

"Never mind how I know you . . . I just do," Amset replied. "Now, what troubles you so deeply, and why do you want out of this marriage?"

Khnumet's eyes followed the flight of a brown marsh hen

from one of the trees to the corner of the temple's roof above
them. She explained, with a shrug of her shoulders, "I guess I'm
like that rather confused bird." She pointed up to a marsh hen
and added, "She doesn't know what she's doing up there on that
roof. Nothing looks like her beloved river banks, and she's probably quite lost.

"The difference between that hen and me is simply that by
the time the sun has set on the west bank, she will have found her
way home. The hen will be safe and happy among the other birds
in the water reeds and papyrus stalks on the edges of the Nile
while I'll still be trying to figure out where home really is for
me." Khnumet sighed and then continued. "And, Amset, what's
worse is that there is nothing *terribly* wrong with my life, nor am
I really lost or mistreated in any way. It is just ..." she paused,
unable to go on for a moment, and then she murmured, "Oh, I
don't know *what* troubles me ... only that I *am* troubled."

Standing up suddenly, Khnumet declared, "But I promise
you, Amset, if you tell me this discontentment and boredom is
normal and I should adjust, that I am being foolish and drowning
in a pool of self-pity, then I will take your words and accept the
fate the gods have given."

"Sit down, Khnumet. Sit down," Amset ordered quietly.
When the girl recovered some of her poise and was settled beside
her, Amset took one of Khnumet's bejeweled hands and toyed
abstractly with one of the gold rings. "Now I *have* heard about a
young wife's boredom, and I understand that, but the time has
come for honest talk. I cannot help you if you give me only parts
of the story. I sense there is much more to your dissatisfaction
with life than merely boring days and sleepless nights ..."

The old woman's eyes pierced Khnumet's very soul, but
when greeted with silence she declared, "Come, come now. The
truth." Still there was no answer from Khnumet.

"Do not try to fool me or stall me with half-truths. These
white hairs have been around a long time, and even now my med-
itation with our goddess Hathor has given me some insight, so
talk to me, child." Amset's irritation began to show.

"What has Hathor said about me?" Khnumet asked with surprise.

The priestess' anger melted almost instantly and was replaced by a short burst of laughter. "Well, for one thing, Hathor has pointed out that you have been married three years, but your belly remains as flat as when you were twelve years old and first danced before me."

Khnumet turned her head away so Amset would not see how close her arrow of truth came to hitting its target.

Amset plodded on: "Actually, my dear, since you were such a favorite of mine, I have asked Hathor about you many times. I've been studying you off and on over the past three years, and I have watched the signs of dissatisfaction raise their ugly heads within you. I wondered when you would seek me out and share your hurt with me.

"But now you're here, asking me to put some purpose into your life, some activity, work, something . . . just anything to help you to escape. It *is* escape you want, is it not?" Amset took Khnumet's smooth and beautiful face in her wrinkled old hands and saw, again, the tears which welled up and spilled down the girl's lovely face.

"Yes, I want to escape," Khnumet confessed. "I swear, by all the gods, I don't know why; nor do I begin to understand it. I have everything, Amset, just everything, yet there is this void . . ."

"I see." Amset's old eyes flickered with a small spark, and she said gaily, "What you *really* need is a little Potiphar running around, or a tiny Khnumet in your arms."

The sharpness of Khnumet's vehement statement, "*No*, that's *not* the problem!" stabbed at the old priestess' heart, and for a moment Amset was caught off balance. But only for a moment. For the shrewd woman sobered instantly and penetrated Khnumet's mask by asking cooly, "Then suppose you tell me *exactly* what *is* the problem?"

Khnumet could no longer dodge the issue so she turned to Amset and said sternly, "You must promise to keep what I tell you a secret between us." The old woman nodded, and Khnumet began pouring out the events which led up to her husband's wounds, his tormented and afflicted soul, and Potiphar's despair at the loss of his manhood. Then finally she spoke to Amset about the needs which burned within her.

"Much of what I've just shared, my teacher, I've never even

voiced to myself, let alone anyone else. I have been content to live my life as faithfully and joyfully as possible. Potiphar is a special man, and I love him with all my heart. Ours is a pure love . . ." She hesitated. "It's just that once in awhile, and more so recently, I think I'd sell my soul to a demon just to have Potiphar lie with me, touch me, and satisfy my needs." She looked up to the roof corner and noted that the marsh hen was gone.

"I've never been with a man," Khnumet confessed, "so I don't know for certain, but it seems to me that some of my pain and discontentment would ease if only . . ."

"He has *never* called you to him?" Amset asked warily, "even just to be with you for a night?"

"No, never," Khnumet murmured.

"You have not thought of taking a lover?"

"No," the girl shook her head. "And I never will . . . though Potiphar suggested it and gave his permission," she added softly.

When the whole story, told in detail, was out in the open between them, Amset sat pensively contemplating the problems facing her former pupil. Slowly, after a deep sigh passed from her lips, the priestess rose, and gently taking Khnumet's arm, they walked to a secluded gate at the far end of the garden to her waiting servants and carrier.

"You must give me time to meditate and reflect on all I've heard today, my child. Then I want you to call on me two sunrises from now."

Khnumet bowed her head in grateful agreement. They reached the gate, and just as Khnumet was about to give her thanks and farewells, Amset whispered, "You know, Potiphar may have been right in advising you to take a lover."

"No!" Khnumet objected instantly, but Amset pursued the idea.

"Passionate desires such as the ones which are beginning to surge within you can start as a small spark; but at any moment, or when you least expect it, the spark can burst into a raging inferno of fire. When that happens you may be powerless to put it out, and then, mind you, child, its flames could destroy you."

Amset knew her words fell on unreceptive ears, but she instinctively began to fear for the girl's peace of mind. Quickly she added, "In the time between now and when I see you, I want you to reexamine your husband's suggestion. If you took a lover you might bear a child. I think that would please Potiphar for he probably longs for a son to carry on his name. Out of his great love for you, I think he would gladly raise and nurture a child that you bore him as if the child were his own issue. It would add a measure of manhood to his soul."

"Oh, Amset," Khnumet wearily sighed. "You don't seem to understand. I will take *no* lover, for I *want* no other man. This desire which throbs so painfully inside of me is for my husband." The tears were flowing again, and she cried into Amset's shoulder, "I do not want someone else . . . I long for Potiphar and him alone."

Amset held the weeping girl and smoothed her long dark hair. "You are right. There *are* some things I cannot understand. After all these years I am still a virgin. This priestess is one of a dying breed who chose to marry Hathor and her temple," she stated with candor, but then warmly she soothed, "Khnumet, you are still my little student, and it pains me to see you like this. I will try my best to find an alternative plan for you."

Amset took a small cloth from the folds of her tunic and wiped the khol which had smeared and streaked the girl's face with black smudges. "There!" she announced, when there were no more traces of makeup on her cheeks. "Now, I want you to go home, and come back as I have said, two mornings from now."

The priestess opened the small wooden gate, and as Khnumet crossed over the narrow street to her servants and litter, Amset called out, "It will work out, child, you'll see." Khnumet managed a wan smile and a faint wave of her hand, but aside from the slight relief she felt for the talk with Amset, things hadn't really changed. She slumped back in the carrier and pulled the curtains closed against prying eyes and was grateful for the semidarkness and the anonymity it brought.

Khnumet made the return crosstown journey unaware of distance or any passage of time. The legs of her four servants carried her from the exquisite alabaster temple, past the walls and sphinx-guarded gates of the palace, through the section of the city where the villas of noblemen lined the avenues, and finally to her own entrance gates. But, to her, the journey was made in an instant. Suddenly she was aware of the dull thud which meant her servants had lowered the litter down in her courtyard. She gathered up her dress and prepared to get out.

Someone, she could not tell who, opened the curtains; and strong hands helped her as she stepped down. The sunshine was a bright fiery contrast to the shaded interior of her litter, and since the late afternoon orange and gold rays were behind him, she shaded her eyes to see who it was.

"My lady."

Khnumet found his deep voice consoling, and taking his hand, she asked, "You are . . . ?"

"Joseph," he answered, and once more his low, quiet voice sent a chill racing down her back. Moments before she had felt herself drowning in deep and turbulent waters, only to reach out and feel strong hands pulling her up and out of murky depths into the soothing sunshine. She was almost glad she was alive.

"Joseph," she repeated, to regain her poise. "Oh, yes, I remember you."

Khnumet had not seen the slave since the day of his arrival. In truth she had secluded herself in her room for the better part of most of her days. Only this morning she had decided to see if Amset or the goddess Hathor could help, so she had ventured out from her home.

Joseph's large frame, topped by his light brown curly hair, handsome face, and majestic blue eyes, came clearly into Khnumet's vision as they stepped into the shade of the portico. *No wonder Zeneb says the household staff calls him Metenu's treasure!* she thought as she realized that on looks alone he was a treasure.

She cast a furtive glance behind her as Joseph exchanged pleasantries with the four carrier servants, and noticed that even with them he appeared to have established a deep bond of friendship. *Evidently he has won everyone's trust,* she mused. *Remarkable!* she added.

Metenu, unsure of where the lady of the house had gone, was relieved that she had returned safely, and he greeted Khnumet warmly as she came through the doorway into the main hall. As she spoke to him, Joseph unobtrusively stepped inside and closed the door behind him.

Khnumet intended to go directly to her room, but Metenu

said, "My lady, I have done as you ordered. Does it meet with your approval?"

"Does *what* meet with my approval?" she asked without any interest, but out of politeness.

"The Hebrew. His hair, beard . . . and I personally tended the wounds . . ." Metenu offered.

"Oh, yes, of course. Metenu, you have done a fine job." She crossed the main chamber and started up the steps without a backward glance.

"I hope Metenu has done a good job for I want to please my lady."

Joseph's voice stopped her mid step. Slowly she turned around to take a better look at this most uncommon slave. Instantly her memory served up a scene from Joseph's first day in their courtyard; and she remembered how even from the beginning, this was a slave who did not speak as a slave.

During the three years she had been Potiphar's lady of the house, she had accustomed herself to meek and obedient servants. She expected no opinions, judgments, or remarks, and got none. She did not abuse her servants, as it was rumored that some wealthy noblemen's wives did, but rather treated them impersonally and fairly. She asked only for truthful, if not somewhat subdued, answers to all her queries and expected prompt service. This slave, even after her very brief encounters, had overturned a whole cartful of traditional servants' behavior.

Khnumet was about to rebuke him for his outspokenness when she thought, with a slight smile on her lips, *He has not spoken out of impudence, nor has he been offensive. In fact, he is not a mindless "Yes" man, and I rather like that.* She looked over at him, standing by Metenu, and pondered, *His only crime just now was that he spoke to me, not as my slave, but as my friend and equal.*

Her thoughts surprised her, and she stood on the stairsteps feeling both silly and slightly embarrassed for no servant or slave had ever affected her like this.

She found herself not wanting to dismiss Joseph, so she said, "Your hair, now cut in the proper Egyptian manner, is . . . most becoming." She faltered a little with the compliment. Actually, she could feel her blood rising quickly within her, and she couldn't help but notice that his well-shaven face revealed a strong jaw line which was softened by a deep dimple in his chin. She had the irresistible urge to touch his face, and most shocking of all, she wanted to be alone with him. Instantly she wondered what he would say and how he would caress her in the privacy of her room.

Joseph's blue eyes, clear and penetrating, were looking directly into hers. Khnumet knew her face was flushed, and she was feeling just a little faint. She was acutely aware that this slave, in only moments, had soothed and calmed her soul; yet Joseph had also fired her passions and moved her beyond what she thought was possible.

She was in danger of losing all her poise when Metenu saved her by saying, "My lady, I have found my replacement in this one." He reached up and patted Joseph's arm and continued, "He is not only strong," he gripped Joseph's upper arm to show Khnumet the well-developed muscles, "but as you know, he speaks, writes, and reads our language." Then the old man folded his arms over his chest and said with unconcealed pride, "Above all, I believe him to be honest, and that quality is as hard to find as Pharaoh's storehouse of gold."

Khnumet recovered some of her composure and said easily, "Well, Joseph, with that kind of an endorsement from one of the best, I'm sure you'll have a brilliant career as a slave." It helped to be flippant with him for it served to hide and disguise her rush of emotions.

Joseph nodded, but as he turned to go he said, "I will serve you, the master, and Metenu, with the best I have to give, and I will work for you not because as a slave I am obliged to serve, but because my God has placed me here and I am to do His will. My life, my lady, whether slave or free man, is in the hands of the God of my forefathers." He paused and then, with Khnumet and Metenu staring at him as if they'd never heard anyone speak as he had, he continued.

"When I was a shepherd over my father's flocks, my God was with me, and I was a faithful shepherd. Now that I am here," he glanced at the large pillars which supported the roof and took in the grandeur of the main room, "God will be with me, and I know once again He will bless my efforts."

What stunned Khnumet the most was that there was no conceit in the tone of his voice, no arrogant attitude, only statements of what he believed to be fact. *What confidence,* she thought. *He believes his God is with him and he does not need to go to the temple to find him. Remarkable,* she said to herself for the second time.

Turning, Khnumet came slowly down the steps towards the two men. "Metenu, bring me some wine," she directed, "and Joseph, you stay here. I'd like to talk with you. I want to know more about a God who seems to be personally interested enough in you to join you in your slave quarters in Egypt."

Metenu soundlessly disappeared. Khnumet sat down on one of the pillow-strewn couches, motioned for Joseph to sit on the floor before her, and the first of many long conversations began.

In the days and weeks to follow they would talk about his God and hers, about his life in Canaan and her life in Egypt, about the Hebrew patriarchs and her Egyptian politics, and about his dreams and her desires. It was to be a time of stretching both the minds and souls of the two young people from vastly different worlds.

It was also the moment when depression began to lift from Khnumet's heart like the early morning mists from the Nile; and joy, as she had never known before, began to fill the air like the fragrant perfume of the water lilies.

24

Only two days later, when it was time for her to keep her appointment with the priestess Amset, Khnumet had experienced a striking metamorphosis, from a despairing caterpillar to a colorfully resplendent butterfly.

Even Potiphar noticed.

"Do you get more beautiful as each day wears on?" he questioned early the morning Khnumet was to report to Amset, as she bade him good-bye in their courtyard. "Or, are my aging eyes playing tricks on me?"

"More beautiful? Me?" she replied coyly. Her laughter tinkled and rang like the small bells in the temple. "It is only your imagination, my husband! Your mind, not your eyes, plays tricks on you."

Potiphar bent to kiss her cheek, and as he rode out the gates and onto the street, Khnumet felt the warm glow of pleasure. He had confirmed what she hoped was true: Joseph's unusual conversations with her and his apparent delight in being with her had suddenly brought on the morning's dawn after what seemed an eternity of dark nights.

Potiphar was right. I am more beautiful, but it's because of Joseph, she thought.

Just outside the temple, later that same day, Amset greeted the surprisingly jubilant young woman with raised eyebrows and, "Now what could have possibly made the difference? Khnumet, you have been gone from here only two days, and I have not been given the opportunity to offer you my best advice ... yet you look as if you are a marsh hen who is no longer lost—but found!"

"It's true, dear teacher! I am found!" Khnumet hugged the fragile old woman gently and kissed her lightly on both her leathery cheeks.

"Don't stand there glowing like that, tell me what has happened," Amset scolded. Then, cocking her head to one side and squinting her eyes a bit, the priestess said confidently, "Ah, ha! I know. You took my advice about taking a lover, and you found one so soon?"

Kknumet laughed, "No, I have not taken a lover . . . I told you . . . I've been found."

"I see. All right, I'll play your game. Who found you?" Amset asked. Her old eyes gleamed with the barest suggestion of a twinkle.

Instead of naming him, Khnumet said almost haltingly, "I've been found by a friend. He is not my lover, at least not yet . . . just my friend. But, Amset, talking with him has opened a window in my soul, and I can't believe how, in two days, he has freed me from the self-pity I was wallowing in and has turned me inside out."

"Who is this magic sorcerer who has managed to enchant you in a mere two days?" Amset asked.

"Just a friend . . . " Khnumet's voice trailed off because she could not bring herself to name Joseph. She wondered how she would ever explain being under Joseph's spell, when he was just a slave. One was not friend or lover with one's servants, *Yet he is so different*, she reasoned to herself.

Amset saved the awkwardness of the moment by saying approvingly, "It does not really matter who found you . . . lover, friend, companion . . . only that he has found you and has *obviously* been good medicine. I need no other details. Your face and your soul's spirits are dancing again, and for me, that is enough."

Relieved that she needed to give no more explanations, Khnumet said eagerly, "I must get back to my home, but I wanted to come and give you my thanks for being such a good listener the other day. You have that rare gift of listening *and* consoling at the same time. I needed that gift. Thank you for it. I have also come back today to pay my respectful gratitude to Hathor for providing my . . . friend."

Amset, her old face wreathed in smiling approval, said, "Come. I'll walk with you." She gestured towards the temple's main entrance, and the two women walked quickly into the coolness of the main hall.

Khnumet always marveled at the painted and gilded columns, the low altar, and the sun's slanting rays which came from the small openings at the top of the walls. It was a tiny jewel of a place, yet nothing was more beautiful than the golden statue of Hathor on the altar. Khnumet sank on her knees before the goddess, and Amset slipped out a side door, leaving her to handle her debt of gratitude in privacy.

Hathor, her life-sized figure covered with a long golden dress and her ornate head crown of cows' horns cupping a round sun ball, rose before Khnumet in the sunlight and shimmered with aliveness. Never had Khnumet seen the goddess in such beauty.

"Goddess of dancing and queen of all gods and goddesses," she began, "thank you for my Joseph. He is gentle, kind, and warm as the sun which caresses you now; yet he is, at the same time, strong as a lion and wise like a sage or a priest of Amun's temple. You have created him wondrously well, and I'll serve you forever for giving him to me."

A small dark thought eased its way across her mind so she said cautiously, "I do not know what the future holds for us, but I beg you to protect our beginnings . . . I fear our time together may be but a fragile moment or two, so help us to grow and blossom quickly."

When she finally left the temple and bade farewell to Amset, she promised that she would return each seventh day to pay homage to her goddess. Khnumet left a curious but pleased priestess waving her good-bye.

The trip home in her litter was a world away from the one she had taken only two days before. Now she left the curtains open and surveyed each street, each house, or statue as if she had just regained her vision. *I wonder how all this looked to Joseph the first time he saw it?* she thought.

When she arrived home she eagerly sought and found him. He was watering the soil around the onion, leek, and cucumber plants in their household garden. "Good day, Joseph," she said as she sat on the edge of a low wall which separated the vegetable garden from the flowering gardens and the lotus pool. "Tell me, what does a Hebrew from the distant land of Canaan think of our forever-sun-drenched land?"

He had not known she was there so he looked up surprised to see her sitting so close. Smiling broadly and dusting sand off his hands, he stood to greet her.

Khnumet instantly forgot every thought she ever had, much less the question she had just asked.

"My lady, this 'sun-drenched land' is quite a departure for me. I think I will always dream of going back to my father's fertile green meadows . . . to the sheep I used to tend, and to the life I used to know, but," he looked around, "I think I *really* like it here."

Joseph went back to pouring water down the rows of plants from his wooden bucket, but said over his shoulder, "My life before was vastly different. You should have seen one particularly high canyon on the side of Mount Gilead. My father pitched our tents there, and that was a part of my childhood which was very pleasant."

When he had used all the water from two large buckets, he took a short stick and began loosening and cultivating the soil.

As Khnumet sat watching his every move, she remembered how Amset had called him a magic sorcerer. *So he is!* she thought as she sat transfixed watching and listening.

"I'll tell you," he was saying as he worked, "when we floated down the Nile on that barge with Asher and the others, I could not believe my eyes! On the shores those massive structures—"

"The monuments to our dead kings." Khnumet found her voice to interrupt him.

"Yes," Joseph nodded in agreement. "They were a sight to see. Especially for this man, born a wandering Hebrew and raised in easily movable tents!"

She let him go on and wished that the sun of the day would stand still so she could listen forever to his voice.

"And you can imagine, after the green fields of my father's country, how amazed I was with Pharaoh's city. The great giant gates to the city, the seemingly endless parade of people, the massive palace, the walls lining the streets and wide avenues, the houses ... what wonders!" Joseph stopped, turned to look at Khnumet, and said dryly, "And not one single tent—anywhere!"

Khnumet laughed, and Joseph put down his digging stick, rinsed off his hands in the water standing around some plants, and came to sit, crosslegged, before her. He resumed his words without asking the customary permission to sit with her, and Khnumet was delighted.

"It was all so much to see! Someday I hope to tell my father of Egypt's grandeur. Wait till I tell him that Pharaoh's palace is guarded by rows of huge stone sphinxes. The only statues I've ever seen were some little stone idols my mother once had ... " He smiled inwardly at the memory of all the trouble those teraphim caused. To Khnumet he said, "To see those great man-faced lions and all the other statues took my breath away! It was overwhelming. I must have been a sight," Joseph shook his head and grinned. "I stood still, and my eyes were only open for staring!"

"You were still staring when you came here," Khnumet reminded him softly. "Remember? You stared at me so hard Metenu gave your left wrist a well-aimed whack."

"That's right, he did," Joseph acknowledged and rubbed his

wrist where the still visible red lines marked the edges of the manacles.

"Why did you stare at me? Had you not seen a woman before? Or was it that I was the first Egyptian woman you ever saw?" She asked the series of questions hoping that his answers would be personal—even his first declaration of his interest in her.

"I stared because . . . " his eyes met hers.

"You stared because?" Khnumet could feel her heart racing and gaining speed within her breast.

"Because . . . you are so very beautiful."

Her throat caught and constricted with joy, but her enchantment dissolved when he added, "Beautiful like I remember my mother, Rachel."

"Your mother?" she managed.

"Yes. Oh, my lady," Joseph sighed with the remembrance, "she was more beautiful than anyone in all of Canaan." Then, looking once more directly at Khnumet, he continued. "Her eyes were a little darker than yours, and her hair lighter, more reddish brown than black like yours; but when I first saw you the day I was brought here, my heart remembered how I loved her." He fell silent and cupped his chin in his hands.

"She lives in the valley of Hebron with your father and brothers?" Khnumet questioned.

"No. She died giving birth to my brother, Benjamin . . . we were traveling to Hebron. It happened in the hills just outside the city of Bethlehem. To this moment I can see it all and hear it all in my head . . . and I still grieve for her."

Khnumet dropped to her knees before him, took his hands from his face and whispered softly, "You need tell me no more. I see it is eminently painful. Joseph," she took his hands in hers and waited for his eyes to meet hers. "Joseph, I can never make up the loss of one so dear, but perhaps here in Egypt, you will find one whose love will lift the grievous weight of this loss from your soul."

He started to say something, but Khnumet put her fingers over his lips. "Hush. Say no more." Then kissing his fingertips she murmured, "I'd like to be the one. I have not offered myself to any man, but you are very special. Come to me whenever your loss or your losses," she thought of his brothers who had sold him to Asher, "become too painful. I care for you, dear Joseph—I care."

It was all she dared say for she instinctively knew that rushing him was not the way to win him. Kneeling so close to him produced an exquisite and momentous explosion within her, but she moved back from him and sat once more on the low wall.

From there Khnumet predicted, "You will not only like Egypt . . . you will learn to love it, Joseph, and it will love you. In fact, Metenu and the servants already love you." *And so do I,* she admitted silently to herself.

Khnumet wondered how long she would have to wait for his love of her to develop, but it didn't seem to matter. She would be patient, and in time he would love her.

"You have been so kind to me." Joseph's words broke into her thoughts. "Master Potiphar, Metenu, the others," he said as he waved a hand towards the house. "They have not treated me as a slave but as a friend."

"I can be more . . . to you," Khnumet announced quietly, trying to stick to her resolve about not rushing him, yet wanting him so desperately.

"More?" Joseph questioned. Then realizing the full impact of her words, he said with tenderness, "There is no need to be more, my lady. My needs are simple. My duties here are clear, and I want nothing more than to serve both you and the master well."

He rose from where he sat and suddenly they were not friends about to be lovers, but only what they had been in the beginning: mistress and slave.

All the way through the garden and back up to her room in the villa Khnumet mentally whipped herself for being so aggressive. She had been given the opportunity to open her heart graciously to Joseph, but instead she had bluntly assaulted him with words. *I spoke too soon and I said too much,* she flailed away at herself.

I will remember the lesson of today, and next time, she admonished herself, *next time I'll find the key to opening his heart, and I'll handle things very differently. He is worth waiting for, and I shall have him.*

25

It was well within Joseph's first year of serving that Metenu came to Potiphar and announced it was time for him to turn over his household duties to Joseph.

Potiphar was in complete accordance with that, so at once he ordered a private banquet, complete with ceremonies to honor the retiring Metenu and to install the remarkable Joseph as overseer.

On the night of the lavish feast the servants, dressed in their finest, were treated as guests. Their heads were anointed with perfumed cubes of fat, and they sat down to be served by hired servants and to eat and drink at tables with lotus blossoms, richly prepared meats, vegetable dishes, fruits, breads, and a generous supply of beer and wine.

Well after the festivities began, Potiphar rose to commence the ceremony.

To the hushed crowd, Potiphar made the master-of-the-house speech and traced Metenu's years of loyal service, from his beginning to his choice, now, of a successor. Eloquently and with great respect, Potiphar spoke of his gratitude to the slightly stooped, white-haired man.

Khnumet was then asked to say a few words, and she did so, but in closing she surprised everyone. With a slight nod of her head to some waiting musicians, Khnumet delighted everybody by performing an elaborate dance for Metenu. None of the servants had seen her dance before, and even Potiphar had not known of her plans. He was stunned but pleased with the graciousness of her gesture.

Khnumet finished with a low bow in front of Metenu and Joseph, and then took her place beside a beaming Potiphar amid a burst of applause and shouts of, "More, more, my lady!"

When the merriment had quieted a bit, Potiphar stood and called Metenu to the main table. The old man, leaning heavily on his walking stick, came forward. He appeared slightly embarrassed, yet he took a gruff kind of pleasure at the exciting events of the evening.

At Potiphar's urging, Metenu began to speak. His voice wavered a little, but as he got into the speech he warmed to his subject and praised Potiphar over and over again, for being the best master in all Egypt. When he sensed he was covering the same ground for the third time, Metenu finally turned from Potiphar and asked Joseph to come forward.

Khnumet was amused at the contrast between the two men. Joseph towered in height over the old man, but the bond of love was obviously thick between them.

Metenu told the audience the oft-told tale of how Asher had tried to sell Joseph for almost three times what he had paid for him, and ended by saying, "If I had known what a valuable man Joseph would turn out to be, I would have paid Asher's outrageous price!"

"You mean *I* would have paid it!" Potiphar interrupted, grinning broadly.

Demurely Metenu said, "Yes. You would have paid it, master." He hid his smile as he bowed towards Potiphar.

Then, turning to Joseph and shifting his mood, he soberly declared, "Joseph, I hereby turn over all my duties and responsibilities regarding the honorable house of my master, Potiphar, and his wife. You will serve them with constant obedience, prompt service, heartfelt honesty and with unrelenting loyalty.

"I now give you my walking stick as an official badge of your position." Metenu shoved the smooth hand carved stick into Joseph's hand, and the servants roared with approval.

"But . . ." Joseph objected, for he understood that an Egyptian, at all levels from the Pharaoh down to the peasant farmer, carried with pride his own walking stick, and to give it up was unthinkable. "I cannot accept this," Joseph protested again.

"Of course you can," Metenu shouted above the clamor. "It was my symbol of command . . . now it is yours!"

Smiling, Joseph gave in, took the stick, and warmly embraced the old man. Immediately, the music and feasting took up where it had left off.

Khnumet watched Joseph carefully. She observed that while he joined in with all the festivities, the jokes, and laughter, and even in the drinking of many mandatory beer toasts to his new position, he seemed to hold himself respectfully aloof from all of them. It was that *set-apart* quality which beguiled and intrigued Khnumet the most.

During the entertaining magician's performance, Khnumet moved over to Joseph's side of the table on the pretense of small talk, but really just to be closer to him. After she congratulated him on his work of the past, she subtly coaxed him into conversing with her by asking, "You seem somewhat subdued tonight. Are you not pleased with your new appointment?"

He flashed his magnificent smile at her, and she caught her breath with the wonder that smile always produced in her. "Oh, my lady, I am very pleased with the honor of the appointment . . . I am just unable to believe it all!"

Khnumet noticed, for just a second, that the blue of his eyes seemed to darken with a remembered memory, and then he resumed. "One moment I was not sure I would see the light of the next dawn. Then I was sold as a slave, and now . . . now, I have been given the most honored position a slave can hold. My times have always been in God's hands, and He has planned each detail; but sometimes, like now, I find it all so surprising!"

"You *are* pleased, though?" Khnumet teased.

"Of course," he replied and nodded his head.

"Tell me, Joseph, is your God always so unpredictable and full of surprises?" she questioned lightly.

"So far that's been my experience," Joseph grinned.

Over the next two years Khnumet had many occasions to remember the short exchange about Joseph's God.

Both Potiphar and Khnumet were startled, amazed, and unable to explain the incredible way Joseph overturned, expanded, and enhanced their fortunes. Success seemed to follow Joseph's every move as closely as his own shadow.

"Scribe, sorcerer, magician, poet, skilled worker . . . what is he?" Potiphar asked Khnumet, with awe edging his tone. "The animals in my stables are not smitten with sickness, and my flocks multiply as if the god of fertility has visited them. The gardens produce more vegetables, including leeks and cucumbers, than ever before; and my crops flourish by the Nile.

"Even the baking of bread, the brewing of beer, *all* take place in an orderly fashion with little or no squabbling between the servants," Potiphar whistled through his teeth. "In fact, the whole staff works in harmony as never before! It is all a wondrous mystery to me." He turned to Khnumet. "Do you realize that as good as Metenu was, Joseph is infinitely better? I have no worries here, no responsibilities. In fact, my only big administrative decision daily is what I shall eat for my evening meal! How does he do it all?"

Khnumet ignored his question for a moment and felt a flare of anger rise in her. *So, my husband, you think you have no responsibilities here except what you will choose to put into your stomach? You are wrong! What of your responsibility to me?*

He was looking at her intently and waiting for her response, and since she wanted no confrontation at that moment, she answered as casually as she could, "Perhaps Joseph has a secret arrangement with his God. He is very devoted to Him, you know."

"Yes, I've heard him speak of his 'living God'; yet he embraces our ways and traditions, while respecting our right to believe in our gods. Joseph's whole attitude seems filled with a remarkable tolerance." In a rare move, Potiphar—euphoric with the success of his household—picked Khnumet up. Easily he swung her around in the small ground-floor chamber and proclaimed, "Actually, my lovely wife, I don't care *how* Joseph does it, or *which* god he serves—only that he is here in *my* house, working for *me.*" He put her down and noticed that for once her hazel eyes were alive with flecks of gold. Still holding her, he asked with a sudden abruptness that surprised her, "Are you happy, Khnumet?"

"Yes, my lord," she answered, trying to be convincing.

"I mean *really* happy?" He tilted her chin up to study her face.

"Of course. I have everything a woman could dream of having . . . a husband, a home, a rich life . . ." Her voice failed her.

"But not *everything* . . . right?" Potiphar said suspecting his failure to lie with her was the probable cause of her obvious unhappiness.

Khnumet quickly said, "Do not pick up that basket of guilt. It is an unnecessary burden for you. I am fine. Besides, what is happiness anyway? I am loved, well taken care of, and now I have the satisfaction of seeing your household prosper beyond belief.

"Surely I should be bursting with happiness over all our good fortunes. Have not the gods brought us together and then prospered our lives with Joseph?" Khnumet left his arms and his concerned gaze to sit on a chair across the room. Then, looking absentmindedly up at the ceiling, she said, "Who knows what Joseph is, as you said, 'scribe, sorcerer,' or just an ambitious, enterprising young man. I only know that he has done small miracles with the staff.

"The Hebrew can untie every entangled knot. He can coax life back into any ailing plant or animal, and he pours his own unique healing ointments over domestic disputes as if he had been a diplomat for Pharaoh all his life."

Realizing that once more Potiphar was intently staring at her, she softened her praise with a subdued, "Joseph's aptitude for work seems to be far above the average Hebrew slave."

Khnumet leaned back in her chair, rested her head against the wall behind her and shut her eyes against any conclusions her husband might have been tempted to draw.

Inwardly her thoughts were painfully precise. She sat there outwardly composed and serene, but the words she was thinking screamed inside her brain with a deafening reality. *Joseph, Joseph, my love, why do you fail to see me? I love you with all the burning passion my heart can hold: yet, you want no part of me! Joseph, please love me . . . please.* Khnumet closed her eyes all the tighter to restrict the tears which might give her away and spill her secret for all to see.

26

In the weeks to follow, Khnumet found herself seeking Joseph out every day. She could hardly wait for the morning's light and the first stirrings of the city and house so she could be with him.

Whether Joseph was supervising the staff of slaves and servants in Potiphar's big house, or managing the activities of the master's vast agricultural ventures, or simply organizing the work

at the stables and chariot shelters, Khnumet would find him.
Once she even managed to concoct a flimsy excuse to visit the site
of Potiphar's huge mud-brick granaries just for a fleeting moment
of conversation with Joseph.

Somehow, even with her constant presence, the young servant maintained a disciplined work pace and never seemed to lose
his attitude of respect when he talked with her. She found it frustrating. Maddeningly so, especially since she had never wanted a
lover until her time with Joseph had melted her resolve.

When Khnumet could no longer deal with his polite and re-
fined behavior, she bundled up her pride, buried it somewhere
deep within her, and risked baring her soul.

She applied her makeup expertly, dressed herself in a simple
white sheat of linen, and wore a plain narrow band of gold around
her head to keep her long dark hair in place. Then, when she was
most satisfied with her looks, she went to find Joseph.

He was alone in the slaves' quarters, sitting crosslegged on the
smooth mud floor with his scribe's tools, tabulating the profits
from a recent sale of grain.

Seeing her, he laid his reed pen down and started to rise in a
formal greeting. "My lady—"

Khnumet pushed his shoulder down and sat quickly beside
him.

He was not unaware of her cool hand on his shoulder: nor of
her costly perfume which floated around him, and of her lightly
scented breath. She seemed to shimmer in beauty beside him.

"Did we make a profit?" she asked, nodding her head towards
the papyrus sheets before him.

"Yes." He finally summoned up an answer, and added, "And
by a large margin." He was relieved her presence had not removed all his mental capacities.

Khnumet reached over and put her fingers across his lips.
"We both know," she explained softly, "that I have not come to
discuss the profits and losses of the grain market."

Slowly Joseph caught the full implications of her words; and
as he did, he immediately straightened up his posture. This in-
stinctive reaction on his part forced Khnumet to tilt her head
back to see him. It was a bad decision, for now her upturned face
smote his soul with its beauty.

"Joseph," she whispered, "why do you always pull away from me . . . or straighten up, as you did just now? Are you afraid of me, or do I displease you? What is it? Am I not desirable?"

He cleared his throat and said hoarsely, "It is not any of those things, my lady. It is only that your sitting here in the servants' rooms . . . is unseemly or rather beneath your station as the lady of the house."

"Nonsense!" she said sharply. "I can *be* anywhere I choose. This is my house. Besides, I think you are uncomfortable in my presence because you do not like me."

She stuck out her lower lip and hoped her pouting would press him into contradicting her.

Instantly he said, "Oh, no! That is not true. You and Master Potiphar have shown me every kindness, and I like you. I like you all very much . . ." In the awkwardness of the moment, he twirled his pen between his fingers.

"Joseph?"

"Yes, my lady." He held the pen still.

"Am I beautiful to you?"

He bowed his head ever so slightly and said softly, "You know you are beautiful . . . you are beautiful to everyone."

"But am I beautiful to you?" Khnumet was leaning close to him, and he could see the rounded forms of her breasts through the gossamer fabric of her dress top. His mouth was dry, and he found it difficult to breathe. Not without some effort, he pulled away from her and got to his feet.

"Help me up." Khnumet held out her hand to him. She grasped it, and in one motion she was suddenly where she had wanted to be for as long as she had known him. Best of all, Joseph's full head of hair, his impressive broad shoulders, and his well-formed body felt as sensual as she had dreamed they would be.

"Joseph, my love, hold me . . . and, just this once . . . lie with me." Khnumet tugged at him, urging him towards the doorway.

He broke her grip on him by the only tactic he knew and once again straightened up to his fullest height. He could breathe again, but his mind was writhing with tumultuous thoughts.

"Joseph," she was saying, "I need you. Surely when you have helped Potiphar with his bath, you have noticed his wounds . . .

can you not see the hopelessness of my situation?" Khnumet realized her pleading was almost to the point of begging, but she had fought the war of frustration for so long she was desperate for victory.

Joseph stood stone-still for some moments, and then gently he put both his hands on her shoulders and held her almost a full arm's length away from him. Looking down into her dark, troubled eyes, he said softly, "My lady, you are asking me to break a very special human trust. My master, Potiphar, has entrusted his entire household to me. He himself has no more authority here than I do. He has withheld nothing from me . . . nothing except you, Khnumet, and you are his wife."

Her heart heard only that he used her name for the first time, and her mind hung on to a thread of hope. Unbidden tears filled her eyes.

"Please don't cry or be hurt, my lady," he continued, using her formal title again. "Besides breaking a human trust to a man, I would be breaking a heavenly trust with God . . .

"Long ago God gave me dreams, plans, all designed by Him. My mother called them high and holy dreams. I do not know when they will come to fulfillment, or how, but I must not betray those dreams."

Khnumet's tears were drying up with the small winds of disgust. She listened as he summed up his argument by saying, "But most of all, I cannot sleep with you for I was taught by my father Jacob, that to lie with a woman outside the bonds of marriage is a moral sin. How could I be a part of a wicked thing like that when it would be a great sin against God?" He finished, hoping his question would show her the logic of his reasoning.

Instantly she retorted, "I can do away with your arguments and simple objections as easily as the river rises every year. In the first place, my husband has no objections to my taking a lover, so you would not be breaking anyone's trust. Are you blind? Secondly, if you please me, it will only enhance your favor in this household." Then, because his rejection was taking large bites out of her soul, she flung at him, "And thirdly, try not to forget, Joseph, I can enhance or annihilate your high and holy dreams of grandeur any moment I choose to."

Hot angry tears returned and spilled down her cheeks so she

turned to leave. However, at the doorway she spit back at him sarcastically, "And by the way, as to your 'great' sin against God ... why would your God call what is so pleasurable a sin? I see no sin in loving and my goddess Hathor would not either. Besides, we could have kept it a secret from God because *I* certainly never would have told on you!" She left him standing there, bewildered, confused, and full of fragmented emotions.

I will never speak to him again, she vowed to herself as she strode angrily up the stairs to her chamber. But even as she said the words to herself she knew she was only putting up a false wall of defense.

Khnumet's studied avoidance of Joseph lasted two days.

Quietly her emotions, painful with needs, could bear the separation no longer, and she went back to Joseph. Her pride was sucked out of her like a leaf which vanishes in a swirling whirlpool, and her shattered soul was a deep well of vulnerability.

Day after day she built her very existence around meeting Joseph. She accosted him in the gardens and the hallways of the house. She waited in the upper chambers as he instructed the servants about their duties, and then stepped out—refusing to let him pass. Other times she let him go only after positioning her slim form against him.

Khnumet tried every method she had ever heard of, and even some she invented on her own, but the long-hoped-for seduction of Joseph failed to materialize.

Late one night when sleep evaded her, she slipped out of bed and onto her balcony. As she looked up to the black velvet sky above she thought, *If only I could get him alone in the right place ... like here in my room.* She left her balcony and surveyed her bedchamber. "The festival of Amun ... that's it!" she cried. Khnumet smiled to herself and felt her cheeks warm with anticipation.

Ten days later, the morning of the festival, Potiphar woke her early. "Khnumet," he shook her shoulder gently. "I must be leaving. Pharaoh wants me at the palace at sunup. Which temple will you be attending today?"

With pretended sleepiness, Khnumet yawned and deliberately slurred her words, "I haven't decided yet, but probably the palace temple ... I don't know."

"Well, I just wanted to give you my farewells. I shall be very late tonight. Please see that Joseph goes with you if you venture into the crowds. There is much celebrating going on, and Amun's fanatic subjects are bound to be a bunch of inebriated idiots. Be careful."

"I will, my lord." Khnumet reached up and kissed him.

She watched Potiphar's chariot leave from her balcony, and when he turned the last corner and was lost to her view, she threw a robe around herself and went directly to the servants' quarters.

"Joseph," she said in a crisp, formal tone, "you will give the servants and slaves a day free from their tasks. Please tell them they are to go out and enjoy the festival of the god Amun. They need not return until sunset. Tell them the master of the house wishes them a pleasant time."

He bowed and was about to leave when she added, "The master has also asked that you remain here with me for my protection. I may pay my respects to Amun at the palace temple this afternoon and, if I do, you are to accompany me."

"Yes, my lady." His obedience pleased her beyond belief, and her mind played with all the "Yes, my lady"s she would hear that day.

The whole morning dragged for Khnumet as if many moons had come and gone. Servants, thrilled with their day off, were nonetheless unprepared to go out, and the morning melted into afternoon until finally most of them went laughing and chattering out the gates.

"Are you sure you do not want me to stay, my lady?" Zeneb asked cautiously, almost afraid she'd have to remain.

"No, absolutely not. You go and enjoy what's left of the day. You deserve a rest from your duties. I insist—no, I order you to go." The surprised girl's mouth fell open slightly, but Khnumet's smile reassured her and with a quick nod of her head Zeneb was gone, eager to be away before her unpredictable mistress would change her mind.

It was mid afternoon before the entire staff finally left. Khnumet had counted and kept track so she would know when she and Joseph would be totally alone.

Finally, amused that her hand trembled rather violently, she

managed to ring her servants' bell. Within moments Joseph stood
in the doorway of her bed chamber.

"I forgot to have Zeneb draw my bath for me, Joseph. Would
you see to it?" Her heart was pounding and accelerating wildly,
but outwardly she was a picture of composure, and she took pride
in her secret accomplishment.

While he filled the tiled pool adjacent to her bedroom, she sat
at her cosmetic table combing and recombing her long silken
tresses. She pretended not to notice his progress, but when she
had calculated that he would be bringing the last of the buckets of
water, she removed the looped golden earrings from her ears,
stepped out of her robe and waited for him just inside the door of
her bath chamber.

As he poured the last water into the pool, she stepped up behind him and said, "Joseph, you have some other duties to attend
to today, and they are here with me." He whirled around to face
her and the bucket clattered against the marble floor. He stood
frozen, as it were, in time and space.

Khnumet—naked and with a husky softness in her voice—put
her arms around his neck and pressed her heavily scented, warm
body into his.

"Come, bathe with me . . . and do not repeat all those foolish
excuses you gave me earlier." Khnumet smiled at him.

"My lady, they were not foolish excuses. This . . . this cannot
be . . ." he said haltingly, trying to look above her head.

"Of course it can," she countered. "I'm commanding you, my
love." She stood on her tiptoes and kissed the edges of his mouth.
Feeling his lips tighten, and guessing that he was about to draw
away, she clung all the tighter to him.

"Don't resist me, Joseph. Give in. There is no one here . . .
just us . . . and the festival was made for loving."

She teased, "You see, I am desirous after all, am I not? You
do want me, don't you, Joseph?"

"My lady . . ." He was embarrassed, for what she guessed was
true.

"Don't call me 'My lady' . . . my name is Khnumet." She
kissed his neck and moved her body sensuously against his.

Finally, as if her words had awakened him from a shocking
dream, Joseph found himself. He took her face in his hands and

said with unprecedented authority, "No, my lady, your name is not Khnumet . . . it's Shechem."

"Shechem?" she repeated. "And who, might I ask, is Shechem?"

He was holding her face tightly and through his own rigidly clenched jaw he said, "Shechem is not a person. It is a place. An evil place. And long ago I was told that if the day ever came when I faced my Shechem, I was to flee from the evil of it!"

Before she could respond and before she could comprehend his meaning, he dropped his hands from her face and turned toward the doorway.

Seeing the back of Joseph's broad shoulders and now fully realizing he was running from her, never to lie with her, raised a volcanic fury within her. His unalterable rejection of her hammered violently against her senses.

Instantly she lunged forward, grabbed Joseph's short tunic at the neck, and vehemently pulled it straight down, ripping it in half. As he continued moving away, the torn part stayed firmly in her hand and glided smoothly out of his wide leather belt.

Joseph never looked back and Khnumet could never recall just how long she had stood there—alone, walled in by the seclusion of shock and stiffly holding one-half of his garment in her outstretched hand.

27

The returning servants heard her screams before they reached the inner courtyard.

Admidst cries of "What has happened?"; "Where is Joseph?"; and "Who has died?" Zeneb pushed through the confused throng of servants milling about the courtyard and ran up the stairs to her mistress's bedroom. The dreadful wailing grew louder.

The servant girl found Khnumet standing on the balcony. She was ranting and raving about "that Hebrew" and waving a torn piece of cloth at the servants below.

"My husband approved Metenu's decision to bring this Hebrew into our house, but he came only to insult us! Egyptian honor has been defamed," she shouted. Khnumet's hair was tangled, and one shoulder strap of her dress was torn off.

"My lady, my lady . . . " Zeneb put her arm around Khnumet and guided her into the chamber. "What happened, my lady?" She cried in alarm as she led Khnumet to her couch.

"He tried to rape me," Khnumet sobbed into her pillows.

"Who? Who would do such a thing?" Zeneb knew that Joseph was always referred to as the Hebrew slave, but she was also confident that her mistress had meant *anybody* but Joseph.

"Who?" Khnumet raised up on one arm. Her black kohl makeup had smeared grotesquely over her face, but she said clearly to Zeneb, "The only one who was here. Joseph, of course!"

"Joseph?" Zeneb stared at Khnumet—seeing her, but not comprehending.

"Do you think I would lie, girl?" Khnumet asked sharply. Then, as if to prove her claim, she held up the torn tunic and said, "See, I fought him off, and this is part of his garment. He heard you and the others were coming back from the festival and he vanished . . . leaving this."

Zeneb stood speechless as her mistress got up off her couch. Trying to smooth her hair and wipe her face, Khnumet walked to her waiting bath and said bitterly, "I will have his life for this humiliating, degrading day. Mark my vow, Zeneb, he will die for what he tried to do."

"Well?" Khnumet looked back at the frightened servant. "Will you stand there all night? Help me bathe!"

Khnumet was still sitting in her bath water, her eyes red and swollen from weeping, when Potiphar rushed breathlessly into her chamber.

Pulling her up out of the pool, he wrapped her in a large drying sheet, dismissed Zeneb and cried out, "The servants came to the palace and said you had been attacked. What has happened?"

"It's true. I was attacked. The Hebrew slave to whom you have given so much authority . . . tried to take over everything you possess, including me." She was crying into his shoulder.

"Hebrew slave? You mean Joseph?" He lifted her chin so he could see her face.

"Yes, Joseph. He tried to rape me." Her voice was flat and colorless. "It was only by my hitting him and by my screams that I was spared. He fled just as the servants returned home."

Potiphar acted as if he had not heard. He merely got up, dipped a small towel into her bath water and wiped the perspiration and grime off his face. He took his time, and when he finished he sat facing her on the edge of the tiled pool. Finally, after a deep sigh, he asked, with a heaviness in his throat, "Khnumet, you are sure it was Joseph?"

"Absolutely!" she said, flaring with defiance. "Look!" She held up the piece of cloth. "It's his! It was torn when I fought with him. He left it here in his haste to get away!"

She threw the piece to him, and Potiphar sat quietly for many moments. He bowed his head as if he were examining the garment, but Khnumet could see his eyes were closed and tears ran down his face. She was shaken a bit for she had seen him weep only once before, and she began to panic as she wondered if his tears were a sign that he sided with Joseph instead of with her.

"Do your tears mean you will be lenient with this slave who shamed me so?" she asked as cooly as she could.

"Lenient? No! I am weeping and venting my anger. Do not fear. He will be punished."

"For my honor, will he be punished in the severest of terms?"

Potiphar knew she meant execution, and while he had supervised and observed many a man's death, for it was a part of his career as a soldier, still he was unprepared to think of demanding Joseph's head on the executioner's pole.

Potiphar began to pace the room, and with each forward stride his frustration mounted angrily within him.

"I am torn!" he blurted out. "Torn by my love for you, Joseph's attempt to violate you, and my ... [he almost said love] my feelings for Joseph."

"Your feelings for Joseph?" Khnumet almost screamed. "What do you owe him? I am your wife. He is only your slave. What about your love for me? Do I not count?

"I want his head, and you have the right and the legal power to do just that! Never had I made any demands on you, my noble husband, but now I am." Then, wild-eyed, she added frantically, "*Destroy* Joseph!"

He rose and left her, and Khnumet felt her knees grow weak for she knew he would seek out Joseph. For a few moments her heart raced with panic for she realized Potiphar would give Joseph a fair chance to tell his side of the story. But, with a confident toss of her head, she said to herself, *It's my word as a wife, against his word as a slave,* and so she contented herself to await word of Potiphar's decision.

She waited for days.

Potiphar avoided her, the servants remained mute, shunning their usual gossip trysts, and Joseph vanished out of the household.

Late one night when she could stand it no more, she burst through the doors which connected their rooms, and asked as calmly as she could, "What have you decided about Joseph, my lord?"

Potiphar was lying on his bed, awake. In response to her question he deliberately rubbed his eyes and wished the dreaded confrontation would go away. When he saw an answer was inevitable, he sat up, propped the pillows against the wall and leaned back against them to face the issue.

Guardedly he said, "I do not deny that what happened to you was a hideous thing, Khnumet. Attempted rape is a crime of great magnitude and ..." he swallowed and then resumed firmly, "When you told me about Joseph's attempt, my wrath toward him knew no bounds."

Potiphar got up, wrapped one of the blankets around his waist, and stood looking aimlessly at the night from his balcony. Khnumet followed him out onto his balcony, leaned against the wooden railing, and waited.

"However," Potiphar looked skyward, "when I confronted Joseph with the facts as I had heard them from you—"

"He told you a pack of lies!" Khnumet broke in loudly.

"No. As a matter of fact, Joseph said nothing in his defense ... nothing at all. Even the servants ... nothing. They would say nothing about Joseph or that day." Potiphar continued to gaze at the star-filled heavens. Then in a voice calm but iced with authority, he declared quietly, "So I made the decision to spare his life." Khnumet gasped. "And I have placed him in Pharaoh's prison. He will be bound in chains for the rest of his natural life."

Without waiting for her comments or remarks, Potiphar moved off the balcony, replaced the blanket on his bed and said into the darkness, "Now that I have told you of my decision, I want it to be understood . . . I will never discuss Joseph with you again . . . ever. He is a closed issue . . . a sealed tomb."

Potiphar's words were almost prophetic concerning their own lives together because his decision never to discuss Joseph that night marked the end of all their discussion about everything.

For the next two years, Khnumet rarely saw her husband, much less talked with him. She made the mandatory appearances at Pharaoh's court dinners, but because of the gauntness of her face, and the dark circles she was unable to disguise under her eyes, Khnumet was the focal point of the court's gossips and rumor mongers. Questions about her mind's health abounded.

During those two years, Zeneb tended her mistress to the best of her ability, but Khnumet's moods soared and descended so swiftly that it was difficult, if not impossible, to make sense of her lady's ways.

The girl had placed her own small couch in the corner of Khnumet's bed chamber so she could be close to her mistress during the night; and so it was that one night Zeneb was almost asleep when, in the semidarkness, she saw that her mistress was dressed and had wrapped herself in a long cloak.

"My lady," Zeneb whispered, "where are you going? It is late. You must not venture out."

Khnumet lit a larger oil lamp from the small flickering one, and Zeneb was pleased but totally shocked with what she saw and heard.

"Zeneb, I will be all right," Khnumet smiled. Her voice had none of the frightened hysteria in it. Nor did it sound flat and dead. She and her voice seemed utterly normal. Zeneb felt it was as though the old Khnumet was back in residence.

"I have an errand to do. I must go to the temple," Khnumet said softly. "I fear I have neglected the goddess Hathor far too long." She patted the girl's shoulder. "Now, you go back to sleep and I will return soon."

"Let me go with you, my lady," Zeneb offered.

"No. There is no need to worry. See, I am well . . . "

"But it is a long walk without your servants or your litter. Let me accompany you," Zeneb tried again.

"Thank you for offering, but perhaps a long walk is just what I need. Now, hush. I will come back."

Zeneb reluctantly agreed, but she lay awake moving restlessly about. When sleep finally did come, it was troubled at best.

28

Khnumet walked quickly through the deserted streets of the city and did not slacken her pace until she reached the elegant, palatial grounds of Pharaoh's palace. Undetected, she made her way past guards, through gardens, and around maintenance sheds and stables until she stood before the iron gates of the royal prison.

"Guard, over here," she said urgently.

"Who calls me?" the alerted guard responded.

"Never mind," Khnumet answered. "Just tell me, is my lord Kharu here tonight?"

"Yes, my lady." The soldier perceived she was a noblewoman and since she called the governor of the prison by name, he was careful to treat her with respect.

"Then get him. I would speak with him."

Kharu's grumbling, which Khnumet heard before she saw him, stopped the instant his torchlight shown down on her face.

Swiftly the gates were opened, and the officer escorted her to a small room in the corner of the main prison building.

"My lady?" He addressed her with curiosity.

"Forgive me for disturbing your rest," Khnumet said quickly, after they were seated at a small table. "I know you and Peheti are loyal and trustworthy friends of my husband. Many years ago he told me of your allegiance to him during times of battles and wars ..." Khnumet searched his face to see if he understood her inference.

"We know of his wounds, my lady, but we have never betrayed the confidence of Potiphar," he said, confirming her words. Then abruptly he peered at her, asking, "What has brought you to the prison at such a late hour?"

"First, I need to know ..." nervously she rubbed her moist,

clammy palms together, "can you be as discreet with my visit to-night as you have been all these years with my husband's afflic-tions?"

Kharu's nod assured her.

"Then I would seek an audience, here and now, with one of your prisoners."

"I can grant that my lady. Who do you wish to see?"

Khnumet kept her eyes lowered and focused on the wooden table before her. Softly she replied, "Joseph, the Hebrew."

While she waited for Kharu to return, Khnumet wondered what Joseph would look like after two years in prison. She imag-ined that his beard would have grown out and that he'd look much like he did the first day she saw him with Asher and Me-tenu.

Finally she heard the clanking of chains and looked up. Kharu held the door open, and there before her, was Joseph. She had been right. His long hair, matted beard, and soiled loin cloth were all as she expected. It was his manacled feet and oozing wounds, however, for which Khnumet was totally unprepared.

"Oh, Joseph!" she cried. His fetters rattled loudly in the still night. He moved awkwardly over to a bench and carefully eased himself down onto it. "What have I done to you?" Khnumet asked, appalled at what she was seeing.

After Kharu vanished into the darkness of the courtyard, Khnumet pointed down at Joseph's swollen, festering ankles and groaned, "Is there no way to heal those open sores?"

"No, my lady." Joseph's first words, spoken in his soft and fa-miliar voice reached out to her. "Nothing can be done as long as the chains are in place. My God has granted me favor with Gov-ernor Kharu, and I enjoy a measure of freedom but my bonds . . ." he looked down at his ankles, "they serve to remind me that I am a prisoner still."

Khnumet was astonished that his brief explanation was unen-cumbered by any trace of anger or bitterness.

"You must hate me for all this," Khnumet said, still unable to take her eyes off his raw wounds.

Joseph sat quietly on the bench and leaned his back and head against the wall behind him. Again his voice was calm and with-out rancor or hostility. He spoke quietly, measuring his words;

and Khnumet sat and listened, caught once again in his spell.

"The past, my lady, is just that ... *past*. I know now that my God prepared me for the chains and dungeon hole of this prison exceptionally well." A slight smile crossed his lips. "In fact, this is not the first time I have been lowered into a pit."

Khnumet leaned forward, her eyes round with unbelief, and asked, "You have been in a prison before?"

"Not prison, but a pit ... my brothers threw me into one ... a long time ago."

Trying to comprehend his words, Khnumet shook her head and blurted out incredulously, "Your *brothers* threw you into a pit before they sold you to Asher?"

Joseph's soft-spoken answer sliced through the torch-lit room like a silent arrow. "Oh, they would have killed me on the spot near Dothan, but Reuben, my oldest brother, suggested an old abandoned water cistern. I like to think he planned to come back later to rescue me ... but before he could ... the others saw the merchant's caravan, and you know what happened after that."

Still unable to take it all in, Khnumet repeated, "Your own brothers did that to you?" Then she stopped—amid her righteous indignation—for her own conscience, fed by two years of pent-up guilt, suddenly renewed its powerful stabbings within her. She retreated to the silence of her mind.

Joseph was looking at her but still remembering the past. When she finally heard him again, he was saying, "Yes, my brothers overpowered me that day and dropped me like a sack of wheat or barley into that deep and frightening hole. I thought I would surely die." He leaned back against the wall, closed his eyes and continued. "My screams went unheeded, the demon-filled darkness pressed in on me, and I remember landing amid the bones and remnants of dead animals. I was covered with insects and dirt, and I shared those wretched hours with two fat snakes which slithered in and around me. I shall never forget the frightening blackness of that pit nor how, at first, I thought even my God had abandoned me."

He looked over at Khnumet and said with a note of triumph, "But, my lady, as I said before, I can see it now so plainly. My God had not deserted me. He was only preparing and teaching me about the bitter realities of living out our lives. Then, you see, because of my past experiences ... Egypt and even this prison have not been so intolerable.

"Please do not be so dismayed. I have some limited freedoms and the governor has allowed me to keep the records and accounts. My lady," he grinned proudly at her, "you are looking at the prison *scribe!*"

"Stop it at once!" Khnumet shouted. "How can you be so complacent with this dreadful place, and where in a dank, rotting prison dungeon do you find forgiveness?" Her tears poured out of her like the mainstream from a shattered dam.

"Please, please, my lady." Joseph pulled his bench beside her at the table. "Do not be distressed. Listen," He took her chin in his hands. "I have put in my apprenticeship according to God's plans, and now I am able to endure because my God is also merciful."

Khnumet pulled back from his touch and dabbed at her face with the edge of her cloak.

"The next thing you will say is that your God is here with you in this prison, now, as well as that loathsome pit your brothers shoved you into."

Her words were colored with sarcasm, but then she had never pretended to understand any relationship Joseph had with his God. Nor could she begin to fathom how lying with a lover could be such a great sin against this invisible God.

Quite unexpectedly the putrid smell of his wounds filled her nostrils and once more she was overwhelmed with her part in all of this. She murmured sadly, "It must be true, what they say about me ... most certainly my mind must have been consumed with madness to have told Potiphar all those lies about you, Joseph."

"My lady, please. What has been done ... has been done. Look, I do not hold you responsible or plan my revenge against you; and neither is there an infection of bitterness raging within me." Joseph's eyes were bright with mercy and forgiveness. He replaced a fallen strand of hair from her forehead and spoke soothingly to her.

But an unnerving shudder of guilt-ridden remorse coursed through Khnumet's veins, and without further words or explanations she rushed from the room and ran blindly into the night.

29

As the first faint lights of dawn filtered down into the columned hall of Hathor's temple, Amset made her daily procession to the sanctuary altar. It was her duty to rouse the goddess for the new day.

The old priestess dropped her tray of sacrificial offerings when she discovered Khnumet huddled at the base of the main altar.

"My child, you startled me!" the old woman called out. "Why are you sleeping here . . . how long have you been—"

Amset drew closer. Khnumet was sitting on the alabaster floor, leaning up against the altar near the golden feet of Hathor. Her head was resting on one arm and she was a picture of peace. Yet something seemed dreadfully wrong to Amset.

The old priestess found it. She stared in horror when she saw that Khnumet's other hand was under the lid of a small basket on her lap. The wicker container was one of many cages which held tiny creatures used in temple ceremonies. Amset suppressed a scream when she remembered exactly what that cloth-lined basket contained.

Her grief was immediate, but the old woman carefully lifted Khnumet's hand out. Slowly and with skillfully fluid movements she untwined the small brown viper from around Khnumet's slender fingers, released the snake to its basket, and quickly shut the lid.

Khnumet's face, now placid and freed from the strain and guilts of life, was even more beautiful in death.

The goddess Hathor, dressed in her golden splendor, towered above them. But even with her sapphire eyes and bejeweled ears, she did not see the two women at her feet, nor did she hear Amset's soft moaning sounds as she cried, "Oh, my Khnumet, why . . . why . . . why . . ."

BOOK
IV
ASENATH

30

"There is no possibility that I can see my way clear to accompany you! The sun shines no brighter or clearer anywhere—even on the royal city of the Pharaoh—than it does in the city of Heliopolis. I'm staying home!"

He knew his wife was halfheartedly teasing him, yet he missed her so terribly when they were parted that he was in no mood to joke about it. With thirty years of practice, he said, "Tuiah, my love, we are not being asked if we would like to spend some days with the Pharaoh. We are being ordered to go. Do you think I want to leave my work and home for some fancied pleasures to be found in the royal apartments?"

Tuiah's lower lip formed into a pretended pout, and jestingly she teased, "Of course you want to go. You probably have some young dedicated temple virgin hidden away in Pharaoh's palace, just eager to lose her maidenhood."

"A middle-aged woman who pouts and whines is just exactly what pushes husbands into the arms of young virgins." Poti-pherah issued the information to the room in general and noted that Tuiah could always lift his moods with her understated wit. Then he grew serious again and said reservedly, "Do you realize, Tuiah, that in all the years I have been high priest here at the temples of On, the Pharaoh has never commanded that we go to the palace for an audience with him? I must ask Asenath what she knows of all this."

He adjusted the multicolored beaded collar around his neck and said gravely, "Something very serious must be going on; otherwise, Pharaoh would not take us away from our extensive duties here."

"Our king is deeply disturbed by his dreams, father."

Poti-pherah swung around and opened his arms to his daughter. He studied the tall, regally elegant girl as she crossed the opulently furnished sitting room. No matter how often he saw her, he always felt a surge of pride for his only child. He marveled to himself that the great sun-god, Ra, had blessed the union of his loins with one so lovely, yet so gifted.

"You think it is only dreams that have caused Pharaoh's crisis?" he asked. "Asenath, as usual your perceptive powers to read the minds of others, even at great distances, has come to aid me in understanding our king." Poti-pherah rubbed the girl's forehead and temples gently and asked, "What secrets do the gods whisper to you about Pharaoh's troubles?"

The young woman kissed his hands and then her mother's cheeks in greeting. She moved a carved ebony chair closer to her mother's, and said unpretentiously, "I think the king has had a dream, maybe a series of dreams, and he has been badly frightened by it all. I may be wrong . . ."

"I doubt that," her father said under his breath, suppressing a slight grin.

Ignoring his note of confidence, Asenath continued seriously, "I sense he has already depleted his collection of sorcerers, occultists, magicians, and local priests to interpret his dream . . . or dreams; and I also think," she looked up to her father, "that none of those people have come up with a reasonable explanation." She paused and then said thoughtfully, "Pharaoh has long been aware of your prominence and your status as the official high priest for Ra . . . now the king calls for you because he is in desperate straits."

Turning to her mother, Asenath said quietly, "It is vital that father goes to the king . . . and who but father is wise enough to advise on matters of the mind and soul?"

She heard her father's low chuckle and then felt his light tap on her head as he declared, "Your mother doesn't see the trip as honorable as you do because Pharaoh has asked that you *and* your mother accompany me. But then," he tilted her chin up in his hand, "you already knew that. Did you not?"

The girl smiled and nodded affirmatively.

"As I see it," Tuiah interrupted, "there really is no great

problem here. Pharaoh needs only you two. He will never miss a "middle-aged wife," so why don't you both go without me? I'll keep the household running, the servants happy, and take as much time in my bath as I want to." She smiled, pleased with herself.

"I might be the high priest at the temple," Poti-pherah groaned good-naturedly, "but around here I just do as I'm told."

He helped Tuiah up from her chair, and with one arm around her shoulders he said, "You win! You get your wish. Asenath and I will go by ourselves; but as soon as we can, I shall return home to plague your life and enlarge your miseries!" Their laughter echoed around the walls, and then Poti-pherah lowered his voice to admit, "But I shall miss you *dreadfully*, my love."

Asenath could not miss the blush on her mother's face. It came easily, as if she was a young girl infatuated with her first love. The moment kindled the fires of an ever-smoldering longing in Asenath's heart.

She could never remember exactly how old she was when she discovered her uncanny abilities, nor when she paid her first visit to the magnificent temple of the sun-god, Ra; but the two events had blended simultaneously, and a love affair with the temple and priesthood had been started.

Poti-pherah, the highest ranking priest in all of Egypt, had named her Asenath, which meant *dedicated to Neit, the Goddess of Wisdom of Sais;* and it had all helped to set her course.

The rich cultural setting of her birth, her influential parents, and her enormous intelligence enabled her to amass a prodigious education, but it was her mysterious gift to perceive the thoughts of others and her unspoiled sweetness of spirit that made her a priestess second to none.

She had responded eagerly to each new challenging year of work in the temple. And even when she watched young women her own age playfully bouncing babies on their knees, or she listened as they chatted about their husbands in glowing terms, Asenath did not experience any regrets as to the road she had chosen to travel, except during moments like today.

Once again, during the spontaneous embrace between her parents, she observed their carefully matured love that had blossomed over the years and wondered if the single life of a dedicated priestess was as fulfilling and rewarding as she had come to believe.

Asenath had little time to meditate on her ponderous questions for within hours she and her father and two servants were given passage on the first available ship sailing southward on the Nile.

Asenath watched the oarsmen as they enjoyed a temporary rest from their labors. The sails were on duty, and strong winds billowed their great expanse. She earnestly wished the winds would vanish. A swift journey could only hasten their arrival in Pharaoh's court, and she already sensed this well-intentioned visit would culminate in failure.

Even my wisdom-filled father will not be able to unravel this tangled web, she thought as she watched the waters of the Nile pushing past her. *Nor will I be of any help. This whole trip is a futile waste of time . . . .*

Moments later she was startled and taken aback by her mind's words because her decisive thoughts declared, *This trip will change every aspect of your entire life. You have been ordained to take this journey since before you were born. You will fulfill your holy destiny.*

Asenath clutched the ship's rail, faced the wind, and tried without success to assimilate the incredible information she had just learned.

31

After their hastily arranged journey, it was the queen, Makara, not the king, who awaited Poti-pherah and Asenath. Their voices echoed and reverberated in Pharaoh's empty throne room. The king was nowhere in sight, nor were his usual entourage, body guards, or the predictably noisy court audience. Only Makara's bubbling greeting—"You two are a *most* welcome sight!"—succeeded in taking the edge off their weariness.

She embraced them warmly and then, pointing to a door left of the throne's raised dais, she directed, "Come—my husband has cancelled his court appearance today so that he may speak privately with you. The king has asked me to bring you to our chambers." Her smile disappeared, and she added, "I fear he is in dire need of both of you, and we will have no peace around here unless you can soothe his troubled mind."

She ushered them through the doorway, past the royal guards, and they walked briskly down a spacious hallway. As the queen approached the royal apartments, two alert sentries sprang forward and instantly opened the vast bronze doors. Makara preceded Poti-pherah and Asenath through a series of chambers and halls until, finally, they entered a small intimate sitting room. There, a few moments later, the king arrived unannounced.

The priest and his priestess daughter rose from their chairs to greet Pharaoh, but both Poti-pherah and Asenath failed in their attempts to speak. They were speechless and stood benumbed before him. They found his physical appearance appalling and his drawn and haggard face haunting.

The king, a slim wiry man when he was hale and hearty, had lost a considerable amount of weight. He could ill afford the loss, and the ashen pallor on his skin only accentuated his prominent nose and sharply etched the hollows in his thin face.

Even his voice had changed. Denied several weeks of sleep, Pharaoh's tone had deepened, and his voice had lost its high-pitched brilliancy. The staccato cadence of his speaking had also disappeared, and his words came slowly, even haltingly.

Wearily and with forced gaiety, the king greeted his friends and made a stab at small talk concerning their time aboard ship. When he could contain his anxiety no longer, he gathered up his strength and blurted out, "Poti-pherah, it is a troubled king you see before you." He searched the priest's face for answers. "I am counting on your wisdom." Then, pointing at Asenath, he added, "and in your exceptional powers to help me.

"Believe me, my friends, I would have never called you away from your labors at the temple of Ra except everyone else I've called on has been unable to put their finger on the heart of the matter "

"Just tell them your dreams, my lord," Makara urged softly.

"Yes, yes," he assured his wife. He began to massage the nape of his neck and then continued. "It is almost as if the gods obscure the meaning of my dreams for their own purposes. At any rate, I can find no one who can tell me why I have dreamed two dreams or what they mean."

"The dreams . . ." Makara said, trying to be patient.

The pharaoh plunged into his oft repeated tale. "In the first dream I was standing on the bank of the Nile when, to my surprise, seven full-bodied, fat, and healthy cows came up out of the river. I watched as they grazed peacefully on the reeds and stalks in the flooded marshes . . ."

"Ah," Poti-pherah interjected, "that is significant already, your majesty. The esteemed god of the Nile, Hapi, would be pleased to give the king fat cows . . . but go on, forgive me for interrupting you."

The king threw an impatient look at the priest and then resumed. "As I observed the seven healthy, well-fattened cows, suddenly I saw seven ugly, emaciated and starving cows come up, once again, out of the same river." He shuddered as he finished describing his dream. "It was so horrible, for those scrawny cows turned on the healthy ones and proceeded to eat them up. They just swallowed the fat ones whole."

"That was all, your majesty?" Poti-pherah squinted his eyes as he peered at Pharaoh.

"No, father. The king said he had dreams," Asenath ventured.

"She is right," Pharaoh assented. "I fell asleep a second time, and once again I dreamed. It seemed that I was in a typical grain field on one of our fertile plains. As I gazed at the scene, I saw a stalk of grain growing up and on the stalk grew seven plump ears of grain.

"But then, the same fate befell the grain as did the fat cattle. Before my startled eyes, a second stalk grew up next to the first. Its seven ears of grain were withered and dried from the bitter east wind, yet they engulfed the healthy stalk . . . the whole stalk was consumed as I watched.

"Everything was so vivid and so real I could scarce believe I was dreaming." The king put his head in his hands and remained motionless in his chair for some time. Finally, he looked over at Poti-pherah and pleaded, "Well, what do you make of it? There must be a meaning to my dreams somewhere. Can you interpret them for me?"

Poti-pherah glanced hopefully at Asenath, but her eyes gave him no help. In a faltering voice he said, "My king, I do not know ... I mean, I have no answers, and my daughter sees no visions. I must tell you in honesty that I do not know what the dreams mean, nor would I fabricate a story based upon guesses to placate the turmoil of your mind. We need to meditate before the gods, but I feel certain that in time," he slipped over to Asenath's chair, "we will give you some answers ... perhaps even on the morrow."

Pharaoh hid his disappointment and was spared the effort to comment by Makara's ever-gracious habits of hospitality.

"My king and I will expect you both at the palace dinner tonight," the queen said tactfully, reminding her husband of the finer points of protocol which he seemed to have forgotten.

The king gave Makara a quick grin and added, "Yes, Poti-pherah and Asenath. If I cannot find answers for my dreams, or sleep during the night any more, perhaps I can enjoy dinner with friends." Pharaoh smiled a thin, polite smile, and then, gesturing with his hands, he bid them take their leave.

Asenath bathed long and luxuriously. The city of Pharaoh was farther south, and the cool water lowered the soaring temperatures and provided a soothing break to her own turbulent thoughts. She had drawn a complete blank in the presence of the king; and even now, refreshed by the ointments of her bath, she still had not the vaguest interpretation of the king's dreams.

The royal dinner was like many others she had attended. She was pleased with herself for as she was escorted to the king's table she noticed the place next to her was empty. Inwardly Asenath smiled for her unique mental abilities were working. She had been able to merely look over at the queen, and at once her powers had told her who would sit there.

"Are we missing a guest?" Poti-pherah leaned over to his left and asked Asenath after she had taken her seat.

"No, father. He will be here. The queen is up to her favorite matchmaking game again," she answered quietly. "Potiphar is to sit next to me."

Almost immediately, Makara left her place and whispered into

Asenath's ear, "In a few moments you will be joined by Potiphar." The girl threw a knowing smile in her father's direction, and he winked in response.

"My husband's most trusted military aide has led a tragic life these past few years. Please do what you can to lighten his heart." Makara lightly squeezed the girl's shoulder.

When the queen was back at her place on the other side of the king, Asenath remarked kindly to her father, "Our darling queen would have me end up as Potiphar's wife . . . little does she know, I desire marriage with no man. I am already married to Ra and his temple."

Her father patted her hand. "Makara means well, and her heart is spacious. Also, Potiphar is dedicated to the king . . . and I am sure our queen thinks of his happiness."

The dinner proceeded routinely and uneventfully. Potiphar, a gracious but somewhat subdued dinner partner, arrived after he had seen to his palace duties. He and Asenath settled into a warm, rambling kind of conversation befitting old acquaintances when suddenly Asenath looked over towards the king. Her hand flew to her mouth, as if in surprise, and then she asked intently, "Potiphar, who is the man serving the king this moment?"

Potiphar glanced up behind him at the servant and said, "It's only Essa. Don't you remember him? He has been Pharaoh's butler and chief wine taster for a long time."

Asenath's mood grew so somber that even her father caught it and asked if she was feeling ill. Assuring him she was fine, she turned back to Potiphar. Then without taking her eyes off of Essa, she said crisply, "Tell me everything about him."

"There's little to tell." Potiphar shrugged his shoulders. "The man is a loyal, highly trusted person. He is devoted to our king. He only has one blot on his record, but even in that he was totally exonerated."

"What did that involve?" she questioned.

Potiphar shifted in his chair and drained the wine from his cup before answering. It was as though he resented talking of things which were part of a painful past. Hesitantly, and with some reluctance, he said, "It was a case of circumstantial evidence . . . Essa was not guilty, but at first it appeared that he and the baker had conspired to assassinate the king. A large cache of poison was found in one of the kitchen storage rooms, and both men were known to have easy access to the room. In due time, however, a thief was captured and he confessed that he had sold the poison to the baker. The baker was executed, and Essa was acquitted of all charges. Pharaoh restored him to his former place here."

Asenath was puzzled because Potiphar's explanation did not shed any light on her newly formed impressions of Essa.

"Why the sudden interest in the king's butler?" Potiphar teased gently.

"Well," Asenath took a deep breath, "you know I have certain . . . talents . . . but sometimes it's hard to put all the facts together. All I know is that Essa, that innocent butler, knows something about Pharaoh's dreams. Of that I am sure. But the how, what, or why of it completely escapes me."

"What a pity," Potiphar mocked, "and all this time, I thought you were really an all-knowing goddess disguised in human form." She pretended she was angry with him, but a short burst of bright laughter escaped and ruined her intent.

"Shall I call him over so you can question him?" Potiphar asked, serious once again.

Asenath responded quickly, "Yes, please."

Potiphar called one of the wine servers, and the lad took and delivered the message. It brought Essa swiftly to their places.

"The wine is excellent tonight, Essa. Lady Asenath would like to thank you personally."

The butler glowed with pleasure.

"Esssa . . ." the young priestess ignored Potiphar's remarks and, pulling all of her powers of concentration together, she met his gaze and said astutely, "Essa, you know that the king is deeply disturbed about his dreams . . . what do you know about dreams that would help him?"

The servant's jaw fell open, and he stammered, "Dreams? My lady, I know *nothing* about dreams. I cannot even recall mine, except . . ." His eyes flashed with the shock of a long-forgotten promise.

"Except, a dream you once had?" Asenath prompted.

"Yes. No. I mean . . . Oh, my lady! Over two years ago, when I was in prison, I had a mysterious dream, and I could not begin

to tell what it meant. But one of the other prisoners asked me why
I was sad of face. I told him my confusing dream, and he interpreted it . . . and . . ." Essa's serving cloth dropped to the floor.
Instantly Asenath read his mind and ordered, "You must tell that
to the king!"

An astonished Potiphar listened as Asenath requested that he
ask the king to withdraw to another room to hear the butler's
story.

The pharaoh had restricted his drinking, so he was alert and
clearheaded. All it took was one look at Potiphar and Essa, and
one brief glance at Asenath's face, and quickly Pharaoh led them
into an antechamber.

Frowning slightly at Essa, the king asked, "Now, what do you
have to say that is so important that Potiphar, Lady Asenath, the
priest Poti-pherah, *and* your king have to hear?"

"Forgive me, your majesty. It was I who felt this man should
be heard." Asenath bowed her head and instantly the king hoped
she had experienced a revelation during dinner concerning his
dreams.

"Speak up!" he ordered Essa in a loud voice.

"My king, only just now have I remembered my sin. I should
have spoken about this two years ago. I made a pledge to someone, and I never kept my promise . . ."

"Yes, yes, go on!" Pharaoh urged impatiently. He sensed that
he was closer to the truth of his dreams than ever before.

Eagerly Essa continued. "Do you remember when the chief
baker and I were put into the royal prison?"

Pharaoh toyed with the short false beard at his chin and then
answered stonily, "I remember. I was convinced that one or both
of you were plotting my assassination. As it turned out, my wrath
and suspicions were well justified."

"Yes, your majesty," Essa breathed quietly, and then continuing he said, "but what I want to tell you is that while we were
awaiting your ruling regarding our fate, both the baker and I had
a dream one night. Neither one of us understood the dreams, so
we told them to a young Hebrew who had been a slave to Potiphar."

Asenath glanced up at Potiphar. He was standing just behind
Pharaoh's chair. She didn't have to read his mind, only his lips,

for he formed the name *Joseph.* She watched him closely and noted that his eyes darkened with what she was sure was a highly painful and unresolved memory.

When she turned her attention back to the servant, the man was saying, "And the Hebrew told us exactly what our dreams meant. His interpretations to the baker and to me were completely correct. The slave predicted, from my dream, that I would be restored to my honored position. He told the chief baker that his dream foretold his death. He told us both that three days later I would be back here, and the baker would be executed and impaled on a pole ..." Essa paused. "Your majesty, it all came to pass as he said." He finished, relieved that he had finally done as he had promised the slave—remembered him to the pharaoh.

The king dismissed Essa after thanking him, and slowly he turned in his chair and faced Potiphar. In a halting voice he asked, "Is that the Hebrew of your household who ... ?"

Potiphar's yes was faint but audible.

"Fetch him from the dungeon. I would see him now, *tonight!*" The royal command was given, and Potiphar disappeared, leaving the king, Asenath, and her father to ponder the incredible events of the past few moments.

Asenath could not stop trembling and when her father's arm came lovingly around the girl's shoulders, she was totally at a loss to explain the hot rush of tears which flowed copiously.

"My child," Poti-pherah said, genuinely alarmed, "what is it?"

"Perhaps she is ill ..." the king leaned foward in his chair and asked if he should send for his physician.

Asenath could only shake her head to answer no, but beyond that there was no explanation to give her father or the king. All she could comprehend at the moment was that it was as if all her life she had walked a single, arrow-straight road which led directly to the temple of Ra. Never had she deviated from the appointed path, never had she lost interest, and never had she even considered another road. Yet tonight, suddenly the road before her divided. Without any hesitation, she realized she would leave the temple's well-marked route and take a different road.

Clearly, what stunned her the most, was that the new road led ultimately to a man called Joseph.

32

Asenath and Poti-pherah followed Pharaoh and his wife, as protocol decreed, back into the banquet hall to await Potiphar and his prisoner. However, when the king was greeted by his dinner guests' polite silence, he was obliged to explain his lengthy absence.

Raising his golden scepter, he announced cordially, "My noble guests, I did not intend to be away from the tables so long; but because many of you are skilled priests, magicians, and sorcerers, I think you will all be interested in what I have just learned."

Asenath sat next to her father and picked idly at the delicate pastries as she halfway listened to Pharaoh tell Essa's story. When she returned her full attention to him, the king was saying, "Normally, I would scorn the help of a Hebrew, especially one from my own prison, but my friends, as you all well know, I have exhausted all the other alternatives. I must know the meaning of my dreams!"

A ripple of subdued approval ran through the audience, and there was scattered applause when Pharaoh added, "Now, I want you all to stay, so finish your wine, and we shall wait together and see. The foreigner from Canaan was right about Essa's dream; perhaps he will be right again."

While the guests speculated on this newest turn of events, the king paced impatiently behind his table on the raised platform.

Asenath, intrigued by the suspense of it all, wished her mother had come with them for the excitement and mystery of these moments could never be adequately retold. In the middle of her thoughts, a somber Potiphar entered the hall.

The hushed and breathless audience waited. The king strode around the table and stood on the front edge of his dais. Everyone gave their full attention to the guards behind Potiphar who flanked their prisoner. Each person in the room watched the slow-paced procession, and no man or woman ever forgot their first glimpse of Joseph.

Asenath, as Khnumet before her, saw the Hebrew's ankles first. They were crusted over with old scars and, here and there, raw and swollen with new festerings. Walking was obviously painful for him. Unsteadily, he made his way across the open center of the banquet hall and stood before Pharaoh.

In accordance with the Egyptians' passion for cleanliness, the prisoner had been hastily bathed, shaved, and dressed in a spotless linen tunic. Asenath thought the slave appeared to be around thirty years of age, but aside from his repulsive ankle wounds and the prison pallor of his skin, her special intelligence decided he was a very special human being. The man was a double for her mind's picture of the most majestic and handsome god she could have ever imagined. Asenath was dismayed at her thoughts, but she found herself enchanted and captivated by the beauty of his countenance. She didn't realize it at the time, but this was only the beginning. Her admiration for Joseph would continue to grow. Before the evening was over she would be smitten and stunned by the whole measure of this man—inside and out.

Pharaoh had little time to observe the slave for he was consumed by his need for an interpretation. Without elaborating further he said simply, "I have dreamed a dream, and no one here can tell me what it means.

"Tonight my butler told me that when you are told a dream you can interpret it. That is why I have called you before me."

Joseph stood on the lower level before the king, his hands behind his back, his head and shoulders held high; and because he had captured the undivided attention of everyone, the low evenness of his voice reached every ear.

"I cannot interpret dreams by myself. It is not in me to do so." He confessed honestly, and then added, "But God will give the meaning to your majesty's dreams, and His favorable answer will establish your peace."

In the stillness that followed, the king stared at Joseph in disbelief. *This slave*, Asenath could hear the king's thoughts, *speaks with a courageous authority—quite unlike any slave—and wisely gives the credit to a god.*

After another moment, Pharaoh went directly to the details of his dream. First he told of the two sets of cattle; then about the two kinds of grain. When he finished, he adjusted the strap on his false beard and declared wearily, "I have told this many times," then gesturing towards the priests and magicians, he added, "but none of them could explain what it all means."

Joseph met the king's eyes with a steady gaze and without any show of arrogance he said, "Your majesty, it is very simple. Both dreams are but one dream, and both of them say the same thing. Your double dreams are God's way of letting you know exactly what He is going to do in the great land of Egypt."

Pharaoh snapped his finger, and a servant brought him a chair. Quickly he collapsed down into it. "God is giving *me* divine instructions?" he asked weakly. He rubbed his forehead, and then said quietly, "Tell me."

The guests strained to hear each word, but even as she waited to hear "God's divine instructions," Asenath knew Joseph would speak the truth. *This slave is obviously speaking out of a glowing spirit, not his own,* she thought.

Joseph's voice, though calm and subdued, has the unmistakable backing of authority in it. The unseen power of this man could only come from God, she reasoned. *This slave's manner commands the respect and instant approval of our king and his advisors. Even my wise father is prepared to hear and take the truth from Joseph.* She smiled to herself at the spectacular events of this incredible evening.

The Hebrew's voice was more animated now as he spoke. "Your majesty, the seven healthy cows and the seven well-formed heads of grain mean seven years of prosperity. The seven emaciated cows and the seven withered heads of grain mean seven years of famine.

"So, you see, God has shown you what He is about to do. The next seven years will be a period of great prosperity throughout the whole land of Egypt. But after the good years, there will be seven years of disastrous famine. The famine will be so great that all the prosperity will be forgotten and wiped out. The famine will consume the land. Even the memory of the rich good times will be erased."

Joseph paused and then, as if he were given new inspiration, he continued earnestly. "That the dream was *repeated* for your majesty means that God has decreed it and that it shall all come to pass very soon."

Pharaoh sat as still as one of his statues. He had no need to verify the dream's interpretation with others because the room was full of assenting, bobbing heads. He collected his thoughts for a moment more and then, because the meaning of his dreams was made so clear, he asked with no small admiration in his voice, "Joseph, what shall I do about this great famine?"

Asenath noted that there was no vacillating or indecisiveness on Joseph's part; nor was he in the least bit intimidated by a king asking the advice of a slave. His instant answer—rational and perceptive—fascinated her and the entire audience.

"My suggestion is that you find an Egyptian man who is both intelligent and discreet. Put him solely in charge of administering a nation-wide plan to gather up the resources of Egypt."

Joseph paused and Pharaoh, amazed at the slave's uncommon insight, sucked in his breath and hoped for more. He did not wait long.

"I think, too, your majesty," Joseph resumed, "you should take further action."

"Further action? Yes, yes, go on!" Pharaoh urged, with mounting excitement.

"Under a leader, you should appoint supervisors or officials to take in one-fifth of Egypt's produce during the seven years of abundant crops. Have them collect that food in the coming good years. They should be instructed to store the grains and produce in the royal storehouses, so there will be enough to eat now and when the seven years of famine come. That way the people and this nation will not perish."

The interpretation ended, and the great hall, crowded with many people, sat silent and hushed. Each man and woman who had heard the sound of Joseph's voice that night was deeply moved by his simple but unprecedented plans. The slave shifted his weight and swayed ever so slightly. Potiphar quickly offered his arm to steady him.

Asenath could not penetrate Potiphar's mind, so she wondered what feelings about this former slave of his were rushing through his veins. She did see clearly that there was a distinct tenderness in the way Potiphar maneuvered Joseph carefully over to an empty chair.

The king called for Poti-pherah and several other priests to discuss who should be appointed to the job. Asenath heard him ask of them, "How can we find such a man?" They murmured amongst themselves, and then Pharaoh asked, "Is there anyone *like* Joseph?" They shook their heads no. "The whole key to success," the king reasoned aloud, "is found in appointing exactly the right administrator. A wise and prudent prime minister could be our savior ... but the wrong man could be a tyrant enslaving us all!" Then, to a man, they united their thoughts and gave their unhesitating approval to the king when he said, "This Joseph is a man *obviously* filled with the Spirit of God."

Asenath reflected on their assessment of Joseph for it was exactly right—this man *was* filled with the very Spirit of God. That any god would infill a human was always up for debate amongst the priesthood. Her father and a few others argued that possibly it could happen, but they also were quick to say that they had never met or seen anyone "filled with God's own Spirit." *The events of tonight*, Asenath found herself smiling, *have introduced us to the first human with proof of God's indwelling.* Her thoughts produced a rare satisfaction within her, but she had no more time to ponder on them for the king rose and she knew he was about to proclaim his decision.

Leaving his chair and the priests behind him, the king stepped off the platform and stood before the Hebrew. Noting that the swelling in the slave's ankles was more pronounced, he motioned for Joseph to remain seated. Then Pharaoh raised his voice, so no one would miss his words or his intent, and said fervently, "Joseph, since God has revealed all of this to you, then it seems to me that *you* are a discerning man and the wisest one in all my land." The king laid his scepter on Joseph's right shoulder and verified, "I am hereby appointing you to be the prime minister of Egypt."

Joseph looked stunned. *But only for a single moment*, Asenath thought. It was almost as if he could never be surprised by anything that happened to him.

The king was saying, "And when you give orders, my people shall obey. Only in matters pertaining to the throne will I be your superior. All of Egypt will be at your command."

Then Pharaoh ceremoniously took off his royal signet ring and, taking Joseph's hand in his, he placed the ring securely on Joseph's finger and said warmly, "Observe! I have put you in charge of the whole land of Egypt!"

The entire hall erupted noisily. Some of the people jumped up from their places shouting, clapping, and roaring their approval.

Others, fearful of how a new leader, especially a Hebrew, would jeopardize their position at court, stood with the crowd and were less than enthusiastic. Hastily they exchanged worried glances and silently hoped their suspicions would not be confirmed. The people had been concerned over their pharaoh's dreams, so they were pleased that someone had restored the good spirits of the king. And there was some satisfaction in that since their king had put the burden of taking care of Egypt on Joseph's shoulders, they now could go back, once again, to their luxurious life at court.

Pharaoh whispered some directions to Potiphar about clothing and having his personal physician tend to Joseph's wounds, and then he instructed the guards to take Joseph to his own royal apartments. When they had gone, he quieted down the crowd.

"My friends, you are free to linger here as long as you like, but I have ordered Joseph to take his rest. I shall present him to the people of Egypt tomorrow morning when I hold court. So stay as long as you like. However," he grinned at everyone, "your tired king is going to retire for the night! This will be my first untroubled sleep in what seems to me to have been ages!" He laughed and waved for his guards to accompany him out.

The king and queen were almost to the door when Pharaoh stopped, turned, and walked back to Asenath.

"It just occurred to me," he said, bending over the priestess, "that had you not been alert and sensitive to my butler, Essa, and his part in all of this, I might not have met Joseph."

Asenath smiled and responded genially with, "Your majesty, I count the opportunity to serve you as an honor." Then, anticipating what the king would now say, she met his gaze and waited.

"What gift can I bestow on you for your timely help?" the king asked, as she guessed he would.

"A husband, my lord. I desire a husband," came her surprising and freshly thought-out answer.

Beside her, Asenath heard her father's sharp gasp, and beside the king she saw Makara's hand fly up to her mouth to suppress a squeal of delight.

"My lord!" Makara quickly grabbed Pharaoh's arm, "It is Potiphar! She means to marry Potiphar! How wonderful!" the queen effervesced.

"True?" Pharaoh questioned.

"No, your majesty," came her candid answer.

Then, very clearly, for the king, queen, her father, guests, and guards to hear, Asenath said vivaciously, "I would marry the Hebrew—Joseph."

Because he was tired, the king said, as briefly as possible, "Granted!" Then he marched out of the hall, went directly to bed, and slept the dreamless sleep of an innocent but exhausted child.

33

She awoke just as the sunrise was being born in the east, and from her palace balcony she watched the sun as it spread its rays over the distant hilltops. Asenath couldn't decide whether it really was as beautiful as she thought, or if the fast-paced events of the night before made it so.

As they were returning to their apartments, after the banquet, she had exclaimed, "Oh, father, it is so right . . . but so unbelievable! One moment I was a single priestess, dedicated to the sun god, Ra, and within hours I have pledged myself to marry the prime minister of Egypt. . . a Hebrew *and* a former slave!"

"I will be hard pressed to explain all this to your mother," Poti-pherah mused, "but I think once she sees Joseph for herself, she will give her blessing. The Hebrew's wisdom is unparalleled. He is a most uncommon man."

They reached Asenath's door, and her father said softly, "Joseph is not only right for you, my daughter, he is right for Egypt. If Pharaoh put all available food supplies into the hands of a self-seeking dictator, our nation could be put out of existence. The key to the survival of Egypt will be in its prime minister; and Joseph, the right man, I am convinced, will be its deliverer." He kissed her and bade her good night.

"Everything shimmers and sparkles so this morning!" she whispered into the rising sun. Then, twirling herself once around the small confines of the balcony, she laughed aloud at the welling up of joy within her.

As soon as she completed her makeup and was satisfied with her dress and jewelry, Asenath slipped out of her chamber, down several hallways, and in through a side door which led eventually to Pharaoh's main throne room. She was pleased to be there early, ahead of the others, so she could catch her breath and even—the gods willing—foresee how things would go.

Though she had been here several times before, Asenath now looked about the resplendent chamber and tried to imagine how it would look in the eyes of a newcomer.

Asenath envisioned Joseph's entrance from the king's door at the far end of the magnificent room. *What will go through his mind when he sees all this?* she wondered.

The walls and ceilings were covered with pale gold alabaster. The light, filtering down from the openings in the walls high above her, illuminated the stone, giving it a translucent glow. *The sun god, Ra, gives his own blessing to this special day*, she silently observed.

An aisle up the middle of the room was elegantly formed by double rows of pillars. Like all Egyptian columns, they were carved and then painted. Pharaoh had many such works of art throughout the palace, but the pillars in the throne room were distinctively different. They sparkled not only with many vivid colors, but with their gildings of bright gold leaf. A thick scarlet carpet flowed like an endless pathway down the middle of the room. It seemed to Asenath that no expense had been spared to create this exorbitant splendor.

On her left, and to the front of the room, stood the king's raised dais. It was carpeted with tiger skins. The rich colors, tawny gold and velvet black, added a spectacular contrast to the

pale stone walls. A pair of young servants, naked and very beautiful twin boys, who held giant fans made of feathers, were already in their places behind the golden throne chairs.

Within a few moments, the guards opened the outside entrance doors, and royal priests, the court's own noblemen and
their wives, specially invited craftsmen, artists, sculptors, musicians, and foreign dignitaries began to line both sides of the vast
hall.

Asenath saw her father, nodded a greeting, and silently indicated she wanted to stay where she was—against a wall where she
could see the king, his subjects and, of course, Joseph.

Suddenly, out of nowhere it seemed, six female singers, without any instruments accompanying them, began to sing. It was
the king's entrance song; and once the women's voices were well
into the melody, the large double doors with posts adorned with
rows of bronze uraeus snakes opened, and Pharaoh, his queen by
his side, promenaded slowly down the length of the long red carpet.

This king, a Hyksos ruler, while not beloved was a just ruler.
He had diligently sought and earned his subjects' respect. Both
he and the queen singled out friends in the great mass of people
and nodded their greetings as they came toward their throne
chairs. They were followed by a handsome stranger who walked
slowly and leaned slightly upon a walking stick.

As she watched the procession make its deliberate way up the
aisle, Asenath finally glimpsed Joseph behind the Pharaoh. Her
heart beat in the most wild and irregular fashion. The sight of
him—looking so changed, even from the night before, and appearing so much more Egyptian—made her knees tremble against
each other.

Has Pharaoh told you about me this morning, my lord? she
asked silently of Joseph.

She could see he was wearing the shendot, a short skirt one
had the right to wear only if Pharaoh decreed it. The sheer white
fabric was edged with a gold and silver embroidered border,
folded at the waist and held together by a carved metal clasp. Joseph's upper torso was bare except for an exquisitely wrought
gold chain which had been placed around his neck. He walked
slowly and managed to keep his posture straight even though he

had to aid himself with his walking stick.

Asenath knew the chain was undoubtedly a gift from Pharaoh and was emblematic of his newly achieved authority, but she wondered who supplied the rather plain wooden walking stick. She had no time to pursue it further because, just as the king and queen took their places on the thrones, Joseph turned his head, scanned the crowd to his right, then his left, and ended his search when he found her.

Their eyes held each other for a moment, and Asenath's thoughts shouted, *So, he knows!* She held her breath. Then, because of what she read in his eyes, she breathed a sigh of relief, and silently she mouthed the words to Joseph, "Yes, I am Asenath."

His acknowledging smile sent an unprecedented chill down her spine, and although she felt faint, Asenath returned his steady gaze and savored the heady tumult of joy which swelled within her.

The king interrupted their moment. He raised his scepter, dismissed all court business, and standing up, so all could clearly view him, he announced that this was a momentous occasion for the people of Egypt.

Pointing directly down at Joseph, the king began his speech, as it was expected of him. The audience soon understood that his words were being spoken merely for political reasons, but were heartfelt as well.

"Behold, this man, loyal subjects of mine, for he and his plans will change the entire course of history for Egypt. He has brilliant insights; yet, humbly he gives the credit to his Hebrew God."

The king adjusted the small panther skin around his shoulders, and then, gravely, to the assembled court he said, "I believe Egypt faces her greatest trial as a nation. Soon, and touching the lives of all her people, we will be engaged in an overwhelming war." A murmur of alarm ran through the chamber. "No," he quickly set their minds at ease, "the war will not be waged on a battlefield, against human enemies, but on our home grounds, against an all-consuming enemy—famine."

A general confusion rippled through the people. Temporary famine, loss of crops, irregular flooding of the Nile, or a few bad years were not new to Egyptians. Why had the king used the words "an all-consuming enemy"?

He understood their whispered alarm, so Pharaoh explained, "A god warned me in my dreams that we are not in for an occasional bad year or for a limited time, when food supplies will run short; but, rather, we will have one year after another of devastating famine for . . . *seven years.*"

The court was stunned. They trusted and believed their king, but they could not begin to assimilate the information they had just been given.

"Last night," Pharaoh resumed, "I told my troubling dreams to this man." He gestured towards Joseph. "And my advisors and I listened as he correctly interpreted those dreams. I believe he has accurately predicted Egypt's future fortunes. No one on my staff had any solutions or plans to prepare for such an immense problem. Yet, Joseph here, in his God-given wisdom, formulated and prepared a battle plan to save our nation.

"There is no doubt in my mind, or in the minds of my priests, even the high priest Poti-pherah, the magicians, and my advisors that Joseph possesses extraordinary powers. He is uniquely gifted with both the mental and spiritual qualities to preserve our nation and to lead us triumphantly through the battles before us so we *will* be victorious!"

The king wiped the drops of perspiration off his brow and then commanded, "My people, behold your prime minister, second in command only to myself!"

The crowd was deeply moved by the king's speech, and they raised their voices unanimously in a chorus of approval. Pharaoh let the ovation go on for a few moments; then he called for silence and added soberly, "I have sealed my oath with this man and have given him my own signature ring. Take a close look at him. He is dressed in Egypt's finery; and when you see him in his royal chariot, you will hail him as prime minister to the king and will bow your knees in homage."

The king snapped his finger and instantly a servant brought him a tray with a large silver cup on it. Pharaoh walked down the three steps of his dais and held the highly ornamental cup out to Joseph. "This is your special divining cup. When you see reflections in the wine or in the formations of the dregs of wine at the bottom, may your prophetic insight be all the more increased. Use the power of this divination cup with your king's blessings!"

Joseph accepted the cup and bowed low before the king. Immediately a servant was at his side to hold the cup for the duration of the ceremonies.

Asenath thought, *Joseph's face is a picture of wonder infused with pleasure. It is as if he understands exactly what is happening, yet he continues to be amazed that it is happening.*

Now the king returned to his throne chair and said crisply to Joseph, "I hereby give you a new name, an Egyptian name. You will be known as Zaphnath-paaneah."

Asenath instantly perceived the need to change his name. She sensed that the king, a little anxious about Joseph's Hebrew lineage, wanted to make Joseph as Egyptian as possible. That could be achieved if enough royal honors and social status were conferred on him. The king knew his court already accepted Joseph, but he desired absolute obedience from the Egyptian people, and he readily understood that they would accept and obey a second ruler only if he possessed enough Egyptian credentials.

It struck Asenath, too, that Pharaoh's immediate granting of her request for Joseph to be her husband was based on the same desire to give Joseph Egyptian credibility. *And,* she thought, *what better way than to marry Joseph into the high caste system of the elite priesthood family of Poti-pherah.*

Unexpectedly, as if the king had read Asenath's thoughts, he smiled and began what ended in being his most grandiose announcement.

"Now, my distinguished guests, it is my unabashed pleasure to tell you that one new moon from today, Zaphnath-paaneah will be married to Asenath, daughter of the high priest Poti-pherah. It will be a royal wedding, and you are hereby all invited!"

If the court had been stunned before, with the fast-moving developments of the morning, they were duly amazed at this announcement; but they caught the spirit of it and simply went wild with excitement over the coming wedding. In Egypt marriage festivities were joyous occasions. Food and merriment were given top priority, even amongst the simple farmer peasants; but a royal wedding—now that was reason for a lavish celebration!

Over the noise of the crowd, Asenath heard the opening strains of the recessional song, sung by the women. The king offered his hand to Makara, and the two of them descended the dais steps down toward Joseph. Then, amidst much cheering, they began to slowly make their way down the long aisle. Jubilation was rampant.

Suddenly, into her ear, Asenath heard Potiphar whisper, "My lady, the king wishes you to accompany Joseph and to be his guest at a private midday meal." Without any words between them, she followed in the path Potiphar made until she stepped onto the magnificent red carpet.

"Good day, my lady," Joseph's first direct words to her were ordinary, but she read hundreds of nuances into them.

"My lord," she responded and took his arm. According to royal protocol, when one processed behind the king, one kept her eyes straight ahead and focused on his majesty; but, for the life of her, Asenath could only look up at Joseph beside her. It seemed not to embarrass him; in fact, by the time they reached the double bronze doors, Joseph was blind to everyone else, save the beautiful woman at his side.

During the simple but exquisitely prepared meal of various fruits, wine, and several kinds of freshly baked breads, Asenath observed aloud, "You will never need that, will you?"

"Need what?" Joseph leaned towards her to catch each word.

Asenath pointed to the king's gift of the silver cup which sat on the table before them.

Joseph smiled and shook his head slightly. "I don't know about you, my lady. You are not only beautiful but perceptive as well." He laughed a moment, and then said softly, "Pharaoh says you read minds. I am beginning to believe it."

"I do read minds," she replied with candor, "and, like you, I interpret dreams, predict the future, and sense others' motives."

"*I* do not," he countered.

"Oh, yes. I remember. You said your *God* does it, and that is exactly why you do not need a cup for divining the future."

"You see, you are *very* perceptive." He shook his head, and a small grin was still on his face. Then he grew thoughtful and added, "Asenath, I want to embrace as much of Egyptian life as possible. I will keep the cup always near for it is a royal symbol of wisdom; but, as you have just sensed, I will call upon my God for predictions, not a silver cup. I fear, though, I have much to learn ..." He paused, and then taking her hand in his, he said carefully, "It is my hope that you will help school me in any area in which I lack knowledge ... protocol, politics, Egyptian attitudes, cultures, belief, and superstitions ... whatever you can teach me will only enhance the work God has set out for me to do here in Egypt."

She marveled at his teachable spirit. Truly great men continually opened their minds to learning, but only the very humble of spirit would ever ask a woman to be their teacher.

"Joseph, I dare say, it is *I* who has much to learn—not you."

He was about to say something else when Pharaoh, looking at them with knowing eyes, said, "I am pleased you two could join us for this meal, but *my* perceptive powers tell me that you would like to be alone. Why don't you stroll about in the palace gardens? You seem to have much to say to each other."

Asenath blushed, bowed to the king, and left with Joseph. They were embarrassed that they had all but ignored the king and queen during the meal, but they had only just discovered each other, and there was much catching up to do. They felt little or no guilt with themselves.

"As well as being intelligent and especially gifted with powers, you also are very beautiful to see," Joseph said sincerely after they had left the palace. Asenath felt her heart catch, stop, and then resume again.

To avoid undue pressure on his ankle wounds, they quickly found a stone bench at the edge of a lotus-filled pool and sat quietly together, without the need of words, for several long golden moments.

She broke the silence by inquiring, "In the court, this morning, and even last night, you seemed, in one way, surprised; yet, not surprised at any turn of events.

"You have been propelled from the prison to the palace with the speed of a shooting star, yet you seem to take it all in your stride. It is almost as if your God foretold your rise to the position of prime minister some time ago."

Joseph looked over the pool and gardens and answered, "Yes. I suppose He did, only I did not recognize it as such."

"He revealed His plans to you in a dream, right?" Asenath asked eagerly.

Joseph laughed. "Right! In fact, two dreams; but I was very young and attached no significance to them ... my family did, however." His voice quieted, and as Asenath looked at him, she saw that his family had jealously foreseen the possibility of his future glory; but that he, in humble innocence, had not until now.

"It all comes together, does it not?" she breathed.

"Yes. I almost laughed aloud today in court when Pharaoh told the people to bow down to me when they see my chariot ... for my dreams, so long ago, were all about people, family, and even things bowing down to me. I stood there this morning thinking, *God has finally interpreted my double dreams, and it is all coming to pass. How incredible!*"

Two large multicolored water birds flew effortlessly overhead. Joseph watched them until they became tiny specks and blended into the sky. When he turned back to her, Asenath said, "My lord, you have told me what you want me to teach you ... and I will, to the best of my abilities, but I must ask something of you."

Joseph turned on the bench, took her hands in his, and replied, "Anything, Asenath."

She took a deep breath and then asked, "Will you teach me of your God?"

She was astounded that her question seemed to trouble him so profoundly, and she was appalled when her mental powers revealed that a long past, completely healed grief had split apart within him.

Asenath was also alarmed by the tears which instantly formed in his eyes. "Have I offended you?" She knew she had not, but it was the only thing she could read into an explanation for his expression.

"No—I am not offended. You just reminded me of my home and some long-ago loves." Joseph cleared his throat and resumed, "I think my mother asked that same question of my father, years before I was born. I see, in my mind's memory, my father, Jacob, taking my mother Rachel's face in his hand..."

Joseph lifted Asenath's chin, cupped his hands around her face, and said gently, "And I can hear him say, 'Yes, dearest Rachel, I'll teach you about the ways of my God, the God of my forefathers. Your gods, my love, are dead ones, made only of stone ... my God is a living, breathing God. This God neither slumbers nor sleeps, but hears, loves, forgives, and has mercy enough to endure forever....' "

Asenath's face was wet with tears as his mouth eagerly sought hers. Joseph's arms went around her, and he pulled her tightly to his chest. Hungrily they entwined themselves together, and a rapturous love of minds, hearts, and spirits was sealed by the living God that day, under the clear blue Egyptian sky.

34

Joseph and Asenath went to their marriage bed.

She, who had never physically desired anyone before, now found herself eager and trembling in his arms. He, who had never known a woman because of his iron-tempered restraint, now opened not only his loins to her but the innermost parts of his oul as well.

Their lovemaking was at once both gentle and powerful. Neither Asenath or Joseph could have ever foreseen anything so gloriously magnificent.

During one of their first nights together, as they talked and sipped wine from a single cup, Asenath purposely brought up the past. Within her lurked the need to wash away the last residue of disquieting thoughts, so softly she said, "The charges which sent you to prison were never true ... were they?"

Knowing someday she would ask, Joseph answered, "No. None of it was true."

"Was she beautiful to you? Really beautiful?" she questioned. He knew she was talking of Khnumet; but, before he could speak, Asenath added, "I saw her once at Pharaoh's court. Her beauty defied description. Surely, at some time, you were attracted to her .. or even desired her ..." Asenath was not trying to entrap him in a confession, but she had heard so many conflicting rumors, she wanted to hear him defend the past and speak in his own behalf.

Joseph leaned back against the pillows of their bed. The doors to the past had been sealed tightly shut. Opening them was difficult, and in past years his silence had become a matter of honor. He had never, to anyone, ever spoken of Khnumet and her accusations. Joseph contemplated a moment and then, when he could see clearly that Asenath was the one person who deserved to know the truth, he replied gravely, "She was *very* beautiful, and you are right; I did desire her. But at that time there was much at stake for me; and when I weighed it out in my heart and mind, I simply could not give in, no matter how tempting she was, for I could not sin against the God of my forefathers."

Asenath moved off her pillows and put her head on Joseph's bare chest. "You seem remarkably free from bitterness . . . yet every time you see the scars on your ankles it must remind you of prison. Do you feel no anger towards Egyptian justice or the woman who caused you such grievous suffering?"

Joseph played with a strand of her long silken hair and caressed her face with his fingertips. Overwhelmed with love for her concern and her caring spirit, he said, "My cherished one, the Lady Khnumet was not the one responsible for my being imprisoned. *God was!*

"It was all a part of His time of seasoning for me. I took my apprenticeship in living when I was thrown into that dungeon. The first day of the iron chains, and in the darkness of that place, I asked myself, 'Has this happened to me *without* God's knowledge or consent?' And, Asenath, my heart resounded with, 'No! *He* knows and consented.' So, I reasoned, He must have a plan! But at that time I never had a dream, a sign; nor did I have any solid proof that He was working . . . only a quiet confidence that He *was!*"

"If it would have been I, I would have been sure my God had abandoned me," Asenath responded coldly.

"I could not believe my God had abandoned me, but I can tell you this: many times the waiting was so painful I felt I was drowning in the black, murky sea of despondency. Never have I known such unutterable days of discouragement. However, now that I know all that God was doing, I cannot be bitter or angry about the past. Nor should you . . . especially when that perceptive, marvelous mind of yours realizes that had I lain with Potiphar's wife, I would probably still be a slave!" He grinned down at her and added, "It pleased God to make me a slave, a prisoner, and an interpreter, for in His time He brought me to Pharaoh and," he paused for emphasis, "ultimately to you!"

Resting comfortably in his arms, Asenath observed quietly, "My husband, perhaps one of the reasons our love is so very sweet is simply because of the amazing timing of God. We have waited so long, and you have suffered greatly; but now, in His time, we are experiencing all the benefits of God's planning."

Joseph's mind went back to his childhood, and he said thoughtfully, "You have just reminded me that my father suffered while he waited so many years for his beloved Rachel. Their love was as ours, so very special; perhaps it is the waiting that transforms an ordinary love into an exquisite one."

She raised her face to his, and Joseph covered her mouth with tiny kisses, as soft as a butterfly alights on a flower, and whispered, "My love, you have been well worth the wait!" Then, in mock sternness, he admonished, "Now, mark this well and remember it: no slave, no prison, no Pharaoh, . . . no Asenath!"

She dissolved into his arms and pledged herself never again to speak of the devious rivers of suffering through which God had surely brought her husband.

Joseph's and Asenath's first year together was incredibly happy and blessed of God, and to add to their bewildered but jubilant delight, God impressed Pharaoh to give them a palace adjacent to his as a wedding gift.

Asenath explored its numberless rooms and found they were elegantly appointed with carved tables, chairs, couches, beds, and consoles. Their marriage-bed frame had been made of several delicately shaded woods and adorned with elaborate gildings of gold. Priceless vases of gold, bronze, and alabaster, in all sizes, were scattered throughout the palace and rare perfumes rose from them. The gentle breezes picked up their scents and wafted the fragrances through the rooms and outside to the spacious courts and covered porticos.

Asenath's bare feet walked over pale pink alabaster floors, on some hallways and chambers, and sank deeply into thick, richly designed carpets or lion skins on others. But their house, modest in size compared to the king's main palace, was still a place of rare splendor. So there, amidst troops of slaves, servants, and officials ministering to their every whim, Joseph and Asenath began their life together.

During that first year, the prosperity and fullness of crops resulted in an explosion of growth. Never had the Egyptian farmers seen such a harvest; but, what surprised them the most was that during the second year their crops increased ten and twentyfold. Expectations of unprecedented prosperity drove the farmers into a jubilant madness, and they toiled even harder and excelled beyond their wildest dreams.

Joseph traveled extensively the first two years. He and his officials visited every section and province of Egypt, always instructing the farmers in the most advantageous techniques of farming. He showed them how to make the land work for them by rotating crops; and, ultimately, how to conserve and save what they grew.

Joseph even tackled the ancient problem of the yearly flooding by the Nile. He ordered dikes to be built and ditches dug to utilize the unusual runoff flow of the river. He and his officials superintended hundreds of the rounded mud-brick granaries, each within its own city or village, which provided easy access from the local grain fields.

When the bulk of his work was over, after the enormous task of educating the farmers, supervising the work on flood control, and building the granaries, Joseph had to make absolutely certain that one-fifth of every harvest was stored away, against the year when the harvest would disappear. The levied tax of twenty percent was exacted judiciously and equally in each province. Joseph made sure of that, so no one could bring charges of discrimination or excess profiteering against him.

Asenath had never known a time of such happiness and all consuming contentment. Each time Joseph left their home, during their first two years of marriage, the experience burned and singed her heart in a painful way; but then his return would bring healing to the rawness of separation, and the memory of his absence would be blotted out.

The only clouds of anxiety which seemed to be visible in the sun-filled skies of Egypt were ones seen by Asenath. Because of her father's position, her life-long association with royalty, and her familiarity with the comings and goings at Pharaoh's court, she knew full well the dark potential of those clouds.

For the better part of his time, it seemed that Joseph was unaware of the controversy he had caused; yet, once in a while, his fatigue and discouragement showed plainly in his face and his words. It was during one of those rare but difficult times that Asenath, using wisely appointed words, began helping Joseph to see and deal with the men of proud nobility who surrounded the throne of Pharaoh. Many were openly jealous of her husband's power and the absolute unquestionable authority the king had vested in him. It was Asenath who took on the task of the staunch, enthusiastic, supportive wife.

Once, when their passionate night of lovemaking did not drive away Joseph's wakefulness and he lay beside her staring into the spacious ceiling of their chamber, Asenath said softly but with penetrating perception, "There are two things I want you to consider, my lord." He rolled over on his side to see her beautiful face more clearly in the moon's light which streamed across their pillows.

"Only two?" he asked with a grin.

"Perhaps three," she teased back. "But now, be serious."

Joseph nodded and slid his arm around her, pulling her to him. Her head rested on his chest.

"Number one," she said, "while you have said nothing, I know you well, my lord, and you are weary of the enormous pressure and burden of trying to carry out all your plans for Egypt. Everywhere you turn, as a foreigner, you face either a loud storm of criticism and opposition or a silent wall of apathy from the nobility or the officials who have royal vested interests and who advise the king. Is not this true?"

Joseph patted her head affectionately and, to his God, he said, "Who but You could have given me such a wise and astute wife?"

She ignored his comment and resumed. "I just want you to remember that you, and you alone, are *eminently qualified* to be prime minister of Egypt. It has been decreed by the living God, and everything is happening as our God has said."

"And secondly?" he asked.

"Secondly, it is now—before the famine and before the people are hungry, when you do not see God working too clearly and you are overworked and burdened—that you tend to forget the high and holy dreams of your childhood. This must not happen! My husband, you are living out the destiny that God has appointed for you . . . do not forget your God-given dreams."

Joseph's eyes misted with tears. Once again she had sounded remarkably like his beloved mother, Rachel. Holding her close, he prayed aloud. "O mighty God of my forefathers, God who has delivered me from the hands of my enemies and set me up as a ruler of Egypt, help me to remember all Your benefits.

"Tonight You have lifted up my doubting, troubled heart and made me to recall Your vibrant promises to me and all the children of Israel. Bless the Lord, You are my strength and my vindication . . . and the wife You have given to me . . . is a woman, rare indeed."

Joseph kissed her dark silken hair, her forehead, and her eyelids, whispering, "Asenath, God has truly blessed me with a wife such as you. I am not only your husband, but your ready and willing slave . . . what gift can I bestow on you to give you a piece of my heart?"

Without opening her eyes, a small smile played across her face and Asenath replied, "Thirdly . . . you already have. You have given of your very self to me, my love . . . for I am with child."

By the time Egypt continued into its fourth year of good, prosperous, and incredibly happy times, Asenath had given birth to one son and then another.

Joseph announced the name of his firstborn would be Manasseh. Asenath knew the name meant *forgetting* or *causing to forget*, but instantly, even as she watched Joseph holding his infant up for all to see, she sensed that the name meant more. Much more. Her heart perceived that God had made up to Joseph for much of the anguish of his youth and for the loss of his father's home. In gratitude, their son's name would mean *forgetting*, not because Joseph had forgotten completely the rejection or the suffering of his boyhood days, but because the memory was no longer able to cripple him with bitterness.

He will always remember those hateful brothers, but how beautiful . . . the living God has removed the poisonous sting. Jo-

seph, somewhere along the line, perhaps when he was a prisoner, dealt with the rejection, and now the memories come and go without hate or rancor. Remarkable!

Ephraim, their second son, blue-eyed and curly haired as his father, was so named because its Egyptian translation meant *doubly fruitful*. Joseph had announced proudly, "He shall be called Ephraim because God has made me fruitful in the land of my slavery, and He has blessed me with two sons!"

Asenath lay back on her pillow, as little Ephraim sucked contentedly at her breast, and took stock of her phenomenal life. *I was fortunate to be born into the highest priestly family of Egypt. I have been given astonishing talents of both mind and spirit. The king himself arranged my marriage to Joseph, the prime minister of all Egypt. I have two fine healthy sons. But, most astounding of all, I have turned from dead and false gods to discover the real true God of creation—Joseph's God—the living God!* The goodness of her life, the blessings of God, which He seemed to shower down on her, and a man called Joseph provided all she ever dreamed or wanted.

The following years brought more of the same contentment. Joseph's work was so successful, the crops so abundant, and the collection of food so effective that it became virtually impossible to keep precise records of the vast amount of supplies on hand. A solidly filled network of royal granaries was so crammed with grain that it was like trying to number the grains of sand on the banks of the Nile. Joseph stopped counting because it was all beyond reckoning.

"God has blessed Joseph, his harvests . . . and now his granaries are filled to overflowing. We are ready for *any* famine!" Asenath said, with proud conviction, to her parents one day.

Shortly after that the seven years—the good and glorious years—of unimaginable prosperity ceased to exist.

At first there was widespread crop failure; then the river failed to flood; the soil was unable to replenish itself for the growing fields; and, finally, the farmers were unable to plant anything in the dry, drought-hardened earth. Prosperity ended—with one year of short supply dwindling down into another year of no supply.

The famine crept slowly over Egypt, like an all-consuming

army of locusts, devouring everything in its path. Egypt was first; the surrounding countries, next; and eventually, virtually no country in their part of the world was left unscarred by its ravenous appetite.

When the people throughout the land of Egypt began to starve, they appealed to Pharaoh for food. He was prepared, and so he sent them to his prime minister, saying "Present your needs to Joseph and do whatever he tells you."

Joseph opened up the storehouses, according to the severity of the famine. At first he sold grain to all the Egyptians and within a short time, he was selling grain to people from many distant lands who came to Egypt seeking relief from the far-reaching famine. Eventually he set up bartering transactions, and the king amassed huge amounts of land and livestock due to Joseph's shrewd business dealings.

So, Asenath murmured to herself as she looked out over the city one night at dusk, *it has all come to pass, exactly as God told Joseph the night at Pharaoh's banquet so long ago . . . a stone god could never have revealed the future or provided the plans for survival—only the real, living One!*

35

The frantic confusion of several hundred men and women at the grain market swirled around Asenath. The travelers, fatigued by hunger and their journey, wandered about in the bewildering crowds of people, and everyone seemed on the verge of violence. Asenath wondered just how wise she had been in joining Joseph today.

She had asked about her visiting one of the grain markets as they had eaten their breakfast. Their table, set outside under one of the great porticos, was a quiet and cool world away from the incredible bustle of activity which spun around her now.

"I plan to visit the storage granaries on the northern edge of our city today," Joseph had said. "Bring a servant or two with you and come at your leisure."

It was a special day and, though she could not put her finger on the exact reasons for her haste, Asenath was dressed and ready to go even before Joseph was in his chariot.

When he saw her eagerness, he kissed her hands and teased, "I think you'll have to ride in the chariot with me! I'm taking no chances with someone stealing your carrier away ... so come!" Their laughter had filled the air, but once they arrived at the granary, Joseph was consumed by the vast number of people, by officials, and by the magnitude of the work.

On some days like this one, Joseph left Pharaoh's palace and the central storehouse to supervise various granaries at distant outpost locations. He made spot checks to be sure officials kept accurate and honest records, and sometimes he even stepped in to transact some business. Joseph was a master at bartering, and Asenath knew he enjoyed getting out from under royal scrutiny to deal directly with the people.

Asenath began looking into the faces of the crowd, and she soon realized by the men's beards and their long tunics that the market was teeming with foreigners. She recognized Midianites, small groups of Canaanites, and others from the countries in the far north. When she saw a great many Ishmaelites line up for their purchase of grain, she made a mental note to remember it for her husband had been brought to Egypt by one of their merchants.

Joseph moved through the knots of foreigners with several officials trailing him. She watched with an affectionate heart as he humbly but circumspectly stopped here and there, talking easily with the men. To his right was Metenu, Potiphar's old servant. Joseph had pulled him out of his retirement because the old man knew a smattering of a dozen different dialects. While the crotchety servant grumbled about being put to work again, his pride in being *Joseph*'s translator knew no bounds, and he positioned himself as if he were the prime minister's shadow.

Asenath wordlessly followed behind her husband. Occasionally he turned casually, caught her eye, winked, and then returned to asking Metenu, "And what country do these men hail from?" all without breaking his stride.

Then, suddenly, it happened. Something about the way Joseph abruptly stopped or the way his head and shoulders snapped upright in firm attention, made Asenath's senses pulsate in fervid expectation.

Joseph was staring at a small cluster of men, no more than a few feet from him. And Asenath understood clearly. Her thoughts screamed out at her. *This is why he visits these outposts! These are the men he has been looking for . . . they are his brothers! He has been searching for them and yearning for word of his father.*

Now Joseph pointed to the group of nine or ten and, in the strong Egyptian language, he asked sternly of Metenu, "Who are those men and where have they come from?"

His voice, harsh and rough, was out of character. Asenath had never heard him speak so sharply. She guessed by observing Joseph's face when they answered Metenu—that the men had not needed any translation of his biting question. She stepped closer to the side of Metenu to get a better look and was overwhelmed by what she witnessed.

The prime minister of Egypt, in his pure white royal linen skirt, his gold chain, and other ornaments, the bejeweled dagger in his belt and the short mantle around his shoulders, loomed in the sunshine like some tall, resplendent and holy god.

The men dropped to their knees before him, and, even before they found their voices to answer him, Asenath surmised two things: They were Joseph's brothers all right; and they had no idea in the world, as they groveled in the dirt at his feet, that this prime minister of Egypt was their brother. *Nor should they! After all,* Asenath reasoned, *they were grown men when they sold him into slavery, but he was a mere lad of seventeen . . . and now he's grown, shaved, and dressed like the king himself!*

"They are from the land of Canaan, and they have come to buy grain," Metenu said routinely, guarding the secret that he knew Joseph was hearing his own Hebrew language.

The sight of the brothers bowing down must have reminded Joseph of his childhood dreams, because Asenath saw a slight flicker of a remembered moment light his face for just an instant. Then, with a shocking violence in his voice, he lashed out at Metenu, "They are spies!" and directly to them, but still in his Egyptian tongue, he shouted, "You are spies. You have stolen into Egypt to see how the famine has devastated the land!"

Their faces drained of color as Metenu translated and then, with hands folded in supplication and voices pleading for understanding, they cried as with one voice, "No! No! We have come to Egypt only to buy food. We are all brothers . . . the sons of one man, and we are honest men. We are not spies, my lord," they protested.

"Yes, you are. All of you!" Joseph squared his shoulders and stood his full height above them. "You have come to spy on the nakedness of the land." His voice threatened their souls with destruction, and Asenath wondered what accusation Joseph would throw at them next. He seemed determined to test them to the uttermost of their limits.

"Sir," Metenu translated for one of them, "great master, there are twelve of us brothers, and our father lives in the land of Canaan. Our youngest brother is there, with our father, and . . . " the man tugged at his beard, "one . . . one of our brothers is dead."

"So?" Joseph spit back. "What does your story prove? Nothing. It is as I have said. You are spies!"

The stunned men watched the ruler as he strode away from them; and, stumbling to their feet, they followed, hoping to continue to plead their case. Joseph sat down on a special chair which had been placed under a coarse linen awning and quietly studied each man.

Asenath stood in the sun, with the curious crowd that had gathered, and realized that Joseph planned to be in the darkened shade of the awning so he could easily see the faces of the men positioned in the brilliant sunlight, who once again dropped on their knees before him.

When he had thoroughly frightened the men and thought he had delayed enough, Joseph said, through Metenu, "I have decided to test and prove your story, and I will do it in this way: As surely as Pharaoh lives, you shall not leave Egypt until this youngest brother comes here! One of you go and fetch your brother. I shall keep the rest of you here, bound in prison. Then we will find out if your story is true or not. If it turns out that you do not *have* a younger brother, then by the life of Pharaoh, I shall know you are spies!"

Before the speechless brothers could appeal their case or beg his indulgence, Joseph suddenly changed his mind and ordered that they all be taken to the royal prison and bound.

Rising quickly, he left his chair, took Asenath's arm, and whispered, "Come. We shall leave immediately."

Not until they were back in the privacy of a small drawing room off their bed chamber did Joseph speak again.

"My knees went so weak out there I thought I'd fall—and, even now, my bones feel as if they have turned to water." He sat on the edge of a small couch, massaging his legs as he spoke. "You have guessed who those men were?" he questioned.

"Truly, they are your brothers," Asenath replied. He slowly nodded his assent.

"The biggest man, with the very dark and full beard . . . ?" she asked.

"Reuben."

"You have been regularly touring these outpost grain store-houses, hoping to hear of them or see them?"

"Yes," he said with a sigh.

Joseph's face, drawn from the emotional strain of his encounter, managed a smile in her direction. "As Pharaoh said, you can read minds. I only hope my inner thoughts were not as transparent to my brothers as they are to you. You are right, as usual. Even going with me today you sensed this would be the day . . . and it truly was." He stopped rubbing his legs and leaned back into the pillows of the couch.

"What a flood of memories gushed over me when I saw them. I knew them instantly, and yet I couldn't believe it was my brothers," he said, shaking his head as if he still did not believe it.

Asenath said firmly, "You were very harsh with them, but, according to Egyptian justice, not hard enough. You could easily have them executed. No one questions your judgment now; and if you said they were spies, that would be all there was to it. They could die for that." Her face softened, and she asked hesitantly, "What will you do with them?"

Asenath moved behind him, helped him sit up straighter, and then she began working her thumbs and fingers into the tense rigid muscles at the tops of his shoulders. She was thoughtful as she continued her massage, and Joseph said, "My love, at this moment I do not know exactly what I am going to do. I threw them all into prison because, as I watched them, I couldn't bear to let even one return to Canaan; yet, I must know the fate of my brother Benjamin." He rested a moment savoring the work of her fingers.

Softly he said, "I know only that I must test them. I have so many questions. Have they changed? Is Benjamin well and whole? Will they protect and love him as I have, or will they sell him, too? And what of my father, Jacob? Oh, Asenath, I long to reveal myself to them—right now. I want to go to the prison and shout, 'It is I, Joseph!' but I know nothing of their hearts, nothing of how God has dealt with them over the years. And I know nothing of my father and beloved brother Benjamin . . ."

Asenath cradled his head in her hands and leaned him against her breast. Soothingly she whispered, "My love, God will give you a plan—just as He has done for all of the starving peoples of the land. He *will*, you'll see. He *will!*"

Three days passed before Joseph went back to the prison and called for the ten men of Canaan to be brought to him. As he related the events that had taken place that day to Asenath, Joseph recalled how he had met his brothers in the confines of a familiar interrogation room and how he had met them with perspiring hands and trembling knees.

"I made it clear that I was a God-fearing man and that I believed in giving them an opportunity to prove their innocence. I also told them that I was willing to take a chance on them, counting on them being honorable men, that only one of them would remain bound in prison chains . . . I would release the rest to go home with the grain for their families. Then," Joseph continued, "I said what they feared the most, for I told them to bring back their youngest brother to prove they had been telling the truth and that, indeed, they were not spies."

Asenath listened, wide-eyed, as Joseph added, "They agreed to this plan of my keeping one of them here, and then—not knowing I could understand them—my brother Judah said to the others, 'Unquestionably, this is all our fault. We are guilty for what we did to Joseph so long ago. We witnessed the terror and agony of his soul, we heard his pleadings from the pit; but we would not listen. Now that agony is upon us.' "

Joseph wept as he related the details to Asenath, but he proceeded on: "Reuben, the oldest of them, reminded them that he

had told them not to take my life. My brother burned them with
his fiery words and spoke through a clenched jaw as he said, 'You,
in your stiffed-necked rebellion, would not listen to me. Take
note, the payment for his blood has come due, and now we shall
die because we murdered him.' " Joseph wiped his face with the
cloth Asenath had handed him and then resumed.

"Of course they still did not know I could understand them;
but I tell you, Asenath, I could bear to hear no more. I fled before
they could see how moved I was by their repentant hearts, and
for a long time I spilled out my pent-up grief and tears in the har-
ness shed behind the prison. I fear I would still be there except
that Metenu and Potiphar found me. I washed and returned to
my brothers."

"And then?" Asenath urged.

"Then I selected Simeon and had him bound in chains, to impress them with my serious intent."

"Why Simeon?" she asked.

"It was fitting." Joseph's voice tensed, "Simeon pushed me,
and his face was the last one I saw before I dropped into the
frightening depths of that dark pit."

Asenath felt the contents of her stomach churn within her;
but she wanted all the details, so she said, "Now Simeon is here
at the royal prison, and your brothers have gone home?"

"Yes," Joseph replied softly. "Simeon is the golden cord
which will bring my brother Benjamin to me. I have sent them on
their way. I also had servants fill up their sacks of grain and, because I found I still love them . . ." He faltered a moment before
resuming. "I had all their money put back into their sacks, and
even added to it for the buying of provisions along their journey."

"Their hearts will fail them with fear!" Asenath predicted.

"Why?"

"Because their consciences are already overburdened with
guilt . . . they will not understand how the money got in there, or
why it is there, and they will be confused if not frightened,"
Asenath suggested.

"Perhaps. But . . . they are my brothers and, while they did
not recognize their now grown brother, I knew them, and, as I
said before, I still love them."

She kissed his tear-stained face and said, "Now hush. You

have gone through enough today. It is enough." Asenath's soft comment served as a benediction on all her husband had said that night.

36

The long, hot days of famine simmered into weeks, and the weeks boiled into one arid new moon after another. But still there was no word or sight of his brothers.

Each daybreak Asenath wakened and watched Joseph as he rose from the restlessness of his sleep to seek the voice of God. She grew familiar with the sight of her husband—kneeling in the open balcony doorway, bending over until his head touched the floor, and hearing him praising and thanking the God of his forefathers. She knew, too, that this man of prayer would end each prayer with the supplication, "O righteous God of Israel, make this the day when I see the faces of my brothers again."

Some mornings she joined him, and, side by side, they poured out their hearts to God. It was one such morning, when they had stayed on their knees for a longer time than usual, that they were interrupted by the chief household servant. Breathlessly Paneb announced, "The men ... the men from Canaan have arrived. They are at the royal storehouse."

As he helped Asenath to her feet, Joseph murmured, "Simeon is here in prison, and I sent nine home." Then, turning to Paneb and keeping his voice as even as he could, he asked, "How many men have come from Canaan?"

When he heard the answer, "Ten, my lord," Joseph whistled through his teeth, swooped Asenath around in his arms, and shouted, "Benjamin! They have brought Benjamin. They have not harmed him! My brother Benjamin is here!"

Joseph readily agreed to let Asenath go with him, although nothing short of a royal edict could have kept her away; but, instead of getting ready, Joseph sat down on their bed.

"We shall take our leisure in getting to the palace," he said as he leaned his head back in his hands on the pillows. "I intend to delay our appearance,' he explained. "When they were here the first time, they acknowleged their guilt in the crime against me; and now, by their obedience in bringing Benjamin here, I think a forgiving reconciliation is possible. However, it suits my purposes to keep *them* waiting."

When they reached the palace, Joseph ordered, "Send the men from Canaan to my court room. I will see them there."

Asenath seated herself on a chair behind one of the side pillars. There she could observe the scene but still be partially hidden. Joseph moved up the steps of the dais and now sat on his throne, nervously snapping the ends of his fingernails together.

All at once the chamber doors were opened. Potiphar and Metenu were followed by the ten men.

Both Joseph and Asenath found Benjamin at the same time.

Asenath located the youngest man instantly. It had not been due to her mental powers, but *rather* because Benjamin's face and form so closely resembled her own husband. She knew, too, that on seeing his brother, Joseph's mind was flooded with childhood memories of his love for his father, and that a fresh grief for his mother rose powerfully within him.

Perhaps it was from his God, but from somewhere Joseph willed iron into his veins, and Asenath listened as he said with no outward display of emotion, "Potiphar, take these men to my home. I have decided to take care of our business there. Tell Paneb they will eat with me, along with you and Metenu, at midday. Instruct him also that he is to personally supervise the butchering and the overall arrangements for I want a special feast prepared.

"Also," he continued, "have their brother released from prison. See that he is bathed and given clean clothes, and have him brought to my house for I would have him join his brothers and me."

Not waiting for Joseph, Asenath slipped unnoticed out of the court and hurried home.

Paneb, a genius in managing their household, threw the servants into a flurry of preparations. A dinner for fifteen would be executed flawlessly; and Asenath knew that by the time the Hebrews reached the outer courtyard, Paneb would have extra servants outside, with basins of cool water, all ready for the first

Egyptian act of hospitality—foot washing.

While she did not understand their language, Asenath knew by their shocked faces that as soon as they had entered the massive iron gates they had surmised the worst: they had been taken to the house of the prime minister! Their spontaneous panic sent Metenu and Paneb over to calm their fearful suspicions.

Asenath finally caught Metenu's eye, and he came out of the courtyard into her house. Excitedly she ordered, "Tell me what happened just now!"

The old man laughed and said, "Their guilty consciences flare for no reason at all. They thought we had tricked them into coming here.

"When they left here the last time, Master Joseph had me return the money they had paid. So, on their first night out, when they opened the grain sacks, they found the money and were at a complete loss to explain it."

"I told Joseph that money would frighten them," Asenath said softly.

Metenu shook his head and, still grinning, he resumed. "They thought that Zaphnath-paaneah wanted them here to accuse them of stealing, and that after that he would imprison all of them."

"Whatever you told them must have soothed them. Look . . ." Asenath pointed out into the courtyard where the men were resting and conversing in a casual way while servants bathed their feet.

"They gave me the payment money back and additional money to buy more grain, and they pleaded my understanding of this mystery. Each man swore he had no idea who put the money into their sacks." Metenu chuckled and then continued. "So I assured them they were not to worry. I gave them back their money, and I told them there was no mystery. Their God, the God of their forefathers, probably put the money in their sacks for we had originally collected the right amount and no more payment was due. Only then would they allow themselves to enjoy this place.

"See!" Metenu pointed to some boxes and baskets. "They have brought gifts from their homeland. There is Gilead balm, thick grape honey which only the Hebrews can make, rich spices, almond nuts, and several vials of myrrh."

Metenu turned slowly and, risking Asenath's displeasure at his asking a far too personal question, he asked, "My lady, who *are* these men that master Joseph pretends he is the cat, playing with the mouse? He taunts them one moment and treats them with a feast the next."

Asenath knew she did not have to answer him; but, because he asked without impertinence and because Metenu's love of Joseph was unimpeachable, she said, "My husband has told no one who they are for the time is not yet right." A small hurt look flashed into the old servant's eyes, and Asenath sought to ease it. Hastily she added, "Perhaps, because he has known you a long time, my husband assumes you have already guessed who the men are."

Gradually the old man pieced the puzzle together and, with gleaming eyes, he said, "Of course! I should have known ... the men are from *Canaan* ... yes, yes." He laid a bony finger across his lips and pledged her his silence.

Several hours later, when all the customs of hospitality had been carried out—the washing, the setting out of gifts, and even the feeding and watering of their caravan of donkeys—Joseph's chariot clattered into the courtyard.

He stood before them in his royal splendor; and once more, it seemed to Asenath, he savored the sight of his brothers bowing to the earth before him and presenting him with their bounty of gifts.

Joseph strolled about, looking at the gifts, nodding his head in approval, and making what he hoped passed for small talk. He was famished for news of his father and family.

Through Metenu, he asked in the casual name of hospitality, "Are all of you married?" He waved his hand at the group, but pointed at Judah for he longed to hear about the well-being of Sherah. Judah shook his head *yes* and then *no* so quickly that Joseph quipped to Metenu, "Ask him if he needs time to think on it!" The brothers smiled, and Levi explained, "Some of us are married, others not; but Judah, he has had two wives."

"You are a widower, then?" Joseph said, with more sadness than they knew.

Judah indicated yes and no again, and Joseph's curiosity flared. "God has blessed me with two wives," Judah explained

"My first wife was young, and when we were in northern Canaan, she left my tents. I think she wanted to live with her own people. My second wife bore me five sons, and then she died."

The explanation was more than adequate, and Joseph, needing time to keep his emotions under control, asked the kinds of questions a dutiful host would: "Are you weary from the journey?"; "How widespread is the famine in Canaan?";"Is the drought continuing?" Then, growing impatient with his pretense, he asked the only question on his heart. "Tell me, how is your father—the old man you spoke of before? Is he still alive?"

Joseph swallowed hard and stared up intently at a far corner of his rooftop. If his calculations were correct, his father was over one hundred years of age, and for all he knew could die at any moment. Unless his brothers had changed, the death of his father would mean a bitter family dispute over their inheritance, and the family of Israel would not emerge as a great nation but as a pitifully shattered remnant of a family. As he concentrated his gaze on the roof they replied, "Oh, yes. Your servant, our father, is alive and in good health." Again they bowed, giving him their respect. Only Metenu saw Joseph's chest heave a sigh of relief.

A moment later, looking at Benjamin, the son of his own mother, Rachel, Joseph asked, "Is this your youngest brother, the one you told me about?" They nodded, and he said, "God be gracious to you, my son."

Asenath, who had observed all of this from a covered porch, was startled to see Joseph leave them unceremoniously and walk hurriedly into the house. She had to run to follow him, but finally caught up to him in their bed chamber. He was on his knees, bent over as though he were praying; but his sobbing penetrated and ground into floor and walls, as if, upon being face-to-face with Benjamin, a large dam had broken within him. The sounds of his weeping filled the enormous room; and, knowing she should do nothing to hinder or stop the venting of his emotions, she busied herself by preparing a basin of water. Asenath waited until finally the heaving of his shoulders subsided, the noise of his sobbing quieted, and the flowing tears were all but emptied out of him.

"My love," she said, offering him the cool, wet towel, "the meal is ready."

Silently Joseph worked and recovered his poise. Then, loving her for her loyalty and wordless approval, he held Asenath in his arms and said, in the same low voice which never ceased to thrill her, "I love you . . . do you know that?"

She kissed his cheek. "I know," she whispered.

Arm in arm they descended the stairs and went into the main banquet room where three tables, set for a feast, awaited them. Joseph escorted his wife to her place at the main table, in the front of the room, and motioned for Potiphar and Metenu to be seated at the second table. Then, because Egyptians never ate at the same table with Hebrews and practiced rigid segregation, the large table at the end of the room was for the men from Canaan only. Immediately his brothers were ushered in.

In simple sign language, Joseph gestured where each man was to sit. They murmured amongst themselves in amazement for he seated each man in order of his age, from the oldest to the youngest. They could only wonder how this ruler knew so much about them.

Waiters served the guests with food from Joseph's table. Asenath was surprised to hear her husband instruct a servant that the youngest Hebrew was to be given the choice morsel of meat he held up. Four more times he sent something extra or something especially good to his brother Benjamin, before Asenath guessed his intentions.

"You are testing them again," she commented as she ate a piece of roasted meat, "and I have it all figured out." Her bright eyes snapped at him.

"Really?" Joseph smiled. "Tell me, then, what am I doing?"

"You are showing a great partiality to Benjamin. Five times you have sent delicious tributes, honoring him; not so Benjamin will think more highly of you, but because you want to see how the brothers take to your display of favoritism," she said smugly.

"And since you know so much what conclusions have you drawn, oh wise wife of mine?" he teased.

Asenath moved closer to him and said with her uncanny insight, "I think they feel no resentment or jealousy for they are eating, talking, and making merry, as if you had never singled anyone out for honor. Joseph, I believe they are changed. Truly changed."

He picked up Pharaoh's gift, the elegant silver divining cup, had it filled with wine, and motioning her to pick up her cup, he declared, "To my new brothers ... may they pass every test as well as they have this one."

"So be it!" She echoed his confidence, and thev drank their wine in bright anticipation of the future.

37

As soon as the first rosy kiss of dawn lightly touched the city's rooftops, the sons of Jacob were on their way home.

Their sacks, filled to capacity and almost bursting with grain, put a considerable strain on their caravan of donkeys; but it was of no consequence to the brothers because nothing could dampen their enthusiasm. They had paid their respects to the man of Egypt once more, and now they were returning to their father with both grain *and* their brother Benjamin. They hurried their beasts of burden along to get home before anything else could go awry.

Joseph watched them from a secluded place on his roof until they disappeared from view within the city streets. When he joined his wife and two sons, Asenath greeted him with, "You are staying at home today, my lord?" She was seated at a small table for their morning meal while the young boys played a game with a servant, nearby.

A slightly mischievous grin spread across her husband's face and, seeing it, Asenath laughed and responded, "I see! You have no intention of letting your brothers go home just yet. You plan to bring them back ... What will it be now? More tests?"

Without answering her, Joseph picked up his older son.

He sat down at the table and gave Manasseh a bouncy ride on his knee. The child's squeals of laughter filled the room.

"Not so rough, my lord!" Asenath cautioned. "He has just finished his meal. Besides, I want to know exactly what will happen today. Now, give Manasseh back to the servant girl so we can talk."

Reluctantly Joseph slid the child down off his leg, then he

whispered something to the boy which apparently tickled Manasseh, because the lad giggled and quickly joined his brother and the servant.

Joseph watched the two boys for a moment, and then he shook a small golden bell on the table before him. Its high-pitched tinkling brought Paneb to his side.

"Paneb," Joseph instructed with quiet authority, "I want you to get Metenu. I have an errand for you two." The servant slipped noiselessly out of the room.

"My, but you are rather devious this morning," Asenath observed aloud with a wink and a wry smile.

Still Joseph made no comment.

When Paneb and Metenu finally stood before him, Joseph spoke with deliberation and gave them his well-thought-out directions. "I estimate that the Hebrew men have nearly reached the outer limits of the city by now. I want you both to use my chariot, pick the fastest horse, and overtake them before they sail away on some barge or disappear on the overland route."

Paneb seemed surprised at the orders, but Metenu's face remained stoic as Joseph continued. "When you find them, stop them and ask why they are acting like this—paying evil for good, when the master has been hospitable and kind to them. Accuse them of stealing my silver divining cup, and let them understand they have done a very wicked deed."

"But, my lord, you instructed us to put your cup in Benjamin's grain sack . . ." Paneb objected, and would have said more, but Metenu shot him a withering glance. Paneb obediently remembered his place.

Bowing low, they took their leave.

Awhile later, as Joseph and Asenath waited in the main reception chamber of their house, they heard the jingling of the caravans' donkey bells. Joseph, seated next to Asenath, reached over and gripped his wife's hand tightly for a moment. Then he pulled away, sat regally back in his chair and with eyes blazing in anticipation, he called for them to be brought in.

Paneb and Metenu ushered the panic-stricken men into the chamber. Judah, the most overwrought of all of them—his tunic torn in a display of remorse—immediately flung himself on the marble floor at Joseph's feet.

Joseph leaned forward in his chair for a moment and then demanded, "How could you do such a disgusting and dishonorable thing?" The formal charges and tumultuous accusations set the men to trembling. "Did you not realize," Joseph continued, ignoring their frightened stares, "that a man, such as I, would know *who* it was who stole my divining cup?"

Judah lifted his head up off the floor but remained prone before Joseph as he implored, "Oh, my lord, what shall we say? How can we plead? Or how can we possibly prove our innocence?" He turned his head slightly and, looking at his brothers, he said remorsefully, "God is punishing us for our sins!"

Then Judah cried out to Metenu, "Tell the master, we have all returned to be his faithful slaves; all my brothers, including the one in whose sack the cup was found."

"No!" shouted Joseph; and so pronounced was his vehemence, Metenu did not have to translate the word. Then, turning to Metenu, Joseph ordered, "Tell them that only the man who stole my cup shall remain and become my slave. The rest of them may go home to be with their father."

Judah's eyes blazed in a flash of horror as he heard Metenu's words. He jumped up and rushed forward to Joseph's chair to plead his case. Intensely he said, "Oh, my lord, give me your permission to speak a few heartfelt words to you. Please be patient with me for just a moment, and let not your anger blaze against me. I know you could doom me in an instant for you are as the pharaoh himself. But listen, I pray you, to my story."

Joseph kept his hand over his mouth and his head slightly bowed as he pretended to listen to Metenu's translation. Then he nodded and indicated that a hearing was granted.

As Judah began to speak, the Hebrew language flowed out of him. The prime minister of Egypt put his head in his hands and leaned forward so no one could see his raw and naked inner feelings. Nor could they discover how deeply moved he was as he listened, while thirty-some years of memories swirled about him.

Judah was overcome by his sense of helplessness, and he whispered urgently before Joseph's bowed head, "Master, you asked us if we had a father or a brother, and we said, 'Yes. We have a father, an old man, and a child of his old age: a young one called Benjamin.' But Benjamin's brother is dead, and he alone is left of his mother's children. This son is loved very much by his father." Judah paused while Metenu translated. Then resuming, the older brother murmured, "Then you said, 'Bring that brother here so I may see him,' but we told you that the lad could not leave his father for Jacob, our father, would surely die. But you, good sir, warned us never to come back again without Benjamin."

Judah straightened up and wiped his mouth with the back of his hand and said contritely, "So we returned to our father and told him all you had said.

"Later when Jacob, our father, instructed us to 'go back and buy a little more food,' we replied that we could not return to Egypt unless he allowed our youngest brother to go with us.

"Listen, good master, for here are my father's words ... exactly as he said them. He told us, 'You know that my wife Rachel had two sons and that one of them went away and never returned—doubtless torn to pieces by some wild animal; I have never seen him since. Now, if you take away his brother from me also, and any harm befalls him, I shall die with sorrow!' "

Judah knelt before Joseph and, raising his hands in supplication, he begged, "Now, my lord, if we go back to our father and Benjamin is not with us ... and seeing our father's life is bound up in that lad ... when he sees us and finds Benjamin is missing, our father will surely die. And then we shall be responsible for bringing down his white hairs in sorrow to his grave."

The brothers murmured amongst themselves in total agreement. Judah silenced them with a look; and then, turning back to Joseph, he offered, "My lord, I vowed to my father that if he let Benjamin go with us, I would take care of him. And I also told my father that if I did not bring Benjamin back, I would bear the blame forever. So please, master, let *me* stay here with you as your slave, and let the lad return home with his brothers. For how can I face my father if Benjamin is not with me?" Judah's eyes spilled over in tears, and with great sadness he added, "I cannot bear to witness what this would do to my father."

Asenath lifted her head suddenly and heard it before the others. It was a low moaning sound which wrenched itself from the depths of Joseph. It finally split the air as Joseph shouted to Paneb and the other servants, "Out—all of you! I would be alone with my brothers."

Asenath caught Metenu's attention and whispered, "You stay here with me and tell me what is said."

Then the moaning of Joseph crescendoed into cries, and still seated in his regal chair, he began to weep violently.

Asenath sensed that the earnest and remorseful, even eloquent, pleas of Judah had stabbed the vital parts of her husband's heart. Whatever Judah had been before, he was not now. It was no secret that this brother had grown into a man of godly character for Judah's compassion toward both Benjamin and his father had just been clearly revealed.

As she stood a little behind Joseph's chair, she understood that the thing which touched her husband the most was the ending of Judah's plea—when he willingly offered his own life to slavery, even to die if need be, in Benjamin's place. She knew, too, that Joseph had given his brothers the severest of tests; and they had passed them beyond his expectations. His tears were the joyous outpouring of relief for a thousand-pound weight of hurt which had just melted off his soul.

Joseph's sobbing shook his body, and it could be heard throughout their whole house. Asenath moved closer to him, but he held her back. He struggled to his feet, and cried out in Hebrew, "My brothers, my brothers—I am Joseph!"

The men, overwhelmed by his Hebrew speech and the meaning of his words, shrank back in utter disbelief. Each man was paralyzed by Joseph's words and his own fearful thoughts.

When Joseph could see they were too stunned to reply, he said loudly, "My brothers!" And then, to help their unbelief and to ease them out of their shock, he added, "Is my father alive?" Still they could not respond.

When Metenu told her what was said, Asenath thought, *He asked that same question before as a brusque Egyptian prime minister. Now he asks about his father as a loving son, and they are beginning to see him as Joseph, their brother, but the knowledge terrifies them!* She was enveloped in the incredible drama which played before her. The hot Egyptian day made the room warm and somewhat stifling, yet she felt a unique surging of cool air around her, and suddenly she knew unequivocally she was standing in the presence of the living God. It would be a moment she would never forget. Momentarily she bent her head and silently worshiped the God of Jacob. When she looked up, she found that the brothers, quaking in fear, had backed away from Joseph to the far end of the room.

"Come over here, all of you. Come closer!" Joseph called when he was composed enough. Slowly they clustered around him, and he repeated, "Look. I am Joseph, your brother, whom you sold into Egypt."

The brothers studied and scrutinized his face, but they still found themselves unable to speak. Joseph continued, "Please, do not be vexed or disheartened with yourselves for selling me into slavery for you were not totally to blame. It was *God's* plan, not yours, to send me here ahead of you to save your lives."

Unexpectedly he sat down, crosslegged on the floor before them, and motioned for them to gather around him. Then, when they were all seated, Joseph explained. "For two years now the famine has been upon us, and you need to know that for five more years there will be neither plowing nor harvest.

"God has sent this Hebrew into the land of Egypt to keep you and your families alive so that one day we shall survive as the children of Israel and be a great nation of people."   •

Metenu translated Joseph's words with excitement into Asenath's ear as she observed the men. The brothers exchanged puzzled glances and shook their heads in amazement as Joseph said without resentment "So, you see, it was *God* who sent me here, not you. It was in His plan to make me a counselor, even an advising father to the pharaoh. It also served God's purpose to make me prime minister of this nation, and so I rule over all of Egypt."

Joseph drew his breath in deeply and then said strongly, "Now . . . I want you to hurry on your way. Go to my father and give him this message. Tell him his son Joseph says, 'God has made me prime minister of all the land of Egypt. Come down to Egypt right away!' Tell him also that he shall be given much land in the Goshen area so that he can be near me with all his children, his grandchildren, his flocks, and all that he has. I will take care of all of our family there."

Joseph gestured his hand toward them all; and then, pointing to Benjamin, he confirmed, "You men have witnessed my promise, and my brother, the son of Rachel, my mother, has heard my vows. For there are still five years of famine ahead of us; and if you do not move down into Egypt where I can see to your needs and support you, your families, and all you possess may come to utter ruin." He paused a moment and then said warmly, "Tell my father all about my splendor and power here in Egypt and how everyone is commanded to obey me ... and then ..." he added softly, "then, as soon as it is humanly possible, bring him to me!"

As the message of the identity and the intentions of Joseph soaked into each man's mind, Joseph reached across Reuben and grasped Benjamin's hand and pulled him close.

Asenath's own tears flowed freely down her face as she watched the two beautiful men embracing, mingling their tears, and renewing their love for each other.

When Joseph finally broke away from Benjamin, he then held and wept with each one of the brothers. All the walls of envy and hate were broken down. For the first time they were united by the bonds of brotherly love, and their surprise was only surpassed by their joy. The healing of souls which took place that day was a miraculous tribute to God's enduring mercy and His everlasting love.

Suddenly, remembering protocol and the social etiquette of the day, Joseph called for Asenath. She rose from her chair and crossed the room to him. With great exuberance, he proceeded to introduce her to each of his brothers. Joseph saved Benjamin for the last; and then whispered to Asenath, "Bring in our sons. I want them to meet their uncles. And tell Metenu to have the rest of the servants come as well."

Asenath and Metenu left the hall, gathered up the boys and the servants, and together they went in to greet Joseph's brothers.

The room was noisily alive with queries about wives, children, and families. News about the country and conversations about all that had transpired in the twenty-two years of separation filled the air.

She knew the loud exchange of information and the sounds of Joseph's weeping had been bound to reach the pharaoh's ears; so Asenath was not surprised, a few moments later, when Metenu's old and shaky voice commanded their attention.

"My lord ..." He directed his words to Joseph. "The pharaoh

has heard the joyous news about your brothers, and he has sent you a message." Joseph nodded for Metenu to continue. "He said he is pleased and happy for you today and so are his officials. He and the noblemen of Egypt rejoice with you on the reunion with your brothers, and they would choose this occasion to show their appreciation to you for all you have done for Egypt. His majesty has requested that you go to the palace and speak with him at once."

Joseph excused himself and left immediately.

Her husband was held in the highest of esteem by the pharaoh, and Asenath wondered just how the king would show his appreciation. *Undoubtedly because Joseph is so unique,* she thought, *Pharaoh believes he has come from a noble and prosperous lineage, so he will grant any favor Joseph seeks from him.*

None of them had to wait very long. Joseph was back in their midst within the hour and his face was flushed with joy.

"My brothers, the Pharaoh himself has asked that you load and pack your animals for travel and return quickly to your home so that you may bring our father and all our family to Egypt. His royal highness said, 'Tell them I will assign them the finest territory in the land of Egypt, and they shall live off the fat of the land.' The king has also sent wagons for you to carry your wives and little ones back here. He said, too, that you should not bother about your furniture in Canaan for the best of Egypt is yours!"

For the next three days the outer courtyard of Joseph's house bristled with activity, much like an over-crowded bazaar on a festival day. Everyone helped to get the brothers off. Joseph gave them the wagons, as Pharaoh had commanded, and a host of servants saw to their storehouse of provisions. Joseph's generosity knew no limits. To each brother, he gave brand new clothing; but Asenath noticed that to Benjamin, Joseph gave five changes of clothes and three hundred pieces of silver. To his father, Joseph sent ten donkeys laden with Egyptian gifts, and ten more carrying grain and foodstuffs for their return journey.

When all was in readiness, Joseph prayed for their safety in traveling; and then, as a parting remark, he said good naturedly, "Have no doubts or disagreements on the way! I want nothing to slow you down!"

Long after they left, and in the privacy of his bed chamber,

Joseph held Asenath in his arms, and feeling doubts rising within him, he ventured, "I wonder if my father, Jacob, will be able to understand all of this. Will he know that what my brothers say *now* is the truth? It has been so long . . . he is old and has many years of thinking that I was dead—"

Asenath covered Joseph's mouth with her hand. "Shush," she whispered. "I can see it all in my mind's eye. Judah and the others will tell him you are alive and the ruler of Egypt. At first, I think, his heart will be hard as stone, but when your father hears Benjamin's testimony and when they give him your messages . . . when he sees the wagons of food you have sent him, his heart will melt. His spirits will revive, and he will come to Egypt straightaway."

Joseph kissed the top of her head and hugged her tightly as he murmured, "Yes, of course, my love. He will come *straightaway!*"

38

By the time one new moon had rounded out in the night skies, then disappeared, and another moon was on its way to fullness, a servant interrupted Joseph's and Asenath's morning meal with "My lord, forgive the intrusion, but your brother Judah is here asking for you!"

Both Joseph and Asenath flew down the steps, into the main hall, and out to the courtyard. Judah, dusty and travel-worn, bowed his head to Joseph and broke into a huge grin. "Our father and all the children of Israel are even now approaching Goshen," Judah said with a touch of wonder, as if—even after making the long trip—he still did not really believe it all.

"Is he well, and has he made the trip comfortably?" Joseph questioned.

"Yes. He is well." Judah put his arm around Joseph's shoulders and then resumed. "At first, when we told him about you, he shut his ears to our words. But in the face of such famine, to see

Pharaoh's wagons loaded with food was ..." he patted his brother's back, "it was *most* convincing."

Joseph took the moment to wink at Asenath. "It was as you said it would be!" he said grinning. He called for stablemen, and ordered two chariots to be brought to the main entrance. Then Joseph said to Judah, "Asenath will ride with me and I shall have my best horseman drive you. We shall meet our father in Goshen."

The horses were the fastest in Joseph's stable; yet their ride through the city's stone streets, and then northeast into the country side, seemed to crawl at a tortoise's pace.

Just as Asenath thought the trip to Goshen would take forever, Joseph turned to her and nodded his head to the north—straight ahead of them.

A large cloud of sand swirled behind a great host of people. "There!" Joseph cried above the clamor and noise of chariot wheels and hoof beats.

Gradually, as they came closer, Asenath could see that the wagons were filled with women, children, and possessions while the sons and older grandsons rode on donkeys. They were followed by all their flocks of sheep, goats, cows, and camels. A quick head count of the main body of people turned out to be about seventy persons. Besides the seventy, there were the wives of Jacob's sons and grandsons and a host of servants. Adding women and children to the seventy, made a spectacular sight. *So these are the children of Israel*, Asenath thought as Joseph reined his horse to a stop.

She never had to ask which man was Joseph's father. Asenath found him immediately. He had ridden in one of the wagons, and during the last mile of their journey he had stood, holding on to the front of the wagon—his white head of hair flowing off his face in the wind and his tall frame, stooped slightly by age—looking like the magnificent patriarch that he was. Asenath loved him instantly.

Joseph left the chariot and ran through the last few feet of sand to help his father down from the wagon.

When Jacob was finally standing before his son, Joseph threw his arms around his father's neck, and the silence of twenty-two years was broken only by sounds of weeping. It seemed that time, people, and even animals stood quietly transfixed that day as the two men held each other and wept.

Jacob was the one who broke their embrace. He stepped back to look at the full measure of his son; and then, lifting up his hands heavenward, he said simply, "I am one hundred thirty years old, not nearly as aged as some of my forefathers, but I have lived a full life. Now, let me die, for I have seen you again, Joseph, and I know you are alive!"

Joseph's face was wet with tears, and he confessed, "Oh, father, how I have longed to see you. I was afraid that you might not make this difficult journey."

Jacob rested both his hands on Joseph's shoulders and said, "I might not have completed such a trip except that I stopped to worship by the old altar I built at Beersheba near the southern boundary. There I sought God's will, offered sacrifices, and remembered the promises I'd been given about all my children. As I slept that night, God visited me in what may be my last high and holy dream.

"Twice He called my name, and I answered, 'Here am I, Lord.' Then the voice said, 'I am God, the God of your forefathers. Do not be afraid to go down to Egypt, for I will see to it that you become a great nation there. And I, your God, will go with you into Egypt and will bring your descendants back again; but you shall die in Egypt with Joseph at your side.'

"My son," Jacob continued, "I have come down to Egypt at God's direction." Then Jacob turned and called for Reuben to bring him "the package." Joseph watched as his father's eyes found Reuben; and then, remembering his father's hip injury of so long ago, Joseph's face was washed afresh in tears as he saw his father limp painfully toward Reuben and then back again.

"Open it," Jacob instructed.

Unwrapped, the linen parcel contained a bloodstained garment. Instantly Joseph's mind was consumed with a hundred memories. "It is my tunic," he said in wonder.

"Yes," Jacob assured him. "The very one Sherah made for you. I have kept it all this time.

"When I first got it and thought you were dead, I wrapped it in linen and never looked at it again . . . until God spoke to me in my dream at Beersheba. That night I opened it up and spread it out before me, and I saw something I had never seen before." The old man smiled, took the tunic and shook it out before Joseph. "See?" he said, pointing to the dark brown stains. "There are many blotches and blood stains, but the garment is not torn or ripped anywhere. I realized it was God's confirmation to me that indeed you were alive in Egypt. For how could you have been brutally killed, torn to pieces by a wild animal, while your tunic, though blood-spattered, was whole and untorn?"

Jacob's eyes were sparkling as he resumed. "I knew, when I really examined the tunic, that God had spared your life and that His promises to me about my children would come to pass! I will not live to see my children multiply as the sands of the sea, but I can die in peace now for I have seen you, dear Joseph, once more!"

Asenath could understand very little of Jacob's Hebrew, but she drank in the scene before her and was deeply moved by the way her husband took the soiled garment from his father's hands. Joseph ran his fingers over the thick embroidery on one of the sleeves, and Asenath marveled at the tenderness in which he folded the tunic to his heart.

Then Asenath and all who stood there that day in Goshen watched as Joseph, the prime minister of Egypt, dressed in his royal garments and still clutching the tunic, knelt down in the pale Egyptian sand. His prayer, first in Hebrew and then Egyptian, thundered out of him.

"Oh mighty God, You have let me come full circle again with my cherished father and brothers. We are united once more, and I can scarce believe it.

"The past years of human hatred, slavery, in prisonment . . . all the suffering . . . they meant it for evil. But You . . . You meant it for good! Blessed be Your holy name.

"Let me never forget to worship and praise the long arm of Your faithfulness. Continue to keep the high and holy dreams of my forefathers, my father, and my own constantly before me.

"And merciful God, I would be as a lamb is to his shepherd, willingly ready to follow and eager to do Your bidding. So, let Your magnificent benefits bless and follow all the children of Israel forever and ever!"

Epilogue

God's answer to Joseph's prayer is found in
The Book of Genesis:
Chapters
Forty-seven through Fifty

Glossary

Listed below is a guide to pronounciations, with some explanations, to add to your reading enjoyment.

Aaron	(Aa-ron)	Master stone craftsman
Abihu	(Ah-bee-hue)	Son of Laban
Amashai	(Ah-mash-i)	Laban's hired shepherd of Padan-aram
Amset	(Am-set)	Priestess at Hathor temple
Amun	(Ah-mun)	King of the gods
Asenath	(Ah-see-nath)	Daughter of Poti-pherah
Asher	(Ash-her)	Son of Jacob and Zilpah
Asher	(Ash-her)	Ishmaelite donkey merchant
Azor	(Aa-zor)	Servant of Laban, Rachel, and Leah
Bedeiah	(Bee-die-ah)	Laban's hired shepherds of Padan-aram
Beeta	(Bee-tah)	Potiphar's chariot horse
Benjamin	(Ben-jah-min)	Son of Jacob and Rachel
Bethuel	(Beth-ool)	Father of Laban and Rebekah
Bilhah	(Bill-ha)	Servant girl to Rachel
Canaan	(Kay-nan)	Promised land south of Mesopotamia
Dan	(Da-nn)	Son of Jacob and Bilhah
Deborah	(Deb-or-rah)	Servant and nursemaid to Rebekah
Dinah	(Die-nah)	Daughter of Jacob and Leah
Dothan	(Doe-than)	City and plains north of Canaan
Eliezer	(Eee-lie-zer)	Servant of Abraham
Ephraim	(Eee-fram)	Son of Joseph and Asenath
Esau	(Eee-saw)	Son of Isaac, brother of Jacob
Essa	(Eh-sah)	Pharaoh's butler
Ezer	(Eee-zer)	Laban's hired shepherds of Padan-aram
Gad	(Gad)	Son of Jacob and Zilpah

Haran	(Hah-ran)	Large city in Mesopotamia
Hathor	(Hat-hoar)	Goddess of women, queen of all gods
Heliopolis	(Hee-lee-o-po-lis)	A city sometimes called On, headquarters for the sun-god, Ra
Isaac	(Eye-zak)	Son of Abraham
Israel	(Is-ray-el)	Jacob's God-given name
Issachar	(I-saw-car)	Son of Jacob and Leah
Jacob	(Jay-cob)	Son of Isaac
Joseph	(Joe-seff)	Son of Jacob and Rachel
Jubal	(Joo-bal)	Son of Laban
Judah	(Joo-dah)	Son of Jacob and Leah
Kharu	(Cah-ha-rew)	Soldier under Potiphar's command
Khnumet	(Koo-new-met)	Wife of Potiphar
Laban	(Lay-ban)	Father of Leah, Rachel, Abihu, and Jubal
Leah	(Lee-ah)	Oldest daughter of Laban
Levi	(Lee-vie)	Son of Jacob and Leah
Makara	(Mah-cah-rah)	Pharaoh's chief wife and queen
Manasseh	(Man-ah-seh)	Son of Joseph and Asenath
Merab	(Mer-rab)	Midwife
Metenu	(Met-ten-oo)	Chief servant and overseer for Potiphar's house
Mimut	(Mim-oot)	Priestess at the temple of Hathor
Nahor	(Nah-or)	Grandfather of Laban and Rebekah
Naphtali	(Na-fah-tally)	Son of Jacob and Bilhah
Padan-aram	(Pah-dan-ah-ram)	The plains of Mesopotamia
Paneb	(Pan-ebb)	Chief servant and overseer for Joseph's house
Peheti	(Pee-hetty)	Soldier under Potiphar's command
Pharaoh	(Fay-row)	King of Egypt
Potiphar	(Pot-ifar)	Royal bodyguard and chief executioner
Poti-pherah	(Pot-ti-fair-rah)	High priest of Egypt
Ra	(Rah)	God of the sun
Rachel	(Ray-chell)	Youngest daughter of Laban
Rebekah	(Rah-beck-ah)	Laban's sister and Jacob's mother
Reuben	(Rew-ben)	Son of Jacob and Leah
Sapher	(Say-fer)	Scribe and teacher to Joseph
Sari	(Sah-ree)	Servant woman of Aaron
Shechem	(Scheck-em)	Ancient city in Mesopotamia
Sherah	(Share-rah)	Girl taken captive from Shechem

Simeon	(Sim-ee-on)	Son of Jacob and Leah
teraphim	(ter-ah-fim)	Small stone gods
Tuiah	(Too-ee-ah)	Wife of high priest Poti-pherah
Zaphnath-paaneah	(Zah-fen-ath-(pan-a-ah)	The Egyptian name given Joseph by Pharaoh
Zebulum	(Zeb-u-lum)	Son of Jacob and Leah
Zeneb	(Zen-ebb)	Servant girl to Khnumet
Zilpah	(Zill-pa)	Servant girl to Leah